THE OTHER PASSENGER

John Keir Cross was born in Scotland in 1914. A prolific writer of scripts for BBC radio and television programs, Keir Cross also published a number of science fiction and fantasy novels for young readers, either under his own name or the pseudonym Stephen MacFarlane. *The Other Passenger* (1944), a collection of macabre tales for adults, remains his best known work, though his contributions to the horror genre also include several influential anthologies, *Best Horror Stories* (1956), *Best Black Magic Stories* (1960), and *Best Horror Stories 2* (1965). He died in 1967.

JOHN KEIR CROSS

The Other Passenger

with a new introduction by
J. F. NORRIS

VALANCOURT BOOKS

The Other Passenger by John Keir Cross
First published in Great Britain by Westhouse in 1944
First American edition published by Lippincott in 1946
First Valancourt Books edition 2017

Published by Valancourt Books, Richmond, Virginia
http://www.valancourtbooks.com

ISBN 978-1-943910-96-0 (trade paperback)
ISBN 978-1-943910-97-7 (hardcover)
Also available as an electronic book.

All Valancourt Books publications are printed on acid free paper that meets all ANSI standards for archival quality paper.

Set in Dante MT
Cover by Henry Petrides

CONTENTS

INTRODUCTION

A Little in Love with the Macabre

On the first pages in the original edition of *The Other Passenger* John Keir Cross dedicates his collection of short stories to the memory of S. T. McF. "a man now dead" and he composes his epitaph:

Here lieth a sad boy
O, he was haunted haunted
By terrible dreams
He knew not what he wanted
And he was a bad boy
Yet, lady, it seems
There were glorious times
When he was a glad boy
And made little rhymes
Here lieth the mad boy
Who made little rhymes

Is it a real epitaph for a real person? No, I very much doubt that. You see, "Stephen MacFarlane" was the pseudonym that Keir Cross adopted for his first venture in fiction as a children's author. With the success of *The Other Passenger* many of those first books were reissued (some were even revised and expanded) under his real name while other books as MacFarlane have all but disappeared. Assiduous hunting through the catalogs of used bookstores led me to all of his early work as MacFarlane and within those pages were the seeds of greatness. Delving into these early books reveals the genesis for the utterly bizarre, wickedly cruel and thoroughly imaginative stories Keir Cross invented for the collection we know as *The Other Passenger*.

For decades I only knew of John Keir Cross as the author of this single volume of unique short stories. I had no idea he had written anything else. My mistake was thinking of him only as a writer of adult fiction. Subsequent research revealed no less than seven books as Stephen MacFarlane and a handful of other children's novels under his own name. All of them show hints of the surreal and eerie worlds he would visit in the stories of *The Other Passenger*. One can find a wealth of the burgeoning talent that would be on display in the mix of crime, supernatural and just plain bizarre stories clearly intended for an adult audience.

His gang of amateur detective youngsters collectively known as the Studio J Kids who appear in a series of three books are menaced by Nazi spies, traitorous Brits and ruthless murderers. The children in *The Owl and the Pussycat* (retitled *The Other Side of Green Hills* in the U.S. edition) are befriended by an elderly gentleman and his little girl companion, both from another dimension, and together they literally do battle with a powerful wizard in search of missing pages from a Book of Secrets that has the power to meld the other dimension with the world we know. This latter book, his last children's book published prior to the collection of his adult stories, is rife with the types of wanton cruelty and dark impulses that flood the pages of *The Other Passenger*.

It seems Keir Cross was spending time honing his craft in the relative safety of a child's world before diving deep into the darkness of human depravity in tales such as "Music, When Soft Voices Die" and "Hands". His love of the supernatural and the power of magic so eerily and often beautifully captured in the scenes between Owl and the children of *The Owl and the Pussycat* transmogrify into nightmarish displays of selfishness and vanity in "Petronella Pan", an especially creepy tale of the desire for eternal youth. One can see echoes of the misanthropic Titus the wicked sorcerer and even a darker version of The Owl in Keir Cross's bitterly pessimistic story "Esmeralda" about a father perversely devoted to his fantasy daughter.

Keir Cross, though not as well known as he should be, has been well respected by some of the more prominent members of the genre fiction community. Arthur C. Clarke, science fiction novelist, remembers him as "the first, I think, professional writer I got to know" and someone "who had quite an influence on me, and encouraged me, I think, to become a pro." From the horror and supernatural community Ramsey Campbell recalls that a seminal anthology edited and with some insightful commentary by Keir Cross preceding each tale "helped shape my view of [horror fiction]" as "a branch of literature." *Best Horror Stories* (Faber & Faber, 1960) was Campbell's introduction to the rich variety that could be had in the macabre short story from literary greats like Graham Greene, Faulkner, and Herman Melville to ghost story and weird fiction masters like Bradbury and M. R. James.

Not long after the publication of the stories in *The Other Passenger* Keir Cross turned to freelance script writing and assisting in radio production at the BBC. In 1949 he landed work as a script writer for the radio program *The Man in Black* for which he adapted several short stories from the work of horror and crime fiction giants like John Collier ("Thus I Refute Beelzy"), Ambrose Bierce ("The Middle Toe of the Right Foot"), Bram Stoker ("The Judge's House") and M. R. James ("Oh Whistle and I'll Come to You"). Richard J. Hand in his study of British horror radio programming *Listen to Terror* (Manchester University Press, 2014) discusses in great detail the skill with which Keir Cross managed to cull the essence of the original writers' stories (often using their own words and dialogue) with the perfect placement of sound effects and musical cues. The distillation of the original work melding with the host's narrative voice (all Keir Cross's own writing) who gave the program its name was one of Keir Cross's hallmarks as a radio script writer. Hand praises Keir Cross's talent—especially his adaptation of William Fryer Harvey's "The Beast with Five Fingers"—and calls the entire series one of the highlights in British horror radio shows. Though short-lived at only eight episodes it was a program that had long-lasting influence. Hand points out that three of Keir Cross's *The Man in Black* scripts were re-broadcast forty years later during the long run of the *Fear on 4* series.

As for the eighteen stories you are no doubt about to devour in this volume I can assure you that John Keir Cross is a devil of a dreamer himself. The range of subject matter is as diverse as those writers whose stories he selected for radio adaptation or the writers he admired in the anthologies he assembled. His work runs the gamut of horror fiction consisting of stories of crime and murder; surreal nightmares and macabre fantasies; one odd blending of science fiction and psychological horror; and two genuine ghost stories. He can be ingenious and chilling ("The Glass Eye" and "Petronella Pan"), witty and poignant ("The Little House"), indulge in black humor ("Absence of Mind") and shock even a modern reader with unnerving examples of wanton cruelty ("Esmeralda", "Hands" and several others). Nearly all of the stories are drenched in a pathos for lonely haunted individuals doomed to cursed lives of their own making. Some of them learn dreadful lessons and pay the price of dreaming too big while others are led down a path of desperation leading to their purgatory or a fate worse than Hell.

Has there ever been a more insanely perverse story of a ventriloquist than that of Julia and her love for Max Collodi in "The Glass Eye"? Not even Ray Bradbury's Riabouchinska or the mad vaudevillian in the film *Dead of Night* come close to the fiendish ingenuity in the finale of Keir Cross's tale.

Tattoos have been a relatively modern subject of terror for writers of the macabre. From H. Rider Haggard's novel of a will tattooed to the back of a woman (*Mr. Meeson's Will*) to Roald Dahl's satire on art collectors ("Skin") to episodes of popular TV series (*The X-Files*' "Never Again") tattoos have always tempted the fertile imaginations of horror fiction writers. "Music, When Soft Voices Die ..." may sport an elegiac allusion to Shelley's poetry but Keir Cross's tale of bewitched African drums, the eerie design etched into their skins and later tattooed on human flesh is anything but a paean. For those with a taste for the exotic this story also has the lagniappe of Zulu mythology along with its lethal inking art.

Keir Cross gives us several variations on deadly sins leading to deadly consequences. Envy and wrath rear their ugly heads in the story of bitterly jealous Adrian Hagerman who lives in the shadow of his brother Charles, a successful poet. "Couleur de Rose" is Adrian's story, the title of a volume of Charles's poetry, and Adrian's poetic way of describing his newfound philosophy. The final paragraphs twist the metaphor into a gruesome literal truth.

In "Clair de Lune", one of Keir Cross's genuine ghost stories, the conflicted and confused narrator muses on the existence of ghosts in this mix of eloquence and prosaic observation:

> "Ghosts are not things—I doubt if they are even people: they are feelings. They are all unaccountable essences—they are your own self sitting gravely and accusingly on your own doorstep. That is why this story is vague and nebulous—all the time it is groping to describe something that is literally indescribable."

Do not be misled by this seemingly obvious statement or its hint of anticlimax. John Keir Cross is a master at capturing and evoking the indescribable, of exposing the forbidden desires and the criminal impulses, of showing us the people who fall in love with the macabre. *The Other Passenger* will take you on a whirlwind tour from dizzying heights of delirium and whimsy to the chasms where lie tortured souls forever lost.

J. F. Norris
August 2017

J. F. Norris's most recent essays on crime fiction have appeared in the anthologies *Murder in the Closet* and *Girl Gangs, Biker Boys and Real Cool Cats*. His writing on forgotten writers and their books has led to reissued books from publishers like Canada's Véhicule Press and La Bestia Equilátera in Argentina. You can read about obscure supernatural and crime fiction (mostly by long dead writers) on his blog, Pretty Sinister Books. He lives in Chicago.

to S. T. McF.
a man now dead,
with this epitaph:

Here lieth a sad boy
O, he was haunted, haunted
By terrible dreams
He knew not what he wanted

And he was a bad boy

Yet, lady, it seems
There were glorious times
When he was a glad boy
And made little rhymes

Here lieth the mad boy
Who made little rhymes

PART ONE

PORTRAITS

Why, 'tis the devil;
I know him by a great rose he wears on's shoe,
To hide his cloven foot . . .

THE WHITE DEVIL

The Glass Eye

THERE ARE THINGS that are funny so that you laugh at them, and there are things that are funny but you don't laugh at them at all—at least, if you do, you aren't laughing because they amuse you: you are doing what Bergson says you do when you laugh—you are snarling. You are up against something you don't understand—or something you understand too well, but don't want to give in to. It's the other side of the familiar thing—the shadow turned inside out—the dog beneath the skin of the dog beneath the skin.

You can take, for example, the case of Julia. Is it possible to laugh at people like Julia? I have never been able to. Yet Julia is funny—there is something monumentally funny in that terrible gaunt shape, in those wide and earnest eyes, in the red, moist tip of that nose of hers that seems longer than any nose in the world. There is something funny in her uncanny genius for saying the wrong thing—but when she does say the wrong thing a whole world of tragic miscomprehension comes to the surface. The blue eyes smile seriously—the whole pose and attitude register the fact that a remark had been made. Behold! Julia seems to say—a remark, my friends, a remark! . . . And everyone shuffles a little and looks the other way, or hastily talks about something else.

For example: Some people with a young baby came to see my wife and me just after we were married. The mother went out for a walk, leaving my wife to look after the child. She suddenly said, glancing at the clock:

"Heavens, it's time I went upstairs to feed Celia's infant!"

And Julia (the blue eyes smiling) looked up from the magazine she was reading.

"Is it bottle-fed?" she asked . . .

Julia is over forty—forty-two, to be exact.

A friend of mine, a man who makes up verse for the magazines, wrote a poem about Julia. He called it:

To Julia: *A song for a lost, mad girl.*

O, she thought she was in China
And a million miles away,
All among the tall pagodas
Where the shining geishas play;

And the mocking-birds were singing,
And the lanterns burning red,
And the temple bells were ringing—
Softly, softly in her head.

And those high and frozen mountains
Brought her comfort in the night—
Golden fish in silver fountains
Wove her garments of delight;

And the rich mimosa blossoms
Scented all the shining air,
And the mocking-birds were nesting—
Quietly, quietly in her hair . . .

Now, I want to tell you a story about Julia. Is it a funny story? I don't know—I just don't know. There are two people concerned in it, and in a sense they were both funny—Julia and this man, Max Collodi, I mean. But I don't think the story is funny. It is grotesque. There is one small twist in it, one odd and unaccountable thing . . .

I must tell you something first. If you call on Julia in her little flat in West Kensington where everything is just so—where the Burne-Jones panels by the mantelshelf harmonize so beautifully with the William Morris design on the wallpaper, where the volumes of the Tauchnitz edition of the Best English Authors smile on you from the bookshelves like rows of well-kept false teeth—if you call on her for tea, say, from the Japanese handpainted cups—you will see, on the mantelpiece, something that will haunt you more than any other thing in that room of ghosts. You will go away with your brows drawn together in a frown and your lips pursed up in an effort to understand, to piece things together. But you will see no more than it can see.

It is the story of that thing that I want to tell you—the story of that unaccountable Glass Eye, nestling on its little bed of black velvet on Julia's marble mantelshelf.

Somewhere in one of the philosophic books of the East there is another story about a Glass Eye. It concerns, if I remember rightly, a beggar who one day asked a philosopher for alms. The philosopher refused and went on his way. But the beggar was a trier and pursued him, shrilly demanding money. He pursued him right out of the city, till at last the philosopher stopped in exasperation and said:

"All right, I'll give you money. But on one condition. One of my eyes is a glass eye. Tell me which eye it is and you shall have all I possess."

The beggar looked at him intently, and at length said solemnly:

"Your right eye, Master, is the glass eye."

The philosopher was astonished.

"Tell me how you knew," he cried. "That eye was made by the greatest craftsman in the world—it should be impossible to tell it from a real eye. How did you know that my right eye was the glass one?"

"Because, Master," said the beggar slowly, "because your right eye was the one that had a compassionate look in it."

Five years ago, when Julia was thirty-seven, she lived in a bed-sitting-room in a narrow-shouldered house between West Kensington and Fulham. It was a small room, with yellow wallpaper stained with damp at the corners. There was a marble-topped washstand with a flowered basin and ewer on it. The pictures on the walls were coloured engravings of old sailing ships—the landlady's father had been captain once of one of those long, slender vessels that had paddles as well as sails. On the mantelshelf was an eight-day clock, and in the tiled hearth stood a rusty gas-ring on which Julia did her cooking.

At this time Julia did not have the reasonably good job she has now. She was clerk to an old-fashioned solicitor, a man named Maufry, who even in the 1940s still wore a square black top hat and wrote to his clients by hand, taking copies by the old moist paper method.

The loneliness and desolation of Julia's life were appalling. She did not know any of us in those days, so she did not have even the slight companionship and relief we afford her. She got up in the mornings, made herself tea on the gas-ring and cooked a slice of toast before the gas-fire. She lunched cheaply at an A.B.C. tea shop, with a book propped up before her. In the evenings she cooked a simple meal—fried some gammon, perhaps, or a chop, and boiled some vegetables (all on the same gas-ring, of course—a complicated conjuring trick this, involving much juggling with pots and pans). Then, having washed up, she read, or wrote letters to her sister in Leicester. And went to bed, generally at ten or half-past.

What went on in her mind? Did she ever gaze at the engravings on the walls and wish she might sail in those vanished ships to unimaginable places? Did she, as she read her books—dull novels by dead authors about people who had never lived—did she ever permit herself to be wafted away in fancy to some other and more picturesque life, in Spain, Italy, Morocco? Did she long for a knock at the door? Did she hope that the young man in the flat above might come home drunk one night and enter the wrong room? Did she look back on the past and speculate on why it was that things had slipped so unnoticeably away from her?

That past of hers . . . Did she realise, do you think, that such lost souls as hers are doomed to fail in everything they touch? She was not a virgin: she had been seduced at the age of eighteen by an elderly Midland business man she never saw again. She had been in love—at one time she had even been engaged (to a young man she had met on a holiday at a sea-side resort). But she never met the object of her love—a lecturer at a church discussion group she had once attended: and her fiancé, after six months' tergiversation, finally sent back her letters and the gifts she had showered on him, and disappeared. The last she heard of him he was living at Liverpool, having married a showgirl from Manchester. So, through the long years, old Maufry got all her devotion, and the small cripple son of her sister got all her love—her chilly and half-frightened love.

Once a year this child was sent to London to live with Julia while his mother went to visit her husband's people in Wales. The spinster curtained off a corner of her room and borrowed a cot from her landlady for the boy to sleep in. She fed him magnificently, took him to cinemas and theatres, bought him toys and books galore. And he, a pale, large-headed child, with eyes like balls of putty, accepted everything unquestioningly. The only reward he ever gave her was a wan, abstracted smile.

It was late one summer, during one of Bernard's visits, that the tragic episode of the Glass Eye began. Julia had bought tickets for the Old Palace Music Hall in Fulham. She and Bernard sat in the red plush stalls indifferently watching the show. It began with an act by two acrobats, a man and a woman in white tights and spangled pantees. The only thrilling moment was when, at the end, the woman climbed a chromium-plated pole that was balanced on the man's chin. She slipped and almost fell. Julia, visualising the white-clad figure falling into the stalls—as seemed inevitable, on top of Bernard's crippled legs—clasped the boy convulsively to her. He looked up at her in surprise, repelled by the smell of camphor from her clothes. She, as the woman on the stage righted herself, felt sweeping over her an immense wave of relief and tenderness. For the rest of the first part of the programme she trembled violently from time to time, looking down at the pale, abstracted boy. If anything should happen to him, while he was in her charge . . . She had an almost uncontrollable longing to touch the boy's bare, warped knees—only to touch him. She had never touched anyone.

After the interval there were some ballads by two stout operatic singers, then an eccentric cyclist took the stage, and then came the high spot of the show. It was announced on the programme thus:

MAX COLLODI
The Gentleman Ventriloquist
with his amazing
Dummy
'GEORGE.'

The curtain rose, and in a moment Julia forgot everything. She forgot Bernard, she forgot the little room with yellow wallpaper, she forgot Mr. Maufry and the high stool on which she sat in his office. Only one thing in the world existed for her—the figure of Max Collodi.

As he sat there on the stage with the spotlight on him it was impossible to conceive anything more handsome. His dark hair gleamed, his jaw showed a slight blue shadow. His moustache was exquisitely clipped, his high square shoulders spoke of great strength. His temples were narrow, his eyes deep set, his chin was cleft, his teeth, when he spoke, shone like jewels.

George, the dummy on his knee, was a grotesque doll about three feet high, with a huge tow head and staring eyes. Its head moved quickly from left to right, its voice was high-pitched and nasal as it answered Max's questions with clumsy wit. Julia did not notice the act—she did not hear the cross-talk, paid no attention to the pathetic little song that George sang. She was staring at the incredibly handsome young man, watching every suave, slightly stiff movement. When the tab curtains swung together at the end of the act she was still staring, motionless, her blue eyes shining, the end of her long nose slightly and pathetically damp. In that one moment she realised that there could be no other man in all the world for her but Max Collodi. All the empty years, the acres of desolation, had been leading up to this glorious climax.

As if she were in a dream she took Bernard home. She gave him some hot Ovaltine and put him to bed in the cot behind the curtain. Then she went to bed herself and lay for a long time staring up at the dim ceiling and listening to the night noises. Footsteps echoed through the open window from the street—the slow, measured footsteps of a policeman, the quick patter of a young man going home, from a dance perhaps, the strolling, mingled footsteps of lovers. Now and again, from somewhere inside the house, a board creaked. A mouse scuttled across the floor—shivering slightly she heard it scraping round the gas-ring, at the spot she had spilt some grease earlier in the day. From somewhere beneath her came the resonant snoring of the landlady.

And all the time, as she lay there, she was thinking of Max Collodi. She could not get his image out of her mind—but she did not want to get his image out of her mind. He was, she reckoned, thirty—thirty-two: only five years younger than she was. What had been his life? Was he (hideous thought—push it under)—was he married? Max Collodi, the Gentleman Ventriloquist . . . A ventriloquist. A man who could throw his voice. A superb accomplishment, it seemed. Thirty-two . . . She, if she took proper care, if she learned to make-up properly, might pass for thirty-five. Was he tall? All the time, on the stage, he had been sitting down—he had not risen even to take his curtain call. But he seemed tall—the broad shoulders vouched for his tallness. Max Collodi . . . A wonderful name—a name full of poetry. Max Collodi. Mrs. Max Collodi. Madame Collodi. Or was it Señora Collodi?

She heard footsteps mounting the stairs outside. The young man in the flat above had come home. Suppose—suppose she *was* Señora Collodi? She was lying in the upper room of their villa in Italy—on the outskirts of Rome. Max had been appearing at the theatre. He was coming home, dead tired. It was his footsteps she could hear dragging up the stairs. In another moment the door would open. He would come in. He would get into bed beside her. She would hold him, she would comfort him, she would send him to sleep.

The footsteps passed and a few moments later she heard the door of the flat above open and shut. She sighed and turned over in bed. Señora Collodi . . .

Next day, Bernard was due to leave for home. Julia got permission from Mr. Maufry to have the morning off and took him to the station. She hardly noticed him. She kissed him good-bye mechanically, then sent a telegram to her sister to say that he was safely on the train. Then she had lunch—and for the first time in years she did not have it at the A.B.C. She went to a small café opposite the Old Palace Music Hall. There was just the chance, as she sat there, that she might see Max going in or coming out.

The afternoon passed somehow. Even old Mr. Maufry noticed Julia's abstraction, but he attributed it to the fact that she had been seeing her nephew off. He himself was not feeling very well those days, so he gave Julia orders to close the office early, set his square hat firmly on his head and went woodenly off to his old-fashioned house out Chiswick way.

Julia, for her part, locked up the office, hurried home, boiled herself an egg by way of supper and then went out—to the Old Palace Music Hall. There, in a ferment of impatience, she sat through the acrobat act, the eccentric cyclist act, the ballad-singing act. By the time the indicator showed her that Max Collodi was next on the bill her heart was beating painfully, her hands had grown warm and clammy, her eyes were staring wide.

"Oh, I'm only a ventriloquist's doll,"

sang the ridiculous George—

"Only a ventriloquist's doll, that's all . . ."

But Julia did not care what George was. It was Max, his master, she was interested in. She stared at the well-groomed, suave, poised figure, smiling so gently and pityingly at George's *bêtises*. She noted the small bow that he gave to acknowledge applause, the gentlemanly restraint of him—so wonderfully unlike the exuberance of most Music Hall artistes. Max Collodi . . . Of course—he was made up. It was possible that off stage he didn't look *quite* so young. Thirty-five, perhaps. Yes—thirty-five . . .

The curtains swung together. The audience applauded. Julia sat still, entranced. They were applauding him—her Max. The curtains parted again. He was still sitting there, bowing a little and smiling, with the fatuous George grinning oafishly on his knee. Max looked straight ahead. By sheer will-power Julia tried to make him look in her direction—she had read of such things being possible. But perhaps her will was not strong enough. Max continued to look straight ahead, at the audience in general. It was impossible to believe that anyone could be so handsome. A woman in front said so in a loud whisper to her neighbour, and the neighbour replied with a sneer: "Yes—too handsome, if you ask me." Julia glared at her fiercely. She could have murdered her.

She walked home slowly. On a bill on the hoarding near her house she saw his name in large lettering—"Max Collodi, the

Gentleman Ventriloquist, with 'George'..." She looked hastily about her to see no one was near, then quickly tore away that corner of the bill. In her room she straightened out the crumpled piece of paper and stared at it for a long time before tucking it away between the leaves of one of her favourite books.

Now I must ask you to believe what may seem to you, a normal human being, the impossible. But remember the thirty-seven desolate years, the long empty hours in that terrible room with its peeling yellow wallpaper and its engravings of long-lost ships. Remember the far-off seduction almost twenty years before, the broken engagement, the square, soulless hat of Mr. Maufry. Remember the solitary meals conjured from that single gas-ring, the cold, unlovely love that had concentrated itself on the distant and unresponsive Bernard. And remember the story of the Eastern philosopher's Glass Eye. That other Glass Eye—the one that now rests on black velvet on Julia's mantelshelf—that is all that remains these days of Julia's affair with Max Collodi. A Glass Eye—a curious, even a terrible relic...

Every night, for the rest of that first week of her passion for Max Collodi, Julia paid her three shillings and sixpence to sit in the fauteuils (as they were called) at the Old Palace Music Hall. She sat with her gaunt fingers picking convulsively at the plush-covered arms of her seat: she sat with her earnest eyes fixed in fascination on the suave spotlighted figure of the ventriloquist: she sat with her long nose twitching, a minute drop of moisture forming always on the red tip of it.

She found, on the counter of a nearby newsagent's shop, a little pile of what professional theatricals call hand-outs—postcard-size photographs of celebrities, with quotations from their press notices on them. Some of these featured Collodi, and without hesitation (but with a furtive look round to see that no one was watching) Julia swept half-a-dozen of them into her hand-bag. They showed the ventriloquist sitting with his dummy, George, on his knee. His signature—a large, bold scrawl—was written across the bottom right-hand corner of the photograph. The extracts from the notices were printed in a column on the reverse side of the card:

"... An extremely skilful exponent of the polyphonic art ..."

"... Mr. Collodi succeeds in convincing us in the course of his exhibition that the term 'artist,' so often misapplied these days, can still be used with accuracy to refer to a Music Hall performer ..."

"... A great, a memorable display ..."

Julia took the cards home and placed them, with the torn fragment of the playbill, in her copy of the *Journal of Marie Bashkirtseff*. She looked at them every night before going to bed. She looked at them every morning before setting off to work.

At the same newsagent's she bought, at the end of the week, a copy of *The Stage*. She knew (from her fiancé in the old days, who had always been interested in theatricals) that show people usually inserted notices in this journal to say what theatres they were appearing in. To her joy, Max Collodi had done this: after his engagement at the Old Palace he was due for a week's appearance at the Pavilion, Finsbury.

Every night she travelled across London and paid her three and sixpence to sit in the fauteuils of the Pavilion, Finsbury.

And the following week, acting as before on the information in *The Stage,* she paid her three and sixpence at the Hippodrome, Streatham.

I said I expected you to believe impossible things. This is one of them: the foolish infatuation of an ageing woman of great ugliness for a Music Hall performer ... Julia was blind. Yet she did not have Glass Eyes. You, perhaps, are the one in the position of the Philosopher in the Eastern tale. She was the beggar—without his wit and acuteness.

The end of it was when Max Collodi was going on tour (as she was informed by *The Stage*) Julia gave her employer, Maufry, a week's notice. She had a small capital, simply invested, accumulated through many years of saving: it was this that, with no thought for the future, she proposed living on while she followed Collodi about the country.

And she did one other thing. She wrote Collodi a letter.

I am not able to quote the letter—I don't know what it said. I know that somewhere in the course of it she asked if she might meet the ventriloquist. And I know that she got a reply, written in the large hand of the signature on the postcard (the hand of an egotist—or a man in need of asserting himself), to say that Mr. Max Collodi was grateful for her praises, but that he never gave interviews.

I know also that Julia went on writing to Collodi. And that he went on replying. And that, as time passed, he seemed to grow warmer towards her—even friendly. Once—in Bradford—he asked her to send him a photograph: and Julia, with great trepidation, sent him a blurred snapshot taken long ago by her fiancé. She appeared in it sitting on a lawn against a background of fuchsia and veronica bushes—very shy, with her head to one side. A very old snapshot it was—a daylight-exposure print on matt paper. They had said, in those days, that it was the dead-spit of her: the bobbed hair caught up in a bandeau of Japanese silk, the frock with no waist that ended above the knee, the earrings of emerald cut glass—they were all very much a part of Julia at twenty-three. And she sent this snapshot to Max Collodi as a portrait—a dead-spit portrait—of Julia at thirty-seven. Close your left eyes, my friends—look at Julia with the Glass Ones.

* * * *

It was at Blackpool that Julia eventually met Max Collodi, in a small hotel in a street off the Promenade—the Seabank Temperance Hotel, Bed and Breakfast 6/6. The meeting was the end of the episode—or the beginning of it.

It happened in this way.

Julia, in her letters to Collodi, kept suggesting that they might meet. In the beginning he reiterated his statement that he never gave interviews. But later, as she grew more persistent and he more benevolent, he began to hint that a meeting might be possible. Perhaps it was the dead-spit portrait. Perhaps he wanted to savour the adulation at closer quarters. It was, I think he felt, worth risking. I said at the beginning of this tale that Max Collodi too, in his way, was funny.

In the letter he finally wrote consenting to a meeting and fixing a time and place, he made, like the true theatrical he was, certain conditions. She was to stay only for five minutes this first time. Later on, perhaps, if she still wanted to go on seeing him, they might arrange longer appointments. And he had (he said) an aversion in real life to strong light, being so much in his professional life under the glare of the limes and the footlights. So the hotel room would be dimly lit. If she did not mind (an arch touch this) being received in a half-lit hotel bedroom by a strange man, with no other chaperone besides his dummy, George, then would she go to the Seabank Temperance Hotel, Mortimer Street, Blackpool, at 10 p.m. on Saturday evening, after his show at the Winter Garden Theatre. And he would be happy to tell her something about himself and to hear, in his turn, something about her.

You will not want me to go into details about the hour and a half that Julia spent that evening before the mirror in the boarding-house at which she was staying. It was a large mirror with a chipped gilt frame. The quicksilver had come off from the back of it in sporadic, smallpox-like patches, and in one corner the glass was warped, so that you appeared curiously elongated in it, as if El Greco had painted you. Nor will I say anything about the agonies that Julia underwent before she could make up her mind what to wear. Did she, in the end, decide that there was no hope of appearing exactly like the dead-spit snapshot? Did she, with an unadmitted joy, bless Max for arranging the dimly-lighted room and an interview of only five minutes? Did she have qualms that when he had said "if she still wanted to go on seeing him," he might have meant: "if I still want to go on seeing you"? It is impossible to answer these questions. I only speculate and tell the story.

At ten minutes to ten Julia was walking to and fro near the Seabank Hotel, waiting for the hour to strike. She was shivering—and not alone from the slight chill of the night. On all sides of her people were enjoying themselves. The town was ablaze with coloured lights, there were a thousand conflicting jazz tunes in the air, from the dance halls, from the piano-accordions and ukuleles of the young men and women who strolled about the Promenade in groups with little white paper hats on their heads that had "Kiss me quick, Charlie" written round the brim. Beyond all these things was the sea, glittering under the lights but cold and detached, no part of the scene at all—the "broad Atlantic" as Julia automatically referred to it, remembering all the books she had read.

She glanced at her watch. It was two minutes to ten. She pushed open the swing door of the hotel and walked up to the reception desk.

An old man, bald, with a hare lip, peered at her. She stumblingly asked for the number of Mr. Max Collodi's room. Number Seven, he told her—on the first floor, stairway to her left.

She blushed a bit as she walked across the hall, feeling his eyes on her back. As she mounted the stairs, taking care not to trip over the worn carpet where it had escaped from the brass stair-rods, she dabbed at the damp tip of her nose with a small scented handkerchief—Attar of Roses from Boots, at 4/6 the bottle. She prayed to God—and she believed in God—that no one would see her. And no one did—if you except the stucco cherubs that decorated the pillar tops of the Seabank Temperance Hotel.

She reached Number Seven.

"O God," she prayed, "help me, oh help me!"

She tapped on the door. His voice came through it to her—unmistakeably his voice, the voice she had heard from her seat in the fauteuils of a hundred different Music Halls.

She repeated her prayer and walked in.

He was sitting facing her behind a large mahogany table. Even in the dim light she could not mistake him: every line of those handsome features was printed deep on her memory.

He inclined his head in the brusque, slightly stiff way she knew so well—it was the bow with which he acknowledged applause in the theatre.

"Dear lady," he said. "Pray sit down."

And she timidly sat down—at the table, facing him. She did not know what to say—what was there to say? To gain time she quickly and nervously glanced round the room. An ordinary room, with flowered wallpaper. There was a high box-spring bed, the striped ticking of it showing beneath the bedcover of lilac damask. There was a wardrobe and a small chest-of-drawers—

and (she noticed, God help her!) a white china chamber pot peeping out from the half-open door of a commode. Lolling grotesquely on a chair to Collodi's left was the dummy, George: a fantastic figure in that half light with its huge tow head and painted smile.

She looked quickly back at the ventriloquist. He had not moved—still held his head slightly forward. He was smiling in his chilly professional way. She remembered the woman in front of her at the Old Palace in Fulham—"too handsome, for my liking . . ."

"Mr. Collodi?" she said, hesitantly. Her voice sounded thin and false—not herself speaking at all, but someone else; someone else in her body, trembling, aching, sick in the stomach.

"Max Collodi, at your service," he replied, still smiling.

And suddenly there swept into her, as she sat there, a terrible, an overwhelming desire. It was a desire she had experienced before, in the Old Palace, when it had seemed that the acrobat was going to fall on top of Bernard—the desire to touch. She wanted to touch Collodi—to touch his hand, his forehead, his blue-tinted jaw. And after those thirty-seven years this craving, gathered and condensed in this one moment, was not possibly to be denied.

She got up. She stood for a moment staring wildly, breathing in hasty, dry gasps. She walked quickly round the table and touched Collodi on the cheek with her gaunt quivering fingers. Then she screamed—or she made the movements of screaming, though no sound came from her but a terrible dry croak. For Collodi, with the fixed professional smile still on his face, toppled sideways and fell from his chair with a crash to the floor.

There was one moment of beastly silence and then there was a scream: but not from Julia or the someone else who seemed to have taken possession of her body. No. It came from the chair where George had been lolling grotesquely. Now, as she stared, it was to see George standing up on the chair, his hideous painted face twisted with rage and fear and sorrow. And, as she stared, she realised that at last she had met Max Collodi, the ventriloquist.

She started to laugh. Sobs of laughter shook her whole angular frame. She stared at the dummy on the floor—the beautiful staring face she had loved so much. And, not fully knowing what she was doing, she gave in to the storm that was wracking her. Screaming terribly, she drove the high heels of her shoes into the padded body and waxen mask of the thing. It still smiled. One of its eyes shot out and rolled across the floor, but it still smiled. And all the time the misshapen being on the chair that was the real Max Collodi, the writer of that bold, assertive hand, the big-headed painted dwarf that had sat on the knee of the thing on the floor, that had spoken in two voices, a fair one and a foul one, working the movements of that handsome mouth and head by means of small pneumatic bulb controls—that misshapen, unlovable creature was weeping. How could he have hoped to get away with it?—he who was, in his own way, as hungry as Julia?

Gasping, blinded by her tears, Julia turned to run from the room. Her foot trod on something round and hard. She stooped half-wittedly to pick it up, then ran down the corridor, past the stucco cherubs, clutching it in her hand so tightly that it socketed itself in her palm. It was the Glass Eye of the thing on the floor—the Glass Eye that now rests, as a terrible relic, on its black velvet bed on Julia's mantelpiece.

* * * *

Well, that is the story of Julia and Max Collodi. I think of it every time I go to see her in that little flat where everything is just so. And I think of that other story about the Eastern Philosopher. And I wonder, every time I look at the thing on the mantelshelf: Which of my eyes is a Glass One?

I think of the thirty-seven years—the forty-two years now. I think of the yellow wallpaper and the vanished ships and the white paper hats on the Promenade at Blackpool. I think of the A.B.C. lunches, the volumes of the Tauchnitz Edition, the broad, cold sea with the lights on it. And I think of my friend's verses:

O, she thought she was in China
And a million miles away,
All among the tall pagodas
Where the shining geishas play;

And the mocking-birds were singing,
And the lanterns burning red,
And the temple bells were ringing—
Softly, softly in her head . . .

There is one more word.

Max Collodi, the Gentleman Ventriloquist, made no more appearances. There are no notices about him in *The Stage*.

But about a year ago I had a letter from a friend of mine who was holidaying in Scotland.

"Things have been brighter here these past few days," he wrote. "A small travelling circus has been visiting the district. One of the clowns is a sad-faced, large-headed dwarf, about three feet high. He calls himself Maximilian. I've seen him several times walking in the village—a fantastic little figure. He has a beautiful voice, which comes (I don't know why it should) as a surprise. He has an odd affectation too (it must be an affectation, for he doesn't do it during his circus act): he wears a black patch over one of his eyes."

My friend did not say which eye. Remembering the Eastern tale I have often wondered. Left?—or Right?

Petronella Pan

A FANTASY

Any time I was near Birmingham I always made an occasion to call on my elderly friend Korngold. He was a jeweller—a stout, ruddy, successful man, with a shop near Snow Hill Station and a pleasant villa in a respectable district beyond Aston.

Korngold was not a married man, and that, I think, was his only tragedy. For he loved children: he loved them with all the weighty, ruddy love of the German-Scottish sentimentalism that was in his blood (his father, a jewel exporter from Bavaria, had married a woman named Flora MacDonald—a descendant, she claimed, of Prince Charlie's Flora).

This flood of love in Korngold expressed itself in a curious way. His hobby was to organise and adjudicate baby shows. His custom was to take a hall every now and then, advertise a baby show in the press, then spend a glorious day surrounded by babies white and babies red—screaming babies, laughing babies, fat babies, thin babies: in short—Babies. He gave a prize to what he considered the most beautiful baby, allowed himself to be photographed by the local press holding it in his arms, and then he retired quite blissfully to his shop and villa till the urge came over him to hold another show.

A strange man Korngold. But I liked him. He exuded benevolence—it did my jaded heart good to talk to him. It stimulated me to marvel at his naïveté. It is no mean achievement, I have always thought, to love a baby—someone else's baby, of course. Korngold's sublimation made a lot of people happy. It oiled the wheels—and God knows, when you look round, the wheels need oiling.

However, to the anecdote (for this, you must understand, is no more than an anecdote. It has no moral, no meaning):—

It was three years ago when I last found myself near Birmingham. An old aunt of mine, who lived in Kidderminster, quite suddenly died (thereby reminding us all with a shock that she had been alive), and I was constrained to go to her funeral. When it was all over I boarded a bus for Birmingham, hoping to shake off the clamminess of death with a bout of Korngold's philanthropy. The old man's shop was closed, though it was comparatively early on a Saturday morning, so I took a tram through Aston and called at his villa. And there a tired old housekeeper informed me that Korngold was holding a baby show that very day in the Congregational Church Hall along the street.

Amused at the prospect of attending one of the old man's love-orgies, I went along to the squat sandstone building. Appropriately enough, on the Wayside Pulpit board outside the Church, were the words: "Except ye become as little children, ye shall not enter into the Kingdom of Heaven." I smiled and entered the hall—shaking off, as I went, the sudden recollection I had of the lowering of my aunt's coffin into the grave (a strange woman, my aunt: it was said in my family that she had been at one time a little rocky in the head—she had had an illusion that she was immortal, she would live for ever . . . however, that is a different story, to be told elsewhere than here).

When I got into the Church Hall that day three years ago I was, at the same time, amused and slightly frightened. Have you ever seen a horde of babies?—a real horde of them, not only one or two together? A terrible, an awesome sight. Squat bundles of flesh, red and raw-looking, clasped to the bosoms of proud mothers. Babies ranging in age from three months to two years—mothers ranging in age from sixteen to forty. The hall sweated love. What could I—a cynic, a misanthropist, a man too aware of the Worm—what could I do in such an atmosphere but cringe a little and wonder more than ever at people like Barrie and Katherine Mansfield?

Babies! My God! So many potential saints, murderers, geniuses, adulterers. Beethoven was once a baby—his little red bottom was powdered and wrapped in soft nappies (if they did such things in those days). Shakespeare was once a baby, Francesco Cenci was once a baby (I can see that most diabolical of all monsters coo-ing and gurgling and sucking gumlessly at a crust—he who, later in life, had to be scraped with sharp boards he was so horny with disease). Think of Henry VIII at the end of his career: an immense, shapeless thing, so putrid that his courtiers were issued with little nose-clips so that they could approach him. The doors of the palace had to be widened, a special machine had to be constructed to lift the hideous mass from place to place. And think of the same Henry at the beginning of his career—the nurses bending over him and crooning lullabies . . . ! Or think, if you want an image so overwhelming that it hardly bears visualising—think that at probably the same time that most famous of all Babes was lying unconscious beneath the gaze of the Magi, another small bundle was being also wrapped somewhere in swaddling clothes: and possibly a man was saying to a woman—"What shall we call him, dear?"—and she replying: "Let's call him Judas—that's a nice name, isn't it, darling . . ."

Babies! And in the midst of them, his red face shining with love and exertion, my good, friend Korngold the jeweller. He had in his arms a pair of twins—was beaming at the mother, a huge-bosomed woman with henna-dyed hair. I thought again of my dead aunt—her bleak bluish face staring waxen from the coffin. She also had once been a baby . . .

As I waited to attract Korngold's attention I noticed, coming in through a door to my right, a woman with a pram—an extremely old-fashioned pram, it was, high in the carriage and over-ornate in its mouldings. She was an elderly woman—a grandmother, I supposed, rather than a mother; silver-haired, flowingly dressed, proud-looking. But it was not she who attracted my attention: it was the baby she wheeled. I have suggested already that I don't like babies—they are not beautiful, not in the least bit objectively beautiful. They are red and wrinkled and repulsive. I run away from them—I, the incurable romantic, the man with secret pictures in his heart of Marie Antoinette, Mary of Scotland, Beatrice Cenci and sweet Nellie Gwynn (bitches all, no doubt, if the truth be told). But heavens!—this child in the old-fashioned pram! I forgot everything in looking at it. I forgot where I was. I forgot the yelling red bundles, the dingy Church Hall with its engravings of missionaries round the walls (David Livingstone meeting Stanley—two old wooden babies in kepis, surrounded by natives with tactful loincloths blowing over all the right places). The little face in the pram was the most perfect, the most exquisitely beautiful face I have ever seen. To describe it is impossible. It was something by Botticelli, something by Raphael, something by the incomparable Leonardo. Intolerably beautiful. I couldn't believe that in that dull hall in that dull town, among those dull dull bundles of red wrinkled flesh, such an angel-thing could be alive. But it was. It was alive, and smiling at me adorably even as I watched it.

I was brought back to my senses by the ripe booming voice of Korngold.

"Malpas! My dear Bob Malpas! How wonderful to see you!"

He was shaking me by the hand, beaming inexorably.

"Hullo, Heinz," I murmured. "Was in Kidderminster, burying an aunt of mine—thought I'd run over to see you. I didn't know you were holding a show, though. I'd better come back when it's all over. I can amuse myself at a cinema or something this afternoon, then perhaps we can dine this evening."

"Of course we'll dine this evening," he boomed. "But before we do another thing, we'll go for a drink right this minute. We've just got time before they close. I could do with a drink—it's hot work in this hall. And I can easily spare a quarter of an hour while my assistants get the little ones classified."

I felt myself being led out of the hall. My thoughts were still confused by the vision of the lovely baby in the old-fashioned pram. It seemed to me incredible that Korngold should be standing so close to it and not be in an ecstasy over its beauty. There was no doubt that it, of all babies there, was the only possible prize-winner. Yet he—that baby-fancier, that expert—hardly so much as glanced in the exquisite creature's direction. No: I am wrong—he did glance, hastily and almost, I thought, slightly embarrassedly. He glanced at the baby and then at the elderly lady. And he gave her a wry quick nod before he turned away with me and took me by the arm out of the hall.

I went with him in a daze, the vision of that small perfect face taking its place in my heart along with Marie Antoinette, Mary of Scotland, Beatrice Cenci and sweet Nellie Gwynn. And ousting them, what's more—ousting even the vision of that other face that was haunting me that day: the blue, transparent face of my dead aunt—she who had thought she would live for ever.

Well, I told you. I told you I was a cynic—a man too aware of the Worm . . .

I did not stay to have dinner with Korngold that evening. It was all too much for me somehow. There are some things I can't stand—not big things—very few big things disturb me. But small things—fantastic things.

I honestly think I was a little bit mad as I travelled back in the train and watched the low Midland country-side go slipping past in the twilight. Quietly, even pleasantly mad. A kind of mild droolling—an innocence and a foolishness, I am sure, was on my face for my fellow-passengers to see. I should, perhaps, have leaned forward in my seat and said to them, in a restrained and dignified way:

"I have just buried an aunt in Kidderminster, friends. Have you ever been to Kidderminster? Famous, they tell me, for carpets. Heigh-ho. They say the owl was a baker's daughter. The owl, did I say? To-whoo, to-whoo! My aunt was a curious woman—she used to say she would live for ever . . ."

I wrote, I remember, a poem in that train, letting it run through my mind to the rhythm of the carriage. It expressed the rare, thin insanity I felt. I called it *A Mad Song,* and the recurring burthen of it ran like this:

Thou'rt mad, thou'rt mad,
Old straw-i'-the hair—
My breeches are torn
And my bum is all bare . . .

. . . And then, simultaneously with the poem, there would run through my mind the conversation I had with Korngold as we drank our ale that day in the little pub across from the Congregational Hall. Even while he spoke, I remember, the vision of that beautiful baby's face was before my eyes. As I raised the tankard to my lips it shone out from the frothy surface of the ale—the way the faces do from the tea in the old Chinese legends. It shone out even while that monster of benevolence—he, Korngold, with no trace of cynicism in his German-Scottish heart—boomed out the text of the wise old Teacher:

"Vanity of vanities—all is vanity and a striving after wind . . ."

"Perhaps," he said quietly, in answer to my question, after he had done laughing (it proves that he was no cynic, that he could laugh at it all)—"perhaps I'd better put it up to you in the form of a story. A once-upon-a-time tale—and you can apply it exactly as you want to. Of course, I can't give that baby the prize—after the first time it would be fantastic, ridiculous. Let me see—I'm now fifty-six—no, fifty-seven. And I began adjudicating at baby shows almost thirty years ago. So you see—however: better to tell you the other way. The story. The once-upon-a-time tale."

He drained his glass and ordered another drink for us both. I, with the mystery of his refusal to give the prize to that lovely baby running all through me and commanding my attention, waited impatiently for him to continue.

"There was, then," he said, "a woman. You must picture her as a very beautiful woman." (I had a composite vision suddenly of Marie and Mary and Beatrice and Nellie). "But vain—inordinately vain." (Bitches all, I remembered, if truth be told). "In course of time she married. She married a very clever man—a biological research chemist. She grew big with child and was delivered of an exquisite babe—the inheritor of her good looks. And behold, all the pride she had hitherto felt in her own beauty she now felt in the beauty of her child. People said they had never seen a lovelier baby, and the woman thrilled as ecstatically as she ever had at a personal compliment. One day she read an announcement of a baby show. She entered her little daughter for it—she was then, I fancy, one year old—and naturally she won first prize: there was plainly no other child to compare with this cherubic one. A little intoxicated by her outstanding success (for the judge had been wildly eulogistic), the woman kept her eyes open for announcements of other baby shows about the country. And the next six months she spent in travelling all over England in a sort of delirium, winning prize after prize. It became, with her, an obsession. It was almost, so to speak, her trade."

The old man paused and gazed mistily through the window of the pub to the Church Hall opposite, with its Wayside Pulpit message plain to view. He chuckled and sipped at his beer.

"Alas," he went on, "there's always a Worm. The woman knew, from her glass, that beauty fades. She knew that her baby was almost two, and that there must be an end soon to the heap of trophies accumulating on her dresser at home. And she was seized with a sort of panic. And a defiance, too, God help her. It seemed to her she was being robbed—something was slipping past her and she could not grasp at it. There were long nights of despair when she lay staring into the darkness while her husband snored dully by her side, with no knowledge of the weeping anguishes that were going on in the same bed with him. Yet it was that very hoggishness and indifference of her husband that in the end gave the woman the idea. One night, as he snored, she thought angrily: 'What does he care, lying lumpishly asleep! He and his wretched researches, his injection into harmless guinea-pigs!' Then she stopped short and drew a long shivering gasping breath. No matter how stupid a woman is she is bound to know something about her husband's work. And this woman, married to a biologist, had certainly, most devilishly certainly—heard of Glands!"

I think I must have gone a shade pale at this point in the story. Korngold laughed and ordered a double whisky. He waited till I had sipped at it copiously before he continued, in a suddenly low and serious voice:

"Of course, no matter how shallow you are, when you really set your mind to a thing you can do it. This woman—well, there are books, you know. And she experimented—she experimented mercilessly, on guinea-pigs, rabbits, rats—oh, anything. And in the end, out of the depths of her stupidity and determination, she succeeded in discovering what, I suppose, scientists have been struggling after for centuries. Her husband would probably have given his right hand to have discovered what she discovered. He, poor man, died at about this time, blissfully unaware of what was going on clandestinely in his laboratory. I don't think the woman even noticed he had died—she was too pre-occupied, too altogether single-minded. And of course—"

The old man shrugged. I stared at him in horror.

"Lord, Lord!" I muttered. "You mean—oh my God!"

I drained the whisky glass and stared out of the window. And I, too, had my eyes on the words of the Wayside Pulpit board.

"But surely," I said at length—"surely the development—"

"She can do some things," said Korngold. "She can read, for instance. She can't talk very well. But then, she hardly needs to, does she? Her life is spent at baby shows."

"And that woman?"

"The mother?" He shrugged again. "I don't think she notices that she doesn't get prizes any more—all the judges up and down the country are wise to her. But it's her life, you see—quite simply it's her life. To show off that beautiful, beastly thing . . ."

I tremblingly lit a cigarette. And when it was properly alight, screwed myself up to the question above all others that I wanted to ask.

"But—how long, Korngold? For heaven's sake—how long?"

"I told you I was fifty-seven," he murmured, after a pause. "Thirty years ago I judged my first baby show. And I gave the prize to—well, why say it? I told you this was a fairy tale and you could apply it as you wanted. For my part"—and he suddenly smiled and straightened himself, "for my part I must get back to the hall now. I've work to do, you know. Come with me, Bob—it'll do that cynical old heart of yours good to see some honest baby-flesh . . ."

So there I was in the train, you see. Quite quietly mad till I got to town. And my relations said:

"And how did the funeral go, Bob? Poor Aunt Elspeth. Poor, dear old soul!"

"Oh fine," I said. "It went beautifully. She looked awfully calm in the coffin—awfully calm, I thought."

We sighed. And I thought of my poem—*A Mad Song*. And then, suddenly, of the last vision of all—what I had seen as I turned, unable to bear it all any longer, and stumbled out of the hall, away from Korngold and the phalanxes of the babies. I did not dare look at the woman with the pram as I pushed out through the press of mothers. But how could I resist looking into the pram—for one horrid fleeting moment?

She was reading, that exquisite small thing. I even saw the name of the book she was reading. It was—final horror!—Proust: *A la Recherche du Temps Perdu . . .*

It was before the calm, quiet mood came on me. I was quite hysterical, I suppose. At any rate, I hardly knew till I had done it that I had torn down the text from the Wayside Pulpit board.

"Except ye become," it said . . .

Thou'rt mad, thou'rt mad,
Old straw-i'-the hair . . .

"Poor, poor Aunt Elspeth," my family said. And I muttered foolishly, over and over again:

"She looked awfully calm in the coffin—oh, awfully calm, I thought . . ."

The Last of the Romantics

He came into The Parrot every afternoon. He was very old, very mild-looking, with wide blue eyes. He wore a high cravat with a jewelled pin. His hair swept back from his pink forehead—very soft hair, it was, and silvery. He looked like the traditional musician—the waiters and some of the regulars even called him Maestro.

But most of the clients—and particularly the sentimental ones—called him The Last of the Romantics.

He ordered tea for two every day. They knew him in The Parrot, of course—there was no question of anyone looking askance because he had no companion. They brought him a little white pot and two cups. He set them out most elaborately—one for himself and one at the vacant place opposite him. Then he poured—but into his own cup only. He stirred gently, with a slow, quiet, deliberate movement. Then, with a dignified smile, he raised his cup to his lips, inclined his head very slightly to the empty place, and sipped the special delicate brew The Parrot was famous for.

Then he did a curious thing. The Parrot was one of those restaurants with a special little lamp for each table—if you wanted it on you pulled a small chain with a hook at the end of it. The old man, after he had drunk his first cup of tea, and before he poured out his second, lifted the empty cup from the vacant place opposite him. And, still with the dignified smile on his lips, he hooked the handle on to the end of the lamp chain. Then he watched it dangling there, slowly revolving, for the rest of his tea-time . . .

"It must be a very romantic story," sighed little Miss Patillo.

For three afternoons in succession she had gone to The Parrot with Thomson Purbeck. The first afternoon she watched The Last of the Romantics with surprise: the second afternoon she sighed deeply: the third afternoon she delivered herself of her judgment. It was, of course, typical—she was incurably a sentimentalist: perhaps just a little soft. That may have been why Purbeck had chosen to have an affair with her. He liked little soft yielding things—it gave him, he claimed, a great joy to disillusion them.

He chuckled now at little Miss Patillo's remark. His long nervous fingers plucked at a corner of a menu. He lounged back in his chair with his shoulders hunched.

"It depends," he said, "on what you mean by romantic."

"Well—don't you think there must have been ... *something,* Thomson? You know what I mean. He was in love—terribly long ago, of course. And they used to come here every day for tea. And then one day she didn't come—she died, perhaps. Something like that. Or maybe their parents didn't approve of the match. And every day since then he has come here—alone—to the same table. And ordered tea for two, just like he always used to do ..."

"I adore you, Patsy," said Purbeck, looking solemnly into her wide eyes. "I simply adore you. You're wonderful. In three days! ... And what do you suppose he is, my sweeting? What does he do for a living?"

Patsy stole a quick and elaborately furtive glance towards the old man at the table across the restaurant.

"He's retired now," she said triumphantly. "He was a—a schoolmaster. Or—or something in the Civil Service! But he's retired."

Purbeck threw his head back and laughed aloud.

"Glorious, glorious!" he cried. "And I bet if I asked you, you could tell me the girl's name and what her father did and the age of the minister who was all booked up to marry them! Darling Patsy!"

He leaned forward suddenly and took her hand.

"Thomson," she said, "be careful! There are too many people."

"I could eat you, Patsy," said Purbeck. "Mouthful by mouthful—very slowly and deliciously—thirty-two chews to each bite, the way Mr. Gladstone recommended. I'd have those sparkling eyes in a cocktail, on the end of little sticks—like cherries."

She laughed—a shade uncomfortably. And glanced to the mirror on the wall beside her to see that her lipstick wasn't smudged.

"Don't be silly, Thomson," she said. "You are silly sometimes —you say such silly things."

"Patsy, dear," he went on, "if you only knew it you've given me the most wonderful cue of my whole life. If I waited a thousand years I'd never get a cue like that again. I'll always adore you for it—always. After we've been to bed together once or twice we'll probably drift apart, we two—you'll find me with another woman one day. Or we'll have a lovely scene and you'll accuse me of mental cruelty. Maybe you'll cry for an hour or two—I hope you do: I like to feel that a good woman is shedding tears for me. Then you'll recover and marry someone very solid. And later on you'll remember me as something in your life that was a little bit haunting—and, shall we say?—pleasantly unpleasant. You'll possibly even shudder. But I, Patsy—*I* shall remember *you* with everlasting gratitude as The Girl Who Gave Me The Perfect Cue!"

She giggled.

"Silly," she said.

"No, my love—I mean it. And to prove it, I'm going to tell you a story."

"You mean about—him?" she asked eagerly, nodding briefly at the old man, who was now sipping his second cup of tea and watching the empty cup revolving on the lamp chain. "Oh Thomson—I knew I was right! I knew it was romantic!"

"Yes, you were right," he said. "And you were right on other counts too. You were right about his being a retired Civil Servant. And you were right about the love affair, and the pair of them coming here every day for tea. And you were even right that she died . . . But darling, I'll begin at the beginning. And then, remember, I'm going to eat you, very slowly—and starting with your left ear lobe as a sort of *hors d'oeuvres* . . ."

He chuckled again. Then he lit his pipe, chewed thoughtfully at the stem of it for a moment or two, and began, in a very low voice, while little Miss Patillo leaned closer and closer across the table towards him, so that she could wallow in every word.

"In those days," said Purbeck, speaking very much as the Story-Teller—as if Patsy were a child, almost, "—in those days, you must understand, The Parrot was a much smaller concern than it is now. It was very attractive, of course, and it had its regular clientele. Among them was our old friend across the way. Very much younger, of course—it was while he was still working as a Civil Servant. He had his regular table. And every day he ordered—just as he does now—tea for two. Only in those days—"

"She was with him!" burst in Patsy eagerly.

"Yes, dear. She was with him. You must picture her—as I am sure you do—as a very beautiful woman. She was tall and she was dark—she had lovely smooth black hair, with a middle parting, gathered in a little hard bun at the back. Her neck was lovely—white and soft. She dressed exquisitely. And, of course, the Maestro—the old boy—well, putting it simply, he worshipped her."

"I knew it," cried Patsy.

"Of course you knew it, darling," said Purbeck softly. "I'm not really telling you a story—I'm only confirming a whole lot of things you know by that wonderful instinct of yours. But it passes the time, dear—it passes the time . . . I suppose you know about the other man too?"

"The—other man?" gulped Patsy, a little crestfallen. "Oh! . . ."

"Oh yes—there was another man. Not a very pleasant man. His name was—well, let's call him Richardson, just for the purposes of the story. And let's call the woman Valerie—it wasn't her real name, of course, but it suits her very well, as it happens. Right then—there you have the set-up:—The Maestro, madly in love with Valerie—bringing her here to The Parrot almost every day for tea and sitting staring across the table at her as if she were a goddess: Richardson somewhere in the background, very handsome and very suave (I'm sure your instinct tells you he was very handsome and very suave, my darling), and then the beautiful Valerie herself, tall and exquisite. And in love with—now who was she in love with, Patsy? Eh?"

Purbeck paused. His pipe had gone out. He relit it, smiling at Patsy through the smoke as she stared at him impatiently.

"Darling," he said at length, "alas, all women aren't like you. There are very few of them that feel the way you do about things. And Valerie certainly didn't. Oh—not in the least bit. She was a curious woman—very sensual, for one thing. These pale dark women usually are. I don't suppose the likes of you can quite understand these things. I mean, you wouldn't understand if I told you that while Valerie was sitting here letting the Maestro make love to her—while he was talking marriage and building up magnificent plans for them both at that very table over there—all that time, darling Patsy, Valerie was going home in the evenings to——"

"To Richardson!" gasped Patsy.

"You've guessed it," said Purbeck. "The instinct again. She was living with Richardson, dearest. She was his mistress. And all the time there she was, letting the old boy go on and on . . . I don't know how these things happen, Patsy. They just do. People get into ruts—they form habits. Maybe Valerie wanted to break away from Richardson—maybe it was just one of those habitual fleshy ties, you know. She wanted to start up afresh with the Maestro, perhaps. And she just couldn't quite break the Richardson habit. Maybe it was that. Or Richardson may have had some sort of hold over her. I don't know. I can only speculate about this part of the story—there's always one part of a story, you know, Patsy, when you can only speculate. The things we can never really understand—not one of us—are human motives. We can only say objectively that such and such a thing happened. We can only, in the last analysis, relate events."

"Did—did the old man know about Richardson?" asked Patsy.

Purbeck shook his head.

"Not him. At least, not till—— But I'm anticipating, as they say in the books. I was really only at the point where I was telling you about Valerie's relationship with Richardson. I suppose she tried to break things off with him—charitably one must suppose that. There were probably scenes. She possibly told him she wanted him to let her go so that she could marry the Maestro. And he, I expect, sneered at her and said oh to hell with leading a decent life, and then that probably led up to a really big scene, so that it was quite inevitable that——"

Purbeck paused again, smiling at the tense Patsy.

"What was quite inevitable, Thomson?" she asked. "Oh, Thomson—don't be silly! Please! What was it?"

"Of course," said Purbeck slowly. "I'm only *supposing* it worked that way, my dear. It may have been something else. She may have been a vicious woman—women of her type often are. She may have been deceiving the Maestro with Richardson quite callously and deliberately. In fact, when I think of it—I mean, when I look over at the poor old soul there . . ."

He broke off and looked across at the old man at the other table. He chuckled again.

"Poor old devil! Poor, poor old devil! . . . Coming in here for all these years and ordering his tea for two! . . . Sentimental, eh? Or maybe——"

He shrugged. For a moment he seemed to have forgotten Patsy's presence. She tugged at his sleeve to remind him.

"Thomson—*please!* Oh don't be silly! What *happened,* darling?"

"Eh? What happened? . . . Oh—of course. The story. Well, my love—the famous instinct. You were right. You really told me the story, you know—right at the beginning. Valerie—— Well . . . Valerie died."

There was something in Purbeck's tone that filled Patsy with horror. She looked at him for a moment intently, her little plucked brows drawn closely together.

"You mean—that Richardson *killed* her? Oh Thomson!"

"Not quite, my love. Just a little slip on the instinct's part—just the tiniest slip. It was slightly more complicated than that. Oh, it was a famous scene, my dear! The Parrot thrived on it—that's how it really got going. It was notorious for weeks. Of course, it's all very long ago now—it's all forgotten about. But people used to come crowding in here—just to stare and be morbid, you know . . .

"You see, dear, one day, when the Maestro and Valerie were having tea there, at that very table, and he was talking about the future and their marriage and all that sort of thing, the door opened and in came a couple of plain clothes policemen. And they marched straight over to the table, and one of them put his hand on Valerie's shoulder, and then, of course, with the old boy sitting there listening, it all came out—every word of it. That was how he heard about Richardson—after it was all . . . I mean—after she had——"

"Killed him!" breathed Patsy. She had gone quite pale—she held her chubby little hand to her heart.

"It created a tremendous sensation at the time," said Purbeck solemnly. "Oh, immense! The papers were full of it. But it had been—well, a pretty messy and obvious affair, and Valerie—well, I told you, darling—or rather, you told me. Valerie—died . . ."

Patsy was silent, breathing deeply.

"Oh Lord," she said at last. "Oh Lord! She was—ugh!"

She looked across to the table on the other side of the room. The old man had finished his meal and was preparing to go. The empty tea-cup from the vacant place hung quite still at the end of the lamp chain. Patsy shuddered.

"Oh Lord!" she said again. "And all these years he's come in here and ordered tea for two! . . . Oh Lord! Poor old man—and she had been living with Richardson . . . all the time. And then she was ha—— oh Lord!"

She stared, horrified, at the dangling cup.

Purbeck, with a slow smile, leaned very close to her across the table.

"Darling Patsy," he said, in a very low voice, "before I eat you there's just one extra little thing I've got to tell you. It's about the Maestro—before he retired. He was, as you said, a Civil Servant—he was the most curious and terrifying of all Civil Servants. He was—well, you know, darling—someone has got to do it. Has it ever struck you, that? Someone's *got* to do it, darling."

"What?" she asked dazedly.

He looked at her for a long time with his intangible smile.

"He was the Public Hangman, darling," he said at last.

There was one long terrible scream, and then Patsy began to have hysterics. Purbeck leaned back in his chair again.

"Yes . . ." he said slowly. "It all depends. It all depends on what you mean by romance . . ."

Clair de Lune

A GHOST STORY

"You must come," said Christine. "You simply *must,* my dear. It's the most wonderful place. You meet such interesting people . . ."

There was a copy of the *New Statesman and Nation* under her arm. I loved Christine. She was almost too typical—if you encountered Christine in a book or a play you would say she was overdrawn. She was large and very pale. She dressed outrageously. She had a high-pitched humourless voice. If you sat on top of a bus with Christine, people looked round the moment she began to talk: if you went to a cinema with her (she would only go to French or Russian films—or perhaps to a Disney festival in a News Theatre), she would whisper penetratingly about "trends" till people went "ssh" on all sides. Christine was "in on" things. When I first knew her it was education. Then she had religion for a time (but she called it "scientific humanism," or something). Then there was town-planning—"reconstruction." It was all—she said—part of a "widening horizon." It was "awareness."

I loved Christine; and felt, in a queer helpless way, sorry for her. I believe that at the root of her there was a quiet, kind, ordinary human being. She had had one big love affair—beautifully worked out—with a married man. His wife was away—abroad for a time. Christine and this man sat for two months or so discussing the situation from all angles. In the end, when, in the light of scientific humanism, they had decided that an affair would be justified, they went to bed together. When the wife came back they would explain: they were intelligent people: Christine would give up the man, whose first duties, of course, lay with his wife and children. It would be a tableau beautifully illustrative of the virtues of enlightenment.

The wife came back. The great confessional took place. Christine sat forward in her chair, her brows drawn together. The man stood before the fireplace (I think it was at Letchworth he lived), and explained lengthily. The wife poured tea and listened. When it was all over she said:

"I see, George. Two lumps of sugar, isn't it, Christine? . . ."

A week later she—the wife—went off with another man, who apparently had been in the offing for a long time. The husband lived with Christine for a month, then he had another explanation tableau (not at Letchworth this time, for he could hardly live there with Christine, could he?—enlightenment notwithstanding). It was Christine's turn to say: "I see, George."

"Somehow it didn't work," she said to me long afterwards. "We weren't in tune. But I admired George's integrity so much—he was so straightforward and honest about it all . . ."

And I looked at her big sad white face and pondered deeply. Either she had great courage or else she was just plain stupid.

But this story isn't really about Christine. She only started it all when she said, in that high plangent voice:

"Do come, my dear. You'll meet such interesting people . . ."

"Christine, darling," I said, "—do you see that roadman sweeping up dung over there? He is an interesting person. He has two legs, he has two arms, he has a heart and a pair of lungs. He has a wonderful arterial system and an epiglottis. He is a fascinatingly interesting person."

"Don't be stupid, Harry," said Christine. "You know what I mean. There's a woman down at Crudleigh who once met George Moore."

"Do you mean that she *hasn't* an epiglottis, Christine?" I asked mildly.

She looked at me, her brows pulled together. Tony came in at that moment and gave her a great hearty slap on the behind.

"Hullo, Chris," he cried. "How's the horizon, eh?—still widening?"

She blinked and looked sad. I felt sorry for her again and cursed myself for a sentimentalist. I always do curse myself for a sentimentalist and a fool. If I hadn't been so sentimental the whole strange business of the Crudleigh ghost might never have happened. At least—However . . .

Crudleigh was a long low house with a thatched roof. It was

very old. At one time it had been a whole row of cottages. Downstairs there were several long narrow rooms—a music room, a writing room, a discussion room. They were furnished with hand-made plain oak tables and stools, rough Indian mats, and yards of coloured hessian.

Upstairs were many little bedrooms. Bare wooden floors, more mats, divan beds with hand-printed fabric coverings, rough baked pots and vases in the windows for flowers, a few tasteful books, more hessian, and some small selected pictures—woodcuts mainly, or prints from lino-blocks.

In the grounds were many outbuildings. Far-off, buried among the outbushes of Crudleigh Combe, was a small solarium where you could sunbathe in the nude. Nearer at hand, across the croquet lawn, was a shed with some potters' wheels in it. A small brick building in the back yard housed a hand-loom. A hut at the foot of the salad garden contained a little turning lathe and an old-style hand printing press.

It was pouring with rain when Christine and I arrived. We walked through the woods, she with her big swinging stride that threw her flared skirt out in great ugly sweeps, I scuttling a little behind, dodging the drips from the trees. Except for the swishing of the rain through the leaves, everything was quiet and somehow mournful. Now and again I would stumble against a big yellow fungus and it would go rolling in pieces among the undergrowth.

Just before we reached the house we heard quick footsteps behind us, and as they got nearer there came the sound of hasty breathing. I looked round. A young man was running towards us along the path. He was dressed in a singlet and running shorts which clung to him closely, sopping wet, showing his gaunt ribby figure. His earnest face looked like a horse's.

We stepped aside and he swung past us, with a grunt of recognition for Christine.

"That's Hector Lowe," she whispered to me. "He must do his five miles a day—always, wet or fine."

I said: "Oh—what an interesting person," and we walked on.

We eventually entered the long low lounge. An immense log fire smoked dismally at one end of it, and round it, in a semicircle, sat a little group of people. One of them, a tall willowy woman with black tousled hair, advanced to meet us. She was dressed in a little Chinese jacket with a long clinging skirt, and her hands and ears were laden with jewellery.

"Christine, darling," she murmured, in a husky, mournful voice. "How enchanting of you to come. And this is your friend?"

Christine introduced us. The woman was the famous Tess Beauchamp, who owned and ran Crudleigh. She showed me to the others—I say "showed" deliberately, for her whole attitude seemed to imply that I was something dreary, brought in almost by accident, that had to be put up with. The people round the fire looked up desultorily. They were a strange-looking bunch: an old man with a patriarchal beard, dressed in a green velvet jacket (a Mr. Belarius), a young man named Dobson, who absently fingered a lute, two women, both gaunt-looking and with drooping, heavily-mascara'd eyes, and a young angular girl who wore a turban of green silk and was engaged in cutting the leaves of an exotic-looking book with a carved pearwood paper-knife.

"Now do sit down, you two," finished the Beauchamp. "Mrs. Fletcher is just telling us about the first time she met George Moore."

We sat down—Christine on a hessian-covered pouf, I on a hard, perfectly flat wooden stool that gave me hell after the first ten minutes.

Mrs. Fletcher—one of the mascara-eyed women—talked on and on and on about George Moore. It seemed that she had been his sole confidante—their conversations must have been interminable. Dobson, as a constant background, fingered his lute. The young man with the horse face—Hector Lowe, the runner—came in, having presumably completed his five miles, and then we all drank weak China tea from handleless home-baked cups.

Christine sat on her immense behind, her skirt flaring out all round her, her brows drawn intensely together. I suffered a damnable torture from my hardwood stool and wished myself a thousand miles away.

We had been sitting like that round the bleak fire for perhaps half-an-hour. Outside it was already growing dark. The rain had stopped and a light damp breeze was in the air, slowly dispersing the grey, low-lying storm-clouds. A big cypress just outside the window opposite me swished gloomily against the wall, as if engaged in a slow rhythmic dance. Mrs. Fletcher's carefully modulated voice went on and on, with occasional husky interjections from Tess. And I felt, creeping over me as I sat there, an unaccountable sense of sadness. I felt isolated and forlorn among those strange folk in that old bare house. I began to wish I had never acceded to Christine's request to meet the "interesting people"—I was annoyed with myself for having been so weak—and for having been sentimental enough to feel sorry for Christine. She was all right, I reflected, as I watched her drinking in everything that Mrs. Fletcher had to say. She would go on—there would always be something for her to do: there would always be literary and debating societies who would welcome her as a member—perhaps she would write a book one day, for one of the Left Wing Clubs. And the others too—the interesting people; old Mr. Belarius, half-asleep, fingering his white beard: Tess Beauchamp, chin on hand, so that her rings were shown off to their best advantage (vast heavy rings they were—Celtic jewels in silver mountings): young Dobson, his lute set aside for the moment, his head turned so that we could see his profile (he tried to look, I am certain, like the misty photographs of Rupert Brooke that frontispiece the *Collected Poems*): the girl with the turban—she was Dobson's sister, I discovered later, and her name was Sylvia—all tight and bleakly virginal, clasping her knees in her hands and staring into the smoky, sizzling fire . . . They were all all right—there was no need to worry about any of them: they had some sort of plan of campaign—they knew what they were doing. Either all this was a phase they were passing through, in which case it did not matter, or it was something they had arrived at, in which case it did not matter either. But still, as I surveyed them, I felt the unaccountable mournful sadness—the same sadness I had felt in the damp woods as Christine and I made our way to Crudleigh: the same sadness of old things, and decay, and quiet forlorn places.

Thinking of the woods I turned for a moment to look at Hector Lowe, the runner. He was the strangest of all the Crudleighites. He sat bolt upright in his chair, munching slowly at a raw carrot. His long horse face was puffy and drawn-looking—it seemed to me, at a venture, that his five miles had exhausted him. As I looked, he solemnly crossed one stringy leg over the other and struck his knee sharply with the edge of his hand. He did this several times, testing his reflexes: and apparently the result was not quite what he had hoped for, for he sighed and shook his head, then brought out a little book and wrote something in it. I smiled, and was on the point of looking from him back to Christine, when something else attracted my attention. Faintly, ineffably faintly, and thin and tenuous against the low monotonous voice of Mrs. Fletcher, I had heard a chord of music.

I looked at Dobson, thinking that perhaps he had picked up his lute again. But no: he still sat balancing his profile—and the lute lay on the floor where he had placed it, in the little dark corner beside the fireplace. I thought I must have been mistaken in thinking I had heard the music; but even while I looked at the instrument, with the pale lifeless firelight reflecting from its polished belly, again there came the ghostly chord—a melancholy interval, exactly in tune with the unaccountable sadness I was feeling. And just for a moment I had the impression—an astonishing, fleeting impression—that lingering over the lute strings in that dark corner were two white emaciated hands.

I looked more closely and they had gone. I stared at the circle of listeners again, but they were all intent on Mrs. Fletcher's recital. I blinked my eyes—they had been playing tricks on me in the bad light, I decided. Yet just for a moment, unmistakably, the hands had been real—small, pale, infinitely delicate: and sad—as sad as the chord they had plucked.

I shivered. I had a sudden uneasy sense that all was not well—there was something just under the surface in that strange house. Somewhere, lingering in the background, were other things—there was at least one other guest at Tess Beauchamp's party.

I stirred, found my voice, and suddenly threw a banal remark into Mrs. Fletcher's monologue. The guests all looked at me disdainfully—Christine blushed as if she were ashamed.

We went through to the dining room and had something to eat—not before time, as far as I was concerned. We sat at a long refectory table, on forms, and ate first some soup in wooden bowls—a thin, saltless vegetable brew—then had salad and brown bread with peanut butter, and finished with some dried fruits—dates, figs, and brown and withered dehydrated bananas. I still felt hungry at the end of the meal, and took an opportunity, when all the guests had their attention fixed on something Tess was saying, to slip two hunks of bread into my pocket—it would always be something to gnaw in my bedroom later on.

After the meal we trooped into the music room, and old Mr. Belarius sat down at a harpsichord there and played—quite pleasantly, I thought. Then Sylvia Dobson took up a recorder and, accompanied by her brother on the lute, blew her way tensely through an arrangement of the Purcell *Golden Sonata*. Half-way through I managed to signal to Christine to come outside with me.

We walked slowly about on the damp croquet lawn in the dusk, with the sweet sound of the recorder coming through the windows to us. I had a mallet in my hand, and now and again shot a ball absently towards a hoop.

"Tell me, Christine," I said, "what is the history of Crudleigh?"

"It used to be a row of cottages," she said. "They were built round about 1820—it was some sort of housing experiment, I think—a group of London ladies financed it—blue-stockings. Then round about the middle of the century a set of artists took them over and started a colony—the Crudleigh Water Colour Group—they had the same sort of ideas as the Pre-Raphaelites a little later on. Then in 1880 the cottages were reconstructed into one long house and some friends of William Morris's took it over. Tess bought it about three years ago, after it had been lying derelict for a time, and started running it as a guest house."

"For interesting people," I gibed. "No, what I meant, Christine, was—has anyone died here? Committed suicide, or been murdered—you know the sort of thing."

She looked at me strangely.

"Good heavens, Harry—what on earth put ideas like that in your head? Of course not—at least, I've never heard of any such thing."

I started on another tack. I sent a ball scooting through a hoop, then straightened myself, swinging the mallet.

"Tell me, Christine," I said, "why does Tess use wooden

dishes? And why does she serve the food in them without salt?—that dreary vegetable soup, for instance?"

"Really, Harry! You know perfectly well that wooden dishes are a hundred times healthier than any other sort—besides, Tess makes them herself on the turning lathe—it's one of her crafts. And as for salt—if you took any interest in dietetics you'd know that mineral salt is bad for you: all the latest books say so. If you cook vegetables properly you don't need it—and it's far better for you without."

She went into a long statistical report about the latest situation in dietetics. I listened as patiently as I could. When she had finished she said:

"Anyway, Harry, why did you ask? It's not the sort of thing I should have thought you would have been interested in."

I remained swinging the mallet a long time. Then I said:

"Christine—in very old books—not the sort of books I suspect you've ever read—there are such things as witchcraft recipes and so on. One of them tells you to use wooden dishes and to cook without salt—that is, if you suspect that there are evil spirits in your house."

She stared at me, her brows drawn together.

"Harry! You *are* mad!"

I shrugged and put down the croquet mallet. We walked a little way into the Combe. The grass was wet and the woods were solemn and still. Occasionally there came the little patter of drops of moisture on leaves—once a shiny quiet grass snake glided away from beneath our feet. There were now only a few straggling fingers of cloud in the sky—the little breeze had died. A faint lingering pink showed over the low hills to the west, some stars were out, and the nearly full moon was poised almost straight above our heads. From the house, far-off, there came the thin sound of the recorder: Sylvia was playing, now, an arrangement of *Au Clair de la Lune*.

We walked in silence back to Crudleigh. As we rounded the corner into the yard I heard deep breathing again, and occasional heavy gruntings. It was Hector Lowe. He was dressed in his singlet and shorts again, and, with his horse's face intently drawn, was engaged in a vigorous shadow-boxing.

"He does it every night and morning," whispered Christine as we passed him and entered the house.

"He'll wear himself out, that man!" I muttered.

I lay in my little room, unable to sleep. I had eaten my hunks of bread and dipped into every book in the hanging bookshelf above my bed. Now I lay on my back, smoking a cigarette and staring at the ceiling.

And once more there crept over me the indefinable sadness I have mentioned. Something elusive was in the air, something fragrant yet full of a dark foreboding. I tried to pin it down: I was, I knew, subject to moods—time and again in the past I had felt elated or depressed for no real seeming outward reason. But this was altogether different—was at once intenser and more nebulous than any mood I had ever experienced. It was a lyrical, elegiac sadness—a sense of things lost and gone away: a feeling of growing old, I might almost say—yet what reason had I, at thirty, to feel that I was old? And all the time, as I lay there, I saw in my mind's eye the two little hands fluttering over the strings of the lute, and heard quite clearly the forlorn thin chord they had sounded.

I finished my cigarette and stubbed it out in a small ashtray of hand-beaten copper. Then I switched the light out, turned over on my side, and tried once more to sleep. But the effort was useless. I lay wide-eyed, staring at the moonlight as it fell across the bare boards of my room.

I thought of the strange people on all sides of me. I wondered what dreams they were having—Christine, for instance, her white sober face set determinedly (for I imagined she approached sleep in the same way she approached everything: very intensely, working it all out). Or the curious Hector Lowe—was he lying on his back or his side?—which was more correct according to the latest health journals? Was he making notes even in his sleep of the number of breaths he took per minute? Was young Dobson presenting his profile to the moon? Was Mrs. Fletcher wandering in the Elysian fields arm in arm with George Moore, listening to his latest confessional with a look of immense sympathy on her gaunt face? Or Sylvia—what dismal virginal visions did she have? A free-love affair (sooner or later she was doomed to such a thing) with a young poet? She meets him at a gathering of the Young Communists' League—they go to Unity Theatre—they stand at a Promenade Concert staring a miniature score—they sit in the gallery at Sadler's Wells during the Ballet season . . .

I sighed. The night was warm. The window—a swing lattice—was only slightly open. I pushed back the bedclothes and went across the room.

The night was still and lovely. Before me, spread out in a long gentle slope, was Crudleigh Combe, the leaves all silvery in the moonlight and seeming to stand out quite individually on the trees and bushes. The air was damp, although the sky was almost empty of clouds—it was plain that more rain was on the way. It manifested itself in a slight creeping ground mist that blurred the edges of the shadows.

I lowered my gaze—then suddenly gasped and gripped the window sill tightly. Again I could hardly believe my eyes—again I felt that what I saw was no more than a trick of the weird light. But there was, as I stared, no possibility of mistake. Below me, standing just beyond the croquet lawn, was a young girl. I thought for one brief moment that it was Sylvia Dobson: but that illusion went immediately. The girl on the lawn was smaller than Sylvia—infinitely more delicate and more slender. And her face was ineffably beautiful—pale and forlorn-looking in the moonlight.

For a full minute I looked at her—and it seemed to me that she, as she stood with her hands at her breast, was gazing equally seriously at me. And then I made a sudden resolution. I knew that just under my window was one of the many Crudleigh outbuildings. In a moment I was over the sill and had lowered myself on to its sloping roof. Then I had scrambled across the tiles and was running over the lawn.

But she was gone. In the brief interval while my back was towards her she had slipped away. I stood disconsolately facing the spot where she had stood—and again the sadness was all over me and around me. Far-off, deep in the woods, an owl cried desolately.

This time there was no question of illusion. I *knew* that she had been standing there, quietly, staring up at me. And I knew something else, too: that the small beautiful hands that had been held at her white bosom were the same hands that had hovered over the strings of Dobson's lute . . .

I went back to bed and lay for a long time thinking in the silence. Towards dawn the threatening clouds at last assembled, and I eventually fell asleep to the low swishing of the rain in the trees.

What is a ghost? There isn't any use any more in arguing whether there are such things or not. I know, quite simply, that there *are* ghosts—and more than ghosts. I have seen and felt far too much to be able to hold any other opinion.

Yet most accounts of ghosts are wrong—no matter how circumstantial they are, they are wrong: indeed the very fact of their being circumstantial makes them wrong. Ghosts are not things—I doubt if they are even people: they are feelings. They are all unaccountable essences—they are your own self sitting gravely and accusingly on your own doorstep. That is why this story is vague and nebulous—all the time it is groping to describe something that is literally indescribable. Nothing spectacular happens—there is no sudden horrifying dénouement in which the girl in the garden turns out to have died violently and unhappily at Crudleigh in the past—all my baiting of Christine on that point sprang only from ignorance. Yet the girl in the garden *is* the story—and though I have not seen her since that visit of mine to Crudleigh, she has haunted me quietly and terribly and with an aching persistence through all the years between.

Who was she?—what was she? Unanswerable questions. I know nothing about her—except that now, in my mind, she is more real than any of those ghosts of Tess Beauchamp's: old Belarius, the two Dobsons, Mrs. Fletcher—even Christine.

I did not even know—definitely—that first night I saw her that she was a ghost. After all—was it impossible that a real girl should have been standing in the garden looking up at my window?—a girl from the village, perhaps, or a guest I had not met either in the lounge or the music room? I may have imagined the hands—

perhaps my mind had invented them as a distraction from the boredom of listening to Mrs. Fletcher: and only my damned sentimentalism associated them with the girl in the garden . . . Yet there was more in it all than that. There was a *feeling* that there was more in it than that. Not fear—not once in the whole strange business was I afraid: except perhaps when—— But no. Even then it was horror and not fear.

And I knew definitely, next evening, that she was a ghost—and I knew something else too. And it is something I still know, and cannot escape from.

. . . She was standing in exactly the same position. Expecting her I had stationed myself at the window, with my raincoat over my pyjamas. The night was cloudy—only occasionally the moon broke through and lit up the whole quiet scene. It was in one of the dark intervals that I first became aware of her—as an uncertain shape just beyond the croquet lawn. Then the clouds parted and she was there, fully revealed, very small and frail, with her little hands at her bosom.

I opened my window wide and leaned out, staring at her. She did not move. And, cautiously this time, I lowered myself over the sill and on to the roof of the outhouse. Keeping my eyes fixed on her, I edged my way over the slates, till eventually I stood facing her, with only the lawn separating us.

For a long time I stood there; then, with my heart beating a shade more quickly, I walked slowly over the wet grass until I was no more than a foot or two away from her.

She was frightened. Her eyes were large, she was trembling. Her small white hands were all the time picking nervously at her dress—hovering at her bosom as I had seen them hovering over the strings of the lute. What could I possibly say to her? She was a ghost—I was as alien to her world as she was to mine. Quite quietly and suddenly, as I stood there, I saw how immense was the gulf between us. There was no real communication—she was a different thing—she existed on different terms. And all round me was the dead weight of utterly helpless sadness that had oppressed me since my walk through the woods to Crudleigh.

Her trembling stopped and she heaved a great sigh. Then she turned and made a little movement away from me.

"Wait," I said—foolishly, for how could I know if she would understand me? But the exclamation came involuntarily.

She stopped: and then, very slowly, she moved back close to me. She looked at me with a curious, almost compassionate expression in her large eyes. She was beautiful in the dim light—her face small and wan, her frail figure so neat and trim in the elegant little gown she wore.

Her lips did not move, but she was speaking to me—I knew what she was saying. I set it down here—as I shall set down our other conversation too—as speech: but it was not speech—after that first "Wait" of mine I never again opened my lips to her, but communicated in the sense, as she did to me.

"It is not you," she said. "Not you at all. Why did you come when it was not you?"

"Who are you?" I asked her. She remained unresponsive, staring, and plucking at her dress. Then she suddenly shuddered.

"It is not you," she said again. "It is not you they are waiting for."

"Who are They?" I asked.

For a moment she did not reply. Then she shivered again and said:

"The Black People—the Other Ones."

A cloud covered the moon. There was a little rush and flicker as a small bat darted over my head. I started—and suddenly all about me there was a sense of icy coldness and menace—the whole air was full of menace. I looked round quickly. Nothing—only shadows, and her dim outline before me. But for a moment—only for a moment—perhaps communicated to me by my contact with her—there was the knowledge that we were not alone. Other things were round us in the quiet corner of the woods—they were pressed tight on all sides, invisible: and they were not as I was—or even as she was.

The cloud passed. I looked at her. Her eyes were wide and full of tears. Then, as it were impulsively, and without saying anything, she put out her small hand and seemed to touch me on the cheek. I had a sensation of a breath—something diminutive—soft, but infinitely cold: and then, quite simply, she was not there—she had gone, as if she had never been before me.

The grass was wet through my thin slippers. I was chilled,

though in my bedroom earlier the night had seemed warm. The trees and bushes rustled as a sudden corner of the breeze swept through them.

I went back into the house—slowly, not quite in my proper senses.

From that time on I lived two separate lives at Crudleigh: a superficial one as one of Tess's party, and a deep and secret one when I thought of the girl in the garden. When I first arrived with Christine it had been my intention to stay for only a few days—long enough to fulfil my duty to her. But now the time dragged on and I could not bring myself to leave—God knows what Tess Beauchamp and her guests thought of me, for they must have seen in a hundred ways that I had nothing really to do with them. I moped through their queer little rites and ceremonials—old Belarius's harpsichord sessions, when he played arrangements of his own of old unknown folk songs and dance suites: Mrs. Fletcher's anecdotes (she was writing a book on George Moore and used sometimes to read passages from it to us, in a high nasal chant): the Dobsons in full spate as duettists, he on his lute and she on her recorder. Mrs. Fletcher's friend—the other gaunt mascara'd woman (a Miss Delaware) made and operated puppets; and sometimes there were performances in the long lounge, when Miss Delaware disappeared behind the screening of a small stage and jerked her dolls through long symbolic plays, with Tess Beauchamp reading all the male puppet parts in her deep husky voice. On occasions like this I went into a kind of dream. I had no interest in the small grotesque figures before me—or in the other puppet-figures, the audience: I was all the time letting my mind dwell on the image of the girl in the garden. I went over and over the conversation we had had, I pondered every expression I had seen on her face. In some strange way, now that I had seen her, had been so intimately close to her, I no longer speculated about who she was, or what she was. I knew, with absolute finality, that she was a ghost—not the ghost *of* anyone, but simply a ghost: something else. It was not a question of believing or disbelieving—not even a question of wondering why. She was a ghost, and there was an end to it.

And she haunted me. The days passed, and since that conversation in the garden on the second night of my visit to Crudleigh, I had not seen her. I waited at my window, shivering in my raincoat, till dawn sometimes. But she did not come. I looked for her, peering into the bushes beyond the lawn till my eyes were strained and aching—but there was no shape—no sign or shadow. I looked for her; and I looked too, sometimes, with a sort of horror, for the Others that she had talked about. But there was nothing in all that time—only on occasions, as I stood there, the sense of sadness—and another sense too, now, mingling with it: a sense of menace and foreboding.

Yes, I thought of her all the time. Her small sweet face was before me—I could not escape from it. The memory of the little caress she had given me compelled my imagination always. As time passed I realized that I did not want anyone else but her—not in the whole world: she was all my life. It was the others that were unreal.

—All, that is, except Hector Lowe. As the days went on I found myself developing an almost morbid interest in this strange man. Perhaps it was because, in another way, he was as much cut off from the Beauchamp crowd as I was—we had an affinity in our separation. The truth about him, it seemed to me, was that he was just not interested in people. He thought of nothing but himself and his health. His room was next to mine, and sometimes, in the early mornings, I would hear him battering at a punch-ball, or working desperately at a little stationary rowing machine that he had. I would see him from my window, darting through the trees of the Combe as he ran his five miles. I would come across him shadow-boxing in a corner, or sitting testing his reflexes, his long face drawn and worried as he made little entries in his notebook.

I tried, once or twice, to draw him into conversation; but all the time we talked his eyes were darting about distractedly and he was plainly thinking of something else—perhaps the number of calories he had in him, or the exact amount of roughage he would be having with his next meal.

"Where did he come from?" I asked Christine one afternoon when we were walking in the village. But she, usually so well-informed about people at Crudleigh, could on this occasion tell me nothing.

"He was here at the time of my last visit," she said, "—about three months ago, that is. I don't think Tess had any knowledge of him before he arrived—he answered one of her advertisements in a magazine—you know—Attractive Guest House, Approved Food Reform Society."

Then she added, to my slight surprise:

"He frightens me a little, you know, Harry."

"Frightens you, Christine? I shouldn't have thought that anything could frighten you."

"Oh yes. There's something—well—unbalanced about him. He isn't at peace with himself."

"Are any of us?" I asked.

"Oh yes," she said solemnly. "Lots and lots of people are at peace with themselves, thank heaven. You are, for instance, Harry."

I smiled ruefully.

"Am I, Christine? I'm glad to hear it."

She drew her brows together in her intense way and added:

"Yes—you know what you want."

"And what is it?"

"I can't tell you that," she said, in her most solemn voice. "Perhaps you don't even know yourself, Harry—consciously. But it's there all right. You know."

Poor old Christine! Big, clumsy, hopelessly wrong on almost every point. But it was impossible not to adore her.

I remembered, as we walked on—she, as usual, swinging her skirt about her hips as she took her big gauche strides—I remembered with a kind of irony the phrase she had used to attract me to Crudleigh:

"Do come, Harry. You'll love it. You meet such interesting people . . ."

Well, it's an old tale now—all over and done with. Nothing remains. A few keepsakes and remembrancers and that is all. Some snapshots Christine took of Crudleigh before they pulled the old house down, a water colour I did from the window of my room of that little corner of the Combe beyond the croquet lawn. And the letter I had from Hector Lowe—that curious pedantic letter in the wavy handwriting: faded and worn now with the years, it has been folded and unfolded so often.

And the terrible sense of loss and sadness that I feel when I think of the girl in the garden. I sit now, for example, staring out of my window on this April evening, with the sky smoky and pink, the outlines on the roofs and chimney pots all hazy in the Spring mist over the city . . . and it is as if, all the time, I am groping unhappily to pin down, only for a moment, the whole nebulous sense of her. But she has gone. She haunts me, there is no escape from her—but now it is only as a memory that she haunts me: a memory of things that have slipped away and are lost—intangible things: sunlight on the wall of a nursery, the scent of a visitor who came to tea, the solemn sweetness of one's very first love affair. The memory of a shadow in moonlight. And that is all.

I saw her only once again during my visit to Crudleigh: and for some years the full horror of that last meeting so compelled me that all the quiet sadness of my real feeling for her was swamped. But fortunately the horror could not last for ever. I can write of it now—as I must write of it—in perfect detachment. There is no question of understanding it—I can relate and no more. Who the Others were—what they were—I have no inkling. It was only that just for a moment I seemed to see the other side of the coin—the shadow of the shadow. There was a hole in the air . . .

It was a week after the conversation I had had with her at the edge of the Combe. All evening I had been standing at the window, looking out. Downstairs there had been one of Miss Delaware's puppet shows, and, after it was over, young Dobson and his sister stayed on in the lounge, playing the lute and the recorder. The thin sounds came up the stairs to me as I stood shivering a little in the darkness; and I found my mind full of the image of the little white hands I had seen the very first night of my visit to Crudleigh. Eventually, towards midnight, the music stopped, and I heard the two players creeping stealthily to their beds.

The night was dark. After a few days of fair weather the rain had come back, and the air was full of the rhythmic whisper of it. Next door, from Hector Lowe's room, I heard the continuous light creaking of the rowing machine. He was doing his last desperate exercises before going to bed.

I stood for perhaps an hour longer, and then, worn out, I went to bed. For a little time I tried to read, but my mind would not stay on the printed page before me, and towards two o'clock I fell into a heavy doze. My last sensation, I remember, was a recurrence of the unearthly sense of uneasiness and foreboding that had afflicted me since first I heard, from the girl in the garden, of the Black People. I started up once at a rustle and scurry from somewhere overhead, then sank back again to the pillow, telling myself it was only a rat in the raftering of the old house.

I do not know how long I slept—an hour, perhaps, or a little more. It was a heady, stupid sleep. I know I was dreaming, in a vast struggling way—but what the dream was I have no recollection. There were heavy, blanketing layers of consciousness—I was like a man smothered and held down.

And then, I remember, I slowly became aware of things—uneasily and unhappily. I fought back through the layers to the surface. And even before I was fully awake—while my eyes were still closed—I knew that she, the girl in the garden, was with me. There was no mistaking it—she was with me, and she was calling to me.

I opened my eyes. She was standing by the bedside—I could see her quite distinctly in the dim light from the corridor that came through the skylight above the door. Her small face was pale—even paler than I remembered it: her whole attitude was agitated—she trembled. She wrung her hands mournfully—she was weeping.

I sat up in bed, staring at her, not yet properly conscious. A slight moaning breeze had sprung up outside and was circling the house, whistling a little under the old eaves and rustling the ivy and Virginia creeper against the walls. The casement curtains billowed and flapped into the room—and again, overhead, the rat went scuttling along the rafters. And as I looked at the wan figure before me in the dusk I was filled suddenly with an immense, a mortal, horror. Not at her, but at the something else that now I felt to be all about us—pressing in on us in the darkness, foul and malevolent, making the very air all black and restless. And I longed, as I lay there, weak and sweating under that terrible sense of doom, to reach out my arms and put them round the trembling small figure. But it was not possible—no contact with her was possible. At the most, from her, there could be the soft diminutive caress she had given me in the garden—not a touch, but rather a breath: a little ghostly gesture across the abyss . . .

"It is time," she said. "They are waiting. It is time."

I did not answer. I wanted to scream out—to make some noise to break the terrible spell. Yet I was bound, in a curious and hideous way, to silence.

"The Black People?" I asked her at last, fighting to make the contact.

"Yes. It is time. They are coming."

We remained for a long while looking at each other. Her eyes were wide and glistening, her little mouth was quivering. Then suddenly her trembling stopped. She stiffened—her whole attitude was one of immense, intolerable horror. She put out her hand and touched mine as it lay on the counterpane. I was filled with a terrible icy coldness. And as I gazed at her she screamed—not aloud, but through the sense, the way she spoke to me: a high, beastly, silent shriek that bored through my brain like a white cone.

And simultaneously, with my ears, I heard filling the air a hoarse, strangled, gasping sound—animal-like, horrible in the silence. And I *knew* at last that the Others were with us in that room—sweeping past us like a black wind. Invisible, horrible beyond all powers of description, dark, greedy, malevolent things, pressing in on us as they passed. Before me there opened an immense gulf—I reeled helplessly on the verge of something unutterably beastly. Then they were gone. The gasping ended in a long hoarse sigh. It was over—whatever the agony, it was over. I lay back weakly on the pillow. The little cold hand was withdrawn. I turned my eyes for a moment to look at her—and

I knew it was the last glimpse I would ever have. The horror had gone out of her face. She still trembled, but her expression now, in the dim light, was infinitely sad and full of pity. Her small white hands were at rest.

I closed my eyes. When I opened them again she had gone. The room was empty. I fell asleep, exhausted. I knew nothing, understood nothing—except that it was all over, at last. Whatever terrible thing had happened in that old house was finished. There was nothing but peace in the air—and the old forlorn sadness. As it were, in the atmosphere, there was the thin lost chord of music she had sounded on the lute . . .

I was awakened at eight o'clock by old Mr. Belarius. He was agitated—clad in a camel-hair dressing gown, with his grey hair and beard all wispy and matted.

"Anderson, Anderson," he cried, as he shook me,—"for the Lord's sake come quickly! Young Hector Lowe has hanged himself!"

I was out of bed and into a dressing gown in a moment. Outside, in the corridor, Tess Beauchamp and Christine were huddled together with pale frightened looks on their faces. Tess wore a long clinging kimono, Christine clutched about her a shapeless blue overall. Her hair was stuck with curlers, her complexion, without a trace of make-up on it, was blotchy and pimpled.

All this detail I took in, irrelevantly, as I pushed past the women with old Belarius and made my way into Hector Lowe's room. Young Dobson was there before us, staring stupidly upwards into the corner behind the door. I followed his gaze. A rope had been slung over a small old rafter that crossed the ceiling diagonally, and swinging slowly from the end of it, his feet about ten inches from the ground, was Hector Lowe. The long horse face was red and bloated, the eyes bulged out of their sockets, the whites of them quite purple. It was a beastly sight. I averted my gaze.

"I came up about a quarter of an hour ago," said young Dobson, in a low helpless tone. "I wanted to borrow one of his diet books—he told me last night he'd lend it to me if I came up this morning. I couldn't get any answer when I knocked at the door, so I opened it and walked in, and—and—"

His voice trailed away and there was a long silence. I saw the frightened faces of the two women framed in the doorway. It was old Belarius who spoke first. He cleared his throat and then said nervously:

"Anderson, he—he left a letter for you. It's over there—on the table."

I looked dazedly to where he was pointing. A small parchment-paper envelope rested against some books. It was addressed: "Henry Anderson, Esq., Personal," in a thin angular scrawl.

I opened it absently and started to read. I was aware of a whispered conversation behind me, and furtive sniffling noises as the two men cut down the body. Outside, after the rain, the sun was shining. The air was fresh, a bird sang lustily in one of the bushes in the Combe. But these things impinged on me incidentally: my whole attention was focussed on the letter.

This is what I read:

"Mr. Anderson,—I am writing this to you because I believe from the few conversations we have had that you will be the most likely to be able to understand what I must say before I commit suicide. But I do not expect you will understand fully—I do not indeed believe that anyone will or can. It is only, in the end, because I must in some way justify this action I am being forced to take to put an end to all the torment I have suffered.

"I am not a healthy man. My earliest recollections are of the sick-room. A long succession of mysterious maladies—shaded lights, medicine bottles, people stooping over my bed and talking in low grave tones. My father died when I was very young and my mother was morbidly solicitous about my health. Of this part of my life I remember little. There were long journeys, there was a succession of different doctors. I had, in the early days, a private tutor, following on the acid governess who had supervised my first steps in education: but when I was twelve this young man left our household and I was sent to school.

"I will not dwell on the unhappiness of my schooldays. You will understand that as a weakling boy, things were not made too easy for me by my companions. The only reason I mention my going to school at all is to emphasise that from this time on I lived away from home. I saw my mother only during the vacations, and thus we grew very quickly to be comparative strangers to each other. She was a curiously reserved woman. She had very few friends and only one relative—an unmarried sister who shared the house with her.

"I was fourteen when my mother died. At this time my health had improved considerably, I was able much more to lead a normal and an energetic life—it was, I can most certainly state, the only happy period I have ever experienced. Yet this brief interlude was completely shattered by the death of my mother. I went home one Easter vacation to find that my aunt was alone in the house. She said my mother was 'away'—she was nervously evasive of all my questions—perhaps my mother would be back, she said, before I left home for school again. But she did not come back. I moped disconsolately through the holiday, with my aunt making gallant attempts to amuse and entertain me. We avoided mentioning my mother after the first few days—I sensed that there was something terrible and mysterious in the air.

"I went back to school. Two days before the summer vacation was due to start, I got a telegram from my aunt to hurry home. My mother was dead.

"The effect on me was incalculable. We had been, as I have said, almost strangers—there was a reserve between us: yet her death left a great and an irreparable gap in my life. My health again grew bad—I toiled unwillingly through University (fortunately there was no shortage of money—my father had left a lot and it was carefully invested, and administered, on my mother's death, by my aunt). It was at this time I began first to grow morbid about my health—hypochondriacal, I suppose: yet in the light of all that I have since learned, is it surprising that I was so?

"But here again I do not want to dwell on detail. I have set myself a limit of half-an-hour for the writing of this letter. I swore to confine myself detachedly to facts. And so, in order to fulfil my planned design, I must hasten to a conclusion.

"Let it suffice for me then to say that when I was eighteen I made the terrible discovery that has obsessed me ever since and poisoned my whole life. I had often wondered how my mother had died, but had never dared, remembering her previous evasiveness, to question my aunt about it. At this time, however, she—my aunt—fell seriously ill, and just before she herself died, she told me the truth. I write it here as the final—the *only* clue to any real understanding of why I am doing what I must do.

"My mother had committed suicide. For three months before her death she had been confined in a lunatic asylum. And in doing so she had fulfilled, in her generation, the inevitable destiny of her family—and my family. The history, as I then learned it from my aunt on her deathbed, was of a terrible thread running through the whole line—an ineluctable hereditary insanity.

"There is no more to say. My aunt died ten years ago. To describe in detail the agonies of introspection I have since undergone would be impossible. They have ended in the decision I have mentioned. Yet I would wish it to be understood that the decision has been taken for the sake—the sole sake—of putting an end to the torture. It is not the other thing—not that, but, oh, my God, *the ghastly fear of that!* The wakening every morning to the dread that perhaps that day—in some sneaking and to me unnoticeable manner—the time had come for me. I have been a man pursued and beastily haunted. And I can stand no more.

"It is five minutes past three. The rope is ready. I subscribe myself, as my last sane earthly act,

"Hector J. Lowe"

I folded the letter slowly and slipped it into my pocket. The men had cut down the body and had laid it on the bed, covering it with a sheet. Belarius was dazed, young Dobson's face was pale—he seemed sick.

I looked round the room. Already the dull quietness of death had settled over it. The rowing machine lay pathetically motionless in a corner, the punch-ball stood beside it, a blank brown face, it seemed, on a thin and armless body. Thrown over a chair were the singlet and shorts I had seen Lowe wearing when first he passed Christine and me in the woods.

I glanced at his books on the table. They were mostly thin paper-covered pamphlets with titles like *Health and Diet* and *The Importance of Protein*. There was one heavy leather-bound volume, however, with its title in gilt Roman lettering on the spine: *Some Aspects of Hereditary Insanity*. And by the bedside, on a small shelf, was a vellum presentation copy of *The Hound of Heaven*.

I sighed and went through to my own room. I packed disconsolately; and, in the afternoon, Christine and I left Crudleigh.

I have tried, as far as I could, to set down this narrative detachedly and dispassionately. At this distance I think it has been possible—it is ten years since it all happened. There is no explanation—no implication, even. I know nothing. Only the letter remains, and it is a dismal and unsatisfactory index to the tragic agonies of that introspective and neurotic man. He himself is as unreal to me as they all are.

No—I no longer speculate, even. You, if you want to, may form conclusions—you may construct theories about the girl in the garden—you may decide who she was, and who, or what, the Black People were. I, after all this time, only accept it all—it is something that happened—something in which I was involved. There is no explanation—as I said before, I do not even, nowadays, want an explanation. It is all there, in my memory, ineffably—sometimes torturously—haunting. In my mind's eye I see the small white figure beyond the croquet lawn: and somehow, in her whole spirit and attitude, there is the essence of the little French song Christine and I heard as we walked in the garden at Crudleigh: *Ouvre moi ta porte . . . Pour l'amour de Dieu . . .*

Christine is married now. She married a West Country farmer, of all people. She has two children—a boy and a girl. The last time I saw her she had views on child welfare and education. When the children are old enough they will go to Dartington Hall.

Tess Beauchamp is in America. She gave up Crudleigh after the suicide—the publicity embarrassed her. The old house was run for a time by a young doctor as a private nursing home, but somehow the venture never succeeded. Eventually, three years ago, it was pulled down—to accommodate a new road that was being built in that part of the country. I went down out of nostalgic curiosity, and stood disconsolately watching the big dredgers at work over the remains of the croquet lawn.

As for Belarius and the others—I never saw any of them again. Once, at a concert, I thought I saw Miss Delaware, the puppet woman. But it was only a fleeting glimpse and I might easily have been mistaken. There are so many people like Miss Delaware who go to concerts.

No, it is not these people I care about—not one of them. It is not they who haunt me from those days, it is not their faces I see as I sit quietly looking back—at my piano, perhaps, playing Debussy—*Clair de Lune*—because, in association and atmosphere, it captures so exquisitely the ineffable mood of those days when I looked down and saw the girl in the garden . . . But she has gone, there is no use in searching any more.

Only sometimes, as I walk home on a moonlight night, or stand, looking out—sometimes, if the mood is deep enough, I seem to hear as from an infinite distance the small forlorn lute chord. And I have a clear fleeting image of those two little white hands. And I find myself wishing—

But no. It is all past. I know nothing.

Absence of Mind

ALL THINGS are affairs of degree. Each man has his own tragedies and his own joys. And their depths can be measured only in relation to the man's own experience. That is why people as trivial as Mrs. Carpenter are, in their own way, as tragic victims of the Other Passenger as Dr. Faustus or George Gordon, Lord Byron.

Yes, consider Maud Carpenter. Consider her well. She had her own type of the agenbite of inwit.

Mrs. Carpenter was absent minded. She could never resist telling people just how absent minded she was. "My dear," she would say—"it's really *appalling*. I can't *begin* to tell you how bad it is. It sometimes positively frightens me." And then she would recount some incident to illustrate her absence of mind—an interminable story involving shadowy uncles and aunts, brothers and sisters, cousins and half-cousins.

Mrs. Carpenter had other interests besides her absence of mind. There were sewing parties, knitting parties, canteens, missions for home and abroad, socials, whist-drives—all of them connected with the Church, the vicar of which, Mr. MacNaughton, was a patient listener to Mrs. Carpenter's stories. So her life was very full. She hardly noticed that her husband—in business in the north of England, though she lived in the south—never wrote to her: seemed, in fact, to have drifted out of her life altogether. Nor did she seem to notice that her daughters had left home, and that her aged mother, whom once she had pressed to come and be looked after, had gone off to live with another daughter in Wales. Mrs. Carpenter noticed nothing: she was too busy with her social duties—and in being absent minded.

Once a month or so, Mrs. Carpenter went up to London for a day's outing. She made it a ritual. The day was planned in advance: an arrival at about half-past ten, coffee, a tour of the shops, lunch, perhaps a matinée or a picture show in the afternoon (when she could take off her shoes in the friendly darkness), tea, and a leisurely journey home. "It's my own day, dears," she would say—"all my very own, to do as I like with. Heavens, I must fly! I'd forgotten all about the League of Helpers meeting! I *must* do something about this absence of mind—it's really too trouble-making . . ."

One outing day Mrs. Carpenter set out as usual for the train to London. It was a delicious morning in late summer, sunny and slightly fresh. As she waited in the little station she felt herself full to the brim of well-being and Christian charity. She reflected on her various activities, her church work, her interest in social problems of all sorts—and she felt indeed that her duty was being done. Looking back on her life she could see nothing to mar its smooth moral course: no shade of real vice, no deviation from the straight and narrow path—well, perhaps an occasional lapse when she was a child, a tiny falsehood, a stealing of apples from the orchard next door . . . But these were diminutive things, mere peccadilloes. Nothing to worry about, nothing to affect her character as a Christian woman.

In the train this mood continued. As she glanced through the paper with its accounts of burglaries, adulteries and crimes of all kinds, she thought comfortably how remote she was from the strange tangle of human sin. One paragraph in particular stimulated her complacency. It described how a woman had been arrested for shop-lifting in a big London store. "Silly creature," thought Mrs. Carpenter. "Of course she was found out. Crime doesn't pay—there's a balance in things. People can't get away from their own guilt. Ah well, poor woman. There, but for the grace of God, goes Maud Carpenter." And she was still sighing when the train reached London.

She had coffee in solitary dignity and smoked a cigarette—a mild one, which she held inexpertly in her lips, pouting as if she were going to be kissed. And then her tour of the shops began: her small dumpy figure moved slowly but inexorably through piles of heaped-up cloths, through rooms of underwear and oddments, through vast halls glistening with pots and pans and full of whitewood kitchen furniture. She fingered fabrics with an expert, faraway look in her pale eyes, sniffed at cakes of soap, popped samples of sweets into her little pink mouth in the confectionery departments. It was all part of her routine, her outing. "It's my own day, dears—my very own, to do as I like with." And it was this, this exquisite dalliance among hardware and drapery —it was this that she liked doing with her very own day. In its solitary, quiet splendour the day was a perfect escape from the confined social flurry of her life at home with all its turmoil and absent-mindedness.

In one or two of the shops she did a little buying—small things, ornaments, bridge cards, a new domestic appliance for cutting carrots and peeling potatoes. And then, towards noon, she entered the big department store in Oxford Street that was her special favourite. Here the piles of cloth were bigger and more imposing than they were anywhere else, the pots and pans shone much more brightly, the whitewood furniture had about it an air of even greater cleanliness and domestic efficiency. Mrs. Carpenter wandered in bliss: at that moment, in spite of her intense Christian charity, she would not have changed place with an Archangel.

It was in the jewellery department that she experienced her greatest joy. Forgotten were the texts about Solomon and all his glory. Here were necklaces, rings, bracelets to grace a million whist-drives and socials. Mrs. Carpenter was forming in her mind an exquisite picture of Mr. MacNaughton partnering her at whist and being unable to concentrate on his hand for surveying her rings and her necklaces, when suddenly she saw—It. It was nestling on a little heap of black velvet, glistening in the bright white light: a perfect little pendant, jewelled cunningly but not elaborately and suspended from a thin, delicately-wrought silvery chain. Mrs. Carpenter coveted the pendant immediately. She put out her plump little hand and touched it, then looked up for an assistant. The girl was at the far end of the counter, talking to a friend, and it was some time before she noticed Mrs. Carpenter.

"Er—how much is this?" asked Mrs. Carpenter, clearing her throat.

"The pendant? Twelve guineas, madam."

"I see. Yes. Twelve guineas. Well . . ." Mrs. Carpenter paused. It was too much. The pendant was exquisite, but twelve guineas was a lot of money. She *had* twelve guineas, of course, and she *did* want the jewel. But still, there were other things . . .

"Yes. I see. Thank you," she said vaguely, and moved away.

"Good morning, madam," said the obsequious assistant.

Mrs. Carpenter moved on, into other, less tempting departments. It had been a beautiful pendant—beautiful: but really it was too much. It would have been nice, for instance, with the slightly décolleté gowns she wore when she was a member of a platform party opening a bazaar or a fête. She saw, in her mind's eye, people in the front rows staring—not at the Reverend MacNaughton as he made his speech, but past him at her, and particularly at her neck and bosom. Well, it would have been nice. But still . . . Mrs. Carpenter sighed and went on her way through the mountains of cretonne, the hats, the posturing wax figures and the shining pots and pans.

Before she went for lunch she walked once more through the jewellery department. The assistant was talking again at the far end of the counter and Mrs. Carpenter was able, unobserved, to put out an envious hand for one quick caress of the pendant. She sighed again, more deeply, and moved away, out of the store this time, to the little restaurant she patronised further along Oxford Street. Beautiful, beautiful. But still . . .

In the afternoon she went to a cinema, walking back past the big store to get to it, and in the darkness she undid her shoes. She sighed joyously at the relief, settled her spectacles more comfortably—she was very short-sighted—and gave herself up to a contemplation of the screen. But something kept her full attention from the mawkish love story she was watching. At first she did not know what it was—something vague and pleasant that her mind was keen to dwell on. And then, suddenly, as her eye caught a glitter from the jewels round the film heroine's throat, she realised that it was the pendant. Yes—the pendant and her desire for it. And thereafter it went on intruding itself. She had only the vaguest notions as to what the film was about: its scenes were interspersed with other scenes woven by her imagination. At tea, too, back in the little restaurant, the pendant was before her eyes—and in the train on the way back home. It glittered from the pages of the evening paper she tried to read, it shone among the trees and houses that slid past the carriage window. And all the time, as she thought of it, she sighed and went on sighing.

Perhaps it was shameful to covet a thing—but she *had* liked the pendant so much . . .

Mrs. Carpenter went to bed early. She always did after her outings, exhausted as she was in body by the walking on hard hot pavements and in mind by the vast pageant of desirable things she had seen in the shops. She undressed slowly, going over in her mind the doings of the day. She remembered buying the bridge cards and the patent potato peeler, and reached for her handbag to put the receipts on the little metal spike she kept for that purpose in her room. As she opened the bag something fell out on the bed and glittered against the pale green of the eider-down. Without her spectacles Mrs. Carpenter could not see it properly. She picked it up and held it close to her eyes. Then it was as if someone were packing cakes of ice round her heart and someone else had installed a lift in her stomach that went down and down and down. It was the pendant. The truth was appalling—terrible beyond comprehension. But she did comprehend it and sat down weakly on the edge of the bed. She must have lifted the pendant—yes, *lifted* it and put it in her handbag in a fit of dreadful absent-mindedness!—because she had wanted it so much! . . .

The night was terrible. In it was fought out to the end a grim moral conflict, comparable only to the conflicts of the ancient saints. When she got over the first ghastly shock of what had happened, Mrs. Carpenter tried, as calmly as she could, to consider how it had happened. The night was hot and clammy in spite of the slight freshness of the morning, and she lay twisting and turning in the darkness, aware that on the dressing-table beside her was the pendant—perhaps, if she had had the courage to look towards it, glowing with the light of evil. There were two possibilities: one, that she had taken the pendant just before lunch when she had walked through the jewellery department (she remembered the assistant at the far end of the counter—had she called her? . . . no—that was the first time): two, that she had gone into the store after lunch on her way to the cinema. Oh this cursed, cursed absence of mind! She had had no idea that it could be so dreadful. After all—she admitted it—it had been . . . well, perhaps a *little* exaggerated in her accounts of it to Mr. MacNaughton and others. There *was* a tendency to forgetfulness, of course, and she *may* have made the most of it for the sake of—well, adding a little picturesqueness to her character (yes—she had to admit it): but this——! In one wild, unbalanced moment she wondered if the whole thing were perhaps some sort of punishment. There had been the few peccadilloes—now that she remembered, something not very nice at school: a theft of something from another girl's locker. And of course—and here she went cold in spite of the heat of the night—viewed in a certain light, this magnified absence of mind of hers, this romanticising of herself for a little cheap dramatic effect—wasn't it really *living a lie?* And wasn't this dreadful blunder through a sudden real attack of absence of mind—wasn't this indeed a visitation? Vengeance is mine, saith the Lord ... Mrs. Carpenter writhed among the hot clinging bedclothes. She was afraid. Even when she considered the high moral trend of her life to date, she was afraid. And she was afraid of what people would say.

Yes, that was it. Suppose she were arrested? She remembered the paragraph she had read in the train about the woman shoplifter. "There, but for the grace of God, goes Maud Carpenter" ... The grace of God had left her: there indeed did go Maud Carpenter. To what? To prison? No good pleading absent-mindedness —worse, worse. They would laugh at her naïveté in offering such an excuse. They would laugh—and they would talk. That was worse than prison—much, much worse. She could hear the thin, viperish voices at whist-drives and socials—Mr. MacNaughton's high indignant tenor, the others, contralto and soprano, as a chorus hissing round him. Mrs. Carpenter a thief. Absence of mind indeed. Tush!—an attempt to fob us off, an excuse built up against the day when she might be found out—as indeed she has been found out. And to think—to *think* of her as the treasurer of the League of Helpers ... Absence of mind indeed!

The anguish was intense, the night interminable. Mrs. Carpenter was beset by evil visions, eternal variations on a theme. All her high record as a church and social worker—all that was lost now for ever. She had sinned, she could see, in attempting to build up for herself a false character—and now (she shuddered at the word) she had *stolen*. She had stolen something that she had coveted. All was ended. *Hic jacet Maud Carpenter.*

Then suddenly she saw a gleam. Suppose—she hardly dared breathe it to herself—suppose she did nothing? It was unlikely that the shop people would have noticed the theft immediately—otherwise why had she not been accused and arrested before she left? And that being so, who was to connect the disappearance of the pendant with her? Even supposing they did suspect the little fat woman who had asked the price of the pendant—how were they to know that woman's name? . . . Her heart leapt, and for the first time that night she lay still, perfectly still. There was a chance. She could hide the pendant—bury it, burn it—and say nothing . . . For a moment—one exquisite moment—there opened before her a vision of the blissful continuance of her career after all. And then she realised that it was false, that it was not to be. She saw that she was a Christian woman—and besides, if she were found out, how much worse it would make the case against her if it were disclosed that she had tried to cover up her tracks. She remembered her thoughts of the morning: there was a balance in things, people couldn't get away from their own guilt . . . She was a Christian woman. She was Maud Carpenter—and Maud Carpenter was a creature of high integrity. Maud Carpenter would play the game. She had decided—suddenly and finally—on the higher ethic. And if people talked—well, she was prepared for it. She—Maud Carpenter—would be able to hold up her head without shame. She would know—and she alone—how this night's temptation had been conquered. After all, this was what it was all about—this was why one went to church and disciplined oneself in philanthropy—to be able to make high ethical decisions. Yes—let them talk: Maud Carpenter was of nobler stuff than would heed them. The course was set, the game had to be played. To-morrow she would go to London. She would go to the shop. She would return the pendant. And—she would confess.

Towards dawn, Mrs. Carpenter fell into an uneasy sleep. Before she did so she stretched out her hand to touch the pendant by her bedside. It was cold and hard to the touch—seeming somehow, to Mrs. Carpenter's inflamed imagination, malignantly vindictive.

Next day, Mrs. Carpenter took the morning train to London. She was in a dream. The ice-blocks were still round her heart, the lift was still going down in her stomach.

She went straight to the store in Oxford Street. In the jewellery department, where she stood helplessly surveying the counters, she was approached by an urbane shopwalker. In the minute detail with which, one is told, the condemned observe, she noticed a small stain on the lapel of his otherwise immaculate coat.

"That one," she said helplessly—"that assistant." And she pointed to the girl who had told her the price the day before.

The shop-walker beckoned and the girl came forward.

"Yes, madam?" she asked. Mrs. Carpenter wanted to faint, but she held her courage high.

"I've come," she said, in a thin croaking voice. The assistant was smiling blandly. What knowledge had she of the immense spiritual turmoil expressed in that high, hoarse whisper?

"I'm sorry—I ... I didn't know—I didn't mean to ..." Mrs. Carpenter almost broke down. But with an immense effort she took the pendant from her handbag and laid it on the counter.

"I—I don't suppose you remember me," she said.

"But of course, madam—of course I remember. Madam was in the shop yesterday." The assistant's face wore a strange expression—half puzzled, half suspicious.

"There it is—take it back," went on Mrs. Carpenter incoherently. "I didn't mean to steal it."

"Steal it, madam? *Steal* it?" The girl was horrified. Then she smiled.

"But madam—surely you remember? You bought it—yesterday. You said not to bother putting it in a box. I can show you the copy of the receipt." And she suddenly laughed. "Madam must be very absent minded. Really she must. She must suffer indeed from absence of mind ..."

The shop-walker was in time—only just in time—to catch Mrs. Carpenter as she fainted.

Hands

My life was a black charnel. I have caught
an everlasting cold . . .

John Neville had been teaching for three years; six months' relief in a small school in the south of Scotland, two and a half years in Cruach Academy in the north. He taught English, and there were two masters above him in his section—Grant and Hamden. Hamden was the senior. He was fifty-five, thin, tall and dry. His hair was lifeless and untidy, it dangled in a sort of limp hook over his collar at the back. He had a habit of wrinkling up his thin nostrils as if in a continual sniff of disapproval, and his watery, pale blue eyes seemed always strained and painful. But it was his hands that fascinated Neville. They protruded from his eternally frayed cuffs, long and gaunt, with huge knobbed knuckles and bulging veins.

Grant was different in every way. He was beefy and good-natured, he made fatuous broad jokes and roared with laughter over them, he was lenient with his pupils and lamentably incompetent. He was married to a big vulgar woman as coarse as he was himself. Hamden was unmarried—he was (his own word) a misogynist.

Neville did not like either of his colleagues. He could tolerate Grant more easily than Hamden, but Mrs. Grant gave him an uncomfortable and overpowered feeling. The only woman he had ever really liked (apart from his mother, whom he had adored) had been a fellow-student of his at St. Andrew's University: a girl named Rosemary. But that was all far off and on another planet. On this planet were only the enormous fleshy bulk of Mrs. Grant and the huge abominable hands of Hamden: and of course the children—the serried ranks of the children, hastily scrabbling through Addison and Steele and Shelley and Keats.

2

"Dear Herbert,—It is after eleven o'clock, but I do not feel like going to bed. Perhaps it will relieve my mind to write to you for a bit. Yet what do I mean when I say it will 'relieve my mind'? I don't think I'm unhappy—I know I'm not. Only bored—interminably, unbelievably bored. Yes, I'm a very odd fish. I went to the cinema to-night, then had a glass of beer and went for a walk. I went up the hill and sat on the grass. It was very quiet. A mist was over the town, then beyond it the mountains, very dim and mysterious and majestic. There were long fingers of purple cloud with the gleam of the setting sun through them, then a mauve and pale blue sky with some half-hearted stars. When I came down I found that my old landlady had gone to bed and left out my usual glass of milk. And here I am. To-morrow we start the tests for next month's exams. You know:—'Put the following poem into your own words. What did the poet mean when he said . . .' etc. etc. Ugh! Think of it—I've been here for almost three years. Is it any different teaching in England? I don't suppose so.

"Hamden is unbearable. I think I could kill him easily. I probably shall some day. Making out the test papers seems to fill him with a dismal dry ecstasy. He asks me for suggestions, but never pays any attention to them when I make them. He's writing a text-book, you know—on précis construction. Grant keeps on saying 'he needs a woman, you know—not good for a man.' Then he says—'so do you, Neville.' I passed his house on my way down to-night, and that gross cow of a wife of his was pulling down the blinds in the front room. You could see everything she's got against the light.

"I wish we could meet and have a long talk, like in the old days. I feel very cut off here. I try to keep abreast of things by reading, but really it isn't easy if you can't argue it all out with someone, and of course there's no one here. To-night's an example. I got some of Schopenhauer's essays from the library and meant to have a quiet evening with them. Then suddenly I couldn't seem to be able to focus my attention—I had to get out. So I saw a wretched American film instead. I couldn't tell you what it was about—it's a sort of dope to sit in the dark and stare at the screen.

A young couple in front of me kept whispering and fondling each other—holding clammy hands—and there was an old woman beside me who went on sighing and weeping over the sad scenes.

"There's a drunk man just passed outside the house singing *Annie Laurie*. I think I'll have to try to get down to Glasgow this week-end—I need a break: I might call and see MacDowell—haven't had a chat with him for—oh, eighteen months. I think a bit of his cynicism would do me a lot of good . . ."

3

In the Cruach Public Library one evening Neville met Miss Tainsh, junior Modern Languages mistress. She had joined the staff of the Academy the term after he had, and as newcomers they had been drawn together for a little while. But now it was some months since they had talked.

They left the Library together, Miss Tainsh carrying a novel by Arnold Bennett, some poems by Hardy and a book of Scarlatti's music. Neville had a volume of Shakespearean criticism and a book about Kant. They walked along the street, chatting about school topics.

Miss Tainsh was small and quite pretty. She had a nervous, forlorn manner, and a way of venturing her opinions tentatively, as if in constant fear of being proved wrong in whatever she said. Neville was abstracted. Once, as they chatted, he glanced down at her and appraised detachedly her wide eyes and moist pink lips.

"If one liked to exert oneself," he thought, "one might, quite easily . . ." And then: "But after all, why exert oneself?"

After a time Miss Tainsh said, in her hesitant way: "I hear you had a—difference of opinion with Mr. Hamden to-day."

"So it's gone round already," said Neville bitterly. Then he added: "I suppose they told you we'd come to blows?"

"Oh no," she said quickly. Then, hesitantly again: "You—didn't, did you?"

"Of course not. We—disagreed, that's all."

"He must be rather a difficult man to get on with," she ventured, after a pause. "I've only spoken to him once. He's very uncommunicative, isn't he."

"He's dead," said Neville vehemently. "He's got no opinion—nothing—that hasn't been out of fashion for fifty years. We had our tiff over these wretched test papers. He said I'd marked them too leniently. I told him they were too ridiculously difficult and pedantic for any child."

"They said that he—threw a book at you."

"He threw my corrected papers at me. I left them lying on the floor and walked out."

They reached Miss Tainsh's home. She lived in a small half-villa with her mother.

"Would you—care to come in for a cup of tea?" she asked, stumbling as always over the words.

"No thanks. I'd better get home—I've got some more papers to correct."

As he made his way towards his lodgings he passed Grant's house. Mrs. Grant was in the front garden, watering the flowers. The earth had a sweet smell in the cool summer dusk.

"Hello, Neville," called out Mrs. Grant, in her bluff, larger-than-life way. "George tells me you've been rowing with old Hamden."

"Oh, it was only a difference of opinion. Nothing much."

She laughed noisily. "What about coming in for a glass of beer?" she called. She had set down her watering-can and was wiping her hands on her apron. He saw how tight her skirt was round the behind and how beefy her calves were.

"No thanks. Got to get home—papers to correct you know."

In his room he sat on the edge of the bed, thinking. First of all, Miss Tainsh. Her first name, he knew, was Miriam. Then, Mrs. Grant. He had heard Grant call her Florence. Then, Hamden. He thought of him as he had sat at his desk, complaining in his high, querulous voice about the marking of the test papers.

"No dam' good, Neville—no dam' good at all."

Then the thin nostrils wrinkling, the watery eyes straining through the old wire-rimmed spectacles, and the great gaunt hands fumbling awkwardly among the foolscap sheets.

Neville saw nothing ahead of him. It would be another ten years before Hamden retired. Then Grant would became senior master and he would slip into Grant's job, and some new young devil would come in his place as junior. Suppose he went to another school—the same sort of life would wait him there. He might marry—someone like Miriam Tainsh, if not even Miriam Tainsh herself. Grant had said: "You need a woman, Neville." A half-villa. Miss Tainsh's mother a permanent guest in the back room. A visit to the Grants'. Beer and cards—Miriam playing Scarlatti as a diversion.

And then his thoughts drifted and he found himself thinking of Rosemary, his old flame of University days. He remembered how they had sat hand in hand on the beach at Montrose one day after a bathe, listening to the remote sigh of the surf. He remembered the first time he had kissed her—how they had clung together so passionately for a moment, the air full of the perfume of night-scented stock and someone, far-off, playing the *Donauwellen Waltzes* on an old piano. His thoughts went further —to his mother. He got into bed and lay staring into the darkness. Lost worlds.

"A bloody sentimentalist," he said to himself. "It's all past. Leave it alone. Do something. Face up to things. Don't be a bloody sentimentalist."

4

Some weeks went by. One evening Neville went to the Grants' for a meal; one Sunday afternoon he had tea with Miriam Tainsh. At the Grants' he ate enormously, then sat suppressing his indigestion and laughing in a strained fashion at Grant's coarse jokes. At Miss Tainsh's he sat with his tea-cup poised clumsily in his hand, making some sort of conversation with Miriam and her mother. Mrs. Tainsh was a little deaf and the inanities of the conversation had to be repeated in a shout into her ear. Both visits were exhausting in the extreme.

He went out one evening for a long walk. There was a spot about three miles from Cruach where the road fell down on one side in a sheer drop to the waters of a long, gloomy loch. There was a strong wooden fence along the side of the incline, and for a long time Neville leaned on the top bar staring into the black water far below. He couldn't swim.

It began to rain—the thin, chilling rain called Scots mist. He walked back to the town with his collar upturned, soaked to the skin by the time he reached his lodgings.

5

Every morning Neville's landlady gave him porridge, bacon and egg, hot rolls and butter and strong sweet tea. He always sat for ten minutes after the meal, reading the newspaper, while the landlady hovered about the kitchen making attempts to start conversation.

He read about international unrest, and it all seemed fabulously remote from Cruach, from this small room with its old-fashioned range and its over-abundant ornaments.

"Will the school holidays be comin' soon, Mr. Neville?" asked the landlady.

"What? Eh? Oh yes—next week, Mrs. Duthie. Next week."

He went on reading and sipping his tea. An acute situation in the Balkans. War in China. Threats of war in Europe.

"Is there something organically wrong with my brain?" he wondered. "I can't grasp this, I can't cram it in. If I were living two hundred years from now I could master it as history, I could teach it. It would be more real than it is at the moment . . ."

He finished his tea and walked down to the school. There was a note for him in the masters' common room. Hamden wanted to see him before school began. He put on his gown and mortar-board and made his way to the senior master's room.

Hamden was sitting back in his swing chair when he went in. His great gnarled hands were clasped at his chin and he swung himself slightly from side to side, so that the ancient chair creaked monotonously.

"Ah, Neville, I wanted to see you. Sit down, sit down."

He waved vaguely at a chair and Neville sat down, saying nothing, waiting resignedly for whatever it was that Hamden had to tell him. The senior master cleared his throat and picked up a pencil from the desk. Then he peered suddenly at the younger man and said:

"Look here, Neville, I'm damned sorry we've had—well, words this term."

"I'd forgotten it already, Mr. Hamden," said Neville. He was staring at the huge knobbled hands as they played with the pencil.

"Quite. Of course. What I mean is—well, it's no dam' good having rows. I mean—school life's trying enough as it is. I mean—you're young . . ."

"So are the pupils," said Neville. It was like a dream—the graceless movements of the hands fascinated him. An acute situation in the Balkans. War in China.

"Quite so, quite so," said Hamden in his dry way. "That is why we are helping them to grow up, Neville. Anyway, don't let's quarrel. I've no doubt your views will change."

The conversation went on with desultory apologies on both sides. Then, in the distance, they could hear the bell for the first period. Hamden put down his pencil.

"Well, I have sixth-year boys. Let's shake hands on it, Neville, eh?"

They shook hands and Neville went to the door.

"A holiday will do you good," Hamden called after him. "I think you're a bit run down—don't look healthy. School life makes you like that, you know. I'd a devil of a time my first three or four years."

Neville looked back at him—at his yellow, stretched face, his lank hair, his stooped, rachitic frame.

Then he went to his third-year boys and tried to interest them in *Twelfth Night*.

6

"Dear Herbert,—Another week of it and then, thank God! a break for two whole months. I don't know what I'll do with myself. I have a feeling that I might go to Montrose for a fortnight or so, and then perhaps down to the border. Is there any chance of your being in Scotland? If so, let me know and we'll try to arrange a meeting.

"Hamden made a heavy-handed attempt to smooth things over this morning. Really I wasn't interested—he's too fantastic altogether. A figment of my imagination—or of his own, I don't know which. Anyway, we shook hands for what it was worth.

I don't know how we'll get on when school resumes. Oh well, what the hell does it matter after all?"

"Did you meet Miriam Tainsh when you were here? I can't remember. She's quite nice—I talk to her now and again. Negative, but not disturbing. She's grown unaccountably friendly with Mrs. Grant—I can't think why. You couldn't imagine two women more unlike. Well, maybe that's the reason. Tainsh spends a lot of time round at the Grants', at any rate. Queer: one can never forecast things.

"Don't be surprised at anything. I feel queer these days, as if on the *verge* of something (can't put it any more clearly than that). Well, maybe I only need a rest and a change. It is a bit of a job giving oneself continuously to insatiable youngsters (I wish I could even take the noble view of schoolmastering) . . ."

7

There was a boy in the third year named Elder. He was oafish and unlovable, good at nothing at all. But if there were any jokes to be played, Elder was always mixed up in them. His jokes were clumsy and pointless, but he had a reputation among his classmates nevertheless and so did his best to keep it up.

On the morning after his interview with Hamden, Neville went to the classroom where he was taking History. When he went in the boys were sitting in unusual quietness. Then he saw that someone had scribbled some fatuous verses on the blackboard. He immediately suspected Elder but said nothing and went over to the board and picked up the felt duster. He rubbed at the verses and immediately a long smear of thin liquid glue appeared on the blackboard. There was a suppressed titter from the boys. Neville stood for a minute wearily gathering patience, then he turned round with the expression of martyrdom he always assumed on such occasions. And at that moment the door opened and Hamden strode in.

He peered at Neville standing with the duster in his hand, then at the smear of glue, then he surveyed the suddenly timid boys. His thin nostrils wrinkled and the tight skin round his mouth began to twitch a little.

"Come out the boy who did that," he quavered, pointing at the board with one of his long crooked fingers.

One or two of the boys glanced involuntarily at Elder, whose face gave no doubt at all about his guilt. Hamden's long arm swung round until it pointed at him.

"You—Elder. Was this your doing?"

Elder said nothing, he only blushed unhappily.

"You can come and see me at the interval," went on Hamden. Then he turned to Neville. "I wanted to see you about something but it can wait till later. Meantime I'll send in the janitor to clear up that mess."

He went out, and there was a little restless movement through the class. Neville went up to his desk and began the lesson in his listless, resigned way.

When the bell rang for the eleven o'clock interval, Neville went straight to Hamden's room. The boy, Elder, had already arrived. He was standing with his hands behind his back, staring unhappily at the three-thonged strap that lay on Hamden's desk. Hamden himself was looking through some papers. He glanced up and blinked as Neville entered.

"Well?" he asked. "Do you want to see me?"

Neville nodded brusquely.

"I want to know what you propose to do to Elder," he said. He was speaking mechanically, with no rage, no feeling at all. But he seemed to have a set course of action, dictated by something outside himself altogether.

Hamden leaned back slowly and his chair creaked. He stretched out his arm and picked up the strap, then began passing it through his hands, twisting his gaunt fingers through the thongs. Elder seemed surprised but dumb.

"To do to Elder," repeated Hamden slowly. "To punish him. Of course." Then, wrinkling his nostrils: "Have you any objection?"

Neville nodded again. Now he was a little surprised at his own actions.

Hamden said nothing for a moment, then he rose slowly from his creaking chair and came round the desk.

"Come here, Elder," he said. "Put out your hand."

Elder glanced for a moment at Neville, then he began to move forward, stretching out his hand as he did so. Suddenly Neville advanced. He stopped Elder with a gesture, then went up to Hamden and, with a sudden effort of strength, twisted the strap out of his hand.

There was an intense silence. Hamden and Neville faced each other, the older man blinking in fury. His face was yellow, the tight skin twitched, he was trembling slightly. Then suddenly he said, in the high, querulous tone he adopted when he was moved:

"Leave the room, Elder. Leave the room, I say."

The boy went out, scared and embarrassed. The two men continued to stare at each other, then with a sudden gesture Hamden went back to his chair and sat down heavily.

"Really, Neville, you go too far," he said.

"Elder is one of my pupils," said Neville in a low voice. "It's up to me to give him any punishment he deserves. I won't have him tortured out of all proportion to what he did. It was only an end of term joke. It doesn't warrant *that*."

He threw the strap down on the desk. The heavy, stiff leather uncoiled itself slowly.

"I'm responsible for all the English pupils," said Hamden. "If you want to know, I determined to punish Elder myself because I knew you'd do nothing."

"I would have punished him," said Neville quietly, "but in my own way."

"Cha!" Then Hamden suddenly raised his voice. "It's no dam' good. I won't have it. I tried to talk to you yesterday, Neville. By God, if I didn't think you were run down I'd take the whole matter to the authorities. You know dam' fine how Dr. Christie views insubordination."

"You can do what you like," said Neville, shrugging.

He went out. In the corridor he saw Elder, still dazed and sheepish looking.

"You can come to my room, Elder," he said. And there he took his own strap from his desk and gave the boy three good strokes across the palm. Then, when Elder had gone, he threw down the strap and sank into his chair. The bell rang for classes, but it was a full ten minutes before he rose and went along to the classroom.

8

That evening he called on the Tainshes. Miriam answered the door. She was startled and vague.

"Mother's gone down to the church—it's her mid-week service night," she explained.

He looked round incomprehendingly at the lifeless furniture and ornaments. There were bits of old-fashioned china, some photographs (one of Miriam as a child, another of Miriam in her degree cap and gown), a screen before the fireplace with some stags painted on it in oils, and an aspidistra in an old Delft pot. A book of Haydn sonatas was open on the piano.

Neville sank wearily into a chair and leaned back on the hand-worked antimacassar.

"Oh God, I'm tired!" he said. Miriam stood flutteringly before him. He realized she was asking if he wanted a cup of tea.

"Tea? No . . . No, thank you."

There was a silence. Miriam was searching for something to say. He could see that she didn't understand his mood but was aware that any of the usual social gambits would be out of place. So she was helpless and embarrassed.

"I expect you won't see me next year," said Neville suddenly.

"Why not?"

"Hamden will have me booted out. We had a colossal row to-day. I thought he was going to strike me."

"Oh . . . Oh . . ."

That was all she could say. She had seated herself gingerly on the edge of a sofa.

"Well, what the hell does it matter?" he went on bitterly. "I don't care. There's bound to be a war in any case soon. There'll be air raids. We'll all be blown to bits."

"But where could you go? I mean—what would you do?"

"Do? Oh there's a world outside Cruach. There's always something to do. I don't know . . ."

There was silence again. Then she ventured tentatively:

"Why don't you get on with Mr. Hamden? I mean—oh, I know he's difficult and all that, but if one sinks one's own personality——"

"Hamden isn't the half of it. He's only a sort of—a sort of crystallization. He gives all the unresolved bits of me some sort of 'local habitation and a name.' What I'm fighting against isn't Hamden—it isn't even Cruach. It's—oh, well. Forget it all."

"Fighting . . . I don't know what you mean by 'fighting,' " she said timidly.

"Neither do I," he said with a sudden snigger. He got up to his feet and began to walk restlessly about the room. She was still sitting on the edge of the sofa, following him about with her wide startled eyes.

"What's this?" he said abruptly, stopping for a moment before the piano and fingering over the first theme of the sonata. "Haydn . . . Tum-ta-ta-ta-ta-ta-tum . . . Why do you go to the Grants'?" he asked suddenly, turning to her.

"I——" she was nervous, his sudden jump from subject to subject was ununderstandable to her. "I——just go. Mrs. Grant—asks me."

"That cow! Oh well. I shouldn't have thought you'd have anything to say to each other."

"Well—school. She's all right."

He had stopped in front of her and was staring down at her. Suddenly he said, inconsequentially:

"You have lovely hands, Miriam. Soft and white and beautiful. Lovely hands."

He could read the fear in her big eyes.

"Miriam——" he began. But he didn't know any longer what it was that he wanted to say. He was inarticulate, his mind was blank—except that he knew of something that was there, struggling desperately in the background to make itself clear.

"No it doesn't matter. I've forgotten. I'm sorry I'm like this. I'll have to go."

"But what's the matter? I mean—can't I help you?"

"No. I don't know. I haven't felt like this before—not as strongly. There's something wrong. Maybe it's only because I need a rest—I've been working too hard over these wretched tests and exams. I wish——" He hesitated.

"What?" she asked.

"Nothing. I'm going. I'm sorry if I've disturbed you."

He went to the door. But something stopped him. Whatever it was that was tormenting him, he seemed to have been goaded to the limit of his endurance. He felt as if his chest were bursting, and his eyes were hot so that he could hardly see. Then he was aware—in a strange, impersonal way—that he was kneeling on the floor with his head in Miriam's lap, sobbing uncontrollably.

She did not know what to do. She kept on saying: "John—John—what is it, John? . . ."

His sobbing spent itself and he was still. In the silence he could hear the ticking of the cheap clock on the mantelshelf. Her lap was warm. He could feel a slight trembling in her legs.

"O God," he said suddenly. "I'm sorry."

She did not say anything. She seemed very small and curled up inside herself—on the defensive, he found himself thinking, always on the defensive. It was no good, something had gone wrong. No sort of relationship between them was possible. He was ashamed of his sudden lack of control. He did not want to say anything more to her. He felt himself alone. Explanation—even to himself—was impossible.

"Good-night," he said abruptly. He went to the door and walked, a little unsteadily, down the garden path.

And now he gave up finally any attempt to understand himself—to understand anything. He felt like an automaton. He had some vague sense of being directed and controlled—he knew in a queer way where he was going and what he was doing. And resistance—even if he wanted to resist—seemed foolish.

9

He walked through the dusk slowly but with determination. Without having to think he took the right turnings. In ten minutes he had reached his destination—a small house standing alone at the end of the road leading up to the school.

He rang the bell and waited. There was silence, then a fumbling sound as a door-chain was unhooked, and he was facing Hamden—Hamden grotesquely clad in a short dressing-gown of stiff silk, blinking in the dusk at his unexpected visitor.

"Neville," said the senior master at last. "Come in. This is unexpected. I couldn't recognize you."

Without a word Neville followed the older man inside. He heard the rustle of the silk dressing-gown and the shuffle of Hamden's slippered feet. Then he was in a study, lit dimly by a big standard lamp—a statuette of a buxom Eastern girl holding up a torch.

"Sit down, sit down," said Hamden. "'Pon my soul I don't often have a visitor. Sit down." He fussed around for a moment or two, pushing things nervously about with his great hands. They seemed more than ever grotesque as they protruded from the sleeves of the dressing-gown.

"He thinks I've come to apologise," thought Neville. "He's getting ready to crow. Well, let him, let him." Aloud he said: "No thanks. I won't sit down. I wanted to see you for a moment."

"Have a cigarette," said Hamden. He leaned over the desk for the box. His lanky grey hair hung in its curious hook over his collar.

Neville held the cigarette to the match that Hamden offered. Then he looked round the room. It was comfortable in a heavy, Pre-Raphaelite way. There were numerous books, some chairs of mellow leather studded with brass nails, a few pictures, a rack with pipes of various sizes and ages. The desk itself was solid and expensive, well polished, though covered with innumerable small ink-stains. It was littered with books and papers. There was one heavy glass paperweight and a big, decorative paper-knife of brass. The blade was long and slender and reflected the light from the houri's torch in a dull bar against the gloss of the desk.

"Well, now," said Hamden, with a thin conventional smile, "what can I do for you, eh?"

Neville made no answer. He looked straight into Hamden's pale strained eyes. He felt nothing at all. But still he knew what he would do.

The silence grew uncomfortable for Hamden. He coughed, his nostrils twitched. With his knobbled fingers he took the cigarette clumsily from his lips and turned to the desk to look for an ash-tray.

Quickly Neville leaned forward and picked up the paper-knife.

With a surge of all his strength he drove it into Hamden's back. And there was an extraordinary rush of feeling, an enormous blinding sensation.

"Finished, finished! Oh Christ, finished!"

Hamden was still standing, with the knife protruding from his back. Then he gave a strangled, high-pitched groan and slid along the desk, sweeping some papers and books to the ground. He lay in a warped, incredible attitude for a moment or two, then toppled to the floor, his long thin fingers twitching like the legs of a dead frog.

Neville stared at him for a long time as he lay there in painful immobility. Then his lips curled back from his teeth in a terrible dry snarl. He knelt down. He grasped the handle of the knife and levered it with a slow and beastly deliberation from the wound. The same unconscious force that had motivated him ever since he had left Miriam Tainsh caused him now to hear, without emotion, the soft, sucking, squelching sound the knife made as it left the wound.

He leaned back on his haunches, gasping a little—the knife had been buried deep, it had clung powerfully to the flesh, as if held by hands inside. He looked at the blade, glinting red beneath the houri's lamp. Not sharp—but sharp enough. He had strength—the thing inside him had strength.

And now his eye travelled to the oozing wound in Hamden's back: and, from the wound, over the black stiff silk of the dressing-robe to the hands stretched out on the hearthrug. They had stopped twitching—lay open, grasping: vile white things with the blue veins standing out in relief, the short hairs on the fingers black and stiff against the skin.

Little bestial grunts came from him. He went forward on his knees. He hacked, he stabbed, he sawed with dreadful strength. The small red veins stood out on the whites of his staring eyes. He sobbed. He sweated terribly. The muscles of his thighs ached. The hearthrug was a charnel.

But the thing inside him was singing.

10

"Good Lord!—Neville! What's the matter, man? You're ill—you look ghastly."

Neville pushed past Grant into the hall and thence into the florid living room. Mrs. Grant was standing by the fireplace, dressed in a huge loose dressing-gown. Her saggy shape was outlined through the thin cloth. Her mouth was open. She stared at Neville stupidly.

"Let me get you a drink, old man," said Grant. "You look all-in. Whisky and soda. Where are the glasses, Florence?"

Neville raised his hand.

"I don't want a drink," he articulated, in an unrecognizable arid whisper. "Listen, Grant—listen. I want you to know. I've murdered Hamden. He's dead. I've murdered him."

He looked at Grant's wide, foolish face—then beyond him to Mrs. Grant. She was standing in the same position, her podgy hands clasped over her stomach. His eyes seemed to focus on her whole huge, bulging and repulsive figure. He began to laugh uncontrollably. He sobbed with laughter. She stared at him in horror.

And the horror increased—she raised her hands to her flabby mouth as she saw him take from his pocket a thing she at first imperfectly recognized. Screaming now he waved it toward her. He held it in one hand and, with the trembling fingers of the other, felt at the bloody stump of it. He found what he wanted—the slimy end of the long tendon. Foam edged his lips as he held the beastly thing out at her and jerked the gristly cord. The mottled, clayey fingers of the hand grasped hideously at the air—like the claw of a chicken when the tendon is pulled.

Mrs. Grant dropped her hands from her mouth. She started to retch, trying to vomit. And to Neville it was funnier than ever. He dropped the hand and sank to a chair. He kept on staring at Mrs. Grant. She filled his universe: Rosemary, Miriam, the ranks of the children—all were lost in the great mountain of her pinky-white bulging flesh. And it was incredibly, fantastically funny. He went on laughing. Grant was pummelling him in an effort to stop his hysteria. But he went on laughing.

II

A letter from Herbert Campion to George Grant:

"Ramornie,"
Eton Bridge,
Chadford,
Derbyshire.

My dear Mr. Grant,

I cannot tell you how shocked I was to get your letter about poor John Neville. It is impossible to believe that it could have happened. It is as well that he knows nothing of it now—they will give him the best of everything in the asylum, I know, and do nothing to bring any memory of the terrible thing into his mind.

I cannot deny that he has always been strange. In his recent letters to me I had the impression of something going on in him, something quite nebulous that was a worry and a goad. But even before these letters there was an unaccountable streak. In our days together at University I was constantly encountering a black wall of terrible morbidity—as if malevolent forces over which he had no control were at work inside. Perhaps it was because of his tragic upbringing. It was a woeful story—did he ever tell it to you? He was born just after the outbreak of the 1914 war. His father was an officer in the army and John's mother, with the child, followed him to whichever town he was stationed in. At the time when he was sent overseas they were living at Sheerness. Two nights after the departure of the father (and on the eve of their own return to her people in Scotland) there was a German air raid on the town. John and his mother were lodging in a small, flimsily built house—sleeping on a mattress in the basement. A bomb fell on them and the house collapsed. John's mother had rolled over on top of him when she heard the whistle. He was completely unhurt, though terribly shaken. She was rather badly injured by masonry. A beam fell right across her hands, crushing them—it was only her indomitable courage that made her able to go on holding herself over John. The pain must have been terrible. It doesn't bear thinking about. One mustn't let the imagination dwell on such things.

The father was killed in France about a month after that. John lived with his mother and her people in Scotland. He was inordinately attached to her. She had to have her hands cut off as a result of the air raid incident. He has often described to me the awfulness of seeing her, beautiful, very dignified, but with special long sleeves on her garments to cover the stumps.

She died when he was twelve. His love for her has coloured his whole life—even to the extent, I remember at college, of his being preoccupied by anyone who bore the same or a similar name. Her name, by the way, was Miriam.

A tragic story, all of it. And now this ending to it. Terrible, terrible.

Many thanks to you, Mr. Grant, for all the trouble you and your good wife have gone to on John's behalf throughout this whole ghastly business. If there is any mortal thing I can do, do not hesitate to let me know of it.

I am, sir,

Your obedient servant,

Herbert Campion.

Another Planet

A ROMANCE

THERE WAS A GIRL called Lily and she met a boy named Harry. They met at a street corner: and after they had talked and laughed a great deal, they walked home together. Harry had very straight shoulders and a hat well tilted to the right. They passed many young men very like him—they might have been his reflections in so many mirrors. But Lily did not notice them.

At the foot of the stair, in the darkness, Harry kissed Lily and ran his hand over her stomach. Lily clung to Harry as she had seen girls do on the films. Then she ran quickly upstairs.

The next night Harry and Lily met again. They walked up and down several streets together and then had cups of tea in a dingy snack bar. After that Harry took Lily home again and they went through the same procedure as on the previous night, only more intimately and passionately. So it came about that Lily was Harry's girl and he was her boy.

Lily had had boys before, and she knew that Harry had had girls. But this time there was a difference. For it seemed to Lily that Harry lived on another planet. How could she have explained? His straight shoulders were not the same as other boys', his tilted hat was not the same as their tilted hats. Other young men used words like "bitch" very frequently. So did Harry—but in a different way. When he said: "So-and-so is a bitch," he said it from another planet.

So they walked along many streets together, and drank many cups of tea, and saw many films. They were very intimate at the foot of the stairs and in other dark corners. Lily knew that Harry had been intimate with other girls in dark corners, and she had certainly known other boys: but she hated to think of that somehow. She didn't think of it, then. She had Harry—although he still seemed to be on another planet. It was, indeed, as if everything were happening on another planet.

One night Harry got drunk. He was out with some of the boys. One of the boys disagreed with something that Harry said. Harry repeated his statement more loudly and the boy punched him on the chin. So Harry kicked the boy in the stomach, and stood over him pugnaciously, waiting for him to rise. But he did not rise. His face turned purple and his eyes stuck out of his head like Bristol marbles. They discovered later that the kick in the stomach had caused hernia.

One of Harry's friends told Lily that her boy was in prison. But she didn't believe him. Later, she heard people say that Harry was probably going to be hanged. She didn't believe that either: it was happening on another planet. She sat in a large room while men in wigs talked at great length about Harry, who stood in a box, very pale and frightened. And it seemed to Lily that the ways of this other planet were inexpressibly strange.

They did decide to hang Harry. To Lily, of course, this was simply fantastic. She visited him in prison for a few minutes, but she knew he wasn't there at all, really.

"I'm sorry, Harry," she said, over and over again, stroking his hand through the bars. "Oh, I'm sorry, I'm sorry!"

Harry did not move. He stared at her as if he were dead, with his eyes like Bristol marbles. But suddenly his face twisted and his lips writhed.

"Get away, you bitch—get away!" he screamed. And he tore his hand from her. Then he fell down on the floor of his cell and began sobbing.

"I'm sorry, Harry," she said. "Oh, I'm sorry, I'm sorry!"

They led her away. She knew that she hadn't been speaking to Harry at all, that it had all happened on another planet. She could almost have laughed at all the misunderstanding that was going on.

They told Lily that Harry would be hanged on a certain morning, very early, and she got up and went down to the prison. It was on another planet that a hanging was taking place. Harry would come out to meet her very soon.

But he did not come. The appointed time passed and Harry did not come. So Lily set out to look for him. She walked along all the dingy streets and peered into all the snackbars. She knew she would meet him. Now and then, among the young men with straight shoulders who passed and repassed, she thought that perhaps . . . but no: not Harry.

At night, Lily found herself beside the river. There were very few people about and it was dark. She looked over the parapet. The river was dark, too, and cold. But Lily did not care.

A policeman saw her.

"Hey," he shouted, "what are you doing?"

He started to run towards her, still shouting. But Lily did not hear him. He was on another planet.

Liebestraum

"Now king David was old and stricken in years; and they covered him with clothes, but he gat no heat . . .

"So they sought for a fair damsel throughout all the coasts of Israel, and found Abishag a Shunammite, and brought her to the king.

"And the damsel was very fair, and cherished the king, and ministered to him: but the king knew her not . . ."

THIS STORY IS ABOUT a man named Mackenzie, a sanitary inspector.

Mackenzie lived in a small town in Lanarkshire in Scotland, with his wife Bella, who was two years older than he was. He was small and undistinguished, with dirty grey skin and thin wiry hair. He had a small moustache, wore dark-coloured clothes and striped shirts, a bowler hat on working days and a cloth cap on Saturday afternoons and Sundays.

Mackenzie's house was number twelve of a row of houses that were all exactly alike. It was small and of black brick, there was a little plot of sooty grass at the front and a yard, or "green," at the back. Inside there were four rooms, two downstairs and two upstairs. The downstairs rooms were: the kitchen or living room, which had a sink and a small range for cooking, and the parlour, which was chilly and musty because it was seldom used.

Mackenzie married when he was twenty-seven. For eleven years he lived with Bella neither happily nor unhappily—they simply lived, going to the pictures once a week, sitting on either side of the range the other nights. There were no children—Bella had said even before they were married that she did not want any children.

Eleven years after the wedding Mackenzie discovered that Bella was fond of another man. She was seeing him in secret and, in the phrase of the district, "carrying on with him."

Mackenzie was not profoundly disturbed—he was not fond

enough of Bella for that. He was, more than anything, disconcerted: he did not quite know what to do. He wondered: Should he go away and leave Bella and the other man to their own devices? Should he go on and turn a blind eye? Should he strike a firm attitude and have a scene?

In the end he decided to go on and turn a blind eye. After all, he had his job. The only thing was that he found himself, to a certain extent, in a humiliating position. He felt himself in the way, he had an urge to go out, to stay away from home so that Bella could have a certain amount of freedom. She knew that he was aware of her liaison and he could feel her adopting an uncompromising attitude. So, in his discomfort, there was nothing for it but the pub in the evenings.

The situation became a routine. The neighbours knew, but after a time they accepted things and no more jokes or protests were made. Everything was smooth and a part of life. Bella cooked for Mackenzie, she washed and mended his clothes. He went to work, to a football match on Saturday afternoons, to the band in the park on Sunday evenings.

For two years things went on like this and then there was a sudden change. Hamilton, the man that Bella was in love with, was killed in a colliery accident. Mackenzie got the news one midday when he was going home for a meal. He entered the kitchen with some diffidence. Bella had plainly been crying, but she put his beef and potatoes before him without ado. He ate in silence for some minutes, then he said:

"I've just heard about Robert, Bella. I'm richt sorry."

She put a plate of sago pudding on the table and then suddenly ran out of the room. He heard the door of the parlour opening and shutting and then a low rhythmic sobbing. He did not know what to do. He ate the sago slowly, then he got up and took a step towards the parlour. But he stopped before he reached the door and stood for a moment in doubt, picking his nose absent-mindedly. The sobbing stopped after a time and he stood poised on the balls of his feet, listening for some movement. After about three minutes he got fidgety and tiptoed through the hall, picked up his hat and went out, closing the door behind him with exaggerated caution.

After the death of Hamilton, a change took place in Mackenzie's relations with Bella. In some strange way he felt himself, as it were, superior to her. The feeling was never crystallized, it was only a vague sense of remoteness. Having formed the pub habit he kept it up, so that Bella was left alone in the evenings. Nowadays she was limp and patient—resigned. She got up and made Mackenzie's breakfast, she washed his clothes and had his boots repaired. At night she lay beside him in bed, staring for long periods into the darkness while he snored dully.

About a year passed and Bella was taken ill with pneumonia and died suddenly. Mackenzie was dazed. Bella's sister, a Mrs. Murdoch, appeared in the house and took control. The sanitary inspector found himself in black, he found himself in a car following the hearse, he found himself by the graveside listening to the earth falling heavily on the hollow coffin. Then he was alone.

He decided to give up the house and go into lodgings. So there was a sale to dispose of the few bits of furniture in the parlour and the bedrooms and Mackenzie moved to a room in a tenement flat a few streets away. His landlady, Mrs. Lawrence, had just lost her husband and was expecting her son, who was in the army, to be transferred to the Far East. So she made Mackenzie very comfortable, she occupied her mind in devising good meals for him, in working out little details which he hardly as much as noticed. But he contented Mrs. Lawrence very well as a lodger: to her there was something distinguished about a sanitary inspector.

Mackenzie at this time was forty-one. There were grey streaks in his hair and moustache, he had taken to wearing spectacles. He was very unobtrusive. When he was at the pub he sat in a corner with an evening paper, at his lodgings he kept to his room. He felt a vague urge towards some sort of edification and bought himself books with titles like: *Things Everyone Should Know, Can You Speak Correctly?* and so on. These he read most studiously, making notes in a careful copperplate style. Thus:

"The word kinetic may be defined as 'of, producing or depending upon motion.' Steam possesses kinetic energy or motion, since it can be used to work machinery."

"Cut-glass was invented by Caspar Lehmann, jewel cutter to Rudolph II, Emperor of the Holy Roman Empire."

"Grass is green because nature has found that this is the colour best suited to its mode of existence."

One day, when Mackenzie went to his lodgings for tea (he had his meals with Mrs. Lawrence), he found that there was a visitor. This was a girl of fifteen or sixteen, very pretty and graceful, with fair hair and large glistening eyes. Mrs. Lawrence introduced her as Jessie Dean, explaining that she was the daughter of an old school friend of hers. The girl smiled and blushed a little. Mackenzie made some remarks about the weather and concentrated on the scrambled eggs that Mrs. Lawrence had put before him.

Throughout the meal Jessie talked vivaciously to Mrs. Lawrence. Mackenzie found himself listening intently, though he knew none of the people she was talking about. He stared across the table at her, at her smooth skin, the small pink tip of her ear, her white teeth as she smiled. When he had finished eating he rose, said good-night to Jessie and went down to the pub. In his corner there he kept on seeing her young fresh face in his mind's eye.

"Jessie," he said to himself thoughtfully. "Jessie ... Jessie Dean..."

About a week later Mrs. Lawrence asked him if he would like a ticket for *Iolanthe,* which her church choral society was presenting at the town hall the following night.

"You remember Jessie Dean that was here last week?" she said. "She's in it, you know—in the chorus, of course. She has a grand voice."

Mackenzie bought a ticket. He sat beside Mrs. Lawrence in the hall. The opera bored him, he did not quite know what it was all about. All he did was wait for the entry of the chorus and then keep his eyes fixed on Jessie. She was very pretty, dressed all in white, with a sparkling circlet round her bright hair.

When he got home he sat abstractedly sipping the tea that Mrs. Lawrence made.

"I do hope you enjoyed it, Mr. Mackenzie," said the landlady. "Did you notice Jessie? My, she is pretty."

"What?" said Mackenzie, looking up. "Oh yes. Yes—it was fine."

In his room he took out a writing pad and began to write in his meticulous copperplate.

"My dear Miss Dean——"

Then, after a long reflection, he decided that the "my" should go, and began again on another sheet of paper.

"Dear Miss Dean,—It may seem strange to you to get an unexpected letter like this from someone you have only just met once, and indeed it is very bold of me to be writing it."

He paused, gnawing the end of his pen. Then he went on:

"I went to the Town Hall to-night with Mrs. Lawrence and I really must say that I enjoyed it very much. I am not very 'musical,' in fact I have never been to a concert before, but I must say—"

He hesitated. *What* must he say? He saw that he had used the phrase before, in the previous sentence, and sought feverishly through his memories of *Can You Speak Correctly?* for some solution. But he could think of nothing. He tore up the letter angrily, undressed and got into bed.

There, in the darkness, he gave himself up to despair. He was forty-one—forty-two in three months' time. He was small, his face was sallow and ugly, he wore thick spectacles, he was a widower. When he had been married his wife had been unfaithful to him . . . Then he had a vision of Jessie in her white fairy costume, her face flushed with excitement as she sang. He fell asleep after he had heard a church clock strike three.

The following Sunday, when he came in at tea-time, Jessie was sitting with Mrs. Lawrence. He felt himself going hot round the collar. Jessie smiled at him warmly.

"I was telling Jessie you were at the concert, Mr. Mackenzie," said Mrs. Lawrence. "She says they're doing *The Gondoliers* next and she might have a part."

"That's fine," said Mr. Mackenzie awkwardly, sitting down at the table. He did not know what to say. He did not want to say anything, he only wanted to look at Jessie.

After the meal he postponed his departure for the pub. He asked for another cup of tea and sipped it slowly as an excuse for staying on.

"Jessie and I were thinking of taking a turn along to the park," said Mrs. Lawrence genially, as a hint to him to finish his tea. He grew hot around the collar again.

"I thought of going along there myself," he lied. "I'd like fine to come with you, if you don't object."

They said they'd be delighted. In the park Mackenzie walked self-consciously beside the two women. Mrs. Lawrence and Jessie kept smiling to acquaintances and every time they did so Mackenzie touched his cap. He imagined, as they passed groups of people, that they were staring after them—there was a small shrinking sensation in his back. All the time he was embarrassed, he kept searching for something to say to Jessie. Once, as they edged past some people on a narrow path, she touched him. A sudden thrill passed through his whole body. The band was playing the overture to *The Barber of Seville:* he thought he had never heard anything so gay in his life before.

"Do you like music, Mr. Mackenzie?" asked Jessie.

"Oh yes. I'm not really very musical, you know, but I must say——" He hesitated. "Oh yes. I like it very much."

Mrs. Lawrence invited Jessie back for another cup of tea. "It's all right," she said, "it's still early. And besides, Mr. Mackenzie can see you home."

Mackenzie felt himself choking with delight. All his feeling seemed to be centred in one small hot pulsing sensation in his chest. As he walked with Jessie through the dusky streets to her home on the outskirts of the town he felt himself growing more confident. Perhaps it was the dark, perhaps it was the fact that they were alone.

At any rate, he succeeded in making conversation. He learned that Jessie's father was dead, that her mother was an invalid. They lived on a small pension Mrs. Dean got from her husband's old employers and the wage that Jessie earned as a filing clerk at the town offices. She had been working there ever since she had left school at fourteen, two years before.

"I don't expect you manage to get out a lot," said Mackenzie boldly.

"Not very often," she confessed.

"Do you like the pictures?"

"Oh yes."

Mackenzie's heart was beating. At last he said:

"I was wondering—would you like to go to the pictures with me one night this week?"

"Well——" She hesitated. They were standing at the close mouth of the tenement where she lived.

"Say—to-morrow night?" he went on hurriedly.

"I couldn't come to-morrow night. I've got a practice of the society."

"Well, Tuesday?"

She shook her head slowly.

"I don't like leaving mother," she said. "You see——"

He nodded. He was humble. Yes, of course. He was forty-two.

"But I *could* manage Wednesday, though—if you made it the first house. Mrs. Lawrence is coming to see mother on Wednesday. I'm sure it would be all right."

He walked to his lodgings with his head up. He wanted to do something spectacular, absurd—to leap up and swing on the crossbar of a lamppost. In his room he hummed softly to himself as he undressed. What could he do? Something different—to mark an occasion, as it were. Something that would elevate him from his routine.

There was a copy of the local paper on the chest-of-drawers. His eye fell on an advertisement. "Mr. Fred King announces that he is enrolling pupils for the Mandoline and the Banjo for the next quarter." That was it, decided Mackenzie. He would learn to play the mandoline. Jessie was musical. In his mind's eye he saw himself playing a selection from *Iolanthe* to Jessie, her mother and Mrs. Lawrence.

He cut out the advertisement carefully and put it in his pocket-book. Then he went to bed, curled himself up with his hands between his knees and fell asleep immediately.

They went to the pictures on the Wednesday. Mackenzie sat staring at the screen, aware only of the young creature beside him. The emotions of the characters in the film seemed thin and false compared with what he himself was experiencing. He wanted desperately to touch Jessie—simply to touch her. It would have been sufficient if their arms could have met on the rest between their seats. But somehow he could not bring himself to make any movement; he sat quite still—even controlling his breathing. When the lights went up between the films he turned with an awkward, tentative smile. She smiled back at him warmly.

"I liked that picture fine," she whispered, and he experienced an immense glow of satisfaction, as if he had made the film himself and she were praising him. He had bought some sweets for her and he put his hand gingerly into his pocket for them, but for some obscure reason he hesitated to pass them over. What could he say?—without seeming clumsy? "Here's some sweeties for you, Jessie . . ."? "Here—I bought you these . . ."? No. He decided to wait till the lights went down. But when the lights did go down he still did not withdraw his hand from his pocket.

When the show was over they walked towards her home, he silent and restrained, she talking animatedly about her favourite film stars, about people in the choral society and so on. He was amazed before such vitality. It seemed to him that he had not lived before at all. His life with Bella had been a shadow existence. Their way to Jessie's home led them past the house where he had spent his fourteen years of married life, and it seemed to him that he was meeting a ghost or hearing a far-off dismal echo. There, in the light of the street lamp, was the gate he had opened and closed so many times, the bleak little plot of grass, the shadowy porch with (and he saw it clearly in his mind's eye) its blistered paint, its knocker in the form of a devil's-head, its small brass plaque engraved MACKENZIE. Now there would be a different name, of course, there would be different furniture, different curtains. Someone else would be sitting before the range, some other woman would be standing in Bella's place by the sink. And yet he had a strange sense that if he walked up the path and knocked at the door, Bella would come and answer it—and beyond her, in the kitchen, he would see Mackenzie, the sanitary inspector, reading the evening paper.

They reached Jessie's home. He was going to raise his hat, say good night and walk off quietly when she made the suggestion he had been half-expecting and even dreading a little.

"Aren't ye coming in to see my mother, Mr. Mackenzie? Mrs. Lawrence'll be there and she'll be expecting you to see her home."

They climbed the stairs to the first floor of the tenement and she led him into a small cosy kitchen. Mrs. Lawrence and Mrs. Dean were sitting with tea-cups on their laps. Mrs. Dean was a thin, shrunken woman, wrapped in an enormous grey shawl. Her eyes were pale and set very deep, she wore a small knitted skullcap because (as she explained to Mackenzie later) she suffered from violent headaches.

When Jessie introduced Mackenzie to her she smiled wanly and offered him a thin hand.

"It was very good of you to take Jessie to the pictures, Mr. Mackenzie," she said. "Now you must sit down for a while and have a cup of tea."

Mackenzie sat down, mumbling something. Mrs. Lawrence and Mrs. Dean went on with their conversation and Jessie turned over the pages of the *People's Friend*. He sat silently with his knees together, balancing his tea-cup. As Jessie bent over the paper her hair fell before her face and he had an almost uncontrollable urge to lean forwards and run his fingers through the beautiful fair waves. And then he had a glimpse of himself in a wall-mirror. There was a mark round his brow from the rim of his bowler hat, his tie was awry, his skin seemed rough and sickly. He was suddenly self-conscious and spilt some of his tea on his trousers.

He walked home with Mrs. Lawrence. She was voluble—he heard her voice going on and on as they went through the deserted streets.

"My, but Jessie's a pretty lass," she said as they neared home.

"She is that," said Mackenzie, nodding. Then, after a pause, he went on hesitantly: "Hasn't she a lad?"

"Well—there's many that would like to be her lad," said Mrs. Lawrence, smiling. "But Jessie's level-headed—and she's got her mother to look after. She's got mair in her head than lads. There's plenty of time for that yet."

After that Wednesday it became a routine for Mackenzie to take Jessie to the pictures once a week. He formed the habit too of going to meet her after the choral society practices on Monday nights. When she came out of the hall he advanced shyly from the doorway where he always hid himself and then they strolled homewards. One chilly night she put her arm in his and snuggled close up beside him, and he found himself hardly able to speak because of the sudden pulsing tightness in his chest. On another occasion the practice finished early and she suggested they should take a short walk before going home. They went to a small park just outside the town—a little patch of open ground among the collieries. It was a clear frosty night, with a beautiful ringed moon. Everything was silent—the sound of their footsteps seemed to move away and die in faint echoes among the distant slag heaps. The big wheels and towers of the mine-heads were outlined clearly against the sky, a rat went swimming across the moon-path in the pond of waste water where Mackenzie had fished for sticklebacks as a boy. Far off, on the other side of the town, they could see in the sky the red glow from the big furnaces of the steel works. It made Mackenzie think of his old childhood conception of the end of the world—an immense blaze, and nowhere to run to to escape from it: and he found himself half-wishing that it might indeed be the end of the world—that it might finish here when everything was quiet and he had Jessie beside him. He glanced at her furtively. In the moonlight her skin seemed transparent, her eyes were wide and glistening, her lips were slightly parted. He did not know what he felt: it was not like anything he had ever known before.

And all this time Mackenzie was expanding in other directions too. Now he went very seldom to the pub—he spent his free time in reading his books on self-education and in practising the mandoline. He had one lesson a week from Mr. Fred King and had quite rapidly reached the stage where he would fumble through pieces like *A Little Waltz* and *Air by Haydn*. His attitude was one of dogged perseverance. He strummed at a phrase till his fingers knew what to do of themselves. When the music said *piano* he suddenly played softly, when it said *forte* he just as suddenly played loudly, with no attempt at any sort of gradation. Always he had a vague vision before him—of himself nonchalantly tuning up his mandoline and dashing off some piece of great difficulty while Jessie looked on admiringly: or he was explaining something to her—not patronizingly, but with an easy air of wisdom:

"You see, Jessie, when a warm wind blows against a mountain slope it is forced to rise into the cooler levels of the atmosphere. Cool air can't contain so much moisture as warm, so the water vapour condenses and falls as rain."

And in this way the months went by. When the warm weather came, Mrs. Dean's health improved a little and she was able to move about, so it was decided that she, Jessie, Mrs. Lawrence and Mackenzie should all go down the Clyde to Rothesay for a day's outing. They set off very early one Saturday morning, laden with sandwiches and thermos flasks. As they mounted the gangway of the paddle steamer at Gourock, Mackenzie found himself expanding in a delicious sense of freedom and adventure. He was wearing a new pair of flannel trousers, a new cloth cap and a white flannel shirt open wide at the neck. He felt the brisk salt air whipping some colour into his cheeks and waved gaily up to Jessie, who had run on ahead and was standing on top of one of the huge paddle cases of the steamer. She was dressed in a bright frock of green material which the wind pressed closely about her slim young figure. Her hair was tousled and she kept pushing it back from her eyes, laughing all the time with excitement.

"Come on up here, Mr. Mackenzie," she cried. "It's grand."

He set Mrs. Lawrence and Mrs. Dean in deckchairs and then went up to join Jessie on the paddle case. On the top step he lost his footing for a moment and she reached out a hand to steady him. He thrilled at the touch of her cool firm skin. Still holding him by the hand she led him to the railing and he stood there blissfully beside her, watching the animated scene on the pier: the stout mothers steering their children through the crowds, the porters wheeling luggage, the excited factory girls, the keelies with hunched-up shoulders and smart felt hats. He felt very young and energetic—he wanted to sing or shout. He found himself half-wishing he had brought his mandoline with him.

Presently the gangway was hauled in, the steamer vibrated and the water immediately beneath them began to froth and swish as the paddles revolved. A sailor on the pier cast off the mooring rope and it fell into the water with a long hissing sigh. The boat began to move. A small orchestra somewhere among the crowded trippers on the deck started playing *Over the Waves* and some screaming gulls slewed round a steward who had appeared from the dining saloon and was throwing scraps of bread into the sea.

"Oh, it's grand, it's grand!" cried Jessie. Her cheeks were full of colour, her eyes were wide, her whole body was alert. Mackenzie felt enormously proud: he imagined that people were looking at them as they stood there at the rail. Against the background of the excited crowd and the garish music it seemed suddenly as if life had a strange glamour: it was like the final scenes of the pantomimes he had sometimes seen as a child in Glasgow—bold and picturesque and full of a vague meaning. A young couple mounted the paddle case and came over to stand beside Mackenzie and Jessie. The boy put his arm round the girl's waist and Mackenzie suddenly felt a sense of affinity with him. He wondered: Should he put his arm round Jessie's waist? Then he realised that she was still holding his hand and it seemed that to hold hands was an infinitely superior way of being affectionate.

The journey progressed. Mackenzie and Jessie went forward to the bows and looked down into the water until they felt giddy. Sometimes they saw the ghostly shapes of jellyfish near the surface, sometimes a long trailer of shining brown seaweed drifted past them. Once they saw a porpoise: it made several jumps into the air, its body glistening in the bright sunlight. Later on they went down into the engine room and watched the big pistons pushing at the cranks of the paddles. Mackenzie debated whether he should begin: "You see, Jessie, steam possesses kinetic energy or motion, since it can be used to work machinery." But before he could frame the sentence naturally into the conversation, Jessie complained that the smell of the oil was making her feel a little sick and they went up into the air.

As they neared Rothesay, Mackenzie, for politeness's sake, went to sit for a moment or two with Mrs. Dean and Mrs. Lawrence, leaving Jessie to roam about the decks by herself for a bit. The two women had found a secluded corner on the second deck at the base of one of the funnels, where it was warm. Mackenzie fetched a deck chair and sat down beside them. The three were quite alone. All the other travellers were on the top deck or in the bows, waiting for the first sight of Rothesay or looking out for *Shamrock* and *Britannia,* the two famous yachts, which were in the channel that day.

By this time the sun was hot and presently Mackenzie fell

into a half doze, lulled by the rhythm of the steamer and the soft drone of the women's voices. His thoughts went hazily to Bella and then beyond her to his childhood. It seemed very near to him these days: little incidents had come back to his memory as if they had happened only a few weeks back. Yet before, when he had been living with Bella, his childhood had seemed lost and remote. For the first time in his life he was overcome with a sense of the strangeness of things—the sadness of time and of death and above all the unrealisable longing for joy to be something permanent and solid, like a pebble, that could be locked away and guarded for ever. He had a sense of panic: it seemed as if things were vanishing away from him, were flowing past and getting lost. Perhaps, if he opened his eyes, all his present joy would melt away too: there would be no steamer, no Jessie, and he would be sitting before the range in that small house of black brick while Bella washed the dishes at the sink. With an effort he forced his mind back to deal with the realness of the moment: the cries of the gulls, the attenuated sound of the orchestra from further along the deck, the voices of the women. But how could one confirm the realness of the moment? He wanted to open his eyes, and then, half-ashamed, he held back. He thought: It *might* be a dream: but I want it to be real, and if I stay like this it will *seem* real and that will be as good.

Suddenly, in a strange half-witted way, he became aware of what it was the two women were talking about. He had caught Jessie's name. He did not open his eyes but now he was awake and listening intently.

"I told her there was no harm in having a lad," Mrs. Dean was saying. "After all, she cannae tie herself to me a' her days."

"That's right enough," said Mrs. Lawrence. "Now that you're a wee thing better it would be the very idea for her. Has she been mentioning anybody in particular?"

"Well, once or twice she did gi'e a bit hint about young Tom Kennedy—in the choral society, you know. He's a real nice lad. I'd like it fine if they got going steady thegither and maybe mairrit someday. She told me he'd asked to see her home one or two nights, but of course Mr. Mackenzie was meeting her, so she couldnae very well say yes."

"Tom Kennedy," said Mrs. Lawrence reflectively. "Now who would he be? I wonder if I know him?"

"Of course—Meg Hamilton's boy. She married Alex Kennedy down at the steel works. You're bound to remember Meg Hamilton—sister to Robert Hamilton, the one that was killed in the colliery accident some years syne. He was the one that was carrying on wi' Bella——"

"Ssh!" the other woman said suddenly, nudging her friend. There was a silence, then the two gossips went on talking in lower voices.

But Mackenzie was no longer listening. The voices drifted away and once more he was asleep and in his dream. It was as if, suddenly, he were fabulously alone and very small, and it was as if, too, he had somehow to cling on to something, something undefinable that had slipped just beyond his grasp. He was on an immense plain. Far off, on the horizon, on the edge of things, were the peaked slag heaps and the mine-heads of a colliery. The sky above them was pulsing and red, and as he looked he saw that it was no reflection from the steel works he was seeing this time, but flames—vast slow flames. And he realised why it was that he felt so small as he stood there. He was a child again—on that vast plain he was a child, quite naked and lonely, and the sky was burning. It was the End of the World.

For a moment he had a feeling of terrible panic. He looked desperately about him for somewhere to run to. But there was nowhere, nowhere.

Then suddenly there swept over him an immense sense of comfort and relief. The distant slag heaps and mine-heads had gone, and in their place now, on the horizon, on the edge of things, stood Jessie. She was smiling and her arms were outstretched. Her green dress whipped round her, writhing like the vast flames that were her background.

Mackenzie gave a strange, quiet, muffled sob and started to run across the plain. And Jessie too advanced, still smiling. Yet by now her dress seemed to be writhing vividly and to be growing out from her and to be mingling with the red flames in the sky. They flowed together, and it seemed that the cool green flames of the dress gave their colour to the flames of the burning sky.

And all was green—the whole world burned green, with Jessie's smiling face all shining among the flames.

He still rushed forwards, his arms outstretched. He sobbed. And he was among the flames, but they did not burn, they were cool. As they writhed all round him they did not torment him. They soothed him. His sobbing changed to a sort of laughter. He went further and further into the flames. His consciousness left him, he went deep and deeper into the green fire. He saw, in the flames, a thousand things that he had forgotten, good comfortable things. And all of them shone green.

He opened his mouth and filled his lungs with the green cool fire. And there was nothing more to worry about. It all *was* real . . .

* * * *

The two women gossiped on in low voices. Suddenly they saw Jessie running towards them. Her eyes were bright and she was beckoning excitedly.

"I think I can see Rothesay," she cried. "And we saw the yachts about ten minutes ago—the *Shamrock,* and *Britannia,* the king's yacht."

She broke off suddenly and looked at the empty deckchair beside the two women.

"But where's Mr. Mackenzie?" she asked. "Where's he gone?"

"Didn't he go to find you?" said Mrs. Dean. "I saw him get up a few moments ago, while we were talking. He went over towards the rail. I didn't see which way he went after that, though . . ."

They looked at each other in silence for a moment or two. Then Jessie said:

"He must be somewhere—in the engine room, perhaps. I'll go and look . . ."

She ran all over the ship. But Mackenzie was not to be found. Mystified, she went to the stern and stared back at the expanse of sea they had traversed. The green tossing wake stretched out in a long broad ribbon behind the steamer. Some gulls swooped round her head, screaming. A quarter of a mile away a porpoise leapt into the air.

The little orchestra in the waist of the ship was playing a tinny, garish arrangement of Liszt's *Liebestraum*. The thin sound came back to her as she stood with her hand on the rail, her green frock whipping about her in the wind, her head upraised to drink the salty air.

"He must be somewhere," she said to herself. "He must be somewhere . . ."

Miss Thing and the Surrealist

We lived in those days in a constant turmoil. Artists we were most consciously—Surrealists, moreover, for the Movement was at its fashionable height then. Things have changed a lot however. As far as I know only two of us have stuck to the profession—if you discount Tony del Monte who became an academician (and called himself Antonio). Tania went on the stage didn't she?—and reached Hollywood somehow, I remember (as Howard Darby said, she got into the Temple of the Muses by the tradesmen's entrance). Jo Haycock married someone from Yorkshire (or Wales?) and poor Chloe Whitehead went mad. And of course there's me (but I was only on the verge of things ever).

And Kolensky.

But what happened to Kolensky is what this story is about.

And then there was Miss Thing.

You must understand in the first place that we attached more significance to our lives than to our work. We were concerned with being artists. We looked like artists. We behaved in a manner. Our mode was intended as some sort of gesture—a rude one—five extended fingers at the nose aimed at—what? (All that we secretly were, perhaps, and were afraid or ashamed of.) That was almost what we understood by Surrealism. It consisted as we saw it of a series of outrageous snarls. What we flattered ourselves was *panache* was a sort of temper.

Traces of it all remain. I find shreds still clinging secretly to my own personality—I see large fragments attached to Howard Darby.

It lingers in aspects of style.

Yet amidst all the turmoil of the amorality of it and the picturesqueness of it and the earnestness and (looking back now nostalgically) the glory of it, there were some of us who were serious and good artists. Kolensky I believe was a good artist—and an honest Surrealist. And Chloe. Whitehead had a streak of queer genius somewhere—but she went mad, poor lass, and is out of it all and away.

We had what we fancied was our wit. It was meant to shock.

For example:—Some of us were walking along the King's Road with some people—some cousins of Tania's. We passed a tall house with a woman shaking blankets out of one of the upper windows. Some feathers were fluttering to the ground and the large loose white thing waving seemed like a bleached tongue out of a toothless oblong mouth.

"Oh look," cried Tania, "that house is being sick . . ."

Or again:—We were all talking about Christianity one night with some earnest theological students.

"How could it possibly fail to have an enormous public?" said Chloe. "Look at its founder. He had the best exit in history."

On another occasion I remember Howard took us all to a crowded and noisy little restaurant that we knew of, where there was music and a permanent buzz of conversation. He had just been reading an anecdote about Baudelaire. He waited for a moment when the music stopped suddenly and the clatter dropped for an instant, then said in a loud tone as if continuing a conversation he had been shouting through the din—

". . . but have you ever tasted little children's brains? Ah they're the things. They're very sweet—like little green walnuts . . ."

Yet there were occasions of great seriousness—when suddenly something assumed momentous symbolical significance because, I am sure, of the way we had accustomed ourselves to look at life. I remember one night Jo Haycock and I were sitting talking in my room overlooking King's Road—in the World's End part of Chelsea, I should mention. It was late and wonderfully quiet—towards two a.m. And suddenly in a long gap in our quiet conversation there sheared beastily through the night a ghastly prolonged loud scream. We stared at each other and rushed downstairs.

We found a little shocked crowd on the pavement opposite. Some ambulance men came and the screaming ended when they took away the dreadful forlorn thing. A wretch of a prostitute had flung herself from the top floor of the tall house opposite the one in which I had my room. She had impaled herself on the area palings instead of dashing mercifully to the stone as she had hoped.

Jo and I went upstairs again and made tea. We were sick. We were haunted for days by the long scream of agony shearing out across the big quiet city. All the Surrealistic peering into the unconscious with its emphasis on the lower motives—all the speculation in the world could not satisfy the big strange question about Alice Emmanuel (as the papers told us her name was) and the black body falling through the night to the blunt hideous spikes.

But all this is not any part of the story—at least not directly. I should talk first about Kolensky and in doing so introduce Miss Thing.

But she was Kolensky's big Surrealist gesture. She was a creation—a personality. She was a work of Art—if you concede a work of Art is something made out of nothing—bits and pieces put together and something intangible emerging, that has or takes a life of its own. Miss Thing was that.

Kolensky was forty or forty-five—a cadaverous man with deep sleepy eyes. Indeed he seemed always to be sleeping—to need much more sleep than most people did, yet to sleep in a heavy and poisoned way. A diabetic you might have said though he wasn't in fact. He was a man too who seemed to have secrets. He talked seldom and when he did it was slowly and as if on guard. He wore a beard—it was one of his disguises (I did myself in those days, for there is always a time—at least one time—when you must from yourself disguise yourself. Later on you realise that when you meet your own ghost sitting quietly and accusingly on your doorstep when you go home at night, he must look like you yourself or he has, poor soul, no meaning.)

Kolensky's studio was at the top of a large house near Battersea Bridge. It was as it were a sort of outhouse built on to the flat roof. You ascended to it by the inside stair but the last flight was no more than an elaborated ladder that took you through a skylight. Then you were in the open air. Kolensky's door faced you.

The door was painted Blue. And for a handle—well it is here that we encounter the first of Miss Thing.

The handle of Kolensky's door was a Hand—a white and beautifully made wax Hand. It was held a little open and at the wrist there was a small circlet of lace that covered the join of it to the wood of the door. To open the door and go in, in answer to Kolensky's sleepily-shouted bidding, you took hold of this Hand as if you were shaking it and turned it just like a door handle —which is what it was after all. But to touch that clammy wax unyielding thing was curious—oh curious. People not like us in our valuation of these attitudes turned away.

The Hand then was the first of Miss Thing. The other Hand was inside the studio—but let me take it all in order.

You went in: and like as not Kolensky lay on the bed half asleep. You had perhaps gone to see some of his canvases—quite beautifully powerful things some of them—but it was not to them that your attention was first attracted. No. You saw, my friend, the Rest of Miss Thing—the Rest of the Gesture.

The truth was that Miss Thing (it was Howard's name for the personality she undoubtedly became in our minds) was Kolensky's studio. He lived almost literally *in* Miss Thing. The only thing that was missing was Miss Thing's face—but she needed not a face, that woman—the face is only an index—you give up faces after a while—it is only strangers you know by their faces. Miss Thing you knew by presence and implication.

There were of course the Parts. Protruding inconsequentially from a wall was a beautiful rounded Breast of coloured wax. The other Breast stood on a table. It had holes pierced in it symmetrically all round and flowers stuck out of these like the glass things people in the suburbs use. (Daffodil time showed the Breast at its best I think. Snowdrops made it forlorn, roses made you think of Dowson.)

In the centre of the studio was a large lovely chair with curved legs. These legs ended in two little and beautifully made wax Feet.

The fireplace was very low. The mantelshelf was a plain long board sustained on two pillars one on either side of the fireplace. They were the wax and footless Legs of Miss Thing.

In a corner by the inner door of the studio and also protruding from the wall like the first Breast was a small smooth feminine Belly all waxen. The Navel was a little bell-push—you pressed it and an electric bell rang away in the basement for the desolate old woman who did Kolensky's charring.

A big sideboard stood all along one wall of the room. Stuck on the centre mahogany panel of it were what were unmistakeably recognizable as the smooth and delicately pink Buttocks of the Presence.

Kolensky's bed was a narrow one and old fashioned. On top of the iron rails at the foot of it were the usual brass balls rather tarnished. Equivalently at the head of the bed (as it were overlooking the artist as he slept like Matthew, Mark, Luke and John in the rhyme) were bright wax Eyeballs.

And the other Hand?—to complete the Parts?

When you were visiting Kolensky you went perhaps into the lavatory. At the end of the flush chain and like the one on the door, half open to be grasped, was the other Hand. Here again —to their embarrassment—the uninitiate had been known to turn away.

To us in those mad days that second Hand was the best of the gesture.

But all of Miss Thing we loved. The whole idea was a glory. Kolensky was our king—the noblest Roman of us all. We hardly noticed his canvases. To us he was the man who lived in Miss Thing. He was the true Surrealist—the noblest and only begetter . . .

And so it came about, you see, that when we numbered ourselves we numbered Miss Thing also. She was one of us. She was the unexplained presence we all at one time in our lives feel dogging us—what Keir Cross (a devilish queer friend of mine—a writer) calls somewhere The Other Passenger. A door would open mysteriously in a draught—Miss Thing was in, we said. Some fabulous coincidence impressed us—Miss Thing had arranged it. One of us lost something. Miss Thing—that occult hooligan—had hidden it.

Those beautifully made waxen Parts all stood for a personality somewhere hidden in our own minds. Kolensky had as I've said created something. She—It—was The Secret Sharer, The Incalculable Factor. It was genius to have conceived her and to have carried her out so exquisitely. We grew fond of Miss Thing—we loved Miss Thing. She was our communal Familiar.

We used to say that Miss Thing was able to defeat anyone—anyone. No one could stand up to Miss Thing. Surrealism and Miss Thing combined were uncombatable.

Yet I have a feeling in my heart that Miss Thing was most subtly and most shamefully defeated. Howard and I were talking about it only the other night and speculating.

What after all is Surrealism? Who was the greatest Surrealist of us all?

Was it indeed Kolensky?

Or was it Vera?—Vera the last and the outside edge?

Vera was the woman Kolensky married.

Vera—for truth.

Vera. I write it carefully. V-E-R-A. In writing it so carefully I am confessing a weakness. It is now necessary to describe Vera. But I hedge. I hesitate. Where to begin?

Why did Kolensky marry Vera? Was he mad? There was a theory at one time that Kolensky was mad. Or was he still in his role of King of the Surrealists?

Where did Kolensky even *meet* Vera? That pale ascetic face of his surely never wandered over Putney Bridge or into Wimbledon. It never was poised over flowered teacups in villa drawing rooms. It never opened its thin-lipped mouth to receive small cress sandwiches or slices of Madeira cake. That leonine mop of Kolensky's never rested back on embroidered antimacassars. Those large-knuckled hands never turned over the leaves of family photograph albums.

Yet plainly it was from Putney or Wimbledon that Vera hailed. It was from Putney or Wimbledon that Kolensky like a ravenous Asmodeus snatched her. He introduced her suddenly into our company complete with her lavender scent and her cream lace fichu. And we were aghast.

. . . She was at that time I should say nearer forty than thirty. She was small. She had a round smiling face and a prim manner. Her hair was done in a little bun at the back. When she walked out she wore black cotton gloves and a toque.

She was the incarnation of all we gestured against. And here she was in our midst, all waiting to be gestured at. Yet somehow—

My friend, I am a poor lost sinner. There is nothing I understand. In those far-off mad days when we lived in Chelsea and ate kippers and drank beer and daubed at canvases or struggled with monumental poems I thought in my young folly that I had an occasional inkling as to what it was all about. I thought I knew a thing or two as we stood at twilight on the Embankment looking at the dying sun on the water and the big misty shapes of the pylons and sneered at Whistler and Turner. I was in my eyes an exceeding wise ancient patriarch as I juggled with Ezra Pound and Salvador Dali and turned to Dostoevsky for light reading.

But the day of my deliverance was at hand. Vera had arrived.

Would you believe it if I told you that she still went to chapel after she married Kolensky and came into our midst?—twice on Sundays and once on Wednesday evenings? You could see her prim small figure, like a bird's, go skipping along Oakley Street with a Bible clasped in the chubby gloved hand. She smiled and nodded as you passed her as if you were yourself a Wimbledon spinster—yes even to Jo and to Chloe she nodded, with their sandals and home-woven skirts and enormous blood-red earrings.

We were helpless. We did not know what to do. You see she had done, when she arrived among us, the unanswerable thing. She had accepted us. She liked us!

She liked every one of us. She accepted every iconoclasm with a distant and patient smile. She could no more understand Howard Darby's aphorisms than we could understand her passion for going to church. But they did not outrage her—they did not disturb her.

Even Tania's more suggestive witticisms were accepted. Even Chloe's wildest blasphemous verses raised no more than a faint sweet blush.

Poor Chloe poor Chloe! Mad, mad and with straw i' the hair . . .

And Kolensky?

We said at first that Kolensky would tire of Vera. She had been, we said, a new sort of gesture. He had found her and brought her home as we used often in those days to bring things home from the junk shops—an ornate gas bracket, a hideous vase, a chamber pot with the willow pattern on it—anything for a gesture. Or she would tire of him, we said. The mystery of it all was upon us. Kolensky the polymorphous pervert (as Howard once called him) and Vera the Wimbledon Virgin. She would run away screaming. He would revolt her.

But he did not revolt her. She did not run away screaming. She cleaned out his studio. She cooked his meals. She washed his violent flannel shirts. When we went to see him and sat into the small hours talking monumentally round every subject under and over the sun, she sat quietly knitting and nodding. She looked at him with fond soft eyes. He was we could see the most marvellous thing that had ever happened to her. He was her Golden Boy.

She was, in short, in love with him. And I honestly think now as I look back with some sort of balance on it all that he—yes Kolensky—was in love with her. She was eminently respectable. She was gas-light and horse-hair and plush and aspidistras. She was the doyenne of a thousand vicarage tea-parties. She was Cheltenham Spa. She was Trollope and Mrs. Hemans and Charlotte Yonge and Ella Wheeler Wilcox. But she was Kolensky's Golden Girl.

So we nodded to each other wisely—for we had to be wise about something, with so many illusions crashing madly all round us.

"Miss Thing," we said smiling. "Let's leave it to Miss Thing. She'll destroy Vera. She will avenge us. Miss Thing is not to be trifled with. Miss Thing is not to be accepted as easily as all that. Miss Thing is a Presence and a Personality to be coped with. No one from Wimbledon can live blithely in Miss Thing and disregard her. Miss Thing will rise in her wrath and destroy. Miss Thing will smite and Miss Thing will spare not. Miss Thing is the Final Ally . . ."

So we watched and nudged each other and waited.

We waited.

We waited.

We nudged each other and waited.

Little whispering voices ran all round us as we waited. "Miss Thing," they said. "Miss Thing . . . She will destroy. That clammy wax Hand on the Blue door will one day rend the sweet usurper. Those Eyes on the bedpost will stare her out of countenance as she kneels one night to say her prayers. That Navel bell-push will one day summon an astonished charlady who will discover Vera insane and gibbering on the floor with Kolensky senseless with sleep on the bed and impervious . . .

"Go to, go to!" the voices cried. "There is a rat behind the arras of that respectable chamber of Vera's mind. And the rat is Miss Thing. Go to, go to . . ."

We waited. We waited.

And nothing happened.

Vera accepted Miss Thing. The Presence seemed to be conquered. That little woman from the suburbs remained undisturbed by the monster her man had created. The Presence seemed to be conquered. On Vera's journey there was no Other Passenger.

But yet—(somewhere William Shakespeare says,

> *"But yet" is gaoler to bring forth*
> *Some monstrous malefactor*).

I feel it sometimes in my bones as I look back that Vera conquered Miss Thing in thus accepting her. At other times it seems that after all it was Miss Thing that conquered Vera. The female Achilles of Wimbledon had her heel. She dusted the Parts of Miss Thing each day, she filled up Breast 2 with fresh flowers. But in her vulnerable corner she was wounded . . .

All this, you must understand, was before they took Kolensky away and hanged him.

But now—to the climax. It is called:

DEFEAT

We were sitting one night in Chloe Whitehead's studio. It was a large room with a north light. The furniture was sparse—it consisted for the most part of drawing-donkeys set in a semicircle round the fireplace. There was no fire though it was chilly. It was one of our gestures that we could not afford a fire. So instead the fireplace was filled with beer bottles some full and some empty. On the mantelshelf was a figure of Chloe in the style of Epstein

(Tania's work). On one wall was a portrait in oils of Chloe in the style of Picasso—the Blue Period. (This also was the work of Tania.) On another wall was a mystic Arrangement of circles and lines in the style of Ben Nicholson (another example of the work of Tania).

(The thing about Tania was that she was the only one who didn't know that she borrowed. When she eventually got on the stage I seem to remember it was because she bore a certain fleeting resemblance to John Gielgud . . .)

To continue:—In a corner of the studio was the little printing press on which Chloe did her poems. They were issued in extremely limited editions on rice paper with simple covers in two colours. There were some half-dozen poems or lyrics in each little book and the volumes were titled as they were issued: *Opus 1*, *Opus 2*, *Opus 3*, and so on. She had just finished printing the first batch of *Opus 7* and was reading us the opening poem—a longish lyric in the evocative manner. *The People of the Moon* it was called, I remember.

Tania lay back on the divan with her hands behind her head. Tony del Monte knelt on the floor beside her picturesquely stroking her temples. Jo Haycock was astride one of the donkeys with her eyes closed (she looked like a neat little horse did Jo—some passing fancy by Chirico). Howard Darby was on another donkey with a half-empty beer glass dangling from his hand. I squatted on the floor staring upwards at Chloe who stood leaning against the mantelshelf with her lovely hair falling down all over one side of her face and covering one eye.

(Poor Chloe! It was impossible not to adore her with that deep modulated voice of hers and the green cat-eyes that never rested for an instant. I wonder what undreamt-of Surrealisms she stares at now in the asylum. And are they a patch on Miss Thing?)

She read:

The dead are quickly buried
bury the dead
with tall white candles for remembrance.
Yet let us forget the candles after all

after all we have only a moment.
It is all an approximation.
I could say:
"Do you remember this, remember that?"
But the poignancy is rare
and is not to conjured:
the poignancy is rare
and is not to be perjured.
The dead are better buried
the candles are easily blown out
and the room is easily darkened . . .

(My thoughts went wandering away as the deep slow voice went on. As they so often did those days they circled round Vera. I had a vision of her rising in the morning with her hair in a little pink net: of her cheerfully preparing breakfast: of her dusting those hideous Parts. She goes out for a morning shopping expedition—Kolensky still abed. She returns. She climbs the inner stairway and mounts the glorified ladder at the top of the house. She faces the Blue door. She puts out her soft smooth hand to grasp without a tremor that pale unyielding waxen Thing . . . Ugh! I shudder—and wonder. She accepts. She *accepts!* . . .)

The voice went on:

O you and I were meant for other things indeed,
there was a destiny for us
a shade of something glorious:
some hint and echo from a greater height
for other men to cling to!
Our banner waves diaphanous
is, as it were, an ancient tattered map,
long scrawled upon but splendid,
of countries from an old lunatic dream
and stories never ended . . .

(Vera with a Woolworth's feather duster. As she works perhaps she whistles or hums a tune—a hymn tune from the Wimbledon prayer meetings or the Sunday School in which she was surely a teacher. *We Are But Little Children Weak* or *Jesus Wants Me For A Sunbeam*. She buys some flowers—anemones I fancy. She sets them in the Breast. She steps back with her head cocked to one side like a bird's to admire the effect. She accepts, she accepts . . .)

And suppose that you and I
suppose that we
inept and condescending
gathered our thin resources round about
and, in the autumn, in a willow trance,
sounded our trite alarums to the moon
and led our own dry ghosts but once to dance? . . .

(Kolensky is her Golden Boy. She defeats us all by accepting. The Personality conjured up by those scattered Parts has no effect on her. The years of ingrained respectability, the anti-macassars, the plush and the horsehair, the Madeira cake and the vicarage tea-parties—they count for nothing. She is not defeated. She accepts and conquers . . .)

And now the voice moves slightly up in tone and tempo as the climax is reached. Chloe shakes her head and the hair falls away from the lovely cat-eyes.

The people of the moon are starry-eyed,
They sing sweet songs all day and dance the night:
Their little heads are empty all of brains, their hearts
Are small soft balls of plasticine delight.
And they remember nothing of the earth,
No echo reaches those enchanted lands:
They cruelly cruelly sup on others' blood—and then
Pluck out their lovers' eyes with soft white hands.
But O! I love the people of the moon!
I love their secret smiles and haunted songs

And suddenly Chloe stopped. She looked up. She put her head on one side and listened. We all listened. And in the strange silence that crept all round us with the stopping of the reading voice, we heard a terrible long-drawn scream.

It died away. I looked up—at Jo Haycock. And my thoughts went rushing—as I knew hers also did—to that occasion when we were sitting in my room, high overlooking the King's Road in the World's End part of Chelsea. I had a vision—a hideous one—of the dark falling body of Alice Emmanuel . . .

And now in the silence that replaced the scream we became aware of a harsh low sobbing. It came from immediately outside the door of the studio. And even as we stared at that door and speculated wildly, it swung open and there came—or staggered—into the room a figure we hardly recognized. The lace fichu was askew, the hair was wild, the violet eyes were rimmed with red and streaming with tears.

"Miss Thing," gasped Vera wildly. "Oh God oh God—Miss Thing! . . ."

Our hearts leapt up. We had beheld! The voices had whispered aright. Miss Thing had won! The monument of respectability had toppled.

But literally, my friend. With another wild cry the Wimbledon Achilles fell to the floor in a faint.

My friend, there are layers and layers. Life, said Howard once, is like an onion. You peel the layers and there is no core. It only makes you weep.

All that is so long ago you see. So incredibly far away. A sort of dream. We were glorious in our way I suppose—to ourselves of course as we look back now. It is all over and we have grown beyond it. I grope like Proust among the images.

There are in life no climaxes. In a play the curtain falls at the end of a scene between lovers—and we applaud and cry "Bravo!" In life we have our scene—we embrace. But the curtain never falls. The chair arm sticks into our ribs or our partner has halitosis. And at the height of the scene we need to go to the w.c.

They came and took Kolensky away and hanged him. A fitting end for the King of us all perhaps—that sparse body dangling through the trap door. Perhaps he was even asleep when they set the noose . . .

But there was nothing dramatic about it all. No real climax. It was all accidental somehow. It wasn't that that Vera went to the police about—not that at all.

It was all something else. It wasn't that, that the years of ingrained respectability revolted against. She was horrified when she found out what her visit to the police had done.

Yes, it is all a sort of dream—a far-off dream. I see us grouped round Vera as she lay on Chloe's divan—I see us as shadowy figures, unreal. The little book called *Opus 7* lay where Chloe had dropped it on that high dramatic announcement. I remember glancing down at it and even reading a line or two while they held up brandy for Vera to sip.

Our banner waves diaphanous
is, as it were, an ancient tattered map,
long scrawled upon but splendid,
of countries from an old lunatic dream
and stories never ended . . .

"You mean," cried Tania, "Miss Thing is *real?*"

And Vera sobbing and nodding blindly.

"Yes, real," in a dry hopeless moan. "Not wax at all—embalmed—embalmed! . . . I found out, you see, when I was going through those old papers this morning. I'd no idea—I didn't know. I found the marriage certificate, you see—I found that. And when I looked more closely at the Parts—when I cut into the Legs at the side of the mantelshelf . . ."

She sobbed here wildly. Tania clutched at her throat—to stop being sick.

"And you went to the police?" asked Jo in a low strained voice.

"Yes . . . Yes . . . And they came—oh God!—they came to arrest him! This evening—an hour ago!"

The tears were terrible. She couldn't speak. I thought of the shrieking figure of Alice Emmanuel.

Yes layers, my friend—layers, layers.

"He's gone—he's gone. And I'll never see him again—oh never, never, never!"

My heart twisted round in my breast I remember. She wildly

smoothed her flying hair and gazed at each of us in turn. A curious bleak agony was in her eyes.

"You see, you see," she gasped breathlessly—"it wasn't that—oh Lord it wasn't that! I didn't mean——"

She stopped and gulped an enormous breath.

"It was only—you see—he hadn't told me. It was false pretences. It was a sort of—bigamy. He married me under false pretences. I didn't know, I didn't know. Oh, it was cruel of him, cruel of him! But I didn't mean them to—oh my God! It was only *he didn't tell me he had been married before! It was false pretences—false pretences! That's what I went to the police about! . . .*"

. . . Strange how we've all dispersed and separated. Only Howard and myself left now. Tania on the stage—Jo married. Tony del Monte an academician. And Chloe, poor lass, gone mad.

We went to see her the other day, Howard and I. She was quiet and gentle. She asked for news of all her old friends. We talked in low voices for an hour or so and then came away.

Impossible not to be nostalgic about one's youth. Now that one has settled down it seems—well, never mind. It is only a layer long since discarded.

I was looking at Chloe's *Opus 7* the other day. The last book she ever printed. The last few verses of it come into my mind. I chanted them over and over again to myself as we came back from seeing her the other day.

They say below that I am mad.
Well—mad I am, mad, mad.
And there are other things they say
That I have thrown my life away:
That I was drowned long since and do not know
O there are many whispers from below!
O little white worms have eaten my heart
And devils have picked my brains apart.
Lady, they say I have sisters three
Who have blanched my veins by the olive tree
Lady, O lady, have pity o' me . . .

And Vera? The last I heard of her she was working in a Camberwell mission among what they call Fallen Girls.

She gives her name as Mrs. Kolensky.

And if anyone—some serious boy from the University Settlement—asks sympathetically: "And—Mr. Kolensky?"

She answers, her little prim mouth slightly tightening: "Mr. Kolensky—died, you know . . ."

Valdemosa

". . . and then, in 1839, ignoring all the proprieties, Chopin and George Sand went to Majorca together . . ."

THE CHARTREUSE

The Chartreuse was an immense sprawling building of endless corridors and walls. It was picturesque and a little frightening. Some of it was in ruins. Each small section or cell—the parts reserved for residents—had a garden, walled round to a prodigious height. It was a building hugely futile—deserted, bleak—set majestically between the hills and the sea, with the beautiful rich trees of Majorca clustering all round it as if to crowd it out and hide it from view.

And all the time that they were there, it seemed, it rained. The long dark corridors trickled, the walls sweated, the air was filled with a chilly moistness, the woodwork of the doors and windows was swollen. All things seemed damp and cold to the touch—the furniture, the counterpanes, their clothes—everything. The very bricks were saturated through and through—as Madame Sand once said, even the marrow in their bones was waterlogged.

It was better after the piano arrived (it had cost them weeks of anxious letter-writing, that piano—and 300 francs duty at the *douane*). After that Chopin had something to take his mind away from the God-knows-what strange nightmares that haunted him in that place. It was better, too, purely practically: for the inhabitants, when they heard the pale visitor's exquisite music, were more prone to overcome their prejudices. They even gave them food sometimes—food of a sort, that is: mostly pork that was hopelessly indigestible, and rancid oil to cook it in.

"I have been as sick as a dog," wrote Chopin to his friend Fontana. "I caught cold in spite of 18 degrees of heat, roses, oranges, palms, figs, and the three most famous doctors in the island. One of them sniffed at what I spat up, the second tapped where I spat it from, the third poked about and listened how I spat it. One said I had died, the second that I am dying, the third that I shall die. I could scarcely keep them from bleeding me . . ."

They hardly knew how they went on living. But they did. Chopin composed, extemporised, moped: Madame Sand wrote and went exploring: the children ran wild among the ruins.

MASTER AND MISTRESS

One morning during a brief interval of watery sunshine in the rain, Madame Sand made her way to Chopin's cell. She had been walking with Solange, her daughter, and was dressed carelessly in trousers and tunic, with great workmen's boots on her feet. She strode mannishly over the flags, taking pleasure in the big free rhythm of her stride.

The door of the cell was open and she paused for a moment on the threshold. A shaft of the thin sunlight fell through the archway before her, resting in a narrow band on the esparto matting and just touching the piano in the far corner. At the piano sat Chopin, leaning forward on his elbows, with his dark hair falling down over his arms. He did not move—hardly seemed even to breathe.

Madame Sand made a slight tapping noise on the lintel, but there was no response. Then she moved slowly into the room.

"Frederic," she called softly.

He did not look up. She moved a little closer and her shadow fell on the piano.

"Frederic . . ."

Then, when he still made no reply, she went up to him and laid her hand on his shoulder.

He started round with an exclamation and the sudden movement jerked her back. She put her hand to her breast—a feminine gesture strangely out of keeping with her grotesque man's costume.

Chopin sighed and relaxed.

"It's you, then," he said. "I was startled. I thought——"

He finished the sentence with a shrug and sighed again. Madame Sand, used as she was to the extreme pallor of his face, noticed with emotion that he was even whiter than usual. The skin was drawn tightly over the high bones—it was as if you could have put a finger through his cheek.

"Have you been composing?" she asked mechanically. He nodded and sighed once more.

"Yes, a little."

He played a soft arpeggio. Outside, after the brief sunshine, the rain began again—falling straight down in a heavy persistent stream, as it had done the day before and the day before that.

"Sol and I have been exploring," Madame Sand went on. "We found an old well right at the far end of the east wing, with a sort of fallen-down fireplace in it. Sol wants to go picnicking there—when the rain stops, I mean."

"The rain will never stop," said Frederic solemnly.

"Nonsense." She made an effort at laughing. Then she moved close to him again and put her hand on his shoulder. One knee she raised to rest on the edge of the piano stool, and in this position she gazed down at him—at the deep unhappy eyes of this strange man whose life seemed to have become so inextricably mixed with hers.

"What's wrong, Frederic?" she asked, in a tender voice. "Why do you mope so? Aren't you happy with me? Oh I know it isn't what we'd hoped it would be like here—we hadn't bargained for this wretched rain and all the trouble with that old fool of an innkeeper at Palma. But we have made things as comfortable as we could for you. And I do love you, darling—you know that, don't you?"

"Yes, I know that," said the composer after a pause—awkwardly, and with averted head. He fingered a few notes on the piano.

"This wretched instrument," he muttered. "Pleyel's an insensitive dolt to send me a pile of junk like this."

"Frederic!" she chided. "Pleyel did what he could. You expect him and Fontana to perform miracles. You're lucky to have a piano here at all."

"Then I'm lucky to be here at all. I couldn't live without a piano—no, not another minute in this vile haunted house, with nothing to eat but garlic, garlic, garlic—garlic to frighten the devils away, that's what it is—yes, that's why they use so much garlic in this hell's kitchen: it's to frighten the devils away!"

His voice had risen querulously, and now suddenly he began to cough. His head jerked forwards and he put both his thin hands to his mouth. She handed him a handkerchief that she took from the waist of her trousers, and he spat into it till the paroxysm was over: then sat looking with a blank and childish expression at the little spots of blood on the fine white cambric.

"Ach!" he said at last. "More spittle for the doctors to sniff at! Well, good luck to them—let them stick me with leeches to their hearts' content. I don't care."

Madame Sand took back her handkerchief and crossed over to sit on the low bed at the other side of the cell. Through the open door there came now the pungent scent of the cooking that was going on in the little outside kitchen—garlic, as always. She could hear the children's voices far-off from somewhere outside—Solange ecstatic (perhaps over a newly discovered ruin), Maurice disgruntled and truculent. And her heart was full of trouble. It seemed to her that there was no sort of good in this strange situation, with Frederic so ill and unhappy, the children running wild without companionship or education. Yet what could she do? She had fought with all her energies to provide the ménage with the small degree of comfort it did have—she had overcome the prejudice on the island, the awful stone wall of fear and superstition about Chopin's disease. It was her money, her strength that had made life possible for them at all. And she knew that Chopin depended on her—that she had his absolute and slavish devotion. That gave her pleasure—it gave her pleasure and a sense of power to feel that she was the strong and responsible member. And it gave her pleasure, too, to feel that the strange genius of her "little one" was flourishing and maturing under her care—that the exquisite music he made was born, some of it, out of the turmoil of spirit that she was causing him. But yet——

Now, as she sat looking across the room at him, gazing intently at the high pale forehead, the hooked nose with its sensitive nostrils, the sensuous lips that stood out femininely against the excessive pallor of the skin, she felt, as it were, something missing, some aspect of their relationship that, in a way impossible to describe, was out of key—even, fundamentally, a conflict. It was impossible for her not to compare in her mind this Majorcan escapade with her Italian journey with de Musset. The Frenchman, too, had been an artist—highly strung and impossible: but his flame had been hot and understandable beside Chopin's untouchable fires.

Meanwhile, Frederic had begun to play. He began with a simple tune in the Polish style—a mazurka: but before even the first phrase had gone, the little dance was imbued with his own spirit—the inevitable arabesque, the theme turning ornately to its cadence, the melancholy intervals that were all Chopin. It was impossible not to be touched by his delicacy, gentle and feminine as it was, yet free from all sentimentalism. The woman lay back and let her thoughts wander.

She was, she felt, taking part in some tender scene—some vague situation in romance in which she was victim, yet mistress. A parting from a lover—the end of a love affair. She stood on a balcony, leaning against the stone balustrade: her lover was before her—he was embarrassed, guilty, in the wrong. It was something he had done, something reprehensible, which made it inevitable for their friendship to end. He had just told her how it was—she, torn in spirit, was saying good bye to him . . . And now he went into the house, leaving her alone on the balcony, her head bowed. She wore lilacs on her bosom. A tear dropped on to the lock of his hair that she held in her hand. There was nothing to hope for or look forward to.

Again, she was at some sort of celebration. People were dancing, there was life, colour, movement. And she was there, in the carnival crowd: but not taking part—cut away, it seemed—some sort of forlorn and remote figure. People moved past her—groups would approach her, and their laughter and gaiety would die quickly when they saw her sad face. She heard them murmuring and saw them glancing towards her, whispering her name. It was large, significant . . .

Then suddenly a noise cut into her dream. There was a scuffle of feet on the flagstones outside, and Solange ran in. Her face was wet, her hair was all streaked and plastered against her temples.

"Look, mama, look!" she cried. "I got them from the sacristan—he said I was to count them—I was to count them every day, he said, and I was to say a prayer to the Holy Virgin for Fritz—I mean, Uncle Frederic . . ."

She held up a little string of cheap wooden rosary beads, her face all flushed with excitement and exercise, her voice shrill and plangent against the music.

"Give them here, Sol," said Madame Sand irritably.

"No—I don't want to, mama. I want to say a prayer for Fritz—Maria Antonia said he was damned."

Her mother snatched at the beads and with a little scream of annoyance Solange tried to tug them back. The cheap string broke and the little wooden balls fell to the floor and went rolling into the corners of the room. Solange gave a cry of vexation and stamped her foot.

"He's damned," she cried. "Fritz is damned—he's damned, he's damned, he's damned!"

Chopin had stopped playing. His face was strained. He looked helplessly at the child and then at Madame Sand, who was frowning her anger.

EN FAMILLE

Later, they sat down to eat, Chopin and Madame Sand opposite each other at the head and foot of the table, Maurice and Solange at the sides. Solange had got over her fit of temper, she was vivacious and chatty, asked questions, giggled, till Frederic's nerves were at breaking point and he would willing have garrotted her. Maurice was sullen. He talked about setting off next day to find some eagles' nests. Madame Sand served the food abstractedly.

"The bread's damp again—it isn't fair," grumbled Solange. "It's always damp. I hate it, I hate it."

"For the love of God, be quiet!" murmured Frederic. He sat moodily upright in his chair, fingering a knife nervously and sipping from time to time at some burgundy that, thank heaven, had been sent up to them by the French consul at Palma. His head moved rapidly and continuously from side to side, his bright eyes resting now on this object, now on that. There seemed no repose for him at all. The bright splash of colour made by the bowl of oranges on the table before him irritated him strangely—it seemed harsh, like a wantonly struck discord. When he lowered his gaze to the floor the rough esparto mat made him shiver—he thought of its coarse surface against his skin—a shirt made of esparto, perhaps—an eternal penance shirt . . . He did not know where to look. His mind jumped from subject to subject—his financial worry, his horror of being tricked by the publishers, his distaste of having to deal with money matters at all. He looked across the table at George (Madame Sand, rather—or Aurore: he hated to think of her as "George"), and he felt for a moment a sudden hatred and malevolence—a resentment. As she served he saw nicotine stains on her fingers, and he shuddered at the imaginary whiff of tobacco that came into his nostrils. Yet this passing disgust was replaced immediately by an upflow of affection: she seemed suddenly capable, calm—a refuge. He longed for the children to go away—he wanted to have her to himself, to have her caress him and quieten him . . . And all the time, as a background to these restless and inconsequential thoughts, his head was full of music. There was a constant urge to get up and go through to the piano in the cell—to play on and on, not remembering anything; but perhaps seeing, floating always before him as he played, scenes, incidents, images of his childhood in Poland—of Poland itself: the peasants dancing, the flat quiet countryside, the big colourful fêtes of the noblemen, the long low houses, and perhaps his mother and father talking to each other across the stove. And all these things seemed forlorn to him, and charged with sadness; for he was, he knew in his heart, eternally an exile from them.

Maria Antonia, the servant, came in, shuffling and staggering with a large ashet. She was incredibly frowsy—her hair in damp wisps, partly from the rain that reached her in the small lean-to shelter that covered the cooking stoves outside, partly from perspiration. Her loose, flaccid mouth was twisted in a perpetual rictus-grin, her clothes were filthy from the grease of many cookings. Madame Sand averted her head: more than anyone in the world she hated this terrible servant, whom they could not get rid of.

"Oh," cried Solange, "it's chicken! It isn't pork after all—it's chicken!"

Antonia put the dish down before Madame Sand, stood for a moment grinning and wiping her hands, then shuffled out, her loose mules rustling the esparto mat.

The four looked hopefully at the brown and withered roast chicken before them. It was lean and dry—"as old as God," George muttered beneath her breath.

"I want a leg," cried Solange.

"You can't have it," said Maurice belligerently. "You had leg last time—it's your turn for wing this time."

Chopin sipped at his burgundy. Then his eye caught something and he stared at the chicken with horror. And simultaneously they all became aware that the brown, dried-up bird was covered with fleas.

"Ugh!" cried Madame Sand, her face twisted with disgust. "Antonia—for God's sake come here—Antonia! . . ."

Solange began to laugh delightedly and even Maurice gave a perverted smile.

Chopin said nothing. His lips were drawn tightly together, his hand gripped the knife with a nervous ferocity. Then he got up suddenly and went through to the next room. When Antonia shuffled in, wiping her wet nose with the back of her hand, he was coughing and spitting violently.

George signalled for the chicken to be removed. She leaned across the table, took Chopin's burgundy glass, and drained it at one gulp. Then she rose, lit one of the long thin cigars she favoured, and strode angrily backwards and forwards, puffing at it greedily.

THE GHOSTS

FREDERIC HAD BEGGED Madame Sand not to leave him alone, but in the evening she insisted on going out with Maurice. Solange had a slight cold and was sent to bed.

In spite of the brazier in his cell, Chopin was cold to the marrow. He trembled and started at the slightest sound, peered apprehensively into the dark corners of his room, huddled himself close at the table where he was trying to write. But the effort was great: he could not keep his mind on what he was trying to say to Fontana—he struggled to form phrases in the always-unfamiliar French.

"Indeed, I write to you from a strange place," he began. "It is a huge Carthusian monastery, stuck down between rocks and sea, where you may imagine me, without white gloves or curled hair, as pale as ever, in a cell with doors the like of which Paris never had for gates. The cell is shaped like a tall coffin, with an enormous dusty vaulting. There is a small window, and outside it orange trees, palms and cypresses. Opposite the window is my bed, on rollers, under a Moorish filigree rosette. Beside the bed is a square table, where I write now (though it is so rickety I can hardly use it), and on the table—a great luxury here—there is a leaden candlestick with a candle. Bach, my scrawls, wastepaper. Silence. You could scream—there would still be silence . . ."

He could not go on. He put down the pen and sat back in the chair. The silence flowed all round him, filled with the thousand small voices of the rain. The candle flickered for a moment in a draught. He was filled with a dreadful restlessness of spirit, an overwhelming fear—but of what he did not know. All round him, it seemed, were ghosts and unfriendly spirits. He was aware of the immense shell of the Chartreuse, himself desolate and pallid among the endless empty rooms and the trickling corridors. He stared at the table, and its immobility, the finality of it terrified him. He sank into himself till he did not know any more what he was, or what anything was: but existed, as it were, in a state of suspension, cut off strangely from his memories, his thoughts—all that constituted in normal life the person. It was like being dead and being aware still of the decomposition of the body, the disintegration of the spirit. The very music that filled him seemed something apart, something that had nothing to do with him, that existed elsewhere. The candle before him was his master: the pen he had just put down, and which lay so painfully still on the worm-eaten table, was greater than he was—was a thing, a shape, a meeting-place of qualities. He was, to himself, a mere sensation, intangible, indefinable.

A gust of wind rattled the door and he started apprehensively. The corners of the cell were dark, the high arched ceiling was filled with moving shadows. He rose, trembling, and went to the piano: then hesitated, with his hands over the keyboard, afraid for a moment to make any sound in that terrible silence. Then, mastering himself with an effort, he began to play.

The music restored him a little. But he was still fretful and ill at ease, and found himself longing for Madame Sand's return. He hated her for leaving him—yet would have forgiven her anything if he could have seen her at that moment coming through the door of the cell. Her image was before him: the dark braided hair falling down on either side of the gypsy face, the short lithe figure—the whole heavy essence of her personality. He thought of all their torments since the decision to sacrifice propriety and come to Majorca together: their first ecstasies at the sight of the island, so soon to be changed into bitterness: Gomez turning them out of their cottage (and pestering them to have it disinfected and redecorated): the suspicion and terror with which they were regarded by the natives—both on account of his disease and because they were "unChristian": and then the rain, the endless, endless rain—their removal to the Chartreuse—the bad food, the cold, the loneliness—and above all the blood, the "buckets of blood."

And in all that nightmare, when he was at his weakest, when there was no hope in him, George had been a strength, a power—a refuge. He knew, deep down, that he was not hers, nor she his: but he knew too that here, on this haunted island, he could not do without her—and knew, or suspected at least, half-consciously, that all his life was just such an island, and she a necessity on it.

He stopped playing and shuddered. For a moment the old fear was back—definable now: a fear of ghosts, of the eternal alien spirits he felt haunting this place. He felt stifled—as if he were dead, had been buried alive. It was as if the door had swung open and someone was standing there in the entrance regarding him—no more than that. There was a shadow by the table—a man: a shape on the bed—a man . . . He longed for someone to come to him—someone real, of flesh and blood—even the wretched Maria Antonia with her rictus-smile and trickling nose.

There came a sudden cry and he stiffened with terror: then remembered Solange in the next cell. A slight fever, perhaps, and a nightmare, causing her to cry out in her sleep. With an effort he rose, crossed to the table and picked up the candle. But he hesitated to leave the cell.

"I am Chopin," he found himself saying to himself over and over again, "Frederic Chopin, Frederic Chopin. I am Frederic Chopin . . ."

His foot touched something that went rolling over the floor with a little rustling sound. It was one of Solange's cheap rosary beads.

"I am Chopin, I am Frederic Chopin . . . O God, let someone come, let someone come! . . ."

When he heard the voices of Madame Sand and Maurice from outside he could have wept, so intense was his relief.

HISTOIRE DE NOTRE VIE

MADAME SAND, indefatigable as always, had waited only to change her wet clothes and see Maurice safely in bed, and was now sitting writing. Her pen scratched rapidly over the paper, she held her head slightly to one side.

Chopin sat opposite her at the ricketty table, trying to finish his letter to Fontana. But he found it unbearably difficult—the words would not come: in his nervous exhaustion there was no incentive to write, no incentive to do anything. He pushed the letter aside and picked up instead the manuscript of some of the Preludes that lay on the table. But here again the same languor came over him: the "spider crawl" meant nothing—seemed incomplete and inadequate—a sketch and no more. He sighed and laid down his pen, then sat for a long time gazing at his mistress.

Her energy, her abstraction appalled him. The candlelight, playing on her face, enhanced the darkness of it, emphasised the high cheekbones and the full coarse mouth; so that, with her hair framing the whole countenance, she looked indeed like one of the old monks of Valdemosa. She was, he reflected, thirty-four —a woman with two children and a history of many loves: and he was twenty-eight, and a man of no previous experience. There had, of course, been Constantia, Marie—others: but these were all quite different. Nothing to compare with, for example, her marriage to Dudevant, her liaisons with Jules Sandeau and Alfred de Musset. He wondered about de Musset—the ill-fated journey to Italy—her uncondonable betrayal of the poet. And he felt: It will happen again—she will betray me like that too, suddenly and without warning: and, as always, she will be able to excuse herself—she will have an array of plausible arguments, for herself as much as for anyone. It was I who was fickle, I was the impossible and the volatile one . . . Yet these thoughts he put away quickly. This might all be different. She was aging—it would not be so easy for her in the future. She perhaps wanted something permanent now. There was Nohant—Maurice was growing up—Solange herself would soon be a woman—and therefore a rival. And she—George—was established as a writer, a force in the thought and movement of the day—her future was assured—she might want something stable . . .

Madame Sand paused thoughtfully for a moment and took from her lips the mouthpiece of the ornamental hookah she was smoking. She blew some of the pungent Latakia smoke into the air, and watched it slowly rising towards the arched ceiling of the cell and dispersing wraith-like among the shadows there.

"Where did you go?" asked Frederic, "you and Maurice?"

"Not far. He wanted to see how distant it was to the rocks where the eagles' nests are. But we couldn't reach them—it was too dark and wet."

"An eagle came down into the orange grove to-day," said Frederic. "It was after a small bird. I tried to frighten it away, but it wouldn't go."

"It was your own spirit," she said with a smile. (And he thought: Which?—the eagle or the victim?)

"I must go back," he said suddenly, rising in an access of impatience. "This place is killing me. I hate it with all my heart."

"Patience, little one," she murmured, with an abstracted and almost mechanical tenderness. "It can't last for ever like this—the better days will come. Maurice feels healthier already—and your own health will improve when the weather changes. You'll want to compose—you can't stop the music in you: and you'll forget these terrible days."

"I shall never forget these days," he said bitterly.

He sat down on the edge of his bed and she watched him for a time, puffing again at the hookah.

"I don't know what's wrong with me," Chopin went on, in a low voice. "I can't rest, I can't settle. There's something incomplete in me. I don't understand myself, I don't know anything."

"You know too much," said Madame Sand. "Darling, it's the way with all us Artists" (she did genuinely think and speak so: a capital A for "artists" and "art")—"we're at the mercy of whatever's inside us. We can't help ourselves—we can't expect to be or to act like other people."

"It's more than that," he said. "I'm not talking about music now. Perhaps that contributes. But—there's something else too —all the time there's something else."

She rose and went over to stand before him.

"Perhaps it's me," she said, with a curious smile. And went on, when he said nothing: "Balzac said he was the only man who could ever get on with me—because when he came to Nohant we hardly saw each other. He worked and I worked—he early in the morning and I late at night."

She laughed. Chopin felt for her hand and pressed it against his cheek.

"Don't say that," he said. "It isn't that. I need you—you're all that keeps me sane in this place. I can't live without you."

She withdrew her hand and began gently to stroke his hair.

"Darling, darling," she whispered.

He was quiet for a moment, then sighed and drew away a little.

"How is Solange?" he asked. "Is she better?"

"Only a very slight fever. She'll be over it in the morning. And if the weather's better we'll go for our picnic."

"I heard her call out earlier," said Chopin.

"She dreams a lot. Poor child," went on Madame Sand. "It's a strange life for her too, I suppose. I want to do something about a tutor for her—I can't go on myself all the time trying to educate her."

"She'll survive," murmured Frederic: then he added abruptly: "Aurore, let's go away—let's go back to Paris."

"Not yet, Frederic. Darling, your piano has only just arrived —and you aren't well enough to travel yet—not in this weather."

"I would get better again in France—we could go to Nohant —anywhere. Fontana can get us an apartment in Paris."

"We can't live openly together, dear."

"Then he can find us separate places, near each other." He was eager and animated. "I'll have some money from the Preludes— they can't do me out of it. There'll be enough for a small place—I can give concerts."

She shook her head.

"Not yet, Frederic."

He relaxed.

"I'm sorry," he said. "I'm keeping you from your writing. I'll be all right—I'll lie down for a moment."

He lay back on the bed. She sat down beside him and took his hand.

"Poor little one! There isn't any rest for you, is there . . . I won't write any more, Frederic—not to-night. I shouldn't have left you earlier. But you see, I feel I mustn't do anything to hamper you —I leave you because I feel your genius can express itself more freely when you're alone. It's a torment—but it's bound to be a torment. *Il faut souffrir—il vaut mieux souffrir . . .*"

She was speaking very simply, as if to a child. It was natural for her to do so—she saw, always, the role a situation demanded, and played it automatically.

And he, because of her tone, felt suddenly full of pity for himself—he felt dependent, helpless.

"It won't always be like this," he said at last, with a slight plaintive whine in his voice.

"No—not always, darling."

"The world is hard. I can't deal with it. I must be left alone, that's all . . . I'm in the world like the E-string of a violin on a double bass."

She nodded slowly, and made a mental note of the phrase. And to him too it seemed a good phrase, and with a sort of satisfaction he repeated it to himself:

"I'm in the world like the E-string of a violin on a double bass . . ."

So they remained quietly for a time, with their hands together. The candle was guttering. The hookah had gone out. The smell of the Latakia lingered, dispersing slowly in the damp still atmosphere.

IN THE NIGHT

AND NOW THEY were lying together and he was not afraid any more. Her arms were round him. Now the darkness was a comfort, the sound of the rain came in as an hypnotic murmur. He felt weak, unable to move: but he did not want to move, and there was a deliciousness in his weakness.

His thoughts now were not any more of death and ghosts, the music was no longer sombre, but resolved and quiet. He was home again, in his dear Poland—with his family—out riding. He was a child again. He had built up a miniature platform with chairs and curtains and was imitating an old Jew to the delight of his mother and father. He and his friend Dominic were writing the magazine they had founded: "On the 12th of August a hen went lame and a drake lost a leg fighting with a goose . . ." His old teacher, Elsner, was sitting beside him at the piano, guiding his hands. He was in Berlin, in a crowded room, gazing shyly across to where a young man was talking animatedly to some ladies—Mendelssohn, none other. He was being tormented by the first pangs of love—all the ineffable magic of the first time, remembered elegiacally in other and darker days: Constantia—gone blind now, he had heard—and her young and pretty face had almost faded from his mind . . . Concerts, success, pretty women. The execrable music of Lanner and Strauss in Vienna. And his meeting with Madame Sand at his rooms——

"I am to-day receiving a few people, amongst others Madame Sand . . ."

He sighed. He fell asleep.

Madame Sand, heavy and sated, was going over in her mind some aspects of her work. She contemplated vaguely a novel at some time or another with Chopin as a character—Chopin in, as would seem necessary, a suitably aristocratic setting. Phrases, disjointed and irrelevant, kept coming into her head. "In both mind and body he was delicate . . . he was like the ideal creations with which medieval poetry adorned Christian temples . . . He had an expression both tender and severe, both chaste and impassioned . . ."

His body seemed incredibly frail in her arms. She had a sense of immense tenderness towards him, a feeling of possession. Earlier, when they had been talking, she had had a recrudescence of what had been almost her first feeling towards him—that his genius was hers to control, that she it was who would widen his experience, his whole attitude, who would make him possible—and impossible. Yet there was something else—it was all something else: somehow not what she had meant. Nothing was ever just what one meant. It was as if, all the time, other forces were responsible—she moved as a puppet—Chopin moved as a puppet. They could not help themselves. They were little people, and alone. They were both, she felt, as they lay there in the vast hollow monastery, "like violin E-strings on a double bass . . ."

In the first creeping light of dawn she saw, on the piano, Chopin's manuscript—the "spider scrawl." A Prelude. She tightened her arms round the thin body as she asked herself: Who wrote it? Who wrote it—where did it come from? Not from him—not for a moment from this stricken boy in my arms.

Who is Frederic Chopin? Oh, my God, my God—who is he?

She trembled a little from the cold. It was as if a shadow and the shadow of a shadow had swept through the cell. There were little voices all around her. Faintly, mingling with the sound of the rain, she heard Solange moaning in her sleep. "Mama, mama . . . the beads—I want my little beads. And to pray for Fritz. The beads, mama—he's damned . . ."

"This is his ghost," George whispered in fear, as she looked at the waxen peaceful face beside her. "This is only his ghost, after all . . ."

She fell at last into a troubled sleep. Chopin smiled, coughed a little, and settled himself more closely to her body. The rain went on.

PART TWO

MYSTERIES

... and each thing has its parasite—even the mole. There is a special flea for moles—the mole flea. And there is a strange destiny for mole fleas—they too are blind ...

MACFARLANE'S NATURAL HISTORY

Amateur Gardening

Tuesday, 18th April. In the train. Now that I've started, am actually in the train, it's different. I feel better. If the simile wasn't impossible, I'd say it was like coming out of a tunnel into the sunshine. But when did the tunnel begin? So long ago that I can't remember—can't remember what it was like before. No more than a few disconnected images—Jenny and I on the beach at St. Andrews with those monstrous breakers at our feet, the sound of a portable gramophone coming thinly down from the dunes—the *Ride of the Valkyries* I remember—fantastically irrelevant: Jenny and I at a concert in the Albert Hall—Mahler, it was ... but what did I care about Mahler? I could only feel her warmth beside me, could only hear her breathing through those slightly parted lips, could see nothing but the movement of her fingers on the arm of her chair. Jenny and I at tea in her flat—toasted muffins, tea always that shade too sweet, fantastic little cakes from the French baker at the corner, the Cézanne that was always crooked, the piano, the books—oh, all those books, a little dusty, packed tightly together. Jenny and I at a party, Jenny and I at the theatre, Jenny and I at the cottage ...

Later. I had to stop there. We reached a station and someone got out—stumbled over my legs. But I'd got to a pause anyway. That phrase—"Jenny and I at the cottage." Too significant—painfully. Something that stabs and hurts. How one's life—one's whole life—can cluster round one image, one phrase. A phrase like that. And I have to *force* myself to face it. Those two things coming together—an immense moment. Too immense, really—for me. Look at me, after all. Clerk, twenty-eight, with literary ideas and ambitions. An occasional article in the magazines, two novels, half a dozen poems (unpublished), a diary (*slightly* Katherine Mansfield) and—well, let me be honest—two score letters or so to friends that I hope they'll keep ... That, and the garden.

The garden. That's the big thing. How I've struggled over

all those years to get my cottage and my garden! The advertisements, the useless journeys to see half-fallen hovels, the agents, the landlords and then at last, at last . . .

It's all over now. All that gross and fantastic nightmare—it's finished. There's only the garden now. To have wanted only this one thing all my life—it seems all my life—to have wanted it as madly as I have wanted it, and now to be on my way—finally *on my way!* . . .

I wonder—shall I think of her there?—because she has been there? And will it spoil it? Will those two things, those two parts of me, cancel each other out? No. Foolish. The literary man in the ascendant. . .

What does Dennis feel? *Can* he feel? No, I mustn't think of it—mustn't, *mustn't*. They had to question me, I suppose—the fiancé—always the Sunday Paper suspect. But to have to go through all *that*. It was over between us. We'd fixed it. It wasn't only because of Dennis.

I tried not to see those placards at the station, but my eyes went round to them in spite of myself. I try not to write of these things now but my hands act of themselves. "Trunk crime developments." And I know, I know. Dennis in prison. Poor devil. But why, *why?* . . . Why did he have to . . .

I can't write any more. It's difficult in the train. I want to lie back in the seat and close my eyes. Another forty minutes—an hour and a half, counting the walk. And all that forgotten—forgotten.

A garden is a lovesome thing, God wot . . .

Loathsome poem. But it runs through my head to the train rhythm like a delirium. A lovesome thing, a lovesome thing, a lovesome thing, a lovesome thing . . .

Sunday, 23rd. Berkshire. Rain to-day—otherwise I wouldn't be writing. I've built up the fire and made tea (find it difficult to write—hands blistered from digging—stiff and painful) . . .

Yet what is there to say? The sort of contentment I have can't be expressed in words—one doesn't even want to try to express it. To go out in the morning, to dig, to plant, to sow—it's its own expression. Only—sometimes it's hard to believe it. I mean—

sometimes I straighten my back and look up at the cottage and a sudden terrible fear comes over me that it isn't true, that I'm really still back there in the midst of the nightmare and am imagining all this because of the sheer power of my wish to escape . . . But no. It's gone in a moment. It isn't this that's unreal. It's the other.

There are moments, when I'm digging, when it seems that my mind sets itself to a rhythm—I find myself repeating some silly phrase over and over again—something like: "When did you last see your fiancée," for example. And although it's distorted and meaningless (all mixed up with that picture of the little boy and the Roundheads in the school readers), I get afraid sometimes that there's something *bigger* going on underneath. I mean—oh, I don't know what I mean. I'm afraid it'll ruin all this . . . It's as if my mind were taking revenge on me because I fight and fight and won't let it think . . .

I read that back. Where's the literary man? I've given myself away. I'm *not* content. And because of all that. The *fantastic* irony of it. We *had* finished—I *was* coming here before it happened. And then because Dennis, because Dennis . . . Everything I've ever worked for, all I've ever wanted, knocked to hell! Beethoven's Parcae.

No. I won't give in. I will forget it, put it out of mind. I will, I *will* . . .

I stopped there to light a pipe. The rain's over, I think, but I'm in the mood to go on; or rather—I'm in the mood not to stop.

When I force myself to be honest I know that all the time I've been writing, I've been thinking over that last scene between us—seeing it dimly in my mind, misty and obstructed because of the mental effort to write. As in a glass darkly. (If ever I write the story of all this, that's what I'll call it—*As In a Glass Darkly*.) I remember going to her flat that night, knowing I shouldn't go, that it was already over between us. I had some flowers with me (futile gesture—I'd only bought them on the way to cover something up from myself) and a big slab of the cake she used to like so much. When I went in Dennis was already there. I had known he would be, of course, but somehow it was still a surprise—a surprise that what I had known had been confirmed, I imagine.

Jenny was standing close to the fire—very tall and slim and dignified in a black gown. I gave her the flowers and the cake and then we all three looked at each other in a futile and foolishly antagonistic sort of way. There was nothing to stay for—nothing at all—but somehow it was absurd simply to disappear again. Besides, I wanted to look at them—I wanted to look at Dennis—to see why I'd failed and he succeeded . . .

Later he went over to the piano and began to play—Chopin, the *Fantaisie Impromptu*. During that sickly middle theme he looked across and smiled at her and I could see then, quite apart from all I was legitimately entitled to feel against him—I could see then that there was something *wrong* with him—some quality of mind that was missing, a sort of perverted and impersonal malice that could make him capable of—oh, I don't know. I don't know what I'm talking about. Only there was that thing, and I saw it.

When I left, Jenny came to the door with me. Another example of the terrible flatness of the big moments of life. I said I hoped she'd be happy with Dennis—and all the time I was fighting down the part of me that was saying that she was no more than a vulgar little tart and would leave him sooner or later for someone else, just as she had left me for him. She asked me what I was going to do and I said the cottage. She laughed. "You always liked amateur gardening, didn't you?" she said. What could I say to that? It was the one futile, bourgeois phrase. I suddenly *had* to see her as I'd always hoped she wasn't. Amateur gardening! . . .

Why am I writing all this? I read back, and all the time it's as if I'm addressing someone—even as if I were getting something off my chest. . . *Should* it matter now, after that final revelation about her character? Why should she come and poison this one piece of my life that should be apart? She had nothing to do with me—not this part of me. Not even before, on the beach at St. Andrews, for example. No. I think it was something else. When I was all ready to come down here, for instance, and then had to be held back because of *that*. "When did you last see your fiancée? . . ."

Yesterday I went to the village. I didn't have to. I told myself it was to get tobacco, lest I should run out over the week-end. I bought a paper in the shop. That was why I went—in spite of myself. Hell, if one has known a person—no matter whom—one *is* interested, one *ought* to be interested . . .

They've found the legs. Written like that it's revolting. The legs—and they were beautiful, I used to love her legs.

Why won't it leave me in peace? What had it all to do with me? What right had it to happen at this one particular moment? Because I was once engaged to her. Two things superimposed in time—an accident.

Yet, in a sense, I can write impersonally enough. *Her* death means nothing to me—except in that it has broken up my peace. She herself—what do I care about her? What do I care about Dennis? He's in prison. It's finished.

27th. Thursday. These past few days a new thought has come to disturb me. Suppose they haven't finished questioning me—suppose they come down here, *here!* No—they couldn't. If they must question me, I'll go to them—I'll go back to town. I can't have them here, in my garden. This one thing I must keep apart.

It's getting worse—more difficult. Last night I couldn't sleep. I tried reading, but the words were meaningless. I kept seeing her face on the page, smiling—and Dennis's smile as he looked across from the piano that night . . .

Later. To the village again this evening. They were talking about it in the pub. I wanted to run away—to run and run. And then I wanted to make the big gesture—yes, to tell them I was the fiancé. "Knew her—of course I knew her," I could hear myself say. "Why—I was engaged to her! I've caressed her—I've felt her arms round my neck—yes, those very arms you're talking about, the ones they've just found . . ."

As I walked back a mist was settling over the fields. Last year, when Jenny was with me, I remember we stood at the cottage window and watched it—exactly like that. And I told her about the garden, what I was going to do—how someday, when I had enough money, I was going to give up my job in London and come down here for good, writing and gardening. Oh, all my hopes and dreams . . . And all she was thinking—I know it now: "He was always fond of amateur gardening . . ."

It's late. Terribly quiet. I've let the fire die down almost to nothing. But I can't go to bed. I can't screw up my courage to the point of turning out the lamp. Yet what is there to be afraid of? I've dealt with it all—my mind is settled and balanced. I have my philosophy, worked out, perfectly ordered: there's no room for that sort of thing . . . If I feel like this, what about Dennis? Poor devil . . .

I wonder if anybody ever reads *Trilby* nowadays? Svengali, even after he was dead, exerting his influence . . . Lord, how meretricious that allusion is! I'm losing my grip—can't write, can't think.

I'm cold. One more cigarette. It isn't fair, it isn't fair! If you only knew what I've gone through—all my life! All the beastly humiliation, the desperate struggle to get enough money to get here for good, the shelving of principles, having to kowtow to a set of beastly money-grubbers—and now this!

They're looking for the head. I heard that in the pub this evening—someone showed me a paper. Dennis won't confess—says nothing. Oh God, oh God! . . .

Wednesday, 17th May. No serious rain for three weeks. Much better. By forcing myself to work all day I can keep my mind clear. But it's an immense effort.

Reading back this part of my journal I can see it's all wrong. It's muddy. I want to be more detached—factual. Lots of things have disappeared in the confusion. I used to have a gift for irony, for instance . . .

Two incidents. The first was when my nearest neighbour came over to see me about some wood on my ground. I could see that that was only a pretext: he kept looking at me curiously, with a foolish half-smile, as if he and I shared some agreeable secret. I felt myself getting more and more irritated. He made one or two clumsy attempts to draw me into conversation. Just as he was going he allowed his smile to expand into a fatuous grin. "Excuse me, Mr. Baxter," he said, "but are you the same Mr. Baxter that was a witness in this trunk crime business?" I didn't reply. I wanted to kick him off my land—get his filthy leer out of sight of my garden. "I thought I recognised you," he went on. "And the—er—young lady—she was here with you last year, wasn't she? . . ."

When I look back now the whole incident seems grotesque and irrelevant. He talked as if, as if . . . I mean, there was something so damned matter of fact about his tone—except for that silly smile . . . And then I thought of all that his visit would mean—gossip round the village, people coming out to look . . . Quite suddenly I lost control. We were standing in the doorway and I screamed out something and slammed the door in his face. Next thing I remember is standing at the window watching him walking over the fields. He had a limp. I swear from the set of his back that he was laughing. I wanted to rush out after him and get my fingers round his throat. And suddenly I became aware that I had something in my hand. The wood-axe. I must have snatched it up when I slammed the door. I didn't remember, couldn't recollect . . .

The other thing I don't want to write about. But I must force myself. Small, trivial—an example of how my imagination *is* being affected by all this. All that subterranean part of my mind I keep repressing . . .

Last week—Wednesday—I was working in the garden—sowing seeds at the foot of the vegetable patch. I'd reached the end of the row and was smoothing over the soil, when, quite clearly, I heard someone call from the house that tea was ready. "Coming, Jenny," I called, and then suddenly I remembered and straightened my back. I went, hot—clammy. Yet I could have sworn . . .

I've tried to write these two things impersonally, but even here I've failed. Nothing can reproduce the enormous effect they had on me. Now that I'm quieter I try to analyze them and my reactions to them. I look out into the garden and it seems—did they really happen? I mean—oh, it's impossible. My mind's a jumble. I can't control anything, anything.

I try not to be indignant any more. But how can I help it? It's too great a struggle. Sometimes I think it would be better to submit. But to what? Jenny's dead. And I know, I *know* what she was. One can understand women like that being murdered. It's the only way one can finally *touch* them and keep them. That smile of Dennis's was the desire to touch. I'm not sorry for him. No. Only . . .

Same evening. I shouldn't have begun writing to-day. I had almost won. Now I know I can't win. It will be with me always, always. Jenny isn't dead. Her body may be, but she isn't. I can feel her *inside me.*

They're going to come down here. I *know* it. The papers are full of—questions about the head. They're saying my evidence isn't complete, I must know more. Did I *see* Dennis and Jenny together that night?

They'll come—*here.* This one thing above all others I've fought to avoid. I could weep . . .

20th May. Evening. It's over, over! But *have* I won? Or has she? I said I'd submit, but now that I have, what has happened? She or I? Oh, what magnificent power—reaching on after death—the old mortmain of the feudals! And how can one ever combat it? It's the one tremendous power, the greatest force in life. There's nothing one can do—nothing, nothing . . .

They came, of course. I knew they would. All that part of my mind that was working on out of sight knew it. And I couldn't keep the knowledge at bay—not by gardening. What was her phrase?—"*amateur* gardening." Yet it was that one phrase that defeated her in the end. Yes—it defeated her. I'm sure I've won. Writing here, quite away from it, I can see that clearly.

Let me go back. I'm quite calm—can afford to be. I've risen above the forces of stupidity. I can be quite impartial—even about those few terrible moments . . .

Last night, after I'd eaten, I took my pipe and stick and went out for a walk. It was splendid—a magnificent moon, a few clouds slung low over the horizon. As I went up the little hill that overlooks the cottage I could hear the echoes of my own footsteps in the silence. An owl flew by with big, soft-sweeping wings, and as I stopped to look at it I felt myself—how can I say it?—suddenly secure. Yes—secure. It seemed that nothing could hurt me any more, that I'd risen away and beyond all the grotesque trouble of the past few weeks . . . And then, as I stood there, I became aware of something else. The echoes of my own footsteps were going on! Very softly, behind me, lower down the hill. I looked round. Below me, in the brilliant moonlight, I could see the cottage, the curl of smoke from the chimney, but for the rest—nothing. I listened again. Silence . . .

For several minutes I stood without moving, and then I went on up the hill, still listening. And then, suddenly, it seemed that I was no longer alone. I knew, quite definitely, that someone was walking beside me—a little behind, on the right. It was how she always used to walk . . .

I wasn't afraid. All the time I was telling myself that the inevitable had happened. My mind was taking its own kind of revenge. It was even pleasurable to stand back, as it were, observing and analyzing a subjective state of mind with another and wiser part of that same mind. No. I wasn't afraid. Yet I didn't look round. It seemed—oh, I don't know. I had a sudden vision of myself looking round and seeing something melodramatic and absurd—something from the cheap ghost-stories. Jenny without a head—all pieced together, but without a head. And it was so fantastic that I laughed—out loud, in the silence of the hillside.

And it seemed that that part of me that was imagining her made her say, quite softly and distinctly—

"Why are you laughing?"

"At you," I said. "At both of us."

"Aren't you afraid?"

"Not any more." And suddenly I thought of Dennis, and added: "Have you been to Dennis?"

"No. I don't belong to Dennis."

"But you do to me?—in spite of everything?"

"I *am* you."

And then suddenly the stupidity of that conversation broke completely over me, and I laughed again and stopped walking.

"You know what I am doing now, don't you?" I said, and was surprised to hear how loud my own voice was. I was almost shouting. "Amateur gardening—do you hear? Amateur gardening! . . ."

I turned round quickly and stared. My gaze fell down to the cottage. The hillside was empty.

No. It doesn't do. Why should one try to write it down at all? It's all inadequate. There isn't any game that's worth the candle . . . Yet I could write on and on—saying nothing, but getting something down. It's probably the only reason anyone does anything—for the sake of getting something down.

But where was I? Now that's it's over and I'm free I find my thoughts rambling away out of control—a sort of delirium almost. Yes—last night . . .

I came home—back to the cottage. The kettle was boiling and I made tea. In some strange way I felt almost light-headed. It seemed I could walk without effort—backwards and forwards in the room a dozen times, enjoying it. I felt that if I wanted to I could jump from wall to wall with the greatest ease—like someone on the moon. I didn't know what was happening to me—only that I was free, that it didn't matter any more . . .

How long this mood continued I don't know. I lost all count of time, didn't think of looking at the clock. When at last I went up to bed the clouds had come up and covered the moon. I could see only very dimly beneath me the broad shapes of my garden. The lawn to the left, and beyond it the big dark patch I had been digging. Beyond that, to the right, the small bed on which I had been working that day when I seemed to hear Jenny's voice calling me to tea.

Thinking of her I lit the lamp and, sitting down on the edge of the bed, took her photographs out of my pocket-book. For a long time I sat looking at the heavy smiling lips, the wide nostrils, the exquisite eyes. And that magnificent head was what they were looking for! I tried to picture it as it was at that moment and, as I looked up, saw in the glass that I was smiling. That same smile that I had seen on Dennis's face during the *Fantasie Impromptu* . . .

I undressed slowly and with great care. When I got into bed I lay for a moment or two staring up at the ceiling, and then I turned out the light and closed my eyes.

Did I fall asleep? How do I know? It would be as wise to ask, was I asleep on the hillside? All I know is that in the midst of that feeling of light-headedness there came the realisation of a warmth beside me in the bed. How could I fail to recognise it?

"Is that you, Jenny?" I asked softly.

"Yes. Are you surprised?"

"No. Not surprised. Was it you on the hillside?"

I remember clearly every word—every intonation. It seemed important somehow that I should speak distinctly, that I should miss no syllable of her replies.

"Yes," she said. And then suddenly I seemed to *see* her lying there—smiling heavily, her red lips slightly parted, her head thrown back and turned towards me.

"I was never anything else but part of you, David," she said, and I remember nodding.

"I know. I had to force myself not to see you as you really were, ever. That was the one important thing I had to remember all the time."

She never stopped smiling.

"And did you succeed?"

"No. You were too strong for me."

"Was I, David?" And the smile deepened. I remember quite distinctly then turning further towards her and allowing myself to smile too.

"I've finished with you now, Jenny," I said. "I've had the sign. I know I'm finished with you."

"Are you sure? What are you going to do?"

"I'm going to kill you." And I stretched out my hands and got her by the throat. She did not move—only half-closed her eyes and went on smiling. I began to tighten my grip. This was why I had smiled as I looked at her photograph—Dennis's smile, the smile of wanting to touch finally and irrevocably . . .

Her throat was warm. I could feel the beat of the blood as my fingers sank into the flesh. And suddenly a sort of panic seized me and I released my right hand for something to strike with—the lamp by the bedside, anything. My fingers closed on a smooth, polished handle—the wood-axe, the one I had seized up that day when the lame man came to the cottage. I raised it and struck again and again. She went on smiling.

And suddenly I opened my eyes. It was daylight. From below came the sound of someone hammering on the door. I jumped out of bed and threw on a dressing-gown . . .

On the step stood a plain-clothes detective and two policemen.

They said they had a warrant and wanted to search the house. The detective kept looking at me suspiciously. He was pompous and heavy—blown up with a sense of duty.

What did I care? It was different now. They couldn't touch me. I was beyond them—beyond all the forces of stupidity. What did even my garden matter now? Let them trample over it. I had won —I knew I had won.

They left me with one of the policemen and went over the house. I could hear them in the bedroom discussing Jenny's photograph. I lit a cigarette and offered one to the policeman, but he refused surlily.

The detective came down and glared at me, then he went out into the garden. In two minutes he was back.

"David Baxter," he said pompously, in a low, clumsy voice —"the missing head is buried under the chrysanthemums."

I smiled. Damned fool! One can't cope with stupidity. They were dahlias.

The Little House

I HATE MONEY. I don't hate it for itself, but for what it does to people. Perhaps I have grown into this attitude because I have been working for fifteen years as an insurance agent. In this business things are valuated in terms of money that never ought to be valuated so. Maybe I am over-sentimental—people have always told me I am sentimental and expect far too much of folk. Well, that may be no more than something in my blood: I am a Scotsman—of Highland extraction originally. (The Campbells of Argyll were my forebears, but of course many of them—my family among them—migrated to the Lowlands at the time of the Lorn Wars, when Montrose's men sacked Inverary—so thank Heaven at any rate that my immediate ancestors were not concerned in the Massacre of Glencoe!)

However, that is by the way. I soon had much of the sentiment (perhaps sensibility is a better word?)—I soon had it knocked forcibly out of me when I went into the insurance business. To begin with, in that world you have tables—long lists—of terms in which, in a sense, your Company is preparing to *lay wagers* on the probable length of a man's life! Your Company, so to speak, bets a man so much that he will not lose a leg or an eye in an accident, or that his house will not burn down, or that he will not run over an old lady in his motor car. Perhaps the Company loses the bet (though not very often), and in this case it assesses the value in money of the said loss of leg, and pays up after the necessary forms have been filled in. So you can see that after a time you get into a way of thinking that it is not very *human*. A cynical point of view.

The first time this attitude began really to upset me was when I was working at the counter of our Head Office in the days before I went on the road as an agent. It was my job to interview people who called, and to help them to fill in proposal and claim forms. I remember a ruddy-faced pleasant-looking man came in one day. He was laden down with doctors' certificates and so on.

He was a stone-worker, and his employer was insured under the Workmen's Compensation Act, indemnifying him against injury or sickness among his employees. This man who came in had silicosis, and so was entitled, under his master's policy, to a weekly allowance from my Company. I paid him the money—something like 35/– it was, and thereafter every week he came in and filled up his form. Gradually the ruddiness left his cheeks—he began to look frail, all eaten away. Eventually he could hardly walk through the big revolving door—and his thin white hand, as he signed the form I filled up for him, used to tremble and shiver. Then one day he did not come at all: his wife came instead—a little sweet-faced woman, very quiet. For a few weeks she continued to come in, then suddenly one day she was dressed in black, and her face seemed even paler than usual. She collected the last payment. We took the file away, stamped it "Closed," and put it in a box. And that was the end of that—I never saw her again.

The *idea* distressed me: the whole implication that the man's life was a kind of commodity, you see. It had an assessed value—in terms of hard cash. I didn't like it at all.

So there—that was how I felt. That was how I came to begin to hate money. But the illustration I want to give you of the way the desire for money twists people's whole attitude to things has nothing really to do with insurance—at least, not directly. I am not a writing man, you know, but only an ordinary individual putting down some random thoughts; and so I have been rambling through an introduction instead of driving straight to the point. However, in a sense it is all relevant.

Ugh! When I think of this business of the Little House I want to run away and hide my head! However—it may not affect you that way: it's all a question of point of view.

Let me begin, then, by telling you that all this happened a number of years ago. I, being a Scotsman (and therefore calculated to be able to deal with other Scotsmen better than a Sassenach could), had been transferred by my Company to the job of travelling agent in the Fife and Forfar districts. I liked the work, I must say—it was good to get about and see the country. I was kept fairly busy too, and since there was a commission percentage on most of my work (and I being on the point of getting married and so needing money), I welcomed this fact most heartily.

I don't know if you know the little town of Monteviot? It's a small seaside resort on the East coast of Scotland not far from Dundee. Rather quiet at most times of the year, but suddenly busy during the Dundee holiday week, when all at once it fills up with hundreds of workers from the City, all intent on having a good time. There are few attractions beyond some golf links and a long expanse of lovely sands for the children, with the big icy breakers of the North Sea rolling continually over them. But it is a place to go—it's the seaside.

As it happened I had some important business calls in and around Monteviot, and, on this particular occasion I am writing about, I had to go there for at least two days, in order to get through all this work I had. Unfortunately it was the time of the Dundee Fair Week—the town, normally full of available hotels and boarding-houses, would be crammed to overflowing. I would, I decided, as I motored along the flat coast road, be lucky if I got accommodation at all.

A few miles from the town, as I was motoring calmly along admiring the scenery, my car suddenly jerked, coughed stupidly and then chugged to a standstill. I got out and heaved the bonnet up. Nothing serious, I could see—some carburetor trouble I could easily repair. So I got out my tools and my little motor repair manual (I always carried one—in a travelling job like mine you never knew what sort of trouble you were liable to encounter), and calmly and determinedly set to work.

I mention this accident for only one reason: it held up my progress and made it inevitable that I arrived in Monteviot just on dusk—a time, Heaven knows, when all the boarding-houses were likely to be full to the attics. I felt very down-hearted indeed as I drove along the esplanade road. It was a beautiful night, with the tide far out and the mauve sky reflecting exquisitely from the hundreds of yards of damp flat sand. But I had no eye for such things. I was looking not out to sea, but inland—scanning the To Let signs.

I put my car in a garage and set off on a systematic perambulation. I tried one or two of the better-known hotels, but the proprietors only laughed in my face. "Man," they said, "dae ye no' ken? It's Fair Week. There's folk in the baths, folk on the landings—there's folk even in the coal cellars. Ye'll be lucky if ye find a set-down the nicht."

I cursed my luck and set off on my wanderings again. I tried the boarding-houses, but there they were even more ribald at the idea of giving me accommodation than the hotel people had been. I fell into a mood of hopelessness and despair and started thinking in terms of getting my car out of the garage again, parking it in some quiet corner of the beach, and somehow curling myself up in it to spend the night. But this idea I was far from relishing: I had a big deal to pull off rather early the next morning, and felt that it was important to get a full night's rest on a bed.

I found myself finally in a small, rather squalid street on the North side of the town. Right at the end of it, standing isolatedly in a tiny withered garden, and surrounded by a fence all ramshackle and, in patches, decayed, was a small detached villa with a Rooms sign in the front window. As a last resort I pushed open the creaking gate and went up the path.

The door was opened by a sour, acrimonious man in shirt-sleeves.

"Good evening," I said. "I wonder—have you any accommodation? Anything—it doesn't matter what it is."

He looked at me surlily.

"We're full up," he grunted.

"Oh surely there's *something,*" I said, in my most wheedling tones. "Even if it's only an old sofa on a landing."

"Not an inch," he replied.

I was on the point of retiring when a thin drooping woman made her appearance at the end of the corridor behind him.

"What is it, Cecil?" she called, in a shrill, querulous voice. "Who is it? What does he want?"

(The idea of the man's name being Cecil struck me as grotesque. He was so sour, so yellow in the face—so utterly misanthropic.)

"It's a man for a bed," he called over his shoulder. "I've told him we're full."

She shuffled along the corridor till she stood beside him. Then she peered at me closely out of small, hard, red-rimmed eyes.

"Aye, we're full," she grunted at last. "It's Fair Week. Ye were daft to leave it so late."

"I couldn't help it," I said. "I'm here on business—I'm not with the Fair folk, worse luck. Could you not find me some corner? —I'm dead beat with looking for a bed."

She shook her head slowly and was, I thought, on the point of refusing point blank. But suddenly a queer, greedy, cunning look came into her eyes.

"How much were you thinking of paying?" she said.

"Oh—anything reasonable. What's your usual charge?"

She peered at me again. Then she took her husband's arm and led him back into the passage a little way. She leaned close to him and whispered with a kind of dry, horrid earnestness. He puckered up his eyes and shook his head. But she went on and on at him, and eventually I could see that he was conceding to whatever plan she was putting forward.

It was at this point that I noticed that the couple were not alone in the corridor. A little girl of about five or six was standing just beside the woman. She was a lovely little creature, with big solemn eyes and masses of fair wavy hair. I smiled at her, but she only stared at me in a serious, shy way.

While I was still trying to win the child's confidence, the woman advanced towards me again.

"Maybe we could squeeze you in," she said. "There's an attic. It's only a little room—I don't use it normally. But I'll have to get it ready. And it'll cost you—" (she hesitated) "—a pound."

"A pound!" said I. "For one night!"

"Oh, you needn't come if ye don't want," she said quickly. "I'm not forcing you. But it's a pound if you want it."

"Can you give me a meal?" I asked.

"Breakfast in the morning. But I can't cook for you at this time of night. I'll give you a cup of tea."

A pound for one small room for one night was fantastic. But I thought of lying all cramped in my car—with the important deal to look forward to in the morning.

"All right," I said. "I'll take it."

I made to enter the corridor, but she held up her hand.

"Wait," she said. "I can't let you in yet. I've got to get the room ready. You'll have to go away and come back in half-an-hour. And it's money in advance, please."

"Isn't there somewhere I could sit down?" I asked. "I'm dead beat."

But she shook her head. "You'll have to go away and come back," she repeated. "There isn't a corner—we're full up with folk—every room: and they're all abed."

There was nothing for it but to do as she suggested. I reluctantly gave her a pound note and went away down the path. As I closed the gate behind me I noticed the name on it: "Fairweather." And I thought—My God! Fairweather!—and a couple of sourer-faced so-and-sos I never saw in all my life!

As I walked up the street towards the town I saw, peeping at me from the almost-shut door, the little girl with the solemn eyes. I waved to her cheerily, and had the impression that she was thawing a little: she gave me a small half-smile before she closed the door completely.

I wandered disconsolately about the town. A few drunken men were abroad, and some courting couples, standing close together—mere huddled shapes in doorways and close mouths. I was desperately hungry, but of course no restaurants or even public houses were open. Fair Week notwithstanding. The Scots, you know, take their pleasures solemnly: even when they are off the leash they must circumscribe themselves with rules and regulations. The licensing laws laid it down that places of public refreshment should close at half-past nine, and so, no matter how holiday a spirit was abroad, at half-past nine the town packed up.

In the end I found, in a side street, a small fish and chip shop. The smell of vinegar and hot tallow was nauseating, but I was desperate and went in. A huge Italian woman lolled her sagging bosom on a zinc counter. She was dressed in a greasy white overall and was talking to a girl in an incredibly short and tight skirt. When I asked for chips she said there wasn't any—nothing left but "black puddings" (mottled, sausagy things, made of oatmeal and pig's blood). I said I would have one, and she went to the big tin friers at the back of the shop to get it. While she was gone the brassy girl in the short skirt leered at me horribly. She was a tart of the worst sort, with a little gold chain round her left ankle and hair all streaked and patchy with peroxide. In the naphtha-flare lighting of that beastly little shop she looked ghastly.

I made my escape with the hot and slippery pudding wrapped up in a bit of old newspaper. The only place to go was the beach. And here I had to pick my way among reclining couples, searching timidly for an unoccupied dune to sit on. Once or twice I was heartily cursed—at other times there would be a rustle and a furtive scampering as two dark shapes made off into the dusk from beneath my feet: I think they thought I was a spy from the Watch Committee.

Eventually I found a corner and sat down disconsolately, munching at my black pudding. There was by this time a considerable nip in the air, and I was far from happy. There I was, you see, stranded in that small town, with people enjoying themselves in a dull sordid way on all sides—and I with no real guarantee of even a good night's rest. I distrusted the Fairweathers—there had been something grim and avaricious in their whole attitude. Unpleasant people—except for the sweet-faced little girl.

It was her, I must confess, that I was thinking about as I made my way from the beach back to the small detached villa. Overhead, the sky was a clear cold blue, with a thin crescent moon just rising above the sea. The roar of the incoming tide fell faintly on my ears, and winging away across the damp sands, flying low, was a little flock of wild ducks.

It was all strange—unreal—like a dream. Except for the little girl. I looked forward to seeing her again—it was the only bright spot in the whole programme before me. I loved children, you see—people told me I had "a way with them." And I had seen, even in the small glimpse I had had of her, that the little girl was very sweet—not in the least like her parents . . .

Well, back I went. And I did succeed in drawing the little girl out and having a chat with her. And she *was* altogether enchanting—not in the slightest bit shy once I had broken down the first barriers. When I got to the house Mrs. Fairweather grudgingly asked me in, and led me through the dim passageway to a small squalid kitchen. It was an appalling room—untidy, with a lingering smell of cooking and washing about it. There were two wall beds—big cupboard-like things, with heaps of dirty-looking blankets on them, and patchwork rag coverlets. A clothes-horse stood before the range, with some damp flannel nightgowns and semmits on it, and on a pulley drier at the ceiling there hung, in clusters, some socks of coarse grey wool, brown and discoloured about the feet, and a few sets of long men's drawers, all baggy and darned at the knees—hairy and shapeless things, horrible in the dim light from the gas bracket above the mantelshelf.

Mrs. Fairweather gave me a cup of stewed tea in a cracked and badly-washed mug. Then she went upstairs—I could hear her shuffling along the passageway, grumbling as she went. There was no sign of Mr. F.—I took it he was helping his wife to get my room ready. I was left alone in the kitchen with the little girl.

For some time we looked at each other, smiling. I was distressed at seeing her out of bed so late—in a corner of the kitchen was a small tumbled cot that I took to be hers. I asked her what she had been doing.

"Playing," she said cheerfully.

"With your dolls?" I asked.

"Oh, yes. I've got a lot of dolls—so has Janet."

"And who is Janet?" I asked.

"She's my little sister—not so old as me."

"And what's your own name?"

"Marjorie."

(It struck me as strange that the sour Fairweather should have two little daughters. Somehow one didn't expect it of them—with their hard yellow faces they weren't the family type.)

"Where were you playing?" I asked her.

"Upstairs and outside. Father made Janet a little house, you see—he's a carpenter. And I've been playing there beside her with my dolls."

I felt, I must confess, a bit warmed towards Mr. Fairweather. If he could find time to make dolls' houses for his children, perhaps he wasn't so bad after all. I remembered that his face had not seemed so thin and cruel as his wife's—I remembered the way she had whispered to him in the corridor, he acquiescing: perhaps he was just henpecked?

"And where is Janet now?" I asked the little girl. "Is she in bed?"

"Oh yes—she's been sleeping for a long time. Out there," she added, nodding towards the back door of the kitchen. I took it that there was some sort of little out-house in the yard that the carpenter Fairweather had converted into a nursery for the younger child.

"You ought to be in bed yourself," I said with a smile to the little girl.

"Oh, I'm just going," she said. "I was helping mother with Janet, you see, so I couldn't go earlier."

At this moment Mr. and Mrs. Fairweather shuffled into the kitchen.

"Your room's ready," muttered the woman. "You'd better go up. It's late—we want to bed ourselves."

I gave Marjorie a good night and followed Mr. F. upstairs, he holding a candle in his cupped hand, so that the shadow of his crooked and stooping frame leapt grotesquely on the wall as we mounted. We climbed to the very top of the house, and then he led me along a short corridor. From behind the doors on either side of it I heard snoring—the other guests, I supposed.

There was another very short flight of steps at the end of the corridor, and at the top of them a small door, painted a dull brown colour. Fairweather pushed this open and stood aside for me to go in.

"Here y'are," he said gruffly. "It's no' palatial but it's a bed. The wife'll call ye in the morning. What time would suit?"

"Half-past seven," I answered. Then I added: "Your little daughter is charming, Mr. Fairweather. You must be very fond of her. Is the other one as nice?—Janet?"

"Janet?" he said, in a strange, stupid tone. "Oh—her . . . Oh, yes—yes . . ."

He stood for a moment peering at me. I had the impression he wanted to say something. Then suddenly he turned abruptly away.

"Good night," he said, and shut the door—with, I thought, unnecessary violence. I heard his footsteps going down the little flight of stairs and along the corridor.

I shrugged, then turned to survey the room. A gas bracket was on at a peep above the mantelshelf and I turned it up full.

It was a tiny room, very bare. The bed was small, covered with a white heavy lace counterpane, badly in need of ironing. The wallpaper was faded and wan—a design of small pink flowers on a yellow background. There were two pictures—one a dark oil painting in a gilt frame of some sort of landscape, the other a tinted photograph, bound in passe-partout, of a little girl of three or four. She was rather like Marjorie—the same wide solemn eyes. I took it to be Janet.

I undressed, turned the light out, and got into bed. And there I lay for a long time, unable to sleep. I don't know what it was —there was a strangeness, an uneasiness all about me. I had a recurrence of my previous impression that I was living a dream. The Fairweathers were not quite real—the house was not quite real. My whole impression of the dark little town, with the cold sea creeping up to it, was curiously nightmarish. I was haunted by a vision of the two squalid women of the fish and chip shop—the gross Italian with her sagging bosom, the tart leering hideously in the naphtha light. And the black pudding lay heavily on my stomach, giving me heartburn, so that the greasy taste of it kept coming back into my mouth.

To crown all, I was cold. There was an unwelcome chill in the bed. I remembered the Fairweathers saying that the room was not often used, and certainly it had, all about it, the unhappiness of an unlived-in place. Yet there was even something more than that—an atmosphere—a clamminess. The cold was not an ordinary cold—it was the bleak, impersonal cold of the sea I could hear in the distance outside. I wondered who had occupied the room in the days when it had been used. Had they felt this penetrating chill?—was that, indeed, why the room was out of use? —because it was incurably damp? And the Fairweathers had let it to me, for the sake of the money they were getting—knowing I was desperate for a bed, and therefore willing to run the risk of a cold or rheumatism?

In the end, exhausted as I was, I fell asleep. My last thoughts, I remember, were of Marjorie. I hoped I would see her in the morning—she seemed the one sane, healthy thing in the whole peculiar set-up. Perhaps I would see Janet too? I had a vision of them playing pleasantly and innocently with their dolls in the little house that Fairweather had made—grotesquely out of place in all the squalor of Mrs. Fairweather's kitchen.

There it was, then. That was the most of life, it seemed to me—things in juxtaposition. That's what it all boils down to in the end. Good things and bad things side by side—the sophisticated and the innocent rubbing shoulders . . .

Well, I am nearing the end of my little story. It is not really a story at all, I suppose—an incident, a situation, no more. It is basically very simple—but, as in the silicosis episode I mentioned, it is the *idea* that compels me: it is the attitude the situation implies and subtends. All I wanted to do was to set down this happening—this adventure, if you will—as an illustration of the point I made when I started writing. Perhaps my own sense of values has got a bit twisted? It may be the old Scottish sensibility: perhaps, when I think of Janet and Marjorie, I go over-sentimental (I always was so fond of children, you see); or perhaps, when I think of the Fairweathers, I go cynical—as a result of the insurance years. Oh well—it doesn't matter. I'm out of insurance now—retired these past eighteen months . . .

Mrs. Fairweather banged surlily on my door at half-past seven. I got up, feeling cramped and stiff and not particularly well rested. I washed and shaved as best as I could in cold water in a little bathroom I found at the foot of the small flight of stairs. Then, at a quarter-past eight, I went down for breakfast.

It was served in the front downstairs room of the villa—converted suddenly, I could see from the bundled mattresses and blankets in a corner, from somebody's temporary bedroom. One or two guests were already eating when I arrived—a small man with pince-nez, unshaven, who hid himself behind a morning paper, a large woman with a set, grumbly face, and two young girls (one of them, to the large woman's plain disgust, in a wrap and mules).

Mrs. Fairweather put some lumpy porridge before me, and a pot of weak tea, and then a pair of dry salty kippers, cooked in vinegar. The memory of the black pudding of the night before was still closely with me—I did not relish the food in the slightest.

Just before I finished my breakfast the four other guests got up and went out, the small man leaving me his newspaper. I was left in the dining room alone—the other guests in the house were plainly late-risers. I glanced through the paper, finishing my tea, and was on the point of getting up to go myself, when I saw a small figure regarding me from the doorway.

"Marjorie!" I cried—brightening immediately at the sight of her small solemn features. "You're up and about early."

"Oh yes," she said, advancing a little way into the room. "I have to be up, you see, when mother begins to get the breakfasts."

"And what about Janet?" I asked. "Is she still asleep?"

"Oh yes. She's outside."

"With the little house?"

"Oh yes." She nodded vigorously.

"I'd like very much to see Janet's little house," I said. "I've got to go in a few minutes—do you think it would disturb her terribly if you and I went round to visit her?"

"Oh no," she answered solemnly. "It would be all right. We could go out the front door and then round," she added, after a moment's pause. "Maybe mother wouldn't like us to go through the kitchen when she's busy with the breakfasts."

I nodded and rose. She took me by the hand quite confidently and led me to the front door. I was, I must confess, looking forward to seeing Janet—and also, strangely enough, to seeing the doll's house. The more I thought of it the more intrigued I was at the idea of the surly Fairweather going to the trouble to make toys at all for his daughters. Perhaps his acrimonious manner was only some kind of shyness?—he was, maybe, quite gentle and domesticated underneath?

Marjorie, chatting cheerfully all the time about the various dolls I would see, led me round the house and into a small yard at the back. There were various sheds and outbuildings and many planks of timber lying about—a notice at a back entrance to the yard read, I perceived: "C. Fairweather, Practical Joiner."

"Now," said Marjorie, lowering her voice to a whisper, "this way. She's in here."

She made for the smallest of the sheds—the one nearest the house. It was hardly, I remember thinking with some indignation, the sort of place I would want to put my daughter to sleep in, no matter how crowded I was for accommodation. It suddenly dawned on me that it must have been Janet's nursery I had spent the night in—the Fairweathers' greed had done the child out of a bed! Yet I suddenly remembered their saying that the room had been out of use for some time—and I remembered the clammy dampness I had felt in the sheets.

Marjorie pushed open the door of the shed and we went in. I blinked in the sudden dusk.

"There it is," said Marjorie, "—over there. That's the little house."

She pointed over to a corner away from the door. By this time my eyes were a little bit accustomed to the gloom, and I saw, lying on a bench, the little house—a small boxlike thing of plain wood. From the position of its sloping roof it seemed to me to be lying on its side.

"But where's Janet?" I asked, looking round.

"Oh, she's *in* the house," said Marjorie. "Come over and look—it's all right, you won't disturb her."

She dragged me towards the bench. Then suddenly I shuddered and released her warm little hand. I stopped dead and stared—at the small, calm waxen face, so like Marjorie's, that I could see before me in the little house!

The little house, my God! I saw what sort of a little house it was that Fairweather had made for his younger daughter. A little house she would live in for a long time.

It was a plain small coffin!

And all the time, as I stared, Marjorie was chattering on:

"She was upstairs, in the attic, sleeping in bed there, till Mummy and Daddy heard you were wanting the room. Then Daddy brought her down here, and we put her in the little house he'd made for her just after she'd fallen asleep. She's been asleep for an awful long time—and she was terribly ill before she fell asleep—I wish she'd wake up. But I think they're going to take her away somewhere today—I heard Mummy and Daddy saying so this morning. But I hope she comes back, and then we'll both be able to play with our dolls in the little house, the way I was doing before we put her in it last night."

She broke off suddenly, with a little "Oh," and looked past me to the door. I turned round. The Fairweathers were standing framed in the morning sunlight. She was erect, defiant, with her hands folded over her apron—he was shuffling and shaking his head embarrassedly.

We looked at each other for a long time. Then Mrs. Fairweather said, in a low, cold, even tone:

"You'd better go, Mr. Campbell."

I did not reply. I walked past them into the house. I got my coat and case and went away. I did not look back once as I walked along the street towards the garage where I had parked my car.

You see what I mean? It's money—the way it twists your senses of value.

I'm glad I'm out of insurance. It was beginning to make me think like that myself—I was beginning to assess things in terms of cash. But I don't think, even if I'd been in insurance for a hundred years, that I would ever have got to the way of thinking the Fairweathers did.

Think of it—for one extra pound! That little creature lying dead in the attic, waiting to be buried. And they moving her out so that they could let the room!

I suddenly knew why it was they had wanted me out of the house for half an hour. And I knew—God help me!—why my bed had been so cold.

Ugh! It's the *idea* of the thing, you know . . . And poor little Marjorie, talking quite blithely about the Little House, and about Janet being asleep. And probably thinking it *was* a doll's house that Fairweather was making—and playing quite happily with her dolls in it till they put her little sister there . . .

Well, maybe my friends are right. Maybe I *am* sentimental and expect too much of folk.

Esmeralda

A NIGHTMARE

Mr. Felix Broome lay on his back, wide-eyed, unable to sleep. Beside him his wife, Nancy, snored raucously—a long complicated snore, starting with a sigh and ending with a staccato nasal grunt. Mr. Broome, with a horrid fascination, followed the sound through all its convolutions, waiting desperately for some variation in the rhythm.

Mr. Broome was forty-five. A small man, round-faced, with a little brunette moustache. His mouth was thin and loose. He had false teeth but never wore them—he found them uncomfortable: jam pips constantly lodged behind the plate, irritating him beyond endurance. He was bald; and, since Nancy hated him bald, he wore a toupee, slightly curled.

The room in which he and Nancy were lying was above the little newsagent and tobacconist shop he had. It was in a side street in Notting Hill—not far from the Portobello Road—a bright, neat shop that did good business. Mr. Broome loved it dearly. He loved the smell of it—a smell all compact of newly printed paper, cheap sweets in cardboard boxes for the children (liquorice all-sorts, wine gums, dolly mixtures, sen-sen cachous, chocolate macaroons and whipped cream snowballs)—and, above all, tobaccos: thick black plug for chewing, tangled shag for those who liked to roll their own cigarettes, sickly yellow curly-cut, artificially scented flake, and half-a-dozen goodly mixtures in brown earthenware jars with tops that were moulded in the shapes of negro heads. Many a time, when the shop was empty, Mr. Broome would lift the top of one of these jars and sniff lovingly at the richness within. Many a time, when no one was looking, he would slip a dolly mixture or a jelly baby into his little loose mouth and suck at it noisily and enjoyably. Or he would furtively bury himself in one of the serials in *Peg's Companion*.

He even, on one occasion, wrote a surreptitious letter to a

character calling herself Wise Woman in one of the girl's papers he sold. He signed himself "Worried" and said:

"Dear Wise Woman,—I have been married for fifteen years but am, I am afraid, very unhappy. It is not that my partner and I have any open differences, it is just that we do not seem suited to each other. We have no children. Our tastes are not dissimilar, but somehow we do not hit it off. Somehow we seem to have very little to say to each other, and so in the house there is often an atmosphere of strain and discomfort. What can I possibly do to relieve the situation?—my partner is a Roman Catholic, so divorce is out of the question, even indeed if there were any ground for divorce, which there certainly is not. Yours sincerely, etc. . . ."

And next week, under a reproduction of his letter, he read Wise Woman's reply in small type:

"Dear Worried,—Alas, the sort of situation you describe is only too frequent nowadays. In so many lives I see Romance being supplanted by Boredom and Indifference. It is a pity you have no children—it is the tiny hands of children that more than anything else in the world smooth over the difficulties of married life and re-establish it in its full sanctity. They join together hearts that have drifted apart. Is it too late to think of adopting a child, if you cannot have one of your own? If this is not possible the only other thing I can suggest is that you should *try* to *find a common interest*. Are you fond of going to the Theatre or the Pictures? Make a habit of going once a week with your partner. I take it you yourself are not a Catholic?—try, nevertheless, to take an intelligent interest in your partner's religion. Make conversation, plan little surprises. And with luck and determination you will yet succeed, dear Worried, in salvaging your lives. Yours in sympathy—Wise Woman."

Mr. Broome remembered this advice with bitterness as he lay listening to Nancy's snoring. "Make conversation, plan little surprises." As if it were possible to make conversation with Nancy!

As if it were possible to plan little surprises for Nancy! He hated Nancy—the truth of the whole matter was simply that: he hated her. He hated everything about her—he hated her voice, he hated the way she dressed, he hated her vast podgy face with its sagging cheeks, he hated the smell of her. He who was so sensitive to smells—to the rich exotic smell of tobacco and the fresh clean smell of printed paper—how could he be expected to stomach the sweaty odour that came from Nancy?—all mingled with Woolworth's scent and pink gin? He hated every single thing that she said and did. He hated her very name. Nancy! If ever a name was unsuitable it was that. Nancy! Applied to the vast flabby hulk lying beside him it was grotesque. And names, he knew, were important—either directly or indirectly—ironically. There was his own name, for instance, Felix: meaning happy (there was an example of irony if you liked!). Or there was Miss Ickman upstairs—her first name was Cynthia, and Cynthia had been the Goddess of Chastity—could anything be more ironically suitable for that bleak and rigid virgin? Or there was—but here all irony vanished and Mr. Broome sighed in the darkness—a little sigh that was swallowed up and lost in the vast nasal sigh of Nancy's snoring—there was Esmeralda . . .

Nancy stirred and grunted. She heaved the bedclothes more firmly about her, and Mr. Broome's right foot was uncovered. With a patient sigh he wriggled the blankets over it again.

He did not want to think quite yet of Esmeralda—not quite yet. There was a deliciousness in holding back—in savouring the moment when at last he would permit himself to think of her. There were many stages to be gone through before he could sink finally into the dream that began: "If only . . ."

There came a creaking of a door from Miss Ickman's flat above. Lord, Lord—was she going to play the piano—at that time of night! He strained his ears, dreading to hear the familiar sound of the screwing up of the piano stool (Miss Ickman gave lessons, so the stool was never at the right height when she herself wanted to play). It came—and a moment later the sound of a Strauss waltz drifted down through the ceiling to him, the bass grotesquely magnified. Oh hell, oh hell! Now Nancy would waken—and Nancy awake was just one degree worse than Nancy asleep.

Yet, as the music went on, he found himself, in a way, welcoming it and enjoying it. The gay dancing rhythm brought into his mind a clear and exciting vision. Never mind if the vision was borrowed from a part of the dream that strictly speaking should come later. Esmeralda . . .

The snoring stopped suddenly in a long succession of short staccato grunts. Mr. Broome held his breath. Nancy heaved herself over on her back.

"Felix," she grunted. "My God, is that bitch at it again! Stop her, Felix—knock on the ceiling."

"It's only eleven o'clock, my love," said Mr. Broome quietly.

"It must be later than that. Besides, it's after half-past ten that you're not allowed to make a noise. Knock up, Felix—go on."

He sighed. But he knew the routine too well. He got out of bed and, shivering, went over to the corner behind the door and picked up a long broom that lay against the wall there. Then he mounted on a chair and thumped with the end of it on the ceiling.

"Louder, Felix—louder," hissed Nancy.

He thumped again, rhythmically. The playing stopped. The lid of the piano slammed shut angrily. Mr. Broome stepped down, wearily returned the knocker to its place, and crawled into bed again.

"Thoughtless old bitch," grunted Nancy.

"Go to sleep, my love," said Mr. Broome absently. "Go to sleep . . ."

She snorted and turned over on her side. He had a sudden whiff of her loathsome smell. It made him feel sick. But with a curious meekness he lay still, waiting. Her breathing grew slower and heavier. Once more the snoring began.

Fifteen years of it, he thought—fifteen years of it! Why had he ever married her at all? (Yet he did know the answer to that—it belonged to the later part of the dream.) In any case, at the beginning she had been different. She had not been bulky, the way she was now. She was kinder in disposition, her voice was softer, she dressed quite passably well. On the honeymoon he had even been quite proud of her. He remembered once, as they came in from a bathe, he had overheard two men saying, as they looked her wet figure up and down: "A fine buxom body, that"—and he had thought: "Yes, and it's mine—all mine . . ." He had thought that too, before, looking sideways at her as they knelt before the priest in the little Catholic Church in Notting Hill: "A fine buxom body, and it's all mine . . . What if I do have to sign a paper and say that our children are to be brought up in the Catholic Faith? It doesn't really matter. The main thing is that we should have children—and with that fine buxom body belonging to me, that should be the easiest thing in the world! . . ."

And now for fifteen years the buxom body had belonged to him. It had steadily grown less attractive—he had wanted it less and less. But conversely, by an irony, he had wanted the fruits of it more and more. And now he knew, finally, that there never would be any fruits from it, he hated the vast bulk with all the vehemence he had. His letter to Wise Woman was the only outward expression his hatred had ever had—and heaven knows that timid effusion was a poor enough index to his feeling.

Mr. Broome stretched out an arm and took a sip of water from the glass he kept beside his bed. A mouse stirred and scuttled in the quiet room. Outside he heard a late bus go slowly along the street. Nearer at hand a drunk man was singing mournfully, and a policeman's slow footsteps went clop-clop on the pavement. He closed his eyes. The moment had come at last—he had gone through all the preliminaries. If only . . .

If only, if only . . .

. . . She was exquisitely pretty. She was dressed in a diaphanous white frock. Her hair was fair—there was a little ribbon of pink silk in it. She was only thirteen, but not one member of the gigantic audience but was captivated and enchanted by her. She danced on and on, a small delicious figure in the glare of the footlights. A man in one of the boxes threw her a posy of flowers and she acknowledged it prettily, with a little curtsey woven into the dance. Some women behind Mr. Broome in the dress circle put their heads together and began whispering. By straining his ears he could just make out an occasional word of what they said:

"Exquisite . . . Enchanting . . . Like a little fairy . . ."

The dance ended. She swept one long and beautiful curtsey and the curtain slowly fell. The applause was enormous, terrifying. The curtain went up again and she was standing there, radiant in the light, blowing kisses to the audience. People were on their feet, cheering and clapping. The stage was covered with flowers. He felt like crying he was so moved.

And as he mingled with the crowd leaving the theatre, he heard again the two women talking behind him.

"Yes, dear—her name really is Esmeralda. Esmeralda Broome—the daughter of a little man who keeps a tobacconist's shop in Notting Hill somewhere. She's adorable, isn't she?"

Oh God, thought Mr. Broome. Oh God! If only . . .

The snoring went on remorselessly. Mr. Broome was almost weeping. If he turned he could see, in the light that came in from the street, the dark shape of Nancy's head on the pillow. She lay on her back again, with her mouth wide open. Fifteen years!

He suddenly drew in his breath in a quick gasp. He lay perfectly still, staring with dilated eyes at the ceiling. Then he quietly raised himself to his knees. Still staring, he picked up the pillow he had been lying on. For a moment he stayed poised, holding it in his hands—then, with a small animal grunt, he lunged forward and crammed it on to Nancy's face.

The snoring stopped. He lay on the pillow, grunting and moaning, pressing it down with all his strength. She began to struggle—little inarticulate sounds came from beneath him. She heaved her enormous bulk on the bed—his nostrils were filled with the smell of the sweat and cheap scent. Still lying on her face, and grunting in little ecstatic gasps, he pushed his hands down under the pillow and fumbled for her throat. He felt the muscles of it twitching convulsively beneath his fingers. He squeezed with all his strength, and his fingers went deep into the flaccid flesh.

He lay like that for a long time. There was a mounting, rushing noise in his ears, like wind, or tumultuous applause. Outside he heard the clop of the feet again, as the policeman repassed the house. And he realised suddenly that all was quiet—there was no movement at all beneath him.

He rolled himself back into his own place in the bed. He listened to the silence. Then, exhausted, but with, somewhere inside him, the applause going on, he fell into a deep stupid sleep.

* * * *

He opened his eyes at a quarter-past six. For a moment he lay looking at the creeping dawn light that came through the window. Then, quite quietly and detachedly, he remembered all that had happened the night before.

He turned and looked at Nancy. The pillow lay over her head. Curiously he lifted a corner of it—then replaced it with a shudder: the face beneath was swollen and ugly—the veins stood out in purple ridges, the teeth showed right through the upper lip, so great had been the pressure.

Mr. Broome got out of bed. He went over to the window and stood there thoughtfully, scratching his backside. His striped flannel pyjamas hung from him loosely—he was a small and grotesque figure in the sick light.

A few people were astir in the street. A man with a bonnet and muffler passed briskly, a blue enamelled tea-bottle sticking out of his pocket. A little hawker's cart went by, the pony nodding dejectedly in the shafts, the driver half-asleep. A lean dog sniffed round the dustbins.

Mr. Broome was surprised that he did not seem to have any feelings. According to the magazines in the shop downstairs, what he had done was spectacular—people wrote stories about murderers. And here was he, in real life, a murderer—and he felt nothing—nothing at all. He had even, he remembered, fallen asleep after killing Nancy. Fallen asleep! There was no end to mystery—things never worked out in life the way they did in books.

He dressed slowly and carefully, spending a long time in settling his tie at the mirror. Before him, on the dressing-table, was Nancy's array of scent bottles. He smiled wrily as he uncorked one of them and held it to his nose. But there was work to be done, he suddenly recollected, and he set the bottle down again and went briskly out of the room.

Underneath the shop there was a deep earth-floored cellar where Mr. Broome kept old boxes and papers. Here he worked furiously for about an hour. At the end of that time there was a hole some three feet deep in a corner of the room. Mr. Broome surveyed it with satisfaction, then he went upstairs to the bedroom again.

Nancy still lay quietly on the bed. This almost surprised him—he had half expected to find her sitting at the dressing-table making herself up. But the enormous bulk was quite motionless—the pillow was still in position.

He stood surveying her for a little time. Then, bracing himself to the effort, he put his hands under her armpits and dragged her from the bed.

She was enormously heavy. He thought with irony, as he looked along the bulging figure, swathed in a nightgown of pink chiffon, of the remark the two men had made on the beach: "A fine buxom body, that . . ." Well, it was buxom no longer—mere clay and no more. Nancy could no longer demand his services for her body, when she had been drinking too much pink gin. There would be no more weeping agonies of resentment—no more vows of "I won't give in to her, I won't, I *won't*"—and then giving in to her, and regretting it, and feeling ashamed and weak next morning. It was all over now. He had beaten her at last, after fifteen long years.

Somehow he got the huge sagging lump down the stairs to the cellar. He dragged it heavily, walking backwards at an angle—Nancy resting on her heels, her huge yellow toes pointing to the ceiling. With a final heave he toppled it into the damp hole he had prepared, then stood back panting.

He went up into the shop to look at the time. It was a quarter to eight—in a quarter of an hour's time the shop should be open, if all was to seem normal. With a feverishness in his movements now, he rushed downstairs and shovelled the earth over the body. Then he replaced the boxes and papers he had cleared from the corner when he was digging the hole. A last look round to see that all was normal and he went upstairs, smoothing his jacket and straightening his tie as he climbed. By two minutes past eight the shutters were down and the shop was open.

"Good morning, Mr. Broome," said the van boy who delivered his bundle of papers. "All right?"

"Couldn't be better, Bert," said Mr. Broome.

"And Mrs. Broome O.K.?"

"Oh yes." And he smiled in his little loose toothless smile. "She's in the pink, Bert—in the pink . . ."

Now all that day, as Mr. Broome worked on in his shop, he was thinking. He began in the morning by thinking how strange it was that he was so calm. He, Felix Broome, forty-five, a man of no importance, had committed a murder. He who had never been able to make up his mind to do anything had at last done one supreme and dramatic thing. He had killed his wife and buried her in the cellar—yet behold, he was calmly going about his business as if nothing had happened.

Where was the sense of guilt that was supposed to overwhelm murderers?—where were the agonies of remorse that were said to assail them? If he felt anything at all it was a sense of relief—and occasionally, mingling with it, a sense of power and achievement. Later on in the day this feeling increased. Sometimes, as he handed a paper or some tobacco to a customer, he felt like leaning over the counter and saying:

"Excuse me, sir, but I thought I would just like to let you know that I have murdered my wife. We had been married for fifteen years and I hated her, sir—she stank. So I murdered her, sir—she's downstairs in the cellar now, under three feet of earth. Anything else, sir—some pipe-cleaners, matches?"

He pictured the sensation—the startled customer scuttling from the shop and calling a policeman. And, later on, the headlines in the papers—papers that would be sold over the very counter on which he leaned. Wise Woman would get a shock if she knew that Worried, to whom she had given such excellent advice, had finished actually by murdering his partner! "Plan little surprises" indeed! He had planned one of the biggest surprises in history—he, Felix Broome—a man of no account and a dreamer.

At this point, as he leaned on his counter, Mr. Broome sighed deeply. It need never have happened. The fifteen years of misery need never have happened. If only—if only . . .

And there came into his mind a sudden image of a white whirling skirt. Esmeralda—she would have solved it.

At lunchtime he went to the little room at the back of the shop and cut himself some bread and cheese and boiled some tea on the gas-ring. And as he chewed his meal slowly (having put in his false teeth for the purpose), he began to think over a plan of campaign. One thing was clear—he had to get out of London. And in some way he had to disguise himself. If he left off his toupee and wore his false teeth continuously, that would make a considerable difference to his appearance. Then he could shave off his moustache. Fortunately, no photograph of him existed—he had always had a horror of cameras. And he had no relatives—at least, only one: a cousin in Canada—and she had not seen him for twenty years.

He would go, he decided, to the North of England—to Bradford, say, or Burnley: one of the vague black cities, on the top of the map, he had often heard of but never visited. Upstairs, in a hole in the mattress (the very mattress on which Nancy had died), he had almost three hundred pounds—his savings. With this sum it should be possible to start a little tobacconist's shop.

It was indeed curious, he reflected again, how calm he felt. He was quite confident that he would not be found out. As soon as it grew dark he would close the shop, gather together his few more precious belongings, and simply disappear. It would be some days before anyone got suspicious because the shop was closed —there was no one likely to call. If he put a card on the door —"Closed till further notice"—that would satisfy Bert the van boy and Miss Ickman upstairs. Eventually, no doubt, there would be a search—an advertisement about the missing Mr. and Mrs. Broome would appear in the Sunday papers. Perhaps one day the police would discover Nancy's remains in the cellar—but what would it matter? By that time he would have started his new business in Blackburn or wherever it was—he would be comfortably established under a new name and with a different appearance. What could he call himself? Black? Thomson? Clarke? There was, he remembered, a significance in names. What about Nancy's maiden name—Gilbert? Too obvious, perhaps—a clue that might give him away. Yet he could always use it as a first name. A sudden curious allusion came into his mind. A few days before, he had been reading an article in one of the cheaper and more spectacular weeklies—*The Real Bluebeard,* it had been called. And he remembered that the name of the famous wife-murderer had been Gilles de Rais. Why not call himself Gilbert Ray? A good name—and a significant one. Gilbert Ray, Tobacconist and Newsagent . . .

Chuckling to himself quietly, he took out his false teeth and went back into the shop. He popped a jelly baby into his mouth to suck by way of dessert. Then he sniffed lovingly at one of the earthenware tobacco jars. It was a pity, he thought, that he would have to leave his carefully-collected stock. But still—it was only for a little while. It would not take him long to gather more—when he started up again as Gilbert Ray.

There was little doing in the way of business during the afternoon. Mr. Broome found himself looking forward to six o'clock, when he could put up the shutters and start disguising himself. He had a lot to do. He had checked in a timetable that there was a train to Blackburn at 10.15—everything had to be ready by then.

He started putting up the shutters at ten to six. Then he went into the back shop again and fried himself an egg. He was just on the point of going upstairs to the bedroom to start on his disguise when he had a sudden uneasy thought. Had he bolted the shop door?

As he went through to examine the lock a sudden whiff of Nancy's perfume filled his nostrils. He paused—then shrugged and moved on to the door.

Surely enough, by an oversight, he had forgotten to fix the snib. With a little grunt of annoyance he stooped to remedy the mistake. And suddenly he had an overwhelming sense that someone was standing just outside. The feeling was powerful—ridiculous but powerful. A little ashamed of himself, he swung the door open—and then his little eyes grew round and his loose mouth sagged open stupidly.

A little girl in a white dress was standing facing him—a little girl whose long hair was tied charmingly in a bow of pink ribbon. And as he stared, she swept him a low and graceful curtsey.

"Esmeralda!" he gasped.

"How do you do, dear father," she said with a smile. "May I come in?"

Still smiling at him sweetly, she walked past him into the shop. He shivered—and again in his nostrils he felt a distant whiff of Nancy's Woolworth's perfume. He closed the door with a slam, locking it with trembling fingers. Then he turned and followed the little girl up the stairs in a daze.

* * * *

And now they were sitting in the bedroom facing each other. She was exactly as he had pictured her so often—petite, exquisitely pretty, with small, quick gestures. She sat primly on the edge of a chair, her feet barely touching the ground—and all the time she smiled.

As for him, he did not know what to say or to do. He felt dazed—unable to comprehend what had happened—unwilling even to try to comprehend it. Was it a dream? Had he stupidly fallen asleep—at the very moment when he ought to be packing feverishly for his flight to Blackburn? He remembered how he had fallen asleep just after he had murdered Nancy—a curious, stupid thing to do. Was he perhaps a little bit mad? After all, there must, he thought, be something unusual in a man who suddenly murders his wife—who sets about covering up his tracks with the care and calmness he had given to the task that day. He did not know—he did not know anything: except that Esmeralda, about whom he had thought and dreamed so often, was now sitting in some unaccountable way before him, smiling at him. And she was lovely—she was only thirteen, but she was lovely. He almost felt like weeping.

He realised that she was speaking to him.

"Dear father," she was saying, "don't be surprised that I have come to you at last. After all, there was only one thing ever that kept me away."

He looked up at her. Her smile was rigid—in a way it was a

little frightening. He almost wished that she would relax it—yet he realised that in his dreams she always had been smiling. He had never seen her with any other expression.

"You mean——?" he said dazedly: and she nodded.

"Yes. Mother. But she's safely out of the way, isn't she? Oh I always hoped you'd do that to her someday, father. She was such an ugly bitch!"

There was something hideous in the way she spoke—it alarmed him. She was only thirteen. His brain was in a whirl—things were growing wild and grotesque and somehow beyond his control. If only she wouldn't smile!

"You see, father," she went on, leaning forwards a little, "I would only have been the same as her. You signed a paper, you know—do you remember? Fifteen years ago! . . . You said that any children you and Nancy had would be brought up to be like her. It might have been all right at the very beginning—she was quite presentable then, wasn't she? And she didn't stink."

"I don't know what you mean," he gasped.

"Oh you do—of course you do! Do you think I don't know you, after all these years? You liked her body a lot at the beginning. Do you remember the first time you saw her without her clothes on? That time when you went to Brighton for a day and missed the last train home?—and you went to an hotel and registered as Mr. and Mrs. Broome? It was before you were married, father."

Her tone was arch and horrible. He felt himself sweating slightly under the collar.

"I hated her body," he said, in a muffled little whisper.

"Not at first, father," she said. "You can't pretend that you hated it at first. It was only later, when she began to—well, father" (and she sank her voice to a low salacious whisper), *"when you began to grow old!"*

There was a long silence. Mr. Broome felt a curious nightmare listlessness in all his limbs—he was weak and helpless. Things had suddenly turned inside out—it was not what he had ever meant—not it at all.

"Who are you?" he gasped at length. "Are you a demon?"

"Father, dear!" she remonstrated. "I'm your own dear daughter! Don't you recognise me? You've seen me a hundred times in your dreams—you've heard people talking about me. I'm Esmeralda, father dear."

"You're not," he said, speaking thickly, with an effort. "You aren't Esmeralda. Esmeralda is a little girl—I mean, I've always thought of her as a little girl—if I could have—I mean, if Nancy could have . . ."

She laughed—a shrill, stagey, impersonal laugh.

"Oh father, father! You haven't known in the least bit what it's all been about, have you! You've thought it was all something else. You've sat in your shop and you've read the stories in the magazines, and you've thought it was all something else altogether! Poor old father! Shall I tell you something, father? Shall I tell you the story of your life?—the real story of your life?"

He stared at her, unable to speak. She went on smiling. And she got down from her chair and walked over towards him till she was only a yard away from him. Then she knelt down on the floor and leaned back on her heels—still smiling.

"Do you remember, father, thirty years ago? You were fifteen—you had just left school. You were apprenticed to a draper in the Harrow Road—Carradine's. You were very shy, father—oh terribly shy. You used to blush if anyone spoke to you. And the girls called you baby-face, father—do you remember that? Do you remember Miss Dobie, father?"

"Stop it—stop it," he groaned.

"Oh father—I'm only beginning! You can't stop me now—there's such a lot to say. Don't you remember—the ladies' combinations?"

She laughed again—her eyes bright and hard and glistening. He stared at her helplessly, in horror.

"Miss Dobie was twenty-eight, father, and you were sixteen. She was a bitch, wasn't she?—all the men said so. The way she used to torture you—made you go into the underwear window and dress the dummies in Carradine's Special Line in Ladies' Combinations!—in full view of the public, too! Beastly, wasn't it. You hated her, father. But you couldn't help yourself, could you?—she was far too powerful for you. That night when she had you to her room—smuggled you into the ladies' hostel she lived in at Earl's Court—do you remember it, father? You were trembling all the time—it was all so new—you were only sixteen . . ."

"For Christ's sake, stop it!" he cried. "It's filthy—it's filthy! Stop it!"

"It's the story of your life, father. It's why you killed mother. And father——" (and she lowered her voice to a whisper again) "—it's why you created me!"

Mr. Broome held his breath. He was aware of footsteps outside—they came to him as from an enormous distance. It was the policeman beginning his evening beat—walking slowly and comfortably in a sane quiet world.

"Poor father, poor father," went on the crouching figure at his feet. "You hardly knew all this, did you? You didn't ever have a real chance. After Miss Dobie it was Alice. Do you remember Alice? You and she at the Dance Palais, just after your twenty-first birthday? Learning the Charleston. Do you remember that long spangly dress that she wore—cut square at the neck and with a low waist? And when you danced the last waltz, when the lights were low, and you were very close to her—so close that your face was buried in her hair . . . and it filled your nostrils, father—it was like a brown shag tobacco, all stringy, but fragrant—you couldn't get enough of the scent of her . . ."

"You devil, you devil!" said Broome, in a low sobbing voice.

"I'm only telling you, father," she said, gently and ironically. "I'm letting you know, that's all. It isn't what people imagine it to be, is it, father? Nothing is—not quite. People never do things for the reasons they think they do—do they? It's always something else—something nagging on in the background . . . Oh, it was glorious last night—wasn't it, father! That magnificent moment!"

"What do you mean?" he gasped.

"You know what I mean—when you lay the pillow and put your hands round her throat. She was in your power, father—at last it was that way round: someone was in your power—instead of it being the other way—you in someone else's power. That's what made it, wasn't it, father?"

Mr. Broome raised his trembling hands to clasp his temples. Something terrible and unutterably beastly had happened to him

—out of the blue. He had been so calm—so infinitely superior to things. He had worked quietly in his shop all day, he had made his plans, he had been so sure of himself. And now, from nowhere, came this foul and raging insanity. He grew aware of the thin ironic voice going on and on.

"Yes—Miss Dobie, and Alice: and the strange girl you met when you were on holiday that time at Weston-super-Mare—Margie her name was—and Enid, that you met at your cousin's farewell party, when she went to Canada, and finally Nancy. It was always the same, wasn't it, father? Life is always the same thing, happening over and over again. That's what none of them understands, isn't it? Wise Woman has no suspicion that that's the real truth about things, has she? Or she could never write such rubbish about Romance being supplanted by Boredom and Indifference, and the Tiny Hands of Children Reuniting Parted Hearts—now could she? It's all the same thing. I bet if you met Wise Woman herself, she'd stink of scent too—and she'd be like Nancy was when she had had too many pink gins. They wouldn't leave you alone, father—not one of them. They're all the same."

A terrible dry sob came out of the little man on the chair.

"Esmeralda," he cried, "for God's sake don't say any more—don't say it! Go away—leave me. You're different—it isn't you that has been saying these things. Something has happened to my brain—I'm imagining this—it's the strain—it's been too much. I'll go away—just let me get away from this bloody room. It'll be all right then. But don't go on about these things—for Christ's sake, don't say any more."

He remained for a long time with his eyes closed. There was a rushing noise in his head. From infinitely far away he heard the footsteps of the policeman as they passed the house again. He did not dare to look up. Above all things in the world he did not dare to encounter the beastly rigid smile of the creature on the floor.

And then he realised that she was speaking again.

"Poor father, poor father," she said: and it seemed that her tone was different—was quieter and less ironical. "One illusion must be left—it's always the way, isn't it. The strongest man must always preserve at least *one* illusion—and you aren't a strong man, father, are you—you're the weakest man in the world . . . Ah, you don't remember, do you? You can't see far enough down, can you? And even if you could, you couldn't piece things together, could you? They wouldn't make sense, even if you did—things never make sense, not real things. It's all a jumble—it doesn't connect. Yet sometimes, if you look at it all quickly, there suddenly seems to be a sort of thread . . ."

He still did not look up, and she went on quietly:

"The little girl, father—the kernel of it all . . . You were thirteen—it was at school. And do you remember you were made to sit beside her, as punishment? And she smiled at you when the teacher wasn't looking. And she had a little string of cheap glass beads round her throat—and they were green—and she told you they were emeralds. Do you remember that, father, and mark it—*emeralds?* And you were reading a book in school that year—dreadfully dull, you thought, but they made you read it. *Notre-Dame de Paris*. It was about a hunchback. And it seemed to you that there was something infinitely pitiable about that hunchback—there was something wrong with him, he was despised by everyone. He was just like you, father."

There was a long silence. Broome held his breath. The small voice went on.

"Yes, father—they all despised him. Except . . . there was the girl. Do you remember the girl in that book? She was all different. She was poetry, she was romance, she was all the warm and the lovely things, she was beautiful—oh, beautiful! Do you remember her name, father?"

He did not reply.

"Oh come, father! You're bound to remember her name. It was——?"

"Desdemona," he said, in an almost inaudible whisper.

"*Father!* You always got those two mixed up! No—Desdemona was the *other* time. Don't you remember?—the other time you sat beside the little girl. It was when they took you all to the theatre that afternoon—and you were so tremendously excited. You had never been to a theatre at all before—though you had heard about them. You thought you were going to see dancing girls, didn't you, father—but it wasn't anything like that at all. It was educational—it would be, since the school arranged it!—and it was a play—by Shakespeare. It was Desdemona who was the girl in *that,* father. Her husband smothered her. You always got her mixed up with the other girl—the girl in the book—their names were so alike. Don't you remember? *She* was called——?"

"Esmeralda!" gasped Broome.

"Yes—Esmeralda! Clever father! And the little girl sat beside you, father—and she was dressed in white that day—and she had a little bag of sticky sweets, and she gave you some. And do you remember she wriggled in her seat, and her dress slipped up over her knees, and you sat there beside her, father, and you looked at her, and you thought——"

She broke off. In the silence Broome heard, above him, in Miss Ickman's flat, the sound of the piano stool being screwed up. The girl spoke again, and this time all the terrible archness was back in her voice.

"Father—look at me. Look at me, father."

He slowly raised his head. His eyes were staring. She was regarding him with the hideous fixed smile still on her face. And as she knelt on the floor she was pulling her skirt lasciviously over her knees.

"Oh Christ!" cried Broome. "No—no! It's abominable—it's hellish!"

He covered his eyes with his hands. There came an echo of the terrible impersonal laughter. And simultaneously, from above, there floated to his ears the strains of the Strauss waltz he had heard the night before.

An immense shudder shook him. He opened his eyes and rose wildly to his feet. The room was empty. But all about him—suffocating him—was the smell of Nancy.

* * * *

The policeman, entering the little side-street near the Portobello Road, found Broome gibbering at the door of his shop. He went inside with him—Broome seized him and made him go inside. He looked on with stolid interest while the small sobbing figure tore at the loose earth on the floor of the cellar.

And he whistled through his teeth when he saw what the little man, with an expression of mixed terror and relief on his face, disclosed.

Later, when Broome had been taken away, the policeman and his sergeant made a search of the house.

"Blimey," said the sergeant, as they opened the door of the bedroom—"what a stink!"

"Someone's been mucking about with scent," said the policeman.

They found that every bottle on the dressing-table had been smashed. The contents had been splashed over the room—the carpet, the walls, the bed—and then the bottles had been smashed.

"The little chap's hands were bleeding," said the policeman. "I thought it was the digging in the cellar—he went at it like a maniac. But it must have been this. Poor little devil—I couldn't help feeling sorry for him somehow . . ."

Music, When Soft Voices Die . . .

I HEARD OF THE DEATH of Sir Simon Erskine some five years ago, when I was taking a long holiday in my beloved Scotland. I had known him quite well—a terrible man, moody, powerful, irascible. They said he was only forty-eight when he died. Yet, when I had last seen him, about two years before, at the time of the tragic death of his young wife, he had seemed at least eighty. I remember him then, standing in the porch of that huge, bleak house of his, a brooding and lonely figure, holding tight about him the black cloak he favoured, his already white hair blowing round his temples in the eternal winds of that wild corner of Perthshire. He was the last survivor of the Pitvrackie Erskines—the Black Erskines, as they had been called in the old Covenanting days: stern, merciless, religious men, who believed (if truth be faced) in hellfire and damnation and not much else. It was one of the Black Erskines who, with one mad stroke, had swept the head from the shoulders of a young officer who, in his cups, had questioned some religious truths. And another of the clan, on discovering his wife in adultery, had hanged the woman with his own hands, after immolating her lover most dreadfully before her eyes. A terrible, half-beastly family they were, with a long history of bloodshed and cruelty behind them.

About a month after the death of Sir Simon, the factors announced an auction of his properties and effects at Vrackie Hall. I was sufficiently interested to travel in the creaking old bus from Perth to Pitvrackie that day: not only was I keen to see the curious old house again on its storm-swept promontory among the hills, but there was the chance of picking up a treasure or two. Sir Simon had been a man of many accomplishments. He had been interested in a thousand things—in 17th Century Dutch painting, in Romantic English literature of the late 18th and early 19th centuries, and, above all, in unusual musical instruments. He had, too, done much big game hunting in Africa. It was in Africa, in fact, that he met Bridgid Cannell, whom he later married, and whose strange death affected him so terribly. Indeed, let me be honest and say that it affected him almost to the point of madness. There were wild tales of his behaviour during the last two lonely years of his life—tales of how he shut himself up for days on end in the big library of Vrackie Hall, of how the scared servants heard him sometimes weeping aloud, sometimes laughing, and sometimes, as it were in a disconsolate frenzy, beating on a collection of native drums he had brought back from one of his African expeditions. The wild, primitive rhythms, going on through the hours and throbbing into the farthest corners of the dark house, hypnotized him, perhaps, into forgetting his bitterness and the terrible sense of his loss. He was a man whose mind was delicately enough poised as it was, God knows—a man who feared loneliness for what it might do to him, yet who nursed his passions jealously and secretly. Neither Bridgid nor his first wife had near-succeeded in fathoming him—it was as if he needed them, he needed their company and the comfort of their bodies, yet was unwilling to let them have access to the innermost parts of him—a Bluebeard who kept one chamber eternally secret. His first wife, a young Scotswoman of good family, had, after five years of him, run off incontinently with a middle-aged American doctor. The fact that she had no child by him but had been delivered of a son within a year of meeting the American, weighed bitterly with Sir Simon. And when Bridgid died childless, so that he saw the line of the Black Erskines ending with him, he raged vilely against the destinies: and so shut himself up in the decaying house, seeing no one, brooding jealously among those priceless possessions of his, weeping like a spoilt child over his failures, beating insanely on those damnable drums and sending the throbbing, restless voices of them across the valley and against the forbidding harsh face of old Ben Vrackie itself . . .

I reached the house that day of the sale in a battered, irritable condition. Gusts of wet, mist-laden wind had worried at me as I mounted the mud-raddled roads to the Hall from Pitvrackie. Dull clouds sagged over the peaks of the hills that surrounded the house, the pine forests that flanked my path were silent and evil seeming, heavily adrip with moisture. I saw no one, save, at one point, an old cross-eyed tinker who carried, over his shoulder, a long pole slung with dead rabbits, all matted and patchy from the damp. A fawn-coloured, evil-eyed ferret stared at me out of his pocket. I had a fleeting remembrance of an old childhood fear—that ferrets were capable of springing at human throats and sucking the blood therefrom: but the beast, I saw, was chained to the tinker's wrist. I gave the man a greeting but he did not reply—passed on his silent way, his squinting eyes fixed on the roadway before him as he walked.

Vrackie Hall stood back from the road in a large park full of trees and gardens that at one time had been carefully laid out. There was a drive of red gravel. The entrance gates were made of elaborate wrought-iron and there were, above the pillars of them, two eagles, staring at each other with their heads turned sideways. They were made of soft stone that had been eaten away by the weathers, so that they seemed to have a frightful and painful disease. The big house itself, built three-quarters of a century ago on the site of the old Erskine Castle, was a mixture of many styles and periods. There was, first, a large porch way flanked with smooth Grecian pillars, the arch of it embellished by a florid frieze consisting of festoons of fruits and flowers with, occasionally in the midst of them, pot-bellied nymphs in modest attitudes. There were festoons above some of the windows too, and many tiles, glazed in yellow and green, with small fat cupids on them and long formal garlands of flowers. The windows themselves were large, and some of them had inset panes of stained glass at each corner. Those on the front of the house had narrow barred shutters in the French style folded back from them, some a dingy cream colour, others painted in flaky green with white underneath. On the south wall there was an exuberant creeper of a rich glossy brown that merged into fresh green at the top and sides: on the back wall there were espalier fruit trees, pegged symmetrically to the lime-eaten bricks. The roof was tiled with slates of varying shapes, some square, others pointed like diamonds and others curved and scalloped—the layers of these last ones looking like enormous fish scales. And on top of all, overtowering the chimneys, was a domed belfry decorated with still more stone festoons and with, inside it, a small rusted bell that had come from an old monastery of St. Fechan, the ruins of which could be seen among the trees in a corner of the park. That old bell had been rung for three days after the death of Bridgid Erskine—not as a sign of mourning: as a last forlorn hope that its clamour, borne out over the hills, would guide her back through the thick mountain mist that was her death-pall to the house where her distracted husband awaited her.

It was a hideous house, this home of the Erskines. I had often speculated, in the old days, on how it was possible for a man of Sir Simon's fastidiousness to live among its rococo carvings. But he seemed singularly attached to it—it was, he once sardonically said, an embodiment, a projection of his own over-elaborate and tortured mind.

When I arrived that day at Vrackie Hall for the auction sale it was to find a small silent company already gathered in the big lobby. The auctioneer had not yet appeared—he was, I understood, a Glasgow man, one Gregory, famed for his dry wit. But it appeared to me, as I looked round the group in the dark hall, that he would have little opportunity that day for the exercise of it. There were about a dozen serious-faced men and two women, and they talked quietly together in twos and threes. I recognized some acquaintances—one of the women was a dealer in Perth, a Miss Logan: I had been introduced to her the year before in my mother's house. Standing alone in a corner was an old man I had seen at several sales in Scotland before (I was, you must understand, profoundly interested in such things, with an eye for old tapestries). This man, I had the fancy, came from Dundee, where he had a business of some strange sort—we none of us had ever discovered quite what it was, though we knew it to be lucrative and had the impression that it had something to do with drawing or designing. His name was Menasseh, and he was a small, wizened fellow with a large head covered with an obvious toupee.

I roamed about the tables for some ten minutes. There were, I could perceive, even at a cursory glance, some exquisite things. Among the paintings were two miniatures by Koninck that I coveted instantly, and a small landscape by Samuel van Hoogstraaten that I would fain have seen in my rooms in London as a companion to the de Hooch *Study of a Hillside Town* I had acquired at Christie's a year before. There were some beautiful vases from the Delft potteries and a Mortlake tapestry—a copy, unless I was heavily mistaken, of one of Le Brun's Gobelin cartoons. In a corner I saw a most masterly carved lime-wood cravat, attributed, according to the notice on it, to Grinling Gibbons. Among the books was a first edition of Lewis's *The Monk* and a copy, signed by Maturin himself, of that strangest of works, *Melmoth the Wanderer*. There were some Blake drawings too, and some of the Master's hand-coloured prints for the *Songs of Innocence*. And among all these beautiful things, curiously out of place even in that strange house, was Erskine's collection of African drums. I shuddered as I looked at them, recalling the man's mad, grief-wracked thumping of them during the last two years of his life. They were, in their way, I suppose, beautiful enough. The largest ones were made of parchment stretched on hollow hardwood trunks, with primitive designs carved round them. There were two enchanting but repulsive small drums, however, that had for sounding boards polished human skulls. I could see, from a close examination of the larger one, the low brow and long cranium of the primitive. The parchments of these (as were also the parchments of some of the large drums) were held tight by means of small carved ivory pegs, driven in at an angle. The stretched surfaces of them bore a design in coloured dyes—a serpent coiled in a curious way: three coils at the tail end, an erratic figure eight in the centre of the body, and two coils again at the head, with the long fangs pointing downwards. It was the mounting of these skull-drums that particularly attracted me. A small hole had been bored in the forehead of each and the end of a long bent bar of chased silver inserted therein, so that the drums inclined at a convenient angle for the player. The drumsticks—long, polished bones—rested in hollows in the bases of the silver bars. Yes, beautiful things in their way, they were, as they stood there on the table beneath Erskine's trophy heads of buffalo and lions and his crossed game rifles. It was impossible not to be fascinated by them, though they contrasted so strangely with the more delicate products of the less barbaric civilization.

I wandered upstairs, since there still seemed little chance of the arrival of Gregory, the auctioneer. One or two of the buyers were looking at their watches and I heard one of them say something about the "Glasga'" express being late as usual, he supposed. I looked into some of the rooms on the first floor, but most of the portable things had been carried downstairs and the bigger pieces were covered with dust-sheets—they were being sold with the house.

I was standing at the long stained glass window at the end of the corridor looking at the mist-cloaked hills, first through the clear panes and then, to give more interest, through the red and the blue ones, when I heard a step behind me and a cheerful deep voice.

"Hullo, Mr. Ferguson. I didn't know you were coming to the auction or I'd have suggested we travelled up from Perth together."

I looked round and found myself confronting Miss Logan, the dealer I had met the year before at my mother's house. I greeted her civilly and we stood together chatting—talking of my mother first and of what we had both done since our last meeting, and then going on naturally to the things downstairs and Sir Simon.

"You knew him, didn't you?" the big woman asked, and I nodded.

"Oh yes—quite well. A curious man. Impossible to understand."

"I met him once," said Miss Logan thoughtfully. "He made me very uncomfortable—so bleak and cruel, somehow. I was at school with his first wife, you know."

I expressed myself as interested—as indeed I was.

"Was she—well, as volatile in those days? I mean—you know how she went off with the American doctor——"

"Oh yes, I know about that," said Miss Logan quickly. "No—it was really a most curious thing. She wasn't at all like that at school—rather serious and unenterprising, in fact. I could never quite understand it all . . ."

She fell silent, staring out at the hills. Then she added ruminatively:

"A tragic man—tragic. And the last one of that terrible family. What exactly was the story about his second wife?—do you know it? I've heard odd rumours, of course, but I was in France at the time. I never heard the real truth of what happened to her."

"Nor did anyone," I said shortly. "You're looking now at the only one who does know the truth of it all."

"What do you mean?" asked Miss Logan, turning for a moment from the window, at which she had been standing firmly implanted in her expensive brogues.

"Ben Vrackie. That old mountain is her graveyard—and her only father confessor. There were two of them, you know," I went on, "Bridgid and an old friend of Sir Simon's—a well-educated South African negro called David Strange, a lawyer, I think. Simon met him in Cape Town about the same time that he met Bridgid. He was holidaying here with the Erskines and one Sunday afternoon he went out for a walk in the hills with Bridgid. Simon would have gone too, but he had a headache and went to lie down instead . . ."

I paused for a moment, looking through the red pane at the clammy mist creeping and twisting round the summit of the old mountain. Then I continued:

"They never returned. They stayed out longer than they had intended, and in the evening one of those sudden and terrible mountain mists came down. Simon sent out search parties—he rang the old bell in the belfry for as long as the mist lasted—three whole days—as some sort of signal to them. But they never came. They must have wandered for miles—you know how it is when you are lost in a fog—and then slipped and fallen into a gully, perhaps. Their bodies were never found . . ."

"Horrible," said Miss Logan with a shudder. "And that was it, then . . . It must have been appalling for Sir Simon—appalling!"

I nodded.

"It was. He had set such store on this second marriage—the last of the line, you know. Particularly after the tragic disappointment his first wife had been to him . . ."

We were silent. There came a slight commotion from downstairs and, looking over the bannister into the hall, I saw that Gregory had arrived. He was divesting himself of his coat—a large, red-faced man, benevolent in appearance: singularly out of place in that over-crowded room with his big, bucolic personality. He was joking with some of the buyers.

Miss Logan and I went downstairs. The buyers were collecting round the dais that had been set up for Gregory. We joined the solemn, whispering group.

2

I stop my narrative here for a moment. It is not easy for me to write—I am no literary man. The sheer manual labour of setting things down is enormous, to say nothing of the wearing effort of coordinating one's facts and arranging them in reasonable coherence for the reader. The pen moves over the paper, the ink flows, the page fills up. Words and more words, yet somehow all the things one had hoped to say remain unsaid. I sit here at my desk in my sequestered room in London, five hundred miles away from Pitvrackie, struggling to set down something about the beastly things that happened in that hideous house. Why? Is it, with those pothooks on paper, to exorcise the ghosts that have been haunting me since ever I learned the truth about Simon Erskine? I don't know. I only know that for five years I have wanted to do this, I have looked forward to doing this. It may never be read—secretly, I hardly want it to be read. If it is, it can harm no one now. They are all dead—old Samuel Menasseh is dead: even Miss Logan, I learned about six months ago in a letter from my mother, died suddenly of heart-failure in her shop.

And there it all is—all those miles away and all those years away. Above my desk now is the van Hoogstraaten landscape I saw and coveted that day of the sale at Vrackie Hall. I bite the end of my pen as I contemplate it. It stands as a symbol for all the horror I have felt through the years—it is impossible for me to look at the peaceful hillside scene without thinking of old Ben Vrackie as I saw him that day through the stained glass with the blood-red mists all about him. And I seem to hear, in my heart, a throbbing echo of the forlorn music thumped out in the empty, soulless rooms of Vrackie Hall by the grief-torn man who was, so tragically against his will, the last of the Black Erskines . . . Well, it is all an old tale now—older with the writing of it, whether that writing is good or ill. How should I know how best to set the story down? How should I know how to arrange events in a sequence that will give the utmost dramatic value to them? I may emphasize unimportant things, I may hold back on things that should be thrown into relief. I am not a professional. I write for one reason and for one reason only—because I must.

So. I light a cigarette. I return to Vrackie Hall on that day of the auction.

We stood round Gregory, the auctioneer, in a small depressed group. Bidding was good, though the scene was so curiously lifeless in the grey light that came in from the hills through the big windows. Gregory made some valiant efforts to exercise his famous wit, but we were unresponsive—his voice rolled away into the recesses of the hall and the stairway. In the end he gave up. He became mechanical. He lowered his voice, he took to nodding and signalling, the tap of his gavel was almost inaudible. I lost interest after I had bought the van Hoogstraaten and the Mortlake tapestry I had had my eye on. I wandered away from the group of bidders and began to glance through the books. I was turning over the leaves of an early copy of *Vathek* when my eye was distracted by the figure of the strange old man, Menasseh.

He was standing a little to my left, before the table displaying Sir Simon's big game trophies. His attitude was one of extreme horror—yet the horror was grotesque: his small wizened body was rigid, so that the musty black cloth of his coat was stretched tight across his shoulder-blades, his pale eyes seemed to protrude, his toupee had slipped a little awry, giving him an irrelevantly rakish aspect. I went on observing him for some time, then moved over beside him.

"Good morning, sir," I said. "You seem, like myself, to have lost interest in the proceedings over there."

He started, then, adjusting his old wire-frame spectacles with, I noticed, a trembling hand, he said:

"Yes . . . I—I'm afraid I have. I . . ."

His voice trailed away. He glanced back at the table and I followed his gaze—to the drums that were among the African trophies. He coughed. Then he suddenly took off his glasses altogether and started to polish them with an old silk handkerchief.

"I know you sir," he said quaveringly. "I've seen you before—several times."

"I'm often in Scotland," I replied. "And when I'm in Scotland I'm often at the sales. My name is Ferguson. I know that your name is Menasseh—I've seen you frequently too. I take it you're a dealer?—or are you only an amateur, as I am?"

"Eh?" he stammered (it was as if his mind were not focussing properly—he was thinking all the time of something else). "No—not a dealer. Only an amateur, Mr. Ferguson."

He put on his spectacles again and stared back at the drums on the table. His gaze was particularly drawn to the two small drums with the silver mountings. He passed his hand over his brow—his toupee fell even further askew.

"Horrible—horrible," he muttered. "God of Abraham, it's horrible . . ."

He seemed to go into a trance for a moment or two. Then he put out his finger and traced, with the trembling point of it, the singular design of the coiled serpent on the parchment of the small drums. I watched him, fascinated.

"Hideously attractive things," I said, by the way of an opening. "Typical of Sir Simon to have had them—a man of curious tastes. You know how he is said to have beaten on them frantically for hours on end after the disappearance of his second wife?"

"Yes," said Menasseh, in a whisper. "Yes. I know . . ."

"A strange sign of grief." (I was still searching to bring him out—he was, there was no doubt, affected to the very roots by something.)

"A strange sign of grief indeed," he muttered. Then once more he fell distrait. It was a long time before he added, in an almost inaudible undertone: "A terrible sign of grief—terrible and horrible . . ."

I looked at him, drawing my brows together. He was white. He kept moistening his thin lips with the point of a colourless tongue. I wanted extremely to ask him what it was that was upsetting him, yet after all I hardly knew him. I found myself, in the long silence that ensued after his last remark, wondering who he was and what he did (I had forgotten, when I asked him if he was a dealer, how, in the old days, we had speculated on his occupation.) Printing, was it—or drawing? Something of that nature, I recalled. Perhaps it was a little publishing business? Yet it was more than likely I would know of it if it were publishing: that was my own line of business—I knew most of the trade in Scotland. Whatever it was it was lucrative—I remembered having heard that he was a wealthy old fellow.

Suddenly we became aware—simultaneously—that two of Gregory's assistants were moving towards us. Apparently the African trophies were the next item on the catalogue. I glanced quickly at Menasseh.

"Now's the time," I said smiling. "You seem interested in these drums of Erskine's. They're going up, I fancy. Are you buying?"

He gazed at me, his eyes large behind the thick glass of his spectacles.

"Oh no," he whispered. "Oh no. God forbid it . . ."

The two men in green baize aprons were lifting some of the larger drums, preparatory to carrying them over to Gregory's dais. Menasseh, I saw by this time, was looking quickly backwards and forwards in an access of nervous apprehension of some sort. He suddenly leaned close up to me.

"Ferguson," he said, "I can't keep it, I can't. I must tell someone. I want to see you—I must see you."

"We could go outside," I said, a little disturbed, I had to confess, by his urgency. "I shall not be bidding again. Will you?"

"No. No. Not here," he muttered. "Not here—I can't stay here. It has upset me too much—I must go away from here, quickly."

He fumbled in his waistcoat pocket and thrust a card into my hand.

"If you are in Dundee," he said, "if you should be in Dundee—"

"I have to be there at the end of this week, as it happens," I answered. "I have a little business which I am mixing with my holiday. Thursday, I should say—or possibly Friday."

"Good. Good. Then could you call on me? For God's sake could you call on me?"

I nodded: and he, in his nervousness, set his old head nodding up and down too. I fingered his card, looking at the address on it:

SAMUEL MENASSEH

39, THE PORTWAY

DUNDEE

"My business address," he said, reading my thoughts. "But come anytime, anytime this week. I shall be there. I have a little room behind the shop where I live—I only go to my house outside the city at week-ends and so on." Then, reading my thoughts still more deeply, he added: "My business is strange—very strange. Don't be surprised. It's a little—unpleasant. I don't tell people about it—I won't mention it here . . . But come, sir—oh for God's sake I beg you to come! It will haunt me, this—I'll have no peace!"

He said these last words quickly, in a hoarse, strained whisper. Then he turned and was gone. I was left holding his card, staring after him as he hastened over to the massive door. He had left me with an intolerable curiosity—a sense of dismay over his hurried and half-finished sentences.

I was brought back to my senses by the deep, healthy tones of Miss Logan's voice. She was standing, a sane, coherent figure in her brogues and tweed costume, watching the men as they carried the little skull-drums to Gregory's dais.

"Ferguson," she called. "Come quickly. Look at these—they're lovely. I'm having these—by Jove, I'm certainly having these."

I slipped the old man's card into my pocket and went over to join her. She was by this time holding the smaller drum up to the light and examining the silver base.

"Look here," she said excitedly. "What an odd thing. Someone's scratched some verse on the silver—look at it, Shelley, of all strange things!"

She read out solemnly:

"Music, when soft voices die,
Vibrates in the memory . . ."

And she laughed.

"Odd thing to find on the mounting of an African drum, I must say. Your old Sir Simon was a devilish queer fish, if ever there was one . . ."

I had to agree. Above all I had to agree to that . . .

3

Almost midnight. Incredible how quickly the time has gone.

I started writing shortly before seven, and since then have interrupted myself only for long enough to brew some tea at about ten. My pen hand is cramped and painful and my eyes ache terribly from staring at the white paper. Yet I cannot stop—I must go on now.

I look back at what I have written. I feel a sinking in the stomach. How imperfectly I have set things down! A rambling introduction, too much description, a conversation which, on paper, seems disjointed and insane. Yet I have tried faithfully enough to keep a clear head over this nightmare. I have tried to set things in their order, to conjure up some sense of atmosphere. The old house, the death of Bridgid and David Strange in the terrible hill mist, the tragic last months of that haunted, lost man . . . You see, *I* know it all now, I know every shade of it. And this informs every word I write, every thought I have in this quiet room. My pen moves over the paper slowly and carefully—I stop to think before every word. I know all of it—all of it . . .

My remembrances go, irrelevantly, to Miss Logan. By her very inconsequence in this nightmare she is the most grotesque figure of them all. Tweeds, brogues, untinted lip-salve. The more select journals, the Scottish Nationalist movement, long walks on the moors with one of those sticks with spikes on the end and handles that fold open to form a little seat. And her shop with the Chelsea china, the old spinning wheels, the pictures on wood, the churchwarden pipes in bundles, the little ornamental shepherd crooks of green Nailsea glass. And somewhere among all these things, tucked away in a corner, perhaps, when her first enthusiasm for them had waned, the little drums. I do not suppose she even knew of those insane weeping fits of Sir Simon's, when he sent the sound of those drums across the valley . . .

She had met him once, I remember she said. He had made her uncomfortable. She had been at school with his first wife. A quiet girl. She had never been able to understand——

What? How *could* she understand? Miss Logan in her little shop, dying of heart failure. Yet had her heart ever started? A man to her was a companion for a walk on the moors. Of course she had never been able to understand, with her babblings of Shelley. How could she?

No matter, though. She had her shop, with its green Nailsea glass. And over the door of it, in gilt, old-style lettering, one word: *Antiques*.

And now, as I near the end of the story, I think of another shop, a stranger shop. I found it, in the twilight, in a side-street near the docks in Dundee. It was low-fronted, ill-lit by a flickering gas standard at the kerb of the pavement. The window had nothing in it, above the door was no sign to announce the trade or occupation of its tenant. The name, no more, in faded block capitals:

SAMUEL MENASSEH

I knocked, and heard the echo of my knock go rolling into the dust and darkness inside. I waited, impatient. A sailor stumbled in the dusk further along the street, singing in the drawn-out, lugubrious tones of a drunken man. I knocked again, and from inside this time there came the sound of shuffling feet and the undoing of a chain.

He seemed smaller now, the old man, as I looked down on him from the pavement. He wore a loose, grey-wool cardigan and, on his head, instead of the toupee, was a skullcap of black velvet —a little biretta of the sort the cantors wear in the synagogues. I greeted him and he nodded. Then he motioned me to follow him and I went inside.

It would be a mockery to say that I was not, in all desperation, impatient and curious. I remembered too acutely the old man's broken conversation in the hall at Vrackie, the whole sense of dismay and nervous horror that had come from him. In the intervening days since that interview I had seen too often, in my mind's eye, that white wizened face, those long trembling fingers of parchment tracing the design of the snake on the other parchment of the drums. I was consumed by impatience. As I followed him through the dim corridor to the sitting room at the back of the shop, I searched feverishly about me for some sign, some illumination of the mystery of him. But there was nothing. Half-way along the corridor we passed an open door that led into the shop proper. I peered anxiously through it. Dimly glimpsed in the light from the gas standard outside as it flickered through the window, was a counter, exceptionally low. Suspended above it from the ceiling was a long, flexible, snake-like thing—a piece of gas tubing I thought at first, and then had the curious fancy that it was a drill—the cable lead of a pedal drill, such as old-fashioned dentists use. But fantastic to suppose that the man was a dentist. Besides, I had no more than glimpsed the appliance in the gloom . . .

We reached the small sitting room. I stood for a moment opening and shutting my eyes, accustoming them to the light that came from the gas-bracket above the mantelshelf. The room was poorly furnished—a table, a basket-chair by the fireplace, an old dresser, a wardrobe. In the corner a divan bed. Some books in a hanging shelf, a fretwork pipe-rack. And for pictures—

I, so accustomed to the beautiful in pictures, so used to the shaded tones, the colours in harmony, the designs so subtle, so balanced—all the magic of the Masters: I, with my fastidious passion for tapestries and delicate needle-worked panels—what could I make of the monstrous things on the walls of that room of Menasseh's? Unframed, stuck to the plaster with rusted drawing pins, glazed with layers of size varnish—those rioting tortured dragons in wild reds and blues, those posies of purple flowers, those bleeding hearts transfixed with arrows, those fleshy nudes in violent pink, with bellies sagged and scarlet nippled breasts—what could I make of them? And yet, I knew that I knew them—they were, in their style, unmistakable. I searched my memory and then, in a moment, could have laughed aloud. For I had, by a wild coincidence, been thinking just outside, while I had listened to the drunken sailor go stumbling along the street—as it goes, you will understand, when one's mind wanders inconsequently in its own secret places and among old associations—I had been thinking then of a fascination of my childhood: whether that sailor were, as had been the only sailor I had known as a child—tattooed! And I understood the meaning of the drill that hung from the ceiling of Menasseh's shop—I had an image of the dye-charged needle at the end of it stabbing again and again into white, tight flesh . . .

I turned and looked at the old man.

"Yes," he nodded. "Not pleasant, not pleasant. Not a very—

select job, tattooing. I keep it a secret. I have money, you see—it makes money for me. I can gratify my passions for the beautiful things in the sale-rooms. You should see my house outside the town—beautiful, beautiful. Different from this," he added, sweeping his arm vaguely round the room. "Oh different, much different . . . But it makes money, this. You haven't an idea—the people who want it—big men: lawyers—I did a lawyer from Glasgow last week—he came up specially. Women, too. I'm busy—all the time. There's a sort of fascination in it for some people—all sorts of strange and unexpected people . . ."

He went on, rubbing his hands together. It was incredible and fantastic—too much. But at the back of my mind was beginning to throb the idea that has haunted me through these years. On the table in that little room, smaller than those other charts on the walls, but like them painted in brilliant water colours and covered with size, was a design I had seen before. A serpent coiled in a curious way: three coils at the tail end, an erratic figure eight in the centre of the body, and two coils again at the head, with the long fangs pointing downwards . . .

* * * *

Half-past one. Almost finished. A century, since I started to write. How did it go?

"I heard of the death of Sir Simon Erskine some five years ago . . . I had known him quite well—a terrible man, moody, powerful, irascible . . ."

I had known him quite well . . . How did I dare to write that? How could I—or anyone—know him? No one in the world—no one but those half-beast forebears of his. And they, thank God, have gone out of the world—as he has. The line of the Black Erskines is ended, and forever.

I look.at the quiet picture above me. Samuel van Hoogstraaten—a still man, unperturbed. His world a hillside scene in Holland: small square houses, lines on canvas. To my right, on the wall there, is the Mortlake tapestry. And what association have these things with the things Menasseh told me in that room of his behind the shop? . . .

David Strange, the young negro lawyer—the descendant, he claimed, of Kings Cetewayo and Dingaan: for he had, as he showed Menasseh, the royal serpent of the Zulus needled into the dark skin of his breast. And the woman with him in the shop that day, with Menasseh copying the design on to *her* breast, while she flinched at every needle-prick, holding tight with her white hand to the dark hand of the negro . . . The sign of blood-kinship among the Zulus, that serpent. Menasseh had been intrigued by the design of it and had made, on paper, one copy: but no other copy, at any time, on any human skin but hers . . .

My hand aches terribly. I sit back. I look at my fingers as I stretch them out to ease them . . .

I think—oh God knows what I think! Of the two skulls that were the sounding boards of those hellish drums. Of Miss Logan tramping over the moors. Of those other two—of blood-kinship —setting off that Sunday afternoon for a walk on Ben Vrackie. Of Sir Simon saying he had a headache and so being unable to accompany them. Of the neat round holes in the skulls in which were inserted the ends of the silver mounts. Of the rifles on the walls of Vrackie Hall. Of the bodies that were never found. Of the shape of the larger skull, the low brow and long cranium of the primitive—the negro. Of the merciful hill mist that came down on the grim old mountain—red and terrible seen through the glass of that hideous house . . .

Yes, what do I think . . .

Of the two last years of the last of the Erskines, his fits of weeping, his fits of laughing, his fits of——

No. The image fades. The ghost goes out of me. I think of nothing. Except, coming over the years, the echo, terrible in this quiet room, of Miss Logan's cheerful voice:

"Someone's scratched some verse on the silver—Shelley, of all strange things . . ."

Yes. Shelley, of all strange things.

Cyclamen Brown

Among the people I know is a little man who makes his living by writing popular music. His real name is John Summers, but he calls himself professionally Eddie Wheeler. There is a sort of shining innocence about Eddie, and what I can only describe as an unconscious cynicism. He believes in things, profoundly: but he believes along well-worn channels. He lives enframed among conventions. He really does—sincerely—fancy that when he writes a song about mother love, or young lovers who pine for each other beneath the silv'ry moon, or meet each other only in their dreams—he really does fancy that he has done something. He sees himself as a serious artist—the more money he makes from a song, the more serious has he been in the creation of it. There is, to him, such a thing as love, in the grotesque sense in which the word is used in his trade. It moves him very much—every song he writes about it deeply and seriously moves him. His whole life is an emotional cliché.

But he is a wonderful little man in his way. I like him enormously. He lives among racketeers, sharks, and toughs—men who would pimp for their own mothers to make a few pounds for themselves and their tarts—little Eddie Wheeler lives right in the middle of it all, yet remains as innocent as he was on the day he was born. The whole mysterious world of Charing Cross Road revolves round him noisily, and he stays untouched. He is a "natural," in the old sense of the word. I should think he knows more about the song-plugging racket than any man alive. He knows every personality in the profession—who is bribing whom, who got whom to write his latest hit for him for the price of a double scotch and a packet of gaspers, who paid whom a handsome premium for a date at such-and-such a club—it's all of it there, glibly and innocently in Eddie's head. He can tell you where So-and-so gets his dope, where Miss Whatshername had herself aborted, why little Mr. Whosit put his head in the gas-oven. And he'll tell you it all with his little bald head shining, his eyes popping out at you through his thick oval spectacles—and the manuscript of his most recent mother song on the table before him. He looks like Schubert, does Eddie-only, of course, he doesn't write like him.

It was Eddie who told me the story of Cyclamen Brown. Well, it's hardly a story at all, really—there's no plan to it, no design. It is something that happened, that's all—a sudden glimpse into the queer half-world of the show folk. I am only setting it down because Eddie amused me so in the telling of it. It was so typical of him to tell it as he did—between puffs of the cheap little cigars he favours, and with a glass of lager in front of him. And all the time his small forehead perspiring and his blue eyes popping like wet glass marbles . . .

It was one night when I went out with Eddie for dinner. He took me along several side-streets off Shaftesbury Avenue and finally plunged down some area steps, coming to a halt in front of a massive black door. He tapped on it with a coin—three long taps, two short ones, and then a brisk rat-tat-tat-tat. A small shutter slid open opposite our eyes and I saw a man's face peering at us—a thin dark face it was, set above the white triangle of a dress shirt.

Eddie thrust his hand through the opening and showed the man some small token he held in his palm—a little red celluloid check, I discovered it to be later, with a design stamped on it in intaglio—a representation of a cyclamen plant.

The dark man nodded. Then he swung the door open and we went inside, Eddie smiling jovially and peeling off his coat, myself a shade apprehensive, not quite sure if I was enjoying myself or not. We went along a small passage and pushed through a big swing door of painted glass. And then we were in the main hall of what Eddie told me was the Cyclamen Club.

It was a long, low room with an arched whitewashed ceiling. All round it was a raised platform with small tables all crowded together on it, and below this was a polished dancing floor. The lighting was dim—wreaths of tobacco smoke clung round the big pink electric globes overhead. At one end of the hall, on a dais, was a small dance band. At the moment of our entrance a slim young man with oiled black hair was crooning into a microphone—the syrupy tones hung, like the smoke, above the heads of the dancers and diners.

"That's Woody Hunter," said Eddie, as we followed a scantily clad usherette to our table. "He runs the band—and will insist on doing his own vocalist. God knows why—I think he stinks."

We sat down.

"What are you having?" asked Eddie, in his soft lugubrious voice. "Eat as much as you want—don't stint yourself. I've just sold a new song—it's a smasher, a smasher. The best I've done since *The Love Bird Waltz*."

I ordered as good a meal as the Cyclamen offered—and I must confess it was most elegant and satisfying. Eddie himself tucked in lustily to an immense plateful of devilled chicken, washing it down with glass after glass of his favourite lager. Then he sighed, belched apologetically, and settled back in his chair, after lighting one of his thin black cheroots.

"Not a bad little place," he said, looking round him contentedly. "Good food, good music, lots of drink, and nice people. There's Harry Nevin over there—that little man with the tall blonde. Just written a new lyric for Sammy Tolstoy, they tell me. The big fellow just opposite—the one shovelling the spaghetti into him—that's Issy FitzGerald. Used to be the best vocalist in the business, but the snow was his trouble—couldn't lay off it."

"The snow?" I asked.

"Cocaine. Got so bad he had to take it every time before he went on, and then in the days of the big famine, when the boys weren't getting through the police rings with the stuff, he went all to bits. He's all right now, though—went into publishing. Still takes the stuff, of course—once you start you can't stop. You can always tell when Issy gets a yen on—you're maybe talking to him, selling him a number, see, and suddenly he starts to yawn. You think, My God—he's proper bored with this—I'll have to try it on old Salmon . . . But it isn't that at all—he really thinks your number's the bee's knees—it's only that he's got a yen, you see. That's the way it takes them—they yawn and yawn, like you'd think they'd get lockjaw. Then he goes out to the Gents and gives himself a stab or two with the syringe and it's all right, see. It's amazing how desperate they are for it sometimes—I remember

Iris Jackson, the coloured girl who used to dance for Bertolini —remember her?—got killed in a knife fight up in Greek Street about two years ago—well, she had it bad, and one night she'd the devil's own yen and couldn't get a drop of the dope. She was screaming mad—screaming. She smashed up everything in her dressing room—ran round and round throwing things against the walls, and yawning all the time. Bertolini asked me if I could get her any of the stuff, and in the end I said yes I could, I was so sorry for her, and went round to Spike Abel's place and begged a paper-full from Spike himself. What a 'cello player that man was, by the way—that's why he was called Spike, incidentally—cos of the spike on the end of a 'cello. Anyway, thank God, he was drunk that night, so he gave me some dope for Iris. When I got back Iris was out for the count—lying on the floor with her eyes turned up into her head and her skin all green underneath her colour. 'Lord Almighty,' says I to Bertolini, 'how do we give it to her? We haven't got a syringe!' . . . 'Oh, that's all right,' he says, 'I've done this before for her—I know the routine. Have you got a cigarette lighter, Eddie?' . . . Then he got a spoon, you see, and he made me hold it over the flame of my lighter with the dope in it, till it was all melting hot and bubbling. Then he took a safety-pin—just an ordinary safety-pin, and a bit rusty at that—and he opened one of the veins in Iris's thigh. And he tilted this hot stuff in with the spoon and prodded it into her with the pin. It acted like a ruddy miracle. She was up as large as life in three minutes—I've never seen her dance better'n she did that night. Bloody marvellous! Poor old Iris!—a gem of a girl, and oh my God could she dance! But it's just as well she went when she did, and the way she did. Bertolini had it in for her, and once he'd got going it would have been one hell of a sight worse for Iris than she ever got in the knife fight. Remember the big vitriol scandal about eight months ago, when Gloria Baum got a face burn and a half coming out of the Albany stage door?—well, Bertolini was behind that, only they never got him, of course: they got that little man Smithy Watson, but he was only Bertolini's stooge . . ."

Eddie, under the influence of the food and the music and the lager, went on and on like this for almost an hour. I sat back contentedly listening to him—hypnotized. The whole world he chattered about was so utterly alien to me—it was impossible to believe that the people dancing on the floor below me, or eating at the tables on all sides of me, were the very people that Eddie was talking about. They seemed so normal. Perhaps the men were a little paler and suaver than most men, and the women a little more elaborately made-up—altogether harder and tougher than the women one normally encounters. But otherwise they were quite ordinary. It was an awesome thought.

"I don't suppose I'll ever get the hang of this queer life of yours, Eddie," I said, in a gap in his chatter. "It's all so wild, you know—so hopelessly immoral."

"Immoral?" he said—and he looked up at me with a sort of mild sad reproach in his eyes. "Immoral? Oh, my dear, my dear! You don't know what you're talking about—you don't really. No wonder you say you can't get the hang of us. And you never will get the hang of us unless you get hold of the fact that it's morals that's the answer to the whole set-up. It's morals that's the matter—we're most of us *too* moral. Of course, maybe it's *different* morals, but it's morals, my dear—it's morals. What you've got to understand is that we're the most moral folk there are."

"Even that fellow over there?" I asked ironically, nodding towards a red-faced elderly man, who, very drunk, was lolling over a young girl in a corner, pawing at her, while she protested, giggling stupidly.

Eddie followed my gaze.

"Who? Old Fred Burrow? Lord, Lord—I should think he is the worst of the lot of us." And he sighed. "Don't you know old Fred? Written more hit lyrics than anyone else in the business. Started life playing the cornet in a Salvation Army Band in Wigan, then he joined Willie Mulligan's outfit at Manchester and wrote a couple of hits with Willie's pianist, Alf Tucker—you're bound to remember Alf—hanged himself in old Salmon's cloakroom when he couldn't get Salmon to buy a new blues he'd written, and old Salmon said, How considerate of Alf to hang himself like that when there was such a shortage of meat in his family (Salmon would sacrifice anything for a gag, you know—he's built like that).—Anyway, he suddenly repented—old Salmon did, I mean—and don't you remember he advertised in the *Melody*

Maker for somebody to adopt Alf's little daughter, Bessie? It was old Fred Burrow that answered that advert. A tough little morsel Bessie turned out to be, though—my God, old Fred has had a job with her. He gets drunk, poor old soul, and then suddenly, when he's sitting in a pub, he remembers Bessie and how he ought to be looking after her, so he staggers out from the pub and goes round the clubs looking for her, just to see that she's behaving herself. And when he finds her he tries to take her home, see—but Bessie never wants to go home—well, you can see for yourself. That's Bessie over there, with Fred now. He's trying to use force, poor old boy—he always gets so drunk. As a matter of fact, it usually ends with Bessie seeing Fred home . . ."

Before I could say anything else there came a diversion from the orchestra dais. There was a roll on the side drums, and some spotlights at the back of the hall swung down their beams and focussed them on the slim figure of Woody Hunter, the band leader, who was standing at the microphone making an announcement.

"And now, ladies and gentlemen," he said, "I know that no evening at the Cyclamen would be complete for you without a song from the little lady who is your hostess. And so I'm going to ask her to step forward and give you her favourite number—*Dark Red Roses*. I'm happy to be able to say, by the way, that we have the composer of *Dark Red Roses* himself with us to-night—Mr. Eddie Wheeler."

There was a burst of applause and one of the spotlights swung round for a moment to rest on Eddie. I blinked unhappily in the white glare, but Eddie rose cheerfully and bobbed up and down and shook his hands as if he were a prize fighter taking his bow. The light went back to Woody Hunter.

"Didn't know they were going to do that," said Eddie to me out of the corner of his mouth as he sat down again. "Pretty decent, eh. Good number too, the old *Roses*—best I've ever done, I think—since *The Love Bird Waltz*, of course."

There was another tremendous burst of applause from the crowd as there stepped on to the platform a girl with the slimmest and most beautiful figure I think I have ever seen. She was dressed in a long flared gown of a flowing mauve material, with a neat little bodice that cupped tightly over her breasts. The strange thing was, however, that she wore a mask—a stiff silk-paper mask of the same colour as her gown; and it did not only cover her eyes, but her whole face—there was a small opening at her mouth and two little eye-holes and that was all. The effect was extraordinary—the white of her neck and arms stood out brilliantly against the mauve of the gown and the mask, and her whole figure was surmounted by a piled-up heap of platinum blonde hair with one stab of colour in it—a cyclamen flower that she wore just above her left ear.

Woody Hunter held up his hand for silence.

"Ladies and gentlemen, we present your own favourite—the Girl in the Mask—the lovely Cyclamen Brown herself, singing *Dark Red Roses*."

The orchestra struck up the introduction and the crowd applauded again. The girl advanced to the microphone and began to sing. Her voice was low and husky—very pleasant, I thought, in a slow, soporific sort of way. As she sang she swung her hips very slightly—the effect was voluptuous in the extreme. I could see that most of the men in the audience were staring at her with moist eyes and slightly parted lips. Eddie—innocent soul—was beaming like a schoolboy who has had full marks from a favourite teacher—he was more Schubertian than ever, with the white light from the stage reflecting on his spectacles.

"Wonderful girl," he gasped, when Cyclamen Brown had finished singing. "Wonderful girl! Don't you think so, my boy?"

"She can certainly sing," I conceded. "And she has a lovely figure. Does she always——"

The rest of my sentence was drowned by a sound of rhythmic chanting that now came from the crowd, superseding the great wave of applause that had marked the end of the song. It was evidently part of the routine at the Club.

"Take off your mask," chanted the crowd, "take off your mask, take off your mask, take off your mask . . ."

The girl had been bowing. Now she straightened herself—I saw just a pin-point gleam from her eyes through the holes in the mask. She raised her hand to her face and a great "Ah" of expectation went up from the crowd. For a moment she seemed to fumble with the fastening of her mask, then instead, with a quick and graceful little gesture, she snatched the cyclamen from her hair and threw it among the audience. And with a final lascivious shake of the hips she turned and ran off-stage.

There was a deep groan of disappointment from the crowd, mingled with some laughter and applause. Then the band struck up a fox-trot, and before very long the scene in the club was normal again.

"Well, I must say," I murmured to Eddie, "I must say she's clever. That act with the mask was one of the neatest things I've ever seen—more exciting than strip-tease. A very clever idea—you get so interested in her voice and her figure that you begin to long to see her face. I was going to ask you if she ever took the mask off, but I can see that she doesn't—at least on the stage. I suppose she does in private life."

Eddie looked over at me, his little eyes wide.

"Oh no," he said seriously. "I assure you she doesn't."

"Doesn't?" I was incredulous. "Oh come off it, Eddie! That's going too far."

"Honestly," the little man said. "Why do you think there was such a build-up just now, with the mob down there shouting their heads off? It's because not one of them has seen Cyclamen with her mask off—at least, those that have, it was so long ago they've forgotten what she looked like. No—not one of 'em has seen her face. Neither on the stage or off it. It's one of the mysteries of the profession, Cyclamen's mask."

"Then it's a better act than I thought it was," said I.

"Maybe. Only——" (and here Eddie blew a neat little circle of smoke into the air), "only, my dear, it isn't an act. She's got to wear it."

"*Got* to wear it? Why? Is she as ugly as sin underneath?"

The little man blinked. "She's got the most beautiful face I have ever seen," he said solemnly.

I signalled a waiter.

"I can see, Eddie," I said with a chuckle, "that you've got a story to tell me. What's it to be?—another lager?"

He nodded and grinned. I gave the order to the waiter and

then, when the drinks came, sat back in my chair and waited for the little man to begin.

"Of course," he said, "I really shouldn't tell you this story at all. I'm supposed to have been sworn to secrecy—professional etiquette and all that, you know. I don't suppose anyone else in the whole Club at this minute knows the secret of Cyclamen's mask —except Woody Hunter, of course. But then, he's different."

"Why is he different?" I asked.

"Oh, you'll see in a minute. Poor old Woody! I often feel sorry for that man—I really do. He's a good-hearted soul, you know—but my God, what a stinking awful vocalist! Anyway, that's by the way. Oddly enough, by the by, this thing I'm going to tell you is an exact illustration of what I've just been saying about morals. The whole thing is morals—our way of behaving. Unless you get hold of that fact you just won't understand a word of what I'm going to say. It's morals, my dear boy—maybe a little bit different from morals as you understand 'em, but all the same it's morals. Well now—where shall I start? You don't know Joe Mulvaney, do you?"

"I'm afraid I don't," I said.

"Best trumpeter in the business. My God, there's nothing that man can't do with a trumpet—we used to say he must have brass lips. An Irishman, Joe is—but brought up in Glasgow—I suppose that's where he learned those queer tricks of his—a tough bunch they are in some parts of Glasgow—I know, cos I had to spend a couple of years up there some time ago, when I was plugging round the Halls for old Sammy Walters. And my Lord, some of those Glasgow boys!—down in what's it called?—the Gorbals, the Gallowgate. The policemen go about in threes—in *threes,* my boy, not twos. I remember one night in a pub there was a sort of row, and one boy—a tall, thin guy with wavy hair—he whipped off his cap and struck another chap right across the face with it —and there was a weird scream from this second chap, and we saw a long, thin spout of blood all over his face. You see, the first guy—the big one—he had razor-blades fitted all along the edge of the peak of that cap of his—that's a regular trick of theirs up there—or broken beer bottles: you break the bottom off, then hold the bottle by the neck and jab it into another guy's face and turn—hard. Nasty, eh? But you see—Joe Mulvaney grew up among that sort of thing, so I suppose it was natural enough that when Cyclamen . . . However, this is all the wrong way round. Where was I?"

"You really started with Woody Hunter," I said gently.

"Yes—yes. There was Woody. Yes, I suppose it did all start with Woody. In those days, you see, Woody was running a little ten-piece combination outfit down in a club in Park Lane. Very good too—he knows how to run a band, Woody does—it's only that he's such a damned bad vocalist . . . However, never mind that. In this little Park Lane outfit, Woody had Joe Mulvaney playing trumpet for him. Wonderful, too. Folk used to go down just to hear him doing his solo—women, mostly—Joe was a devil for the women. It was the one thing—like Issy FitzGerald with cocaine. He was a big buck Irishman, you know, with slim hips—good to look at—a wonderful dancer, too—exhibition standard and then some. As a matter of fact, he was keener on dancing than on playing the trumpet. That was how the trouble all began.

"You see, one day Joe goes to Woody and he says, 'Look Woody—I've found one swell of a dame—an ace dancer and a hot vocalist too. What about working an exhibition dance spot into the show with me and her, eh?'

"'Fine,' says Woody—'suits me. What's the damsel's name and how is she to look at?'——And Joe says, 'Ann Brown—plain Ann Brown: and as for looks—oh boy!'

"So you see, next morning, at the band rehearsal call, Joe turns up with the dame, Ann Brown—Cyclamen Brown, of course—you've guessed that much—only she wasn't called that in those days. She does a singing audition for Woody, which she passes on her head, and then an exhibition dance with Joe that even made the band boys cheer. All well and good. Woody engages Ann on the spot and everything's set. The new act goes down big with the customers, and it looks as if the Hunter-Mulvaney show is all set for a long and successful run, as they say on the handouts. All fine and dandy, eh? But wait, my boy—just wait.

"Now then, what happened next? I get a bit confused, you know—so much kept on happening just about this time—it was just when I'd written *The Love Bird Waltz,* you know—I remember that, cos Joe and Ann used to feature it in their dance spot—that's how I got to know them so well—I did a special arrangement. As a matter of fact, I've always felt pretty sure that it was that tune of mine that—well, you know what I mean. It was a slow, dreamy waltz, all chromatic and luscious, and when two people dance close together night after night, and the lights are lowered, and —well, my dear, you know, you know. It was simple. It's the way the wheels go round. It just couldn't be avoided . . .

"Mind you, I will say one thing—having a regular girl like Ann made all the difference to Joe—all the difference in the world. It steadied him up—pulled him together. A terrific thing love, you know, my dear—a *terrific* thing. And Ann was such a peach—so good for him. They took a flat not far from my own hide-out in Soho and started to live together—a little top-floor place, it was, looking down Wardour Street. And I don't think I've ever known a happier couple than they were in those days, when it all began. Every song I wrote at that time I dedicated to them—they were the inspiration of them all—they were the tops . . ."

Eddie paused for a moment and lit another of his cigarillos. He looked thoughtfully round the dancing floor. The Club was beginning to empty—I saw, among the couples going out, the elderly lyric writer, Fred Burrow. He was very drunk, and was being supported by the young girl I now knew to be his adopted daughter. The band was playing a blues—I remember Woody Hunter's cloying voice whispering something about:

"Why do you never bring me roses—
Roses aren't much to ask . . ."

"Funny they should be playing that tune," said Eddie eventually, with a deep sigh. "I suppose they're going through all my numbers cos they know I'm here, as a sort of compliment—nice people, as I told you. That was one of my hits that owed its inspiration to Joe and Ann—only, of course, it was after things changed a bit with them . . .

"You see, Joe wasn't exactly—well, thoughtful. You'll know what I mean. He was all right, of course—wonderfully good-hearted. But just a little bit short of imagination. And you know, boy, you've got to have imagination when you're dealing with women—what we call presentation in the business. You've got to have an eye for the little things—you've got to notice when they're wearing a new dress, or if they've started doing their hair a different way—it's all important with women, that sort of thing. And Joe didn't have presentation—he was just a great big lump of virility and that was all. And he thought it was enough, Lord help him. Of course, it was, to begin with. But somehow—I don't exactly know why, or when—somehow things began, after a little time, to change between Ann and him. They used always to be together, for instance—you never saw one of them without the other being there too. But just about this time we began to notice that this wasn't happening any more—quite often you'd run into Ann sitting alone in a corner, or Joe standing the boys a drink in Bertolini's with no Ann beside him. And if you said, 'Hy-ya, Joe—where's Ann?'—he would answer, 'Oh, around, you know, old boy—just around . . .'

"And of course she *was* around. Alone at first, but later on not *quite* so much on her lonesome. She was around with Woody Hunter."

Eddie paused again. The blues had come to an end, and now Woody Hunter had his slim back to the floor again, and was conducting a waltz.

"Thank God!" said Eddie, "that Woody's finished singing, I mean. He's such a *stinking* vocalist! Oh well—can't blame him, I suppose. He *used* to have quite a voice—he was all right as a torch singer *once* upon a time. I mean, before—well, never mind. People are queer, I always say—they're ruddy queer, and you've got to put up with the fact that they're queer, or you won't get anywhere with anyone. Where was I? Oh yes—Woody and Ann.

"Of course, Joe knew nothing at all about this other string that Ann was fixing to her bow. He was just Great Big Handsome Hero No. 1—as dumb as they've ever been made. As far as he was concerned, Ann was still his girl—they still lived in the little penthouse I told you about in Wardour Street. And I honestly think that at the time Ann wasn't so dead nuts on Woody as poor old Woody liked to think she was. Maybe it was just that Woody was the boss, and he was talking big to her about building up her act—maybe even starring her—Woody Hunter's Band, Featuring Ann Brown—if only she'd . . . well—you know what I mean. You know the old routine, even if you are outside the business."

I said I did—I knew the old routine perfectly.

"Of course you do. Well, I think it was all that. And, of course, the fact that things weren't going too well between Ann and Joe. She had a sort of *chagrin,* if that's the word. Poor Joe," went on Eddie, sighing and shaking his head—and blinking several times through those thick crystal glasses of his. "God save his big dumb carcase! Lord, if there wasn't a song already called *Poor Old Joe,* I'd write one to-morrow. I felt so sorry for that guy, the way he messed up his chances! If only he'd had a *little* imagination! But I guess that's what's wrong with most of our folk—all morals and no imagination."

"I'm still waiting for the morals to come into this story," said I at this point. "After all, Eddie, you said it was because it illustrated all that you meant by morals that you were telling it to me. And so far all I've heard about is a dance band trumpeter and a croonette living in sin together in a pent-house in Soho."

"Not so fast, my boy," said Eddie, draining his lager glass and holding up two fingers to a waiter for a refill. "You're an impatient listener, that's what's the matter with you. But never mind—I guess you're outside the profession, that's what's wrong. You'll never quite cotton on. You're like Joe—O.K. at heart, but dumb. My God, was that man dumb! And passionate—too ruddy passionate. An Irishman, you see—and brought up in Glasgow. I suppose it couldn't be helped.

"I was there, you know, when they had their big row. I'd gone up to see Ann with a new number I'd written for her, and somehow—I can't quite remember how—Joe and she got into an argument. All about nothing, it was—but of course, you know how these things grow: one thing leads to another, and before you know where you are you're going at it hammer and tongs. They forget all about unobtrusive little me, sitting there at the piano. Joe yelled his head off—and boy! could he yell!—and Ann just cried and cried. And Joe says finally, in a sort of whine—'Well anyways, Ann—what's the matter with me?—what have I done?'

And Ann cries more than ever and she says, 'It's what you haven't done, Joe boy—that's what's the matter. It was my birthday yesterday and you never said a word—and last week it was the anniversary of the night we met and you forgot all about it. You never remember anything, Joe,' she says, more in sorrow than in anger, as the phrase goes—'Boy, you never even bring me flowers . . .'

"And there Joe stood, like a big mutt, with his face all pasty, like he was going to cry himself. Then he picks up his hat and goes out, see, and I says to myself, I guess this is your cue for exit too, Eddie, and I hops it while Ann is still sobbing her heart out on the sofa . . .

"Well, I don't know, my dear—I don't know nothing. What's the answer? There was Joe, in prison——"

"In prison, Eddie?" I asked, in bewilderment. "In *prison?* But how did he get into prison? Surely you've skipped a lot?"

"Have I?" asked the little man absently. "Yes, maybe I have—I get a bit confused, you know—I'm growing old. It's a battlefield, my dear—it's a ruddy battlefield . . . Anyway, I might as well hurry on to the finish—I can't spin out this yarn all ruddy night. They'll be closing up soon, and I must get home early to-night—I haven't been to bed before two for a whole month, and I've got a song conference with Issy FitzGerald in Salmon's office at ten o'clock. I see that Issy has gone off for *his* beauty sleep, incidentally—either that or he's giving himself a shot or two in the cloakroom . . . Where was I? Joe in prison—no, before that, wasn't it? Yes—when they had their row.

"My God, I'll never forget that day—never, as long as I live (though I don't suppose that's going to be so very long now, I drink so ruddy much and get so little sleep). It was a day and a half, that was—a day and a half, I can tell you. Everything seemed to happen that day. For one thing I was all mixed up in the Iris Jackson affair at Bertolini's—I told you about that, didn't I?—and for another I was supposed to be writing the score of a musical comedy for old Tommy Finlayson. So I didn't get down to the Park Lane club where Woody and Ann were featuring my new number till rather late, you see. And on my way—when I was walking through lower Soho—who should I run into but Joe! And he was wheeling a barrow. A *barrow!* I ask you!

" 'Joe!' says I—'well, what do you know! What the hell are you doing?—fetching the laundry?'

"For a time he never said a word. He just stood there, holding the barrow, swaying backwards and forwards. And I could smell that he was drunk.

" 'Aren't you on to-night, Joe?' I asked him, 'aren't you doing a dance spot with Ann in this new number of mine?'

"And he answered me in a sort of queer husky voice—'Oh yes, Eddie, I'm on all right. I'm just going down to the club now. Only, you see, I've got to take these home to the flat first.'

" 'What are they?' I asked, peering a bit closer to the barrow—it was a darkish sort of night, you see.

" 'They're flowers,' he says. 'She said I never took her flowers. You heard her, Eddie—you was there. And by God, I've brought her flowers!—I've brought her a whole ruddy barrow-load of flowers from a street pedlar!'

"And then he gave a queer kind of grunt and went on. And do you know something, boy? As he passed me I saw why it was that Joe was talking in such a queer husky voice. He was crying, that's what it was—that great big Irish mutt was crying . . ."

For the last time Eddie paused. He blinked round—rather sadly, I thought. The Club was emptying fast. The orchestra had finished playing and the men were packing up their instruments. Woody Hunter was walking off the dais, through the little bead-hung doorway that Cyclamen Brown had used for her exit earlier.

"Well," said Eddie at last, with a sigh. "It's soon told. No sense in spinning things out. I saw it all—and what I didn't see I could guess at. Joe got home with the flowers all right—he stacked them all round the flat. Pot flowers they were—the whole barrowload of them. And he got down to the club in time for his dance spot—he got down a good quarter of an hour before his spot, and during that quarter of an hour he locked himself in his dressing room. Cos why? Well, my boy—I'll tell you cos why. Cos he had found out that Woody Hunter was making advances to Ann—he had found out while he was busy getting drunk that evening before he bought the flowers. Somebody had told him—

there's always somebody in the profession who's ready to tell any tale of scandal or gossip. And Joe, you see—well, just for an hour or so he wasn't an ace trumpeter and a star dancer at all any more: he was just a big tough from the Glasgow Gallowgate. He had a razor-blade, you see, and a little length of adhesive plaster. And there he was, sitting in his dressing room, fixing the razor-blade on to his thumb nail. Nasty, eh? I'll say it was . . .

"It caused a devil of a sensation that night. Well, I ask you! When you go to a club to enjoy the music and dancing, and when you're sitting back applauding the floor show, it isn't exactly *nice,* is it, when you see one of the stars making a leap at another star and slashing out with something shiny on his hand? Is it, now?"

"You mean, Eddie," said I, "you mean—that Joe went for Woody?"

"God no! Don't you understand how people's minds work, boy?—don't you understand *anything* of what goes on in the world? Joe went for Ann! Woody had taken Ann's hand at the end of the spot, see, and was bowing to the customers with her. And Joe's arm swung round and he went slash with the razor-blade, straight at Ann's face. But his arm continued round in its swing see, and there was Ann, standing dazed for a minute in the spotlight, and still smiling—and we could see, right down the side of her face, from her ear to her mouth, that nasty little thin red line. And—because Joe's arm had continued round in its swing—we could see another red line too: right across Woody's throat, and dripping down on to his shirt front before he collapsed."

Eddie rose to his feet, blinking. He motioned the waiter to bring our bill.

"It was morals, you see," he said, as we made our way slowly to the cloakroom. "Morals. Just like I told you. Joe argued, you see, that Ann was his girl—she was his *property,* so to speak. He couldn't keep Woody from muscling in if he wanted to—but he could do his damnest to make his property damned unattractive for anyone that did not want to muscle in. See what I mean? He felt he was entitled to do that—and I suppose he almost was—according to our sort of morals, at any rate. Of course, maybe you won't understand that, but anyway, there it was."

"Do you mean to tell me," I said incredulously, "that Joe knew what he was going to do to Ann and then went and brought her flowers? My God!"

"Why not?" shrugged the little man. "He had to clear himself somehow. Besides—he was an Irishman . . ."

There was silence between us for a moment. Then Eddie sighed deeply.

"Poor Woody," he said. "He had his operation, of course—to the throat. God knows why he insists on singing these days—his voice has gone, if ever a voice had. It was just as well for Joe his razor-blade didn't go any deeper. If he'd killed Woody he'd have swung, or at least had a sentence for Manslaughter—as it was he got away with a spell for Grievous Bodily Harm. He missed the jugular by a hairsbreadth . . ."

At this moment, as we stood by the cloakroom of the Club putting on our coats, I saw, coming towards us along the corridor, Woody Hunter, the band leader. He was escorting the girl in the mauve frock—and she still wore her mask. They nodded to Eddie as they passed us.

"Good night, Woody," said the little man cheerfully. "'Night, Cyclamen darling."

"My God!" I whispered. "I've suddenly seen it! The mask! I see now why she wears it. Because of——"

"Of course," said Eddie. "Well, I ask you! You could hardly appear in public with a razor scar all down your face, now could you? Woody's different, fortunately—his hardly shows if he keeps his head down. A wonderful girl, Cyclamen—wonderful. Of course, she's married now."

"To Woody?" I asked.

Eddie stopped short and stared at me. His blue eyes were wide, his brow was slightly puckered. He was Innocence personified —a little sad, a little puzzled, and very, very eager to explain.

"Oh no," he said. "You don't understand. How could she have married Woody? I told you it was different—it's all morals—all of it—and different morals. You'll never understand anything if you don't grasp that. It's the way people behave, the way they *really* behave. I said they were ruddy queer . . . Ann married Joe Mulvaney. Who else could she marry? She was waiting for Joe the day he came out of prison. And they were married straight away by a special licence from the Bishop of London. A lovely wedding too, it was—I was there—I wrote a special song for them. The flowers! Oh boy—I never saw such flowers! And most of them was cyclamen plants. Ann was mad about cyclamens—so mad about 'em that we nicknamed her Cyclamen Brown. Everything was cyclamens—she wore cyclamen colour, she sunk some of her savings in a club and called it the Cyclamen Club. You see, when she got home from the hospital after that night—when she went up to the little flat in Wardour Street and saw all those cyclamens that Joe had brought for her—well, boy, I ask you! She *couldn't* have done anything else but marry Joe—it would have been immoral . . ."

We said good night to the thin dark man who had let us into the Club. The air was cold. Eddie threw away the butt of his cigarillo and pulled his coat round his shoulders closely.

"Well anyway," I murmured at length, as we made our way towards the Avenue, "Cyclamen seemed friendly enough with Woody Hunter to-night. I suppose they've all let bygones be bygones, eh?"

For a long time Eddie did not reply. Then at last there came a sort of grunt from the darkness by my elbow.

"Friendly? Yes—I suppose so . . . They're friendly all right. As a matter of fact——" He broke off. There was a long pause. Then suddenly he burst out: "Oh what the hell! You might as well know. Of course Ann and Woody are friendly. They're having an affair. They're—well—living together."

"My God!" I said. "But what about Mulvaney—what about Joe?"

"Oh Joe's got his own band these days. He's touring in the North of England. The Leeds and Manchester circuit, if I remember right."

"But—doesn't he *mind?*"

Another long silence. And the sound that came from my elbow this time in the darkness was a kind of sigh—quiet, and almost, perhaps, regretful.

"Well . . . no. Why should he? It's—it's sort of different now, my dear. You know what I mean. Cyclamen is hardly Joe's *girl* any more, now is she? It's sort of difficult to explain. It's not quite the same, you know. They're—oh don't you understand? They're married now, you see . . ."

If I had not known Eddie better I might have supposed that in the darkness by my side he was a little embarrassed.

We walked on. Some drunks reeled past us. Far-off, in an alleyway, a woman screamed. We entered Shaftesbury Avenue. I said good night to Eddie, called a taxi, and went home.

Couleur de Rose

Hagerman washed his face with great care, puffing and blowing as he lathered. Then he groped about for a towel and dried himself. He felt infinitely better—infinitely clearer in the head.

He smiled at himself in the shaving mirror. Now at last the long torment was finished. Charles had gone away. All his life he had wanted that one thing to happen—he had felt himself stifled by the man's presence: his very existence was a menace, a discomfort.

Hagerman slipped on his glasses and went through to his bedroom. He felt he could walk more easily and lightly than he had ever walked before—it was as if he had had a couple of glasses of champagne, or had huge pads of cotton-wool on the under soles of his shoes. He wanted to sing—at last he *could* sing: he could sing at the top of his voice (and it was, he had always secretly felt, a good voice), without hearing Charles's complaining whine from downstairs:

"Adrian, for God's sake shut up! You know I can't tolerate noise—my head aches so. You're beastly thoughtless, Adrian, I must say—beastly thoughtless . . ."

"Oh, Charles has gone away,"

he sang—

"Far, far away . . ."

He held the "away" on a sustained note, then broke off with a chuckle. No whine from the study, no querulous grumble from his brother that he was—"as you know beastly well, Adrian"—in the middle of his new book. He had always hated Charles and his books. He was (he could admit it to himself) in some way jealous. What had he, Adrian, ever been but a sort of hanger-on to the other Hagerman? "Any relation to Charles Hagerman, the author?" people would say. "It's an unusual name, isn't it? . . ."

Well, he had the house to himself now—at last. He could roam through every room without feeling any of the vague guilt that assailed him when Charles was about. It *would* belong to him: his mother *would* leave the house to the elder son—as she had left everything to the elder son. "He's so much more sensible than you are, Adrian—you're far too flighty to have responsibility . . ." Far too flighty—a phrase that had stuck. People called him "the other Hagerman—you know, my dear, the flighty one . . ."

"Oh, Charles has gone away"

he sang—

"Far, far away . . ."

He stood at the bedroom window. The sun was shining gloriously. The whole world seemed to be smiling—the colours were brilliant and warm, the wonderful colours of autumn. Yet yesterday the scene had seemed dull and commonplace enough—yesterday, when he had been oppressed by Charles's presence. He had stood there, he remembered, by that self-same window, listening to the thin mean sound of Charles's flute coming up the stairs. That intolerable flute—his "recreation." He grimaced at the memory of a phrase his brother had kept repeating over and over again, blowing the same sour note at every repetition, so that he—Adrian—had grown to wait for it, grinding his teeth and clenching his knuckles from sheer hate of the man.

But to-day there was no flute. The house was empty. The sun shone. The trees at the foot of the long garden were superbly tinted—wonderful, wonderful trees. The grass was warm—soft, beautiful. And the flowers . . . He could not express himself about the flowers. He had never had much time for flowers before—had never thought about them somehow. He felt a curious tightening in the chest, a little trembling round his heart as he surveyed the heavenly riot of colour.

This was glory. This was—what was the saying?—looking at the world through rose-coloured spectacles . . .

He moved back to the wardrobe and started to look out his clothes. Curious, he thought as he worked, what an extraordinary difference the mere absence of an enemy could make. His whole outlook was different now that Charles had gone—he was, literally, a different man. Yet it had always been so, he recollected. He had never felt truly himself while Charles was about. Odd, then, that he lived with him all these years. Why indeed had he never struck out on his own? His weakness, his flightiness. It was easier to cling to Charles. Because of old ties, perhaps. Their mother had encouraged him to rely on Charles. If their father had lived, thought Adrian, would it have been different? Would he have been the "father's boy"? Would he have had a better chance? Would he have been more independent?—less . . . flighty?

Charles Hagerman, author . . . Adrian Hagerman, hanger-on . . .

He undressed slowly before the mirror. He *looked* different now that Charles had gone. There was a glory about him, too, just as there was a glory about the garden. The rose-coloured spectacles again, he thought with a smile . . .

Looking back he tried for a moment to discover why he had always hated Charles so. Yet it was hideously understandable. He remembered the gibes the older boy had thrown at him about his being unwanted—and those when he was only eight and Charles twelve. Their mother had evidently taken Charles into her confidence—at that age. "Charles is *my* boy," she always said, when people called, fondling him. Even when Charles was eighteen, and his first book of poems had been published, she still said that sort of thing. He remembered that book, "that slim but competent volume," as the advertisements had called it. He had hated it—hated the ostentatious way in which their mother had left copies lying about the house for people to see. "My clever Charles," she always said, with an arch smile, when someone made a comment. "My clever, clever boy—and don't forget, dear —he's only eighteen . . ."

That was more than twenty years ago now, but of all Charles's books he still hated that first one the most. It had been called (and he saw clearly the ornate lettering on the fly-leaf): *Couleur de Rose . . .*

Couleur de Rose indeed! And here was he talking of looking at the world through rose-coloured spectacles! The irony of it—the incredible irony of it!

He laughed, straightening his tie. Well, it was all an old tale now. He had the house to himself. Charles had gone at last, after all these years. He could roam through the old place at will, into every room—into the room that had once been their nursery, into the room that had once been their mother's bedroom . . .

He stopped in the movement he was making of putting away his dirty clothes. His mother's bedroom. It was a room he somehow had never dared enter while Charles was about—yet God knows he had often, secretly, wanted to. Why not go to it now? There was nothing to stop him—nothing. The house was empty, quite empty . . .

He went out to the corridor. Through habit he made as if to close the door of his room quietly behind him, then, recollecting, he grinned and gave it instead a vicious slam. Then, whistling, he stamped along the passage and down the small annexe staircase at the end of it. For a moment he paused before the door of their old nursery. He had a sudden crazy notion that if he opened it, it would be to see, crouching on the floor, at play, two little boys. "Hullo, Charles," he would call, "hullo, Adrian . . ." And go, quickly, before they had time to look up . . . Crazy, crazy, he thought, smiling and passing on. The rose-coloured spectacles. Crazy . . .

And now he reached the dark door of the bedroom—the sacred room. He paused for a long time on the threshold. The old house was silent, terribly silent. Suppose—just for a moment—suppose . . . that Charles came back? Suppose, standing there, he heard, coming up the stairs, the sound of that loathsome flute? No. Foolish, foolish. A weak fancy—typical.

The old door creaked strangely in the silence as he opened it. Even now—even when he knew he was alone—there was an unaccountable reluctance . . .

The room was exactly as she had left it ten years before, when she died. Quiet—ineffably quiet. It seemed misty to him as he stood there, timidly looking round. The sun, coming through the window, rested in squares on the worn and faded carpet. Over there, in the corner, was the little work-table he had seen her use so often. Her treadle sewing machine. On the wall the samplers she had worked as a girl. One of them, he remembered, was embroidered with her own lovely hair—the one she had made just after becoming engaged to his father. His name, twined with flowers. "Edward Hagerman."

Her little nursing chair—inlaid mahogany. The set of doll's crockery she had kept as a rememberancer of her own mother. The blue and gold French china. The ormolu clock. The mother-of-pearl card case. The Spanish shawl cast so casually over the end of the bed . . . And over all, ineffable, ghostly, the delicate lost scent of her, conjuring up an infinity of memories and hopes—and bitternesses.

He sighed and turned to go. Just inside the door was a small occasional table and on it a book. He picked it up idly and flicked open the cover. Then, with his sigh cut short on his lips, he cast it down angrily on the floor and went out, slamming the door. *Couleur de Rose . . .*

He went back to his own room, striding quickly along the corridor past the door of the nursery. Damn them all, then, he felt—God damn them all. He didn't care. What if Charles had had all the success, what if he had been "her" boy? For him, now that Charles had gone, the world was, in its own way, brighter—was different. He knew it was. There *was* glory. It had been a weakness to go into her room—a damnable weakness. He wouldn't give in again—he wouldn't be flighty.

He entered his bedroom and seized his attaché case. Then, singing defiantly, he ran downstairs and went out into the garden, the sunshine. He strode across the grass, past the wonderful flaming flowers and so through the trees to the road.

And all the glory was on him again. He threw back his head and laughed at the sky. This was himself. Now, and for always, he looked at the world through rose-coloured spectacles . . .

* * * *

On the station platform people stared at him curiously, half-frightenedly. But he didn't care. He was beyond them. He looked through the rose-coloured spectacles.

When the train puffed into the platform, throwing out clouds of steam, he saw it, gloriously, through rose-coloured spectacles.

And when, just as he was stepping into the carriage, he felt a heavy hand on his shoulder, he turned and stared at the serious-faced policeman who confronted him—through rose-coloured spectacles.

He had stabbed Charles insanely, driving the knife again and again into his chest and throat—so hellishly insanely, indeed, that the warm blood had spurted out all over his face. And a dry, caking film of it remained—on his spectacles.

That to him, was the glory of it all.

The Lovers

IT WAS YOU, talking about ghosts, that put me in mind of it. She's the only ghost I ever saw, and I didnae ken she was a ghost till after I saw her. At least—I *think* she was a ghost. When I cast my mind back I don't rightly see what else she could've been. Yet the way that man sat there beside her, quite joco—och, it was no' canny, it was no' canny.

But I'll tell ye the story as best I can. I'm no' a tale-maker, but sitting here at our crack over a dram, I'll ha'e a shot at gi'eing ye an account o' it. And if I use the wrong words and suchlike, well, ye'll just have to put up wi' that. Ye'll mind I'm no' an educated man—I had to leave the school when I was twelve to get apprenticed to my trade. We were a big family, you see, and my mother was sair put to it to get enough to fill a' the mouths in the house. So when the chance came for me to be apprenticed to old Mr. MacIlwham the Electrician in Stirling, my mother took it, and I started haudin' tools for the repair men at seven and six a week.

Of course, you must understand that this was all a long time ago. In those days there was not a great lot of houses in Scotland that had the electricity. But it was comin' in—it was like motor cars, it was fair sweeping the land. So old MacIlwham got a good business going in the end—we were aye kept hard at it, not only in Stirling itself, but travelling all over the countryside, you see, because there was so few electricians—and in them days too you hadn't the Corporation to put the current in your house, you had to have all the fitments put in by private firms like ours. (By the way, it was queer me mentioning motor cars just now. This man I'm going to tell ye about had something to do wi' motor cars, if I remember right. I don't know exactly what it was, but it's in my mind that he was someway connected wi' that trade . . . Anyway, we'll come to that later.)

Well now, at the time that this happened that I'm telling ye about, I had been wi' MacIlwham for nigh on eight years. I was a repair man myself by this time, and since I was young and guid i' the health, I got the part of the job going over the country. I liked it fine—I was aye a lad for seeing the sights and meeting folk. And there was plenty o' that—the auld man had mair business than he could rightly handle. We were aye on the go—I've often thought that mebbe it was because I was gey tired and overworked at the time that I saw yon woman at all . . . Oh well—let's not bother with trying to explain it—ye cannae really explain some things. At least—the likes o' me can't—I'm an ordinary working electrician—and I wasn't even that in those days, but just a mechanic repair man that could hardly even sign his ain name and certainly couldn't understand any of the big words folk use when they're talking about this kind o' thing.

Now old MacIlwham had a customer on his books that lived in an old house just outside Dunblane. His name was Gemmell. He had had the electricity put in about ten years before—just before I joined the trade. Old MacIlwham had put it in himself—and I must just say this about the old man, though he was a good master to me all the years I was with him: he was no' muckle good as an electrician. Anyway, what happened was just at this time we began to get letters from Gemmell saying that all the fitments in his house were breaking up, and would MacIlwham's send out a man to have a keek at them. At first the letters were quite polite and business-like, but as the time went on and nothing happened, he began to get angry—he said he was reduced to oil lamps again over most of the house. The old man sent him letters saying he was sorry but there was a terrible pressure of work and so on, and he would send a man as soon as he could. And so it went on like that for a while.

Well, that was the first time I heard of this man Gemmell. He was an oldish man, you know—he had retired from business to this old house outside Dunblane. I wish I could remember what this business of his was. I'm positive it had something to do with motor cars—he had made his money hiring them out or something. I can't rightly remember, though—except that it had something to do with motors. Anyway, it doesn't matter—it's just that ye get a sort of tick—ye know what I mean: something sticks in your mind and ye want to remember it, but it just escapes you all the time. We'll forget it—I'll get on wi' the story.

Where was I?—Yes, I mind—old MacIlwham saying he'd get a man out to look at Gemmell's fitments as soon as he could. Well, the chance came at last. And it happened this way:

I was to be in Dunblane for a big job for a few days, and then I had to hurry back to Stirling. But there was just the off chance I'd be able to fit in the Gemmell house on my way back. MacIlwham wrote to Gemmell and told him this—but he said I'd be so busy in Dunblane that I'd just have to do his job when I could—mebbe I wouldn't be able to tackle it till the evening, for instance. Gemmell wrote back and said it didn't matter when I came as long as I came—I could come in the middle of the night if I liked, the main thing was that the job should be done.

So that was the way of it, and off I went to Dunblane. I got my job done there without bother, though I didn't finish it till well after five o'clock, and by the time I'd had my fish tea wi' the old landlady I used to stay with there—a right douce body she was too, and fine I liked her—it was near half-after six before I reached old Mr. Gemmell's house. And it was winter too—a dark and dreich time yon, wi' the rain slanting down as I got near the house, and me with a long job to look forward to and then a cauld journey back to Stirling when it was finished.

I knocked on the door. It was a queer house—sort of *blind,* if you know what I mean, standing up there against the wild sky, with the big poplar trees swaying and swishing all the way round. And the fact that there wasn't a glim of light coming from inside —on account of the electricity, you see—that made it all worse. It was an eldritch sight a'thegither.

Gemmell came to the door after I'd been knocking for a good three minutes. He was a dour-looking, peering sort of man—suspicious-like. He stood there in the mirk wi' a wee oil lamp in his hand, wi' the door only barely open, spiering at me who I was and what I wanted. When I said I was frae MacIlwham's he gave a sort of grunt and then stood back and asked me ben. I went—but none too happy, somehow. There was a sort of cold and dampness in yon house—an unhealthy spirit somewhere.

I went into the kitchen first. He lit up an oil lamp and I had a look at the fitments. It was exactly the way I had expected—they were just done. What wi' old MacIlwham's skimpit work, and the general damp and decay o' yon house, they were fair fallin' to bits. It was just a matter o' fittin' new ones, and I started on that job straight away, wi' Gemmell fidgetting about in the background like a hen on a hot girdle.

I worked quick, so's I could get finished and away afore it was too late. I got done wi' the kitchen and the upstairs places inside the hour, and then I said to him, The front room—what about that?

"Oh aye," says he. "The front room. Yes. You'll have to do that, won't you."

There seemed to be something on his mind. He stood thinking for a wee, then he says again:

"Yes. The front room. Mphm. Well—it's this way—just along here."

I went after him. Just when we got to this front room he stopped and keeked round at me, as if he wanted to say something. Then he seemed to change his mind and opened the door.

It was a big room, and the minute I went in I felt a queer sort of smell in it. I don't know what it was like—nothing quite wholesome—a sort of camphor smell, but queer, wi' an edge to it. I didnae like it—I just didnae like it at all. There was something about the whole room that I didnae like—a sort of coldness in it, though there was no' a bad wee fire in the grate. It was when I looked over at that fire that I got my shock—though there wasn't any reason why it *should* have been a shock—just somehow I had had the impression, you know, that Gemmell was alone in the house—the way he had answered the door to me, the quietness there had been in the place all the time that I was working. But you see, man, there was a woman in that room—sitting down by the fire. And there was something about her—I don't know what it was—but a something that linked up in my mind in an instant wi' the queer cauld in the air and the unwholesome smell that I told ye about.

She was a woman about eight or ten years younger than Gemmell—a bonny enough wee body, dressed in black. She sat wi' her hands folded in her lap—very straight—on a sofa. And she was smiling—but not at me—she didnae even look at me. She had her eyes fixed straight ahead and she didnae move—she didnae budge an inch. I couldn't see her very clear in the bad light, but I had the impression that she was—och, how can I put it?—no' quite *real*. She had a high colour—she looked, if ye know what I mean, ower healthy—a wee thing too fresh.

Gemmell had come into the room behind me—I could feel him fidgeting about at my elbow. He gave a sort of cough and then he says:

"This is my wife," he says.

"How-do-ye-do, ma'am," says I—but the wee soul never answered—not a word. She sat there just staring ahead, wi' that smile o' hers. She never moved—I was a wee thing frightened.

"You mustn't pay any attention to her," says Gemmell, wi' a queer sort of half laugh. "She's—" But then he hesitated. "Och, never mind," he says, "get on wi' your job."

Then he went over and sat down beside her and he leaned close up to her and then he says, in a very loud voice—a sort of shout:

"It's the electric man, dear. He's come to mend the lights—and then I'll be able to see ye properly."

He laughed his wee nervous laugh again. She never budged —not an inch. And I fear properly got the wind up. I don't know what it was—there was just a wee something about her . . .

Well, I got on wi' the job. All the time I was working he kept his eyes on me—a sort of jealous and suspicious way, I thought —I could feel it. If I glanced over he would give his wee laugh. Dod, man, I hated yon job! That damned smell was in my nose —a sort of—och, the Lord kens what it was! Sulphur it was—or no—was it forma-something? We had it burnt once in our house at Stirling when my wee sister Jessie had the scarlet fever. Something like that. But it wasnae really the smell or the cauld that was worrying me—it was just yon woman. As the time went on I just wanted her to move. I didn't want her to speak. I just wanted her to move. Every time I keeked over at her, there she was, wi' that sonsy wee face a' glowing in the firelight—and smiling, ye ken, wi' him quite joco beside her. It was damnable—there was something about it that was damnable. I wanted to drop my tools and run out o' that terrible house—I didnae care where, just to run.

I got finished at last.

"There," says I, "it's done. Now I'll just switch on the light tae see if it's working, and then I'll have to be going."

He was up like a flash. And there was a sort of feared look on him.

"No," he gasps, "dinnae try it! It'll be fine—I ken it'll be fine!"

"I've just got to check on it," I says.

"No, no. Ye dinnae need tae—I ken ye made a job o' the others, and this one'll be the same. Dinnae bother."

I couldn't understand the man. But what could I do? He was dancing about in front of me, fair jumpit wi' fright or something. Then he turns suddenly and cries:

"The electric man's finished now, dear. He's just going."

And he gives his wee nervous laugh.

"Ye'll tell Mr. MacIlwham to send me his bill," he says. "I'll settle wi' him at once."

And almost before I could get my tools packed up he was bustling me to the door. I keeked back once, over his shoulder—and there she was, in exactly the same position. And the smile was still on her face . . .

Eh, ghosts did ye say? Man, man!

D'ye ken what happened? It gi'es me the jimjams to mind o' it now. But I'll tell ye, I'll tell ye . . .

I was in no healthy mood yon night when I left Gemmell's house. I walked along the road fair sweating, wi' the wind soughing round me in the trees like a warlock's skirlings.

And then, thank God, I suddenly minded I had seen a wee pub as I walked out to the job earlier on, and I thought—Well, Andrew boy, it's you for a dram, and be damned to the train for Stirling for a whiley! And in I went, and cried the dame for a nip.

I got down in a corner to shift it, and presently in comes a wee man and joins me. I was fair in the mood for a healthy crack, and it wasn't long till we was gossiping at it like well-tried cronies. A nice wee man he was too—a ploughman from the big farm up the road, just ayont Gemmell's house.

Of course we talked about Gemmell. The whole thing was too heavy on my mind for us not to. And by this time, ye see, wi' a couple o' nips in me, I was mair inclined to laugh at the old chap, and to feel it hadnae been as queer as I had thought it all at the time. And there I was, just telling the tale—beginning wi' the time I landed, and him coming out wi' his wee oil lamp to the door, and the fixing of his fitments in the kitchen and up the stairs, and then the wee hesitation he gave at the door o' the front room before he ushered me in.

"And then," says I, quite perjink, "we enters, you see, and he introduced me to his wife, and I says, quite polite-like——"

I stopped there and looked up at the wee ploughman. He had given a sort of splutter and a cough—and now I could see he was gaping at me, wi' his mouth open, and the whisky glass trembling in his hand.

"His—wife?" he says.

"Aye, whit wey no'? Ye're gey surprised. Can a man no' be mairrit? But losh, a queer wee woman yon! She didnae move—"

"Guid help us!" says the little man. "His wife, ye say? Guid help us! James Gemmell's wife is dead—she died eight years ago!"

I felt the wee hairs bristling.

"He *said* it was his wife," I says—but a' the time, in my eye, mind you, I had a picture o' that wee body in the dim light—no' moving an inch.

"Janet Gemmell's dead this eight years," says the wee chap dourly. "And it was a sad day for yon man when she died. I never kenned a couple more attached to each other. He fair worshipped her—he wouldn't let her out o' his sight, almost. We used to call them The Lovers . . . Oh man, it shook him sair when she slippit awa'."

I never said a word. The wee man went on, shaking his head:

"Aye, aye. It was a' a bit queer wi' him after she died. If he could've brocht her back from the grave he would've done—he was fair daft on her, fair daft on her, auld though the pair o' them was. We all expected him to have her buried decently in the kirkyard up-bye, but maybe he didnae want to have the thocht o' her so near. He took her away somewhere. And he came back in a big closed motor car about three months after, and from that day to this we've hardly seen him. He stays in the house most o' the time . . . Pair man, pair man!"

I got up and went out, wi' my last dram untouched on the table. I walked into Dunblane for my train, very quietlike in the dark. You see, I *kenned* I had seen her. I *kenned* the two of them had been together there. Somehow, by some devilish cantrip, they were there—the two of them, in that big house—and she dead for eight years . . . Man, man, ye could have slippit the skin off my banes that night, it shivered so loose about me . . .

Well, that was the time I saw a ghost—and as I told you, I never knew she was a ghost till after I had seen her. And I'm just an ordinary sort of man—nae book-learning, as I said.

Oh wait a minute, wait a minute. I've just remembered what Gemmell's business was before he retired. I knew it had something to do wi' motor-cars. Hiring them out, it was. Taxis. That's it. I mind it used to say it on his note-paper when he wrote to MacIlwham. He had a fency professional sort of name for it though. What was it?

Aye—I remember. Taxi-dermist. That was it. Aye—taxi-dermist.

He was just an ordinary wee man in business after all, you see. Was that no' queer?

The Other Passenger

THE SPARKS FLY UPWARD

Sitting like this, with the blank sheets before me, trying to coordinate things before setting them down, I see, above all other images, that wry and beastly figure as it burned: the head lolling grotesquely on the shoulder: the arms outstretched and nailed to the crosspiece of the frame that had, in the children's excitement, gone all askew; and I, only I, in all that cheering company, with any notion of what was behind the leering mask.

The flames rose slowly at first, I remember: then, as the straw and the twigs caught properly alight, roared round the sagging clothes and played on the whole crooked figure. I sniffed the air in a sort of ecstasy of relief—and realised immediately, thinking in grotesque parallel to Lamb's "Dissertation Upon Roast Pig," why I did so . . .

Where to begin? The evening in the fog? The first time I heard the sound of the piano come creeping along the corridor? The scene on the platform of the Underground with Miller, and the terrible scream rushing through the crowd to me? Or further back still, to the first vague premonitions?

I remember, long ago, when I was a student, going to a party. We were very young. We sat round the fire with the lights out, playing a game we called "Horrors." The idea was for each guest to describe the most horrible thing he could think of. We each took our turn—I remember I had something naïve, about a skeleton. It was good fun—we laughed a lot. We had all taken part except one shy pretty girl who sat on the outskirts of the circle. In a silence she said, in a low voice:

"Shall I tell you the most horrible thing I can imagine? You waken suddenly in the night. You have that ineffable feeling that there is someone else—some *thing* else—in the room with you. You stretch out your hand for the matches, to investigate.

And, quite quietly and simply, the matchbox is placed in your hand..."

We all fell silent. As for me, something swept over me—a sudden expression had been given to something I had known always secretly. For the first time I had a real, overwhelming, haunting sense of—well, call it what you may want to: I have my own name.

We go, you see: and with us goes always Another Passenger. He is beside us in every deepest action and speaks through us in every fateful announcement. There is no escaping him or his influence. His voice whispers suddenly in the night, his presence intangibly lingers at our shoulder when we feel ourselves most alone. He is the Man on the Back, the Secret Sharer. He is the Worm that Dieth Seldom, the Great Sickness.

Yet in it all there is, I suspect, a terrible paradox. We do not hate him. We fear him, perhaps: but secretly, in our hearts, we still love him. He may be the Worm: if he is, he is Brother Worm.

We go: and he—the Other Passenger—is always at our side. Always, always, always—to the grave: and perhaps beyond it...

My name, I should tell you, is John Aubrey Spenser. I am a pianist, thirty-five years of age. I was, when all this began, engaged to be married. My fiancée's name was Margaret du Parc, daughter of Georges du Parc, the violinist. She was (perhaps you have seen portraits of her?—there is a famous one by de Laszlo) most exquisitely beautiful. Yet God knows my own remembrances of her now are all vague enough. That has been the most devilish part of it all—I forget things. I forget good things and only remember old agonies. I remember inconsequential torments from my childhood days, for example, and so everything mounts to a deep, ferocious resentment.

I was born in Scotland—an illegitimate child. My father was an extraordinary man—morose, untidy, clever, lazy. He was one of the Spensers of Barnhall in North Perthshire, a big farming family—old puritans, with the fear of God and a love of the Devil in them. My father's father, the head of the family, was a dour, powerfully charactered man: autocratic, hard-working, firm in his belief that a man should beget and keep on begetting. Hence there were fourteen children—my father the youngest.

The old farmer's death was typical of his life—precise, sparing in emotion, with not a word wasted. As my father used to tell me the story, he came in one night from the fields and stood for a few moments silently in the farmhouse doorway. Then he heaved a great sigh and said, in a perfectly matter-of-fact voice:

"Aye, Barnha' will need a new maister in the morning."

Forthwith he collapsed in a heap and by the morning he was dead.

The farm went to my father's eldest brother, Finlay, a typical phlegmatic Spenser. They still tell the story in the Barnhall district of how, when his young son Geordie had been killed in France in 1915 in the First World War, he appeared wild-eyed on Barnhall Station and slammed his wallet down on the booking-desk. He had no hat or coat, but under his arm he carried his big double-barrelled rabbit gun.

"I want a ticket for France," he said. "By Goad, I'll get they de'ils for killing oor Geordie! . . ."

My father was the schoolmaster in a little two-teacher school in the country—the dominie, with the school-house thrown in. A terrible house—damp, draughty, with no drains and a big pump in the yard to provide the water supply. We used to have to wrap great lumps of brown felt and straw round the pump in winter so that it shouldn't get frozen. I used to think it was some sort of live thing when we did that.

When my father got that school his sister Bertha went to keep house for him. She had a maid to help her, and there was my father stuck away in the country with no woman but Aunt Bertha, so he couldn't help going after the maid—there wasn't anything else to do. Anyway, I was the result of that. When my mother became pregnant my father tried to get her out of the way, but he bungled it (as he bungled everything) and my Aunt Bertha found out. There was a scene—my father told me later, before he died, that she gave them both hell—particularly my mother. She had the poor little thing sent to her people and gave her some money, and when I was about two she had me brought up to the school-house. My mother's people were too poor to object—what the hell did they want me for anyway?—and there I was, with Aunt Bertha pretending to the Minister and anybody that was curious that I was her cousin's orphan.

There wasn't any maid in the house now, and as soon as I was old enough to lift an axe, my Aunt Bertha began. I think I was her revenge—against everything. She kept a strap hanging up beside the mantelpiece—one of my father's shaving-strops, with an iron buckle on it. She used to hit me with it if I didn't get the sticks split quickly enough. But that was nothing compared with some of the things she used to do. If I wet the bed she used to make me stand outside in the frost in my nightshirt till she decided it was dry. That was a favourite punishment of hers—making me stand outside in the cold. Sometimes it was so bad I couldn't close my fist to knock on the door and ask to get in again. Another of her punishments was not to give me anything to eat. She would send me up to bed without anything, and I had to lie under one old blanket and listen to her down below in the yard wrapping up the pump. I hated her. She was a big thin woman, very angular, and she used to wear long woollen drawers like a man in the winter time. We went to Church every Sunday and I could hear her singing beside me in a deep man's voice, and sometimes the Minister came to tea and she sat in immense dignity with a big cairngorm brooch on her dress and gave him slices of black bun.

I didn't see much of my father in those days. He hated Aunt Bertha as much as I did. I remember once, during a meal, she was haranguing him, and suddenly he picked up the oil-lamp and threw it at her. It didn't hit her, but the lamp got smashed against the wall and there we were in the dark, dead quiet for a minute or two, and then she began again, just where she had stopped. I was terrified. Then I remember the door opening and my father's silhouette in the frame, and then we could hear him pacing about in the next room, swearing to himself. He used to spend most of the evenings like that—walking backwards and forwards in his study. He drank a lot. Sometimes the footsteps stopped and we heard him muttering, but they would begin again—perhaps, even, he would start singing. You can picture Aunt Bertha and me sitting there and just listening to him all evening, she bolt upright with that great cairngorm at her breast like a huge sore.

When I was old enough to go to school it was worse. I had to do my jobs in the evening or early morning—no matter what the weather was like, I was out in the yard chopping wood, with an old storm lantern to see by. One of my jobs was to empty the dry-closet, and she used to wait till it was dark before she told me to do that. I used to hate going down to the foot of the garden with my lantern and digging a hole and struggling to lift up the bucket. It was so heavy I had to strain and strain, and when I was about eight one of the boys at school told me about hernia, and I was sick with fear every time, but I strained till I was crying because I was so terrified of her . . .

Aunt Bertha died when I was eleven. When she was ill my father and I used to sit downstairs, very quiet, but both of us were hoping she would die. And when she did, the moment she did, I felt guilty somehow—for wishing it—as if I had caused it. Then the next day I thought: O God—no more sticks to break! . . . and I began to cry in a silly relief. And then for a time my father and I managed in a sort of way, the two of us, in the school-house, but with his drinking and some other things too in the district, matters had gone too far with the authorities and my father got transferred. It was no sort of promotion—simply a transfer, to a school in Glasgow. We moved about two months after Aunt Bertha's funeral. I remember helping my father to pack his books. He was most methodical about them—I have often thought how strange that was. They were all classified and catalogued . . . Lord, I can just see him!—standing there peering at some book or other, turning over the pages with his long crooked fingers and his yellow hair falling over in front of his eyes . . .

But all this is irrelevant—except in that it is these old haunting things that I remember nowadays, and nothing of the good times. Nothing of Margaret, beyond the vague association of something warm and good—ineffable and forlorn, too, like an echo. Oh the facts are there—I remember, detachedly, the facts. But nothing of the essence—no hint at all of that since that devil came on the scene and destroyed every good thing between us.

The Other Passenger. The man in the Dark . . .

I remember—it was, most surely, the first time—walking in Bristol. Five years ago. I was booked for a concert and had decided to travel from town the evening before it. The train was two and a half hours late—there was a heavy fog.

When I got out at last at Temple Mead Station it was to find that no buses were running—no taxis, nothing. I set off to walk to my hotel in Clifton. I can't begin to describe the weird, muffled quietness. The fog was so thick I couldn't see the pavement I was walking on. When I reached the City Centre I heard, on all sides, thousands of footsteps. The people were walking home from work—all traffic was stopped.

There were no voices. Occasionally a woman giggled nervously, but no one spoke—there was something awesome in that impenetrable wall of mist. Only those thousands of muffled footsteps going on determinedly and slowly.

I groped my way towards the University. And I remember I was thinking—irrelevantly enough, as one does—of the early days: my breakaway from Scotland after the death of my father, my incredible success with scholarships, my first concert. Impossible to connect myself, as I walked there, with the shivering and weeping boy who had knocked so helplessly on the door of that decaying school-house. Impossible to imagine what Aunt Bertha would have thought—she who had forbidden me to touch the old walnut cottage piano in my father's study till he had interfered growlingly (only for the sake of countering her!) and said I might play if I wanted to—and might even have lessons from Miss Ramsay in the village . . .

I groped on slowly up the hill. And then I became aware that among all those straggling footsteps there was one pair close to my own—almost in time with my own. I peered into the fog. Whoever it was, he was no more than a foot or so away from me.

I made some ineffectual remark—some fatuous statement about the fog and the discomfort. There was no reply. I walked on. The footsteps continued.

And suddenly a curious fear came over me—intangible, but overwhelming and insistent. I reached out my hand. I moved it backwards and forwards. There was no one there—no one at all beside me. Yet all the time—devilishly and rhythmically—the footsteps were going on. And there was, in the yellow mist, a sort of chuckle, and a whisper.

"Spenser—pianist. John Aubrey Spenser—pianist . . ."

I STOP HERE FOR A MOMENT. I read back what I have set down so disjointedly, in such confusion and unwillingness of spirit. What will it convey to a detached reader? Will he have any notion of me?—a picture in his mind? That strikes me as funny—the idea of anyone having a picture of me in his mind. A young man—dark, thin, with narrow temples. It is what they call "a sensitive face."

A young man with a slight Scottish accent. A picture in a reader's mind. When all the time it might be—

Do you remember, in *Peer Gynt,* towards the end of the play, there is the famous storm scene? Peer is on board ship, returning home at last from his adventures. He stands on the deck watching the storm. Then suddenly he becomes aware that someone is standing beside him at the rail—a Stranger. Peer had thought himself the only passenger on board, yet now he falls into conversation with this mysterious travelling-companion. The man bargains with Peer for his body if he should die in the storm. In the end, unsatisfied, he leaves Peer—he goes down the companion way. Peer asks the ship's boy who the Strange Traveller is.

"There is no other traveller," says the boy. "You are the only passenger."

"But someone was with me a moment ago," cries Peer. "Who was it that went down the companion way just now?"

"No one, sir," says the boy. "Only—the ship's dog . . ."

I cannot concentrate. My mind wanders. I cannot assemble my thoughts. If I were anything of a creative artist I would be able to impose an order on all this. Yet can there be order? I am not concerned with creating a work of art—I am putting things down. And I am putting them down as they come into my head —and as simply as I can. I cannot be logical—sequence is only a convention after all: there isn't any time or scene, character isn't a progress. What matters isn't what happens or when it happens, it's the accumulation of *things*—bits and pieces, states of mind, a fragment of an eyebrow, five minutes in a tram-car, a pair of shoes that don't fit, a slap in the face, a kiss, a diseased kidney, disgust at a spittle, a woman's legs, desire, the smell of onions —all these piled and piled on top of each other and represented in descriptions of odd encounters, conversations, the contents of a room, a recorded memory. What matters isn't what happens or what is said or even felt—it's the sense from the whole, the *smell* of it. That's why I must simply write as it flows—as if I were talking to you.

Very well, then: things—the things that surround me as I write.

My room is large. I keep it dimly lit because of my eyes. To my left, in the corner, is my piano. It is the most beautiful thing I have ever possessed. The firelight gleams on the polish. Open as it is, it is like the Winged Victory. I compare it with the old cottage piano in the school-house—panels of green faded silk and two ornate brass flanges for candles.

On the wall behind the piano, arranged in steps, is my collection of Blake engravings—the Job series, beautifully reproduced. Over the mantelshelf a portrait of Chopin. On the right-hand wall a caricature of me by my friend Peter Ellacott and a photograph of the de Laszlo portrait of Margaret. Beneath these my books and my music cabinet. For the rest, furniture—some beautiful pieces picked up in the sale rooms. On the little Chippendale table by the fireplace is a small old photo-frame containing a portrait of my mother—her people sent it to my father when she died. The print is faded, the yellow glaze cracked diagonally across at one corner. She was a little, sad-faced girl, with her hair piled up on top. Round her neck there is a locket. Whose portrait, I wonder? Her son, John Aubrey? A lock of his hair?

The desk I write at is the only thing that has stayed with me through the years. It was my father's desk—I retained it when his few effects were sold at Glasgow. The greenish leather with which it is topped is scored and worn and ink-stained. Scratched roughly on the wood of one of the drawers—as if done absently as he brooded in his strange way—is his name: Edward Spenser.

So, then—my room. I have described it—I have mentioned some of the things that are in it. Yet I have not mentioned—I have not dared to mention——

No. Even now I haven't the courage. I am too compelled by that damnable smile . . .

THE FOG WAS THE FIRST TIME—the first real time. Then there were other things—small things. Then finally——

Look: I must be detached. I must set it down without opinion or ornamentation. I must report. I am Spenser—very well then: Spenser and his friend Miller are in an Underground Station. People move on all sides—faces held up for a moment, smiling or agonized, then whisked away into limbo. Noise. A distant distorted voice crying "Stand clear of the gates." Miller and I arriving breathlessly at the moment a train starts up and moves out. I swear—I am disproportionately irritated by missing the train.

"The next one doesn't touch our station," I say.

Miller shrugs—damnably imperturbable. He suggests we sit down.

"If we can," I grumble. "There's a devilish crowd."

One of the devilish crowd suddenly heaves into me and I swear irritably again.

Miller: The poor fellow couldn't help banging into you with that enormous case. You ought to do something about those nerves of yours, Spenser.

Spenser: I know—I'm sorry. It's overwork—I've been practising too hard. And this confounded weather—rain, rain—all the time it's rain. There isn't any end to it.

Miller: Never mind. We can have a drink at the other end—one of Jameson's special rye juleps. Think of that and sit down and be patient. There's room here.

Spenser: Thanks. Have you a cigarette?

Miller: I think so . . . There you are—and don't throw half of it away, the way you usually do these days. These are special.

Spenser (and I gave a nervous laugh here, I remember): All right —I'll try not to. God—this crowd! You'd wonder where they all get to go to.

(A train is heard approaching in the distance.)

Miller: It's the rain—people prefer travelling underground when the weather's bad. One of those things—must be a headache for the Transport Authorities in bad weather.

Spenser: Here's a train. I don't suppose . . . ?—No, ours is the next one.

(*The train draws up. People move in and out of it. There is even more noise as background to our conversation.*)

Miller: You should take a rest, you know, Spenser—get away for a few days.

Spenser: How can I? You know I have a concert tour coming off. I must practise. It's all right, Miller—I'll be all right once I get the Chopin *Fantasia* into my fingers. And besides—(*I break off and draw quickly at the cigarette.*)

Miller: And besides what?

Spenser: I don't know. One of two things—queer things. You know—like that night you phoned me—that business down at the Six Bells.

Miller: Oh I wouldn't worry about that. It's the sort of thing that might happen to anyone who was a bit overworked.

Spenser: I suppose so. All the same it—it worries me. Sometimes I think—oh, never mind.

Miller: Think what, old chap?

Spenser: Oh—the blues, the blues. (*I hated Miller's unctuousness—his hearty "old chap."*) I find myself thinking sometimes how easy it would be to—well, shove oneself under a train, for instance.

Miller: Don't be a fool, man. Where would that sort of thing get you?

Spenser (*sighing*)*:* Nowhere, I suppose. Forget it, Miller. I'm only talking for talking's sake. I get these periodic bouts of depression—always have done.

(*Shouts: "Stand clear of the doors," etc.; and bustle.*)

Miller: Besides, what about Margaret? Chaps that are engaged to be married can't go about chucking themselves under trains. There *are* responsibilities, you know.

Spenser: Yes, I know. Forget the whole thing, Miller. The train's going out—we're next.

(*The train starts.*)

Miller: You're just about the queerest chap——

(*It is at this point, if I remember, or in the middle of some such fatuous remark from Miller, that there is a sudden scream from a woman.*

A pause in the crowd noises, then they start up more busily. The train moves out and away.) What's that? What's wrong? . . .

Spenser: I don't know—they're all crowding up to the end of the platform. There's been an accident or something.

Miller: I can't see—confound these people! Don't shove, damn you! Come on, Spenser—let's go and see . . .

(*The crowd noises thicken. We push our way through somehow—led on by Miller's morbid curiosity.*)

Spenser: Miller, wait—it's . . . if it's an accident it's hardly——

Miller: Oh, come *on*—don't be squeamish.

(*We reach the end of the platform. A dishevelled and partly hysterical woman is talking to an official.*)

The Woman: . . . but he did—I tell you he did jump! He was standing here—right beside me. They're trying to say I'm imagining it all but I know I'm not. He was standing here, just beside me——

The Official: Who was?

The Woman: The man. And when the train started he jumped down—on to the line—just as it was entering the tunnel. Oh, it was horrible!

(*Her lip quivers. She begins to weep. She is trembling violently. The official looks puzzled. He appeals to the crowd. No one else has seen anything at all. He looks down at the glistening line. He addresses the woman, he touches her arm and tries to calm her.*)

The Woman (*wildly*): But I tell you he did jump, he did! He was wearing a raincoat and a soft sort of velvety hat, and he—

(*She breaks off suddenly.*)

The Official: What's wrong, madam? What are you staring at?

The Woman: That's the man—there!—that's him, in the crowd! That's the man I saw throwing himself in front of the train.

(*A pause.*)

Miller: Spenser—she's pointing at you! This is fantastic, man —she's pointing at you!

. . . THAT WAS FOUR YEARS AGO—nine months after my visit to Bristol and the episode in the fog. There had been other things —little things. One of them I have mentioned already, in the conversation between Miller and myself in the previous section:

Miller rang me up one evening. He was jocose—I thought at first he had had too much to drink. I accused him of that and he immediately became ponderously and jovially indignant.

"My dear Spenser," I heard his reedy voice exclaim, "there *can't* be any mistake. I'm not the sort of chap to go about imagining things. I asked you if you wanted a drink and you shook your head. You had a whisky and soda in front of you, half finished."

"What time was it?" I asked, irritated by his persistence.

"Just before closing time—about a quarter to ten. I went in with Jameson. I said to him 'There's Spenser'—I remember it distinctly, 'cos he commented that he hadn't seen you since he'd met you and Margaret at Peter Ellacott's party last month."

I was in no mood to listen to him going on and on. I repeated that I hadn't been at the Six Bells the night before. He laughed.

"Nonsense, my dear Aubrey—I can't be wrong," he cried. "You've been overworking, old man. You must have started playing your wretched piano, then got up by sheer force of habit and slipped out to have one before they closed. What is it they call it?—amnesia . . ."

I hung up on him finally. And I went thoughtfully over to my writing desk and took up a letter I had had a few days before—from Helen Bannerman, Margaret's friend. I found the passage I wanted and read it slowly to myself several times.

". . . I didn't know you ever came to this part of the country—I mean, you've never even mentioned that you knew my corner of Wiltshire. But there you were, as large as life, coming out of the Post Office. Of course, I pulled up the car immediately and went back, but you must have slipped round the corner and got off in that little two-seater of yours mighty quick—there simply wasn't a sign of you. I asked the old lass in the shop if a man had been in and she said oh yes, you'd bought some tobacco: and when she said it was an ounce of Honeymead I knew it simply must be you. Besides, you were wearing that ridiculous velvet hat you favour—I couldn't mistake it. I must say it's a bit thick for you not to have called—I expect you were fantastically busy as usual, but all the same there are the fundamental courtesies . . ."

I knew in my heart as I stood there that evening that the day before I received this letter I had been thinking I needed a rest.

I had thought that if a few days in the country *could* have been possible . . . But I knew it was out of the question. I had gone stoically on with my work. As far as I could calculate it, at the time Helen Bannerman must have thought she had seen me, I was in a bus somewhere between Knightsbridge and the Marble Arch. Miller's talk of amnesia came into my mind. I had a wild notion to try to trace the bus and ask the conductor if he remembered me. But it would have been absurd. And there *wasn't* any doubt —I could never have had the time to get down to Wiltshire—I had been at an orchestral rehearsal that very morning of the supposed encounter . . .

And then—the scene in the Underground. And Miller's strained, incredulous voice:

"Spenser—she's pointing at you! This is fantastic, man—she's pointing at you! . . ."

Yes, fantastic. Fantastic as I walked home that night through the empty streets. All about me, it seemed, there were little evil whispering voices. I felt ill—I found myself shivering. Fantastic that I kept glancing over my shoulder, fantastic that I strained my ears to hear other footsteps than my own in the long quiet street. Fantastic, fantastic.

I mounted the stairs to my flat, slowly, with a year between each step. I was monstrously weary. There was no reality in me —it was all fantastic. The thirty-five years were fantastic, the appalling effort to get anywhere, to do anything, to break away. I saw the weeping boy standing out in the cold, the cairngorm on my aunt's black dress. I saw my father's silhouette in the frame of the door, I saw the yellow hair fall over his eyes as we packed his books on that last day. My father and my mother—all over with them now, they were gone. The shadows coming together and drifting apart.

And as I mounted that dark stairway, I remember, in the few moments that it took me, there came back, suddenly and sweetly and with infinite poignancy, my first small love affair. Irrelevant —fantastically irrelevant. Part of my weariness and the weight of the years and all that was in me over which I had no control . . . I was fifteen—it was before I left Scotland, while I was still at school. Her name was Ellen. We walked—endlessly, with long embarrassed gaps in our conversation. Sometimes, as we walked, I put my arm round her waist—timidly, and after much debate with myself. Once, when we were resting on the grass after a long evening walk, I began to caress her and fondle her. She did not resist and I pulled her gently back until we were lying together, very close, with my arm under her neck. We were quite still and my heart was beating, and I saw, as I looked at her in the twilight, that her eyes were wide open and shining and her lips were parted. And I found myself, I remember, wanting to cry—to put my face against hers and cry, very softly and without passion or effort . . .

"For he is like to something I remember,
A great while since, a long long time ago . . ."

We go. Somehow we go. And with us goes always that other silent Passenger.

I reached the top of the stairs. I felt in my pocket for the latch-key as I went along the corridor. And then I stood still, my hand outstretched to the door.

Softly, from inside my flat, there came to my ears the sound of a piano. Not my piano—the sound of an old piano: but the music was Chopin—the *Fantasia* on which I was, in those days, so seriously working.

I remember I smiled wryly—I was tired, monumentally tired. I opened the door and switched on the light. There was no fear in me—only an infinite resignation. I knew what I would see—I knew, without hatred, that the old enemy was there—that from now on there could be no peace between us.

He was sitting at my piano—for a moment shadowy as he played. But he rose when I entered, and the music stopped. He advanced, smiling a little. He was, unmistakably, as I had supposed him to be. Dark, thin, and with narrow temples—it was what they call "a sensitive face . . ."

Nowadays I have none of that bland, elated remoteness. Not any more. There's only a quiet rage nowadays—I know what has to be done. Too much has happened, you see—there's been too much to fight against. Too monstrous an accumulation of sheer things. At every turn I've been defeated—defeated over my music, my friends, defeated over Margaret. And defeated hopelessly as I stood in the November frost sniffing the air, with the shrill screams of the children in my ears and the sagging, hideous effigy aflame before me.

I realise suddenly, as I write, that I am speaking as if it were all over and a hundred years gone by. And it was only a few days ago. And it is not all over—not yet—not quite . . .

I looked over at my piano—the Winged Victory. I look up at the portrait of Chopin and think of him, haunted too, in his cell at Valdemosa. I look at the Blake engravings—the book of Job. "Man is born unto trouble, as the sparks fly upward," I remember.

It had been too much of an effort, too great a struggle. I wonder—has my disease been that I have had too deep a grudge? —that I haven't fitted in?—have been, in secret, a chronic enemy of society? But what the hell! It's been a matter of keeping going —of being out of things and fighting to get in them again and keep in them. The only thing you have is yourself, and there you are, just you yourself, and not one other thing caring a damn. It hasn't been circumstances—one rises above circumstances. You just stand there—it's like being God. And suddenly you have a sort of terror, because there isn't anything to show. In the old days, when I was beginning, I used to walk along the Strand or Oxford Street and look at the people and think: Not one of you knows about me—not one of you knows what it was like emptying out that closet-bucket or standing with my fingers frozen in the darkness outside the house. But that was me—and this is me . . . And I could have gone and smashed their heads in with an axe, because I wanted them to know about me . . .

It all ties up. I stretch out my hand—to find a matchbox, to grope in a fog, to open a door. It all ties up.

And you, I suppose, would put me in a text-book. You would have a label on my forehead. You would have me on a statistic sheet, with the size of my collar, the shape of my brow, the state of my digestion. You would want a cause. You always want a cause—you want a cause for war, a cause for peace, a cause for unemployment, a cause for juvenile delinquency and the spread of venereal disease. But what's a cause?—and where does it begin or end?. . .

All I know is that there are people and things and there's movement. I don't believe there's direction—there's only movement. And I'm a person and I've had to go on being a person.

"The sparks fly upward . . ." I think of that sagging figure nailed to the crosspiece—and only I with any notion of what was behind the leering mask.

I HEARD OF HIM AGAIN—I saw him again. For these four years I have seen him and heard him. He has walked beside me quietly in the darkness. He has sat with me here in my room, he has silently pulled at my sleeve at significant moments. I have been aware of him with me at the piano on concert platforms. As I fluffed my music, half-weeping, I have heard his voice whisper in my ear: "John Spenser—pianist . . ." I have, on the point of saying something, looked up—to find him silently regarding me, the quiet and damnable smile on his lips: and my words have remained unsaid. He has gone in my place—he has done, in a hellishly logical way, the things I have secretly wanted to do: and, having done them, has destroyed them utterly for me forever.

I have hated him till I have sobbed my hatred out loud—yet I have, at the height of the agony, looked up for him, expected him: and have secretly rejoiced at finding him.

For me, now, there is nothing left in the wake of his destruction. Peer goes home from his adventures. The sun shines on an empty house.

I know what has to be done. An evening's writing, for the sake of getting it all down somehow, and then—I know what has to be done. On the desk before me—my father's desk—the razor is ready. It too, when it is open, is a small Winged Victory . . .

THE GREAT GROMBOOLIAN PLAIN

HOW LONG AGO since I met Margaret? A month?—ten years?—yesterday?

In actual fact, I find, looking at my diary, it was on the 15th of May, 19—, six years ago. It was at Mrs. Wheeler's house—Rosalind Wheeler, the first friend I had when I came to London. I had met Margaret's father before, of course—we had done some concerts together, and a half a dozen broadcasts. A taciturn, elegant man, I found him, but a fine artist.

Mrs. Wheeler was giving us tea in her house at Notting Hill. She was, in a mild and harmless way, something of a lion hunter. She introduced people by telling you immediately what they did. "This is Mr. So-and-So, Aubrey. He writes, you know. Aubrey is Aubrey Spenser, the pianist, Mr. So-and-So—I am sure you two will have a lot to talk to each other about . . ."

Introduced like that, there never was anything to talk about. Conversation at Rosalind's tea-parties was as dull as anything Letchworth or Welwyn ever produced. But that never mattered—Rosalind had more than enough to say for all her guests.

"This is Margaret du Parc, Aubrey," said Rosalind. "She plays the violin—like her father. Or do you professional musicians prefer to say fiddle? I never know. Anyway, dears, you two are bound to have lots to say to each other, so I'll leave you to it. I see that dear Sylvia Ellacott has arrived—Peter's sister. She sculpts, you know . . ."

Margaret and I smiled wanly at each other. We went out into the garden and sat down in a couple of deck-chairs. Behind her, I remember, was a fuchsia bush, the little artificial-looking flowers bobbing up and down in the slight breeze.

Within six months we were engaged to be married. Rosalind was delighted—to think that it was she who had brought us together! It was at her house we had met! At one of her parties!

"I knew you had lots to say to each other," she cried. "I remember distinctly saying so when I first introduced you . . ."

Now Margaret is no more than a photograph of the de Laszlo painting of her on the wall of my room. There is no bitterness about it—as I said, when I started writing, I can hardly remember. Only the facts. Perhaps (and in admitting this to myself I may, subtly, be touching the very keynote of this whole fantastic thing)—perhaps there was, secretly, from the beginning, a reluctance

—a knowledge that between us there never could be anything satisfactory and permanent. It was an elaborate and lovely pretence—a conceit, in the old Elizabethan sense. It was another way of being successful: Spenser, the shivering boy in the cold, the illegitimate son of a drunken Scottish dominie and a servant girl—and the fiancé of the daughter of Georges du Parc, the violinist.

Yes, I knew that all the time, I suppose—or I tell myself I did. I don't know—I don't know anything at all any more. Like the expanding book-cases in the advertisements—it's all always complete but never completed . . .

We went one summer to St. Ives for a month—Georges, Margaret, myself and Helen Bannerman. We had a house just outside the town, overlooking the smaller of the two bays. To reach the shops you had to go through a labyrinth of small cobbled streets with crooked houses, some with nets hung out to dry on the sills. The weather was windy and beautiful most of the time, with enormous clouds lolloping over the sky like huge Dr. Johnson wigs and a pale green sea (to quote Helen) like a slightly naughty lady coquettishly pulling back the white frills of her petticoats from shining tawny legs. It was like holidaying in a water-colour exhibition, again as Helen said.

"Where is Zennor?" I remember Margaret asking, about a week after our arrival. "Is it far away?"

"Not very," said Helen. " 'A limb of a walk,' according to Mrs. Tregerthen—but she has very short limbs. Three or four miles I should say."

"I'd like to go there. That's where D. H. Lawrence had his cottage, you know. People are very unexpected, aren't they," she added. "One would have thought of something more luscious than Cornwall for Lawrence. I wonder if anyone reads him nowadays?—all that talk about Dark Gods of the Loins . . ."

"I think he was really rather a dreadful man," said Helen with a mock shudder.

"I'm not so sure about Cornwall," I remember I said slowly at this point. "I think it *was* Lawrence's country—the country of his whole generation and attitude. You can see it in his face. Any picture of Lawrence is just like a map of Cornwall. That was his spirit too—rather arid."

"Arid?" smiled Margaret. "Well, that's a new one at least. I should have thought arid was the last epithet one could apply to Lawrence."

"Yes, the last," I said. "After all the rest, the last. Arid."

Margaret looked at me curiously.

"Anyway," she said with a little laugh, "we can walk over to Zennor someday and have a look at it. Apparently there's an inn called The Tinner's Arms where he lived for a bit. Think of it—The Tinner's Arms! It takes all the romance away."

"Lawrence would soon have put it back," I said drily. "He spent his life putting the romance back over things like The Tinner's Arms . . ."

No, the holiday was not a success. I was depressed by the Cornish landscape—the low dry fields with their stone dykes, the bare hills, the derelict towers of the old tin mines. Only the sea I loved—I would sit for hours simply staring at the vast bulk of the water, its magnificent blue, the pure white of the fretting foam. I used to long for a storm—an immense, violent storm, so that I could run out on the rocks and be buffeted by the wind and bathed by the lashing spray. Sometimes, in the evenings, I stood in the garden of our house with Margaret, watching the slow sunsets—the dead, smoky disc sinking behind the horizon and then the changing and fading pastels, mauve and pale green merging to purple . . . and I would debate whether I should tell her, in those uncomfortable silences that fell between us, about the figure I was aware of all the time at my elbow.

I knew what he wanted: I knew, as a small hard fact, what he would make me do. But it was always a matter of putting things off. Impossible not to linger. Because, after all—

No, never mind. It all ties up. One stretches out a hand . . .

"She has gone to the great Gromboolian Plain,
And we probably never shall meet again . . ."

STRANGE. I feel a little light-headed. Beyond it all. Facts—it reduces itself to facts. I could make, almost, a catalogue of facts. Speculation is no longer possible. I no longer think in terms of things like amnesia. How should I explain it? How should I care if he is subjective or objective? You who classify, who label—that must be your task.

It is your task to say:

(1) A woman on an Underground platform has an hallucination that she sees a man throwing himself under a train. It is possible that she was in some sort of telepathic sympathy with the mind of the subject, John Aubrey Spenser.

(2) A man Miller imagines that he sees the subject (John Aubrey Spenser, aforementioned) in a public house, whereas the subject was, to his own certain knowledge, somewhere else altogether at that established time.

(3) A woman Bannerman supposes that she sees the subject one hundred and fifty miles from where, at that alleged moment, he is. The possibility again of some sort of telepathic sympathy between Bannerman and the panel, causing the former—an otherwise healthy and balanced woman—to experience a subjective hallucination (see Dunkelhaus on *Hallucinations,* Appendix II, p. 649) . . .

(4) The panel Spenser—a neurotic type—has the constant sense of another self controlling him and motivating him. The hallucination is so powerful that he contends that this other self has *a fleshy and objective existence*. He even contends that he has touched this Other Self—he has, he says, had his hands (his strong-fingered pianist's hands) round the throat of this Other Self: he has, while the Other Self smiled most damnably *strangled him in this way to death, thereafter causing the body to be burned* . . .

(5) The panel, Spenser, erstwhile pianist, is therefore mad . . .

No. Facts. A catalogue of facts.

Fact 1: A cairngorm brooch.

Fact 2: A picture of a woman with hair piled up on top and a locket round her throat.

Fact 3: A photograph of a de Laszlo portrait.

Fact 4: A letter, in the possession of Margaret du Parc, violinist, from John Aubrey Spenser, late pianist, breaking off his engagement to her.

Fact 5: A footstep in a yellow fog.

Fact 6: A heap of charred straw and old clothes, the remains of a Guy Fawkes bonfire organized by Eric Jameson, a friend of John Aubrey Spenser, as an entertainment for the children of the district in which he lived . . .

Fact 7: A small razor.

WINGED VICTORY

. . . I CAN PICTURE my friends rallying round. I can picture Jameson and Miller meeting in the Six Bells and in a welter of "old chaps" and bovine kind-heartedness saying:

"Poor old Spenser! Gone to bits! What's happened to his playing? Never gives a concert now, does he . . . Queer how chaps disintegrate. Probably needed a woman, poor fellow. I suppose we must do something about him—do something to shake him out of it."

"I'm having a sort of party next week-end at my place at Wraysbury," says Jameson. "Fifth of November and all that. Got to do something. I'm having a Guy and fireworks—for my kids and their friends, you know. Could always invite him down to that. I don't suppose he'll come, but he might, you know. It'd do him good . . ."

I did go down to Wraysbury. Since it is facts we are on now, let me say that I went because I had no heart to refuse. I was indifferent. What did it matter if I went or stayed? So it was easier to go—and I went.

That was a week ago. Since my return on Tuesday I have not once moved out of my flat here. I have—knowing what had to be done—compiled this manuscript. It covers my desk in thirty closely-written sheets. Disconnected, pointless, an amorphous scribbled mass. It was to have been immense—I began, you remember, vastly. The antecedents of the author—the farmer, my grandfather, with his epigrammatic exit line: "Aye. Barnha' will need a new maister in the morning." Then my father and my aunt—a portrait of the author as a child. All in order and as it should be. But somehow in this—as in everything—something has gone wrong. I haven't the heart. All that I had wanted to say (more about Ellen, for example, and more about Margaret)—all these things have gone by the board. I emerge as a sort of inverted Proust: *A la Recherche du Temps Trouvé.*

A paragraph—a rest—perhaps a few moments' dozing—an interlude on the piano—a scratch meal—another paragraph. So it has gone. Not what I meant—not it at all.

And now there is only a little more to be said. It is late, and I cannot—I haven't the heart—to spin it through another night.

In the street it is quiet. On the mantelshelf the clock ticks slowly. On the wall, in steps, the Blake engravings. "The sparks fly upward."

I went to Wraysbury. And He—inevitably—went with me.

FACTS DETACHED. The story of my life in simple facts.

Jameson's house. Large, modern. It must have cost him a fortune. Furnished expensively in appalling taste. A beautiful piano in the lounge on which they urged me (as a sop) to play. "Won't you give us a piece on the piano, Mr. Spenser?" A blue China carpet on the floor, a ceiling tinted in pale green. A Chinese lacquer motif in the dining room—too much chinoiserie altogether.

The Jameson children filled the house with an air of excited expectancy. They showed us the boxes of fireworks, they took us out to the yard to see the Guy, all ready propped on a heap of branches for his next day's martyrdom. He sagged from a crosspiece of old creosoted wood, wretched, limp, with a grinning Scaramouche-like face. I shuddered a little as I looked at him with the yellow straw packed round his feet—to keep him from the cold through the long night vigil before him. In the twilight he was tragic.

We went indoors and the children were sent to bed. We adults played cards for a time, and drank Jameson's special rye juleps. Then, yawning, one by one we went upstairs.

Facts, eh? I can give you the facts. It's all I can give you now, as I sit here writing, so near the end. As in a curious far-off dream I see the facts—unreal—the unrealest things there are.

Opposite the door in the little room that Jameson had given me there was a long wall mirror. I stood on the threshold for a long time regarding myself solemnly. Then I closed the door behind me. I turned to the right and the reflection turned in sympathy to his left. I walked over towards the bed, beyond the range of the mirror-frame. And, smiling, the other figure walked with me.

I sat down on the edge of the bed, infinitely weary. He, still smiling, sat opposite me in a little low armchair of brown uncut moquette.

INDICTMENT 5 ABOVE:—The panel, Spenser, is mad . . .

Am I mad? *Was* I mad in that moment in my room at Jameson's house when all the accumulated rage of the thirty-five years mounted up to a pitch of fury? How should I care any more whether it was hallucination or not? All I know is that he *was* flesh and blood. There was no mistaking that he was flesh and blood when I put my fingers round his throat. There was no mistaking that he was flesh and blood when he sagged limply in my arms and I lowered him gently to the floor.

A thousand things were in my mind—a thousand small humiliations. How should I, among all things listed, list those? Can you understand humiliation? Can you understand the humiliation of simply being the shape you are?—of having the colour of hair that you have? . . .

And, as always, coming into my mind irrelevantly, even at that high moment, there was one disconnected incident. It was before I left school—during my last term, when I was fifteen. In my form there was a boy named Gallacher, a barren, vindictive, twisted creature with a permanent grudge against one of the masters, Rivers, who taught Mathematics. One part of our school was in a very old house and the rooms were heated by huge coal fires in the winter time. It was typical of Gallacher that he should go to grotesque lengths and use this fact to gratify his revenge. He began in the school workshop and in the laboratories, heating pieces of metal and holding them in his bare hands until he could touch iron that was not positively red hot. Then, when he considered himself ready, he chose a day when the Algebra lesson was due to follow the mid-morning interval and put the poker in the schoolroom fire for the duration of the break. When the bell rang for class he lifted the poker out, carried it across the room and set it down on Rivers's desk. Then he went to his seat and sat caressing his cheek with his palm to experience the heat that was in it from carrying the poker.

When Rivers came in he saw the poker lying on his desk and, all unsuspecting, picked it up without hesitation. The pain must have been excruciating, but he gave no sign of feeling anything. Instead he carried the poker back to the fireplace and laid it in the fender. Then he turned and faced us. He was desperately white, and suddenly he threw out his hand towards us so that we could see the great red weal across it.

"You've burned my hand!" he cried. "Look—you've burned my hand!"

And he stamped out of the room. A few moments later he came back, with the Rector and Iles, the Janitor. Iles stationed himself at the door and spectacularly turned the key in the lock. Meantime the Rector had mounted the master's dais and was surveying the class, while Rivers stood by with his hand wrapped in a duster.

"No one will leave this room," said the Rector impressively, "until I have found out who did this abominable thing to Mr. Rivers."

There was silence. One or two of the boys glanced toward Gallacher. He sat with a vacant, stupid smile on his face, rubbing his hand against the edge of his desk. The Rector sat down.

"I'm quite prepared to wait," he announced drily. "I can always get Iles to fetch me in something to eat. You'll have the pleasure of watching me."

Up to this moment I had taken no great interest in what had been going on. But suddenly, I remember, a peculiar and intangible sensation began to grow inside me. I watched the Rector, fascinated, studying his fresh healthy features and following his eyes as they roved slowly round the room. Then suddenly, without my own consent, as it were, I rose to my feet. The Rector's brows went up.

"You, Spenser? Well, well!"

I was aware that the class was staring at me amazedly. I could see Gallacher, still with the fatuous smile on his face. I knew they all thought I was being quixotic, getting them out of a scrape, and that knowledge suddenly began to annoy me. It was not that that was in my mind at all. I did not know what it was, but I knew it was not that.

I was escorted by Iles to the Rector's room. The old man opened a drawer and took out a short, two-thonged strap of tough leather. He passed it through his fingers and looked at me quizzically.

"Was it you, Spenser?" he asked.

I nodded.

"Why did you do it?"

I made no reply. My heart was pounding, I remember, and I could feel my knees trembling slightly. The Rector went on:

"It isn't usual to punish in the fifth," he said slowly. "When it is necessary it means that the punishment must be a heavy one."

He was looking out of the study window, and now suddenly he turned and said quickly:

"Why did you say you did it, Spenser? You know you didn't."

I still made no reply. I stared at him foolishly. And suddenly he made a gesture of annoyance and strode to the desk to pick up the strap.

"Ach!" he cried. "Hold out your hand . . ."

I STEPPED TO THE DOOR and put out the light. Then I drew back the window curtains and stared out over the fields. The moon was full. The outbuildings cast long silent shadows on the silvered ground. I shuddered. The frost glistened and sparkled. I thought —I remembered . . .

I lowered my eyes. In the yard below me, huddled and grotesque in the clear blue light, was that stuffed and tragic figure.

For a moment I stopped breathing. Then, quickly, with sly and quiet movements, I went over to the door, opened it, and listened in the corridor. The house was dead. Leaving the door open I tiptoed back into my room and put my hands under the oxters of the thing on the floor . . .

IT IS LATE—TOO LATE. I fill my pen with ink for the last few pages. I light a cigarette—my last cigarette.

It all ties up. I stretch out my hand for a last cigarette: I stretch out my hand to open a door: I stretch out my hand sadly, as a last sentimental gesture, to Margaret. I was a man who lived in the dark. I stretched out my hand for a light to see by—and a light was quietly and simply given me.

Why should I waste time now by building up the dramatic climax? I should describe, in detail, with a cumulative atmosphere, the nailing of that terrible thing to the crosspiece, the weeping struggle I had to drape the sagging ancient clothes round its limbs, the ecstasy that was inside me as I packed the yellow straw tightly, tightly round the foot of it . . . But there is no dramatic climax. There is only, all about me, a flow of images.

The piano, open, a Winged Victory. That other small Winged Victory on the desk beside me, half-covered with the pages as I write. A little heap, too, of my father's books on the desk: Jevons on *Logic,* two volumes of Carlyle, Renan's *Life of Jesus* . . . the books I helped him to pack on that last day at the school-house when he stood, remote and statuesque, with the yellow hair before his eyes.

No. There is no climax. If there had been—if it might have been over as I stood there with the children's laughter in my ears, looking desperately for some sign, some diminutive sign—looking till the last smouldering fragment of cloth stopped glowing on the heap of charred and blowing ashes . . . if a climax *might* have been possible . . .

Jevons on Logic. What else but devilish logic is there in it? What else but hell's own logic explains and justifies me as I sit here writing in my room? Would this have been written at all if it hadn't been for logic?

I shiver. The fire has burnt out—there is no glow on the polish of the piano. I stretch my cramped limbs. I stare straight ahead. I know what has to be done. I stretch out my hand to clear the papers from the razor. I open it. The delicate blade shines in the dim light from my standard lamp.

I test the edge on the little hairs on the back of my hand. I must remember what I once read in a book—to hold the head forward, not backward, as would seem natural. Otherwise the jugular is not severed, and that would be fatal—for both of us . . .

I PERMIT MYSELF a final jest.

"We, the undersigned, do hereby swear that all contained in this document is true. We affirm that we were born, thirty-five years ago, the illegitimate son of a Scottish schoolmaster and a servant girl. We affirm that we are a thin young man with narrow temples—what is popularly called 'a sensitive face.' We affirm that we are no longer engaged to Margaret du Parc, violinist. We state that we were seen throwing ourself under an electric train, we state that on Monday of this week we underwent ordeal by fire and are, in consequence, purged and purified. We state and confirm these things and sign this document under our hand and red seal this 9th day of November at five minutes to twelve o'clock.

John Aubrey Spenser, *Pianist,*
John Aubrey Spenser, *Pianist.*"

FOR THE LAST TIME I pause. I stare straight ahead. I stare to my left. But not to my right. Never, never, never to my right.

Because he is there! He is there—to my right. There was *no escaping him—no release in the ordeal by fire. He is there, smiling his damnable, everlasting smile. It is he who has written this story!* . . .

I knew he would be there. I knew it when, on Tuesday, I returned from Wraysbury. I knew it as I stood with my hand stretched out to open the door of my flat. Faintly, from inside, I heard the sound of a piano. I could have wept. It was the music that Margaret and I, sentimentally, as one does, had associated always with ourselves—because, as I put it, it was such a perfect description of her.

Debussy—*The Girl With the Flaxen Hair* . . .

www.ingramcontent.com/pod-product-compliance
Lightning Source LLC
Chambersburg PA
CBHW060538310726
48982CB00009B/1305/J

* 9 7 8 1 9 4 3 9 1 0 9 7 7 *